SEA RIFT

J.M. Simpson

Also by J.M. Simpson, available on Amazon.

The Castleby Series
Sea State
Sea Change
Sea Shaken
Sea Haven

Twitter @JMSimpsonauthor
Instagram @JMSimpsonauthor
Bluesky @jmsimpsonauthor.bsky.social

Copyright ©J.M. Simpson 2024

The right of J.M. Simpson to be identified as the author of the work has been asserted by her in accordance with the Copyright, Designs and Patents Act 1988. All rights reserved. No part of this publication may be reproduced, stored, or transmitted, into any retrieval system, in any form, or by any means (electronic, mechanical, photocopying, recording or otherwise) without the prior written permission of the publisher. Any person who does any unauthorised act in relation to this publication may be liable to criminal prosecution and civil claims for damages.

This is a work of fiction. Any references to real people, living or dead, real events, businesses, organisations and localities are intended only to give the fiction a sense of reality and authenticity. All names, characters, places, and incidents are either the product of the author's imagination or are used fictitiously, and their resemblance, if any, to real-life counterparts is entirely coincidental.

This book was written in its entirety by a human, and has no artificial intelligence content.

Cover design copyright ©J.M Simpson 2024

ISBN: 9798320662756

Imprint: Independently published.

In Memory

Brock Rey – Maxie

12.5.2010 – 27.2.2024

My friend, my constant companion, my shadow.

Always by my side, or at my feet.

Run free and chase squirrels, cats, and balls endlessly.

You will be forever loved, missed, and cherished.

I'll think of you chasing balls on the big beach in the sky.

Sleep well, my beautiful, best boy.

Waste no tears over the griefs of yesterday.

Euripides

PROLOGUE

'MUMMY'S COMING!' she screamed.

She could hear her crying. Wailing for her. But she couldn't see her. *Where is she?* Breathless, tearful and frantic, she rushed outside and stopped. Listening. There!

She ran blindly across the car park, her hospital gown flapping in the evening breeze, her bare feet painful on the hard tarmac. Her hand sprayed droplets of blood as she ran from where she had yanked out the stent.

Closer. She was closer. She could hear her.

'Mummy's coming!' she shouted breathlessly, launching herself at the metal fence and awkwardly climbing it.

'Mummy's coming!' A gash opened in her leg, and her gown tore as she struggled over the sharp metal spikes of the fence that led to the woods behind the hospital. But she didn't feel it.

She could hear her. That's all that mattered. She needed to be kept safe. Faintly, she could hear shouts, but she ignored them and kept running. Brambles and thorns ripped her gown and skin as she blindly ran through the woods; stones and sticks on the forest floor dug into her bare feet, but they didn't slow her.

She stopped abruptly. She couldn't hear the noise anymore. She strained to listen. Panting. Tearful. Desperate. She heard a faint noise and ran towards it, the shouts behind her getting louder.

'Mummy's coming!' she screamed. 'Mummy's coming.'

She sobbed as she ran. Gasping, she clutched her chest. The desperation causing her a deep physical pain.

The woods grew dimmer as the pine tree canopy became denser. Then she heard the sound she craved. Abruptly, she changed direction. She glanced behind her; there were people in the distance running after her. *What do they want?* Panicking, she turned back towards the sound of her baby and ran straight into him.

The man was hanging from a noose, strung up from one of the large pine trees. The lifeless body swung away, limply, before swaying forwards again. She felt a cold, lifeless arm brush her face.

The horror she felt was so intense, so all-consuming, that she fell backwards, screaming. She hit her head on a tree stump. Struggling to move, she heard her baby cry again. Her vision started tunnelling; her limbs felt like lead. Terror overwhelmed her. She saw her baby held in the arms of the dead man swinging from the tree. She screamed again.

CHAPTER 1

Nathanial Bennett, known as Nate to most people, was becoming increasingly pissed off.

'Any danger of you looking where you're actually going when you're bringing things in?' he snapped at the removal men.

They had already broken a table and smashed a picture. He looked at the lorry full of his belongings and wondered what the casualty count would be by the end of the day. He rolled his eyes and muttered under his breath as he picked up an abandoned box and took it upstairs. Nudging open the door to the front bedroom, he put the box down, his attention drawn to the view from the window. He sighed with pleasure. Before him stretched the ocean. It was like soul food. He liked to be near it; missed it when he was away; longed for it when he was troubled. After years of travelling with his job as a trainer in hostage and crisis negotiation, he was finally able to put down proper roots, in the place he had lived as a young child.

His phone blared out, making him jump. He dragged it out of his pocket.

'Hello?'

'Ah, Mr Bennett. It's Dr Oakley. How are you?'

'I'm good, thanks. Everything OK?'

'Ah… Yes… Well, no… I'm afraid your wife had a rather serious episode last night.'

Nate closed his eyes, dreading the response. 'Episode?'

Dr Oakley cleared his throat.

'Yes. Most unfortunate. I'm afraid she escaped from the ward and ran into the woods behind the hospital. She slipped past the nurses it would seem. She thought she could hear the baby crying.'

'Again?' He struggled to process the information. 'But you have her there, safe?'

'Well, yes, but there are another couple of issues.'

Nate stayed silent. A trick he often used: the human psyche felt the need to fill a silence with words. The doctor continued.

'Er… It appears that there was a man in the woods. He had hanged himself.'

'Poor fellow,' Nate murmured.

'Well, your wife. She ran straight into him and then fell and hit her head.'

Nate fought to find the right words. 'Is she OK? Well, you know what I mean. Is she OK, considering?'

'Um… she was in a highly distressed state when security found her. I'm afraid we had to sedate her.'

'I'm not surprised. I think that would shake anyone,' Nate said mildly. 'What aren't you telling me?'

'She was convinced the man who hanged himself had her baby in his arms.'

Nate closed his eyes and sighed. 'How long do you think she's likely to believe that after this episode?'

2

'I'm not sure. I want to try something different though. We need to deal with this psychosis in a different way, try some new drugs. I've had a long meeting with some new colleagues. We concluded the approach of new medication, hand-in-hand with some extremely intensive therapy, is the way forward. I think we need to throw everything we have at this. The new medication is reported to be highly effective.'

'How long?' Nate asked. 'How much longer will she be like this?'

The doctor sighed. 'Hard to say, Mr Bennett. She has been with us a while now since… well, since… you know. It could be weeks or months. It depends how she reacts to the new treatment programme and medication. We're going to try a very different antipsychotic drug. It's had staggering results.'

'Can I see her?'

'At present I think it would be better if not, just for the next few days. She was so agitated last time you came. She seemed to blame you for her current situation.'

'I remember,' Nate said flatly.

'Perhaps the weekend? She might be calmer by then.'

'OK. I'll come then.'

'Try not to worry, Mr Bennett. We will get your wife better, so she can come home to you.'

Nate stared out to sea. That was what worried him the most. 'Can you keep me posted? If anything changes and you feel it's OK for me to come in sooner to visit, please let me know.'

'Will do. Goodbye, Mr Bennett.'

Nate ended the call. He leant against the wall. He longed to go for a walk on the beach to clear his head, but the sound of something else breaking had him striding from the room and down the stairs, a murderous expression on his face.

Alone now, Nate stood in the kitchen and looked around. He genuinely didn't know where to start. There were boxes stacked haphazardly; none of them were labelled and a few of them looked like they had been dropped from an upstairs window. In the dimness of the evening, he found the light switch and flicked it on. He cleared a few boxes off the large scrubbed pine table and sat down heavily on one of the Carver chairs.

His stomach rumbled loudly in the quietness; he was starving. A knock at the door had him frowning and tripping around boxes to open it. A woman stood on the doorstep holding a bottle of wine and a foil-covered dish.

'Hi, neighbour.' She grinned. 'I figured you were knee deep in boxes, so I've brought you some dinner and wine as a settling in present.' She suddenly looked horrified. 'Oh shit, please don't tell me you're a vegetarian, or a bloody vegan?'

Nate burst out laughing. He liked the woman instantly.

'Come in,' he said. 'Bona fide meat eater in residence.'

'Phew!' she said, smiling. 'Sure it's OK to come in? I can just leave this and go.'

'Please, it'll be a relief to talk to someone who isn't about to tell me a list of things they've broken.'

'Oh dear, like that was it?'

'Oh yeah.'

He closed the door behind her and gestured through to the kitchen.

'Try not to fall over anything,' he said as she picked her way across the obstacle course of boxes.

'Does the oven work?' She peered at it and twiddled a knob. 'This could do with a blast for twenty minutes or so.' She turned around, her expression triumphant. 'Bingo.' She opened the door and slid the dish in.

Standing up straight, she held out her hand. 'I'm Jenny.'

He grinned and shook her hand. 'Nate.' He gestured to a chair. 'Which neighbour are you?'

Jenny sat down and pointed over her shoulder. 'That place.'

'The hotel?'

'The very same.'

'Wow. It's gorgeous,' he said. 'The builders are in, aren't they?'

She nodded. 'They'll finish in about six weeks, I reckon.' She folded her arms and looked around. 'This place is like a Tardis. I've always liked it.'

Nate's house was a brightly coloured blue, three storeys, and nestled in between Jenny's large five-storey house on the end of Compass Row, and a pair of very grand Edwardian villas. All of the properties faced the beach on one side and the road to the harbour on the other.

'I love it. It was the small office that juts out over the rocks that sold it for me.'

Jenny rummaged in her pocket and brought out two paper cups. She unscrewed the wine and poured. 'Cheers and welcome,' she said, raising the cup.

'Screw top,' he observed, impressed. 'Very wise, considering. Were you a Brownie in a former life? Always be prepared? Dib dib dib and all that?'

She laughed. 'Dib dib dib is Scouts I do believe. I was a Brownie, and a Guide too, but I got asked to leave. Too disruptive apparently.'

He chuckled. 'Look, thanks very much for this. It's really kind of you.'

She waved her hand dismissively. 'It's what neighbours do. We look out for each other here, people become family. They were wonderful to me when I first came.' She smiled at him. 'So, is it just you? Do you have family? Kids? Am I being too nosey?'

Nate shifted in his seat. 'Me and my wife,' he said. 'Although she's not too well at the moment, still in hospital. Hopefully she'll be home soon.'

'Oh, I'm sorry to hear that,' Jenny said in dismay. 'Hard for you to sort all this out on your own.'

'What about you?' he asked.

'Just me and Archie,' she said and then smiled. 'Archie is a rescue dog.' She stood and went over to the oven, peering in.

'You're good to go in about fifteen, I reckon.' She picked up her cup and drained it. 'Nice to meet you, Nate. Swing by next door any time and I hope your wife is on the mend soon.'

'Thanks, Jenny,' he said, genuinely touched by the gesture.

She hesitated. 'Look. Might be a bit full on or too soon, but I'm having breakfast in Maggie's cafe down on Castle Beach tomorrow morning, around eight, with a couple of the locals. They're genuinely lovely folk. Feel free to come and say hi.'

'Thanks, I might well do that.' He grinned. 'Now, all I need to do is find a fork.'

She pulled a wooden knife and fork out of her pocket.

'Dib dib dib.' She laughed. 'I'll let myself out. You get eating. I could hear your stomach from next door.'

'Bye, Jenny.' He watched her pick her way out and heard the door close.

He sat for a while, thinking about his wife, and then moved over to the oven and peered inside. He wondered how he was going to get the hot dish out without dropping it. He searched through a few boxes and found nothing he could use, so in his despair, he took off his jumper and used it as an oven glove.

While Nate tucked in, he thought more about his wife. He missed her with an ache. It had almost broken him when he had to agree to section her. To stand by and watch the woman he loved more than anything in the world be dragged away kicking and screaming was an experience he never wanted to repeat.

Vivienne had spiralled into a deep depression when their daughter was stillborn. She couldn't cope and refused to believe their baby had died.

In the hospital she had become hysterical, repeatedly telling people she could hear the baby crying and she hadn't died. Even when they buried the baby, she became frantic saying that she could hear her crying from inside the tiny white casket. She tried to jump into the grave and to get her out and it was all Nate could do to restrain her.

A few weeks later, Nate found her in the woods behind their house in her pyjamas; dirty, scratched and sobbing, looking for the baby she could hear crying; he had no other option but to section her in a psychiatric ward. Mercifully, Viv's company had superb private healthcare, which had been a godsend.

Four months she had been there. Progress was slow. But Nate had been busy making decisions. He gave notice on the house they were renting and bought a place in Castleby. A place he'd always deeply loved as a child. He needed new roots to get through this with Viv.

She needed a place with stability. No more travelling about, living here and there, depending on where he was working. He felt they both deserved a fresh start. He thought the sea would help Viv heal, help her cope. Help them both move on with their lives. A house that wasn't full of reminders. A house that didn't have an empty nursery sat waiting for the occupant who would never come.

Exhaustion washed over him. He put the dish in the sink and trudged up the stairs wondering which box the bedding was in. After thirty minutes, he gave up and made himself a bed from the box of towels and coats he *had* found.

Nate woke the next morning and wondered why he was lying on his coat. Then he remembered. He sat up and rubbed a hand over his face. He grabbed one of the towels he had been sleeping on and headed to the bathroom.

Downstairs, he looked at the clock and saw that it was just before eight. He thought about Jenny's offer of breakfast and on a whim, he decided he would go and join her. He was under no illusions he needed to make some new friends, especially if Viv was as fragile as he expected her to be when she came out of hospital.

He wandered down the road, admiring the sweep of the pretty coloured houses that lined the harbour and went through the stone archway that led to the beach. His nostalgia was strong today and it gave him a happy glow.

There weren't many people around; the tide was in, high up the beach and he took a moment to breathe in the sea air. Getting a waft of bacon, his stomach rumbled.

Pushing open the door to Maggie's, he saw Jenny sitting at a large table with two other people.

'Nate!' she exclaimed. 'Come and join us.'

Nate moved to stand next to her.

'Guys, this is Nate, moved in yesterday to the blue cottage next to me.'

'This lady saved my life last night with dinner and some wine,' Nate said wryly.

'Found anything yet?' Jenny laughed.

Nate pulled a face. 'Couldn't even find the bedding. I slept on towels and a load of old coats.'

'Pull up a chair,' Jenny said.

Nate grabbed a chair and sat down.

'Right. Nate, this is Foxy. He owns the climbing centre opposite.'

'Foxy, eh?' Nate said, smiling.

'Rob Fox,' Foxy said. 'Good to meet you.'

'And this is Doug. He's skipper of the lifeboat here.'

Doug leant over and shook Nate's hand. 'Good to meet you, mate. Welcome. Are you new to the area?'

'No, I used to live here as a kid, always loved it. Me and my wife travelled such a lot, I'm at the point where I don't want to live out of a suitcase anymore, so we've settled here.'

Jenny turned to Nate. 'What does your wife do then, Nate, if you travel so much?'

'She's an analyst of illegal maritime activity. She spends a lot of time collating reports of illegal pirating, sea terrorism and so on. Occasionally, she's off abroad in various places like the Persian Gulf or the Indian Ocean, working with their coastguards and doing briefings.'

'Wow,' Foxy said. 'Interesting. Is she away at the moment?'

'She's poorly in hospital, actually. She should be home soon.'

'How did you meet?' asked Jenny, forever the hopeless romantic.

'I work in hostage and crisis negotiation. Well, I used to. I was in Somalia trying to defuse a crisis with a tanker and some pirates, and she was there working on a placement monitoring things and working with the ships to make it harder to board – stuff like that. Less likelihood of success when they attack.'

Foxy grinned. 'Those Somalians are pretty ruthless. Refuse to listen to reason.'

Nate noticed one of his tattoos. 'SBS, eh? I probably worked with some of your colleagues a few times when you've come to save the day.'

'My mate Rudi, he lives here now, he was out there for a while. You should have a chat. He *loves* to reminisce,' Foxy said, rolling his eyes.

Maggie, owner of the cafe, appeared in a cloud of hairspray and perfume wearing one of her trademark, epically tight T-shirts, which stretched across her enormous bust. She eyed Nate as she put some mugs down.

'And who is this lovely creature?' she asked, grinning.

'This is Nate. He's my new neighbour,' Jenny said. 'Look after him, Mags, he can't find anything in all those boxes and his wife is away.'

Maggie took up the baton; she loved to add to her brood of people to look after. 'Well, Nate. Welcome to Maggie's. Breakfast is on me this morning.'

'Is my breakfast on you?' Foxy asked, mischievously.

'Oh you!' She swotted him with her order pad. 'Absolutely not. You eat me out of house and home. You can bloody well cough up.' She grinned. 'Now, Nate, what are you having?'

CHAPTER 2

Detective Steve Miller, currently residing in the good books of his Superintendent following the recent discovery and arrest of a high-ranking police officer on paedophile charges, stood in the woods behind the hospital looking at where the body had been hanging.

'They wanted him to be found,' he mused to the PC stood next to him. 'Or someone wanted *us* to find him. Are we sure it's a suicide?'

The PC, who was currently making short work of a bacon roll he had resourcefully secured from the hospital canteen, shrugged and pulled a face.

'Dunno. Murphy said to call him later.'

'Jesus, Jonesey. Do we even know who it is?' Steve asked.

'Ahhh... no. Murph is going to print him, and we'll run them.'

'Any matches from MisPer?'

Jonesey took a close interest in the end of his bacon roll.

'Have you even looked?' Steve asked.

'I'm on it now,' Jonesey said. 'Literally. All over it.'

Steve rolled his eyes. 'Shudder to think what you'd be like if you weren't "on it",' he muttered. 'Bugger off back to the station and get cracking.'

'Guv,' Jonesey said, wandering off to ponce a lift from one of the patrol cars.

Steve took a while to wander around the crime scene. Forensics had long gone, with nothing of any particular note found. He liked to walk a scene when everyone had gone and take it all in and generally have a ponder.

Steve wondered how the man would have hanged himself. Climb the tree, tie yourself into the noose, then jump? There was nothing he might've used to stand on that was kicked away. Plus, the tree looked difficult to climb.

Steve mused as he walked. Why would you pick the hardest tree to climb when there were loads of others that were easier? And why would you choose a tree that was front and centre, in the middle of the main path that ran around the woods. It was impossible to miss him if you were walking up the path. Was this a message?

He viewed the scene critically. It had all the hallmarks of a message being sent. Sighing heavily, he knew exactly who liked to send messages like this, so he drew out his phone and made a call.

'Detective Miller.' A warm voice answered. 'How are you? You performed quite the public service putting that awful policeman away.'

'Hello, Pearl. How are you?' Steve said warmly. He liked Pearl Camorra very much. She was the wife of Mickey Camorra and together they represented the organised crime for the region. Steve had an easy camaraderie and mutual respect for Pearl, and they tended to help each other out to a certain degree. Steve was not naive enough to think he could stop any form of organised crime happening on his patch. Instead he had formed a somewhat reluctant alliance to control it as best he could without knowing too much and keeping all of his activities well within the confines of the law.

He respected Pearl and Mickey to a certain degree: their organisation had high standards. They didn't deal with poor quality drugs, would not deal to youngsters and, invariably for them, any type of violence tended to be a last resort – as far as Steve was aware anyway.

Steve thought it was better to ensure that things outside of his control and in the Camorra's control were safe and good quality. He figured what he didn't know wouldn't hurt him and had a 'better the devil you know' attitude, which unfortunately was at odds with some of his colleagues who would happily sell their soul to put Mickey Camorra behind bars.

'I'm all the better from hearing from my favourite policeman,' Pearl said lightly. 'Now what can I do for you, darling?'

'Hospital woods. Dead bloke in a noose. Kind of has the Camorra stamp all over it. Ring any bells?'

Pearl chuckled. 'Well, nothing to do with me personally, I'm sure. But the others, I'm not so sure. I'll check with the boys and get back to you later. Is that OK?'

'Appreciate it. Thanks. You take care now.'

'Speak soon.'

Steve ended the call and wandered around the woods some more. Although it looked like the Camorra's work, they tended to be a little more subtle. They weren't the kind to leave bodies anywhere for the police to find. Unless they wanted to make the specific point that they had performed a public service to society in general by getting rid of a certain individual. Something they had done on more than one occasion in recent months. Steve leant against a tree and made another call.

'What do you want?'

'That's no way to greet me,' Steve said dryly.

There was a snort from the other end of the phone. 'OK. What do you want, Detective Miller?'

Steve laughed. 'That's more like it, mate. Now, what can you tell me about the guy in the woods? Jonesey is clearly on another planet today. He tells me you came out since it was literally over the fence.'

Jim Murphy, the pathologist for the region, sighed heavily. 'He hanged himself.'

'No shit, Sherlock. I managed to work that out for myself,' Steve said sarcastically. 'My question is… did he do it to himself or did somebody do it to him?'

'I've literally just got back from the crime scene. Can't say yet.'

'Not even to hazard a guess?'

'You know I hate doing that.'

'Push yourself and try new things.'

'I'd forgotten how much you annoy me.'

'You love it.'

Murphy grunted. 'To be honest, I'm not sure. I'll get to it. It'll be a welcome relief to do someone who appears to be under seventy-five.'

'Not enjoying flu season?'

'No.'

'Call me when you have an inkling?'

'Yup.'

Murphy ended the call and Steve stood staring at the tree with his head on one side trying to work out how anyone would actually climb it.

Steve arrived back at the station to find Jonesey outside his office, hopping from foot to foot.

'Got an ID,' he said, grinning.

'From missing persons?'

Jonesey looked confused. 'No. From the lifeboat.'

Steve frowned. 'What?'

'He's a reserve on the lifeboat.'

'How did you come to that conclusion?'

Jonesey grinned. 'Alfie was in changing the tyres on some of the squad cars and he recognised the picture.'

'Tell me you didn't show him a picture.'

'I'm not a bloody idiot,' Jonesey said indignantly. 'I was showing Garland the picture so he could get cracking with looking on missing persons and I didn't realise Alfie was looking over my shoulder.'

'And he said he's on the lifeboat crew?'

Jonesey nodded. 'Cause Alfie's a reserve too, but he said he hardly ever sees the bloke.'

'Do we have a name?'

'Marcus Daly, forty-one.'

'Does Doug know?'

'No one knows yet.'

'I'll go and have a chat with Doug.'

'Can I come?'

'Why?'

'Because it's next to Maggie's and I can go in and get one of her amazing breakfast rolls.'

'I literally saw you eating a bacon sarnie an hour ago.'

'That was breakfast. This will be elevenses,' Jonesey said, waggling his eyebrows. 'Please?'

Steve sighed. 'Go on then.'

Together they walked the short route through the town and around to the lifeboat station. Castleby lifeboat had two full-time staff: Doug, who was the coxswain; and Jesse, the full-time mechanic. After some traumatic and fairly life changing events, Jesse and Doug were now an item.

Steve wandered into the station waving at Nessie, the elderly lady who was Doug's neighbour and also ruled the RNLI shop with a rod of iron. She waved back while she served a customer. He walked down the narrow metal steps, along the corridor and knocked on Doug's open office door as he walked in. Doug looked up from the paperwork on his desk.

'Hey, buddy!' he said, smiling. 'Good to see you. What can I do for you, chaps?'

'Marcus Daly.'

Doug's eyes narrowed. 'What about him?'

'We think he was found dead in the woods by the hospital last night. Hanged himself.'

'What?' Doug looked shocked. 'No way.'

'Way,' Jonesey said solemnly.

'Sure it's him?' Doug asked, doubtfully.

Steve gestured to Jonesey who produced his phone.

'It's not pretty,' he said, showing Doug the picture.

Doug looked at the photo. He walked around to his desk, grabbed his mobile phone and dialled a number, putting it on speakerphone.

'Hi, Doug. What's up?' Came the disembodied voice from the other end of the phone.

'Hey, *Marcus*,' Doug said, looking at Steve. 'Just wondering if you can make the launch on Sunday. We're doing a run with the coastguard's helicopter too.'

'Should be able to. I'm not working. So yes, I'll see you there.'

'Great stuff. Look just quickly. Do you have a brother?'

'Yeah, name's Harry. He doesn't speak to me though. Why do you ask?'

Doug pulled a face at Steve as he replied. 'Friend of mine saw someone that looked just like you. I know you're working on the wind farm, so the likelihood of it being you was pretty slim.'

'Where did he see him?'

'Oh, he didn't say.'

'Hmm. He's into some pretty bad shit. That's why we don't talk anymore.'

'Pretty bad shit… like?'

'He was in rehab for heroin addiction at one point. You know, all the usual druggie shit. The spiral of addiction, nicking to feed the habit, trying to get clean, falling off the wagon. When he stole everything of value from my house, that was it for me.'

'That would do it for me too, I think,' Doug said grimly.

'Look, if you can find out where your mate saw him that would be good. Last I heard, he was in Cardiff, hanging out with some junkies. But if he's here poking around again because he needs a fix or some cash then a heads up would be good. Need to hide the valuables.'

'I'll see what I can do,' Doug said. 'See you Sunday, mate.'

'Cheers, Doug.'

Doug ended the call.

'Looks like it's not Marcus then.'

Steve looked thoughtful. 'Tell me about Marcus though,' he said. 'What's he like?'

'He's a good bloke. Works all the hours which is why he rarely makes a shout. He's some sort of engineer, working out on the new wind farm, so his shifts out there are long. He's a nice guy.'

'Married?'

'Don't think so. He was living with someone, but I couldn't say whether that's still on.'

'Got an address?'

Doug produced a book from his desk drawer and flicked through it. He reeled it off.

Steve glanced at Jonesey. 'If the brother's a junkie he'll probably have form. Even if it's just a caution.' He looked at Doug. 'Thanks, mate. Appreciate it.'

'No worries. See you later.'

Steve and Jonesey left the station and wandered around the path to Maggie's beach cafe.

'I'm thinking you ought to let Alfie know it's not Marcus. You know what a gob he's got on him.'

'OK.' Jonesey rubbed his hands gleefully as they approached Maggie's. 'I'm going all out on one of her heart attack in a rolls,' he announced.

Steve's mouth watered. 'They are good,' he said. 'Get one for me too, will you?' He fished a fiver out of his pocket.

Maggie was delivering plates to a table outside and turned to Steve and Jonesey.

'Well, if it isn't my favourite long arm of the law,' she said, tittering. 'How are you two lovelies?'

'Good thanks, Mags,' Jonesey said. 'I'm starving. My stomach thinks my throat's been cut.'

Steve stood watching Jonesey in amazement. His phone rang and he drew it out. It was Pearl; he moved out of Maggie's earshot.

'I'm almost afraid to answer this, Pearl,' he said.

He heard her throaty chuckle and couldn't help himself but smile.

'I've spoken to the boys. No one knows anything about it,' she said. 'Do we know who it is?'

'We do, but it's not for general consumption.'

'OK. Was he a nice fellow?' she enquired.

'Do you mean did someone do a public service by getting rid of him?'

'Well, I wouldn't put it quite like that,' she said lightly.

Steve smiled to himself. Pearl amused him.

'By all accounts he had a nasty habit and was a little bit of a scrote.'

'So, sort of a public service to taxpayers then,' she said.

'Since when have you ever paid tax, Pearl?' Steve laughed.

'I have been known to on occasion,' she said indignantly. 'Alexy suggested that Jimmy or that dreadful little man Sniffy might know something.'

'Jimmy or Sniffy is my next conversation,' he said. 'Thanks, Pearl. Look if you do—'

'You'll be the first to know,' she interrupted. 'Take care now, I hear the place is full of ruthless thugs nowadays.'

'Thanks, Pearl,' he said. 'You watch out for those ruthless thugs too. Take care now.'

Steve wandered down to look at the sea while he waited for Jonesey. His phone rang again. It was Jim Murphy the pathologist.

'So soon?' Steve said dryly as he answered.

'You said I should try new things,' Murphy said. 'This is me trying new things.'

'Just making calls in general? Or making calls with news to impart?' Steve enquired.

'Smart arse. So, I'm taking a punt.'

'That's trying a new thing, is it? Just to be clear.'

'Yes. Do you want to hear or are you too busy being sarcastic?'

'I'm all ears.'

'I think our friend in the woods was most definitely not a suicide.'

'Oh really? Elaborate, please.'

'I'm not staking the house and contents on it just yet, but on cursory inspection it appears to me that he was dead long before they hung him up there.'

'What did he die of?'

'I've no idea.'

'Trying new things only goes so far then?'

'I need to get him open. That's all for now, folks.'

'Hmm. Interesting though. Is it murder or…?'

'Or what…? A new style of alternative burial?'

'When are you hacking him up?'

'I think you mean, cutting him precisely but respectfully. Couple of hours, I reckon.'

'I think he had history of drugs and rehab, etc.'

Murphy snorted. 'I could have told you that just by looking in between the man's toes. Classic, "oh I'm clean, but actually I'm injecting between my toes, so no one spots it".'

'Right. Don't let me keep you from the stuff you really enjoy.'

'I can't believe the amount of grief I get from you. I ring you up with my early insights and all you do is make snippy comments.'

'Don't forget the element of ridicule too.'

'I'm going. Goodbye.'

'Bye, Murph. Speak later.'

Jonesey appeared with their rolls and together they perched on a bench overlooking the sea, eating in a companionable silence.

CHAPTER 3

Mike Young was standing on the deck of the Tamar lifeboat, sharing a joke with Doug, the skipper, as the powerful engines chugged gently back into the harbour. Mike was twenty-eight, handsome, with dark hair, a short dark beard and large brown eyes. As Mike focused in on the quayside, he was surprised to see Foxy, his boss from the climbing centre standing by the narrow stone steps they were approaching. Doug nudged him, grinning.

'Looks like you're in trouble. The boss is here.'

Mike called out. 'Foxy, you OK?'

Foxy acknowledged him with a thumbs up and grabbed the mooring rope that Mike threw him. Foxy moved quickly and gracefully for a big man. He deftly tied the boat on; his years of experience in the Special Boat Service showing both in his efficiency at tying on the boat and by a few of the tattoos that adorned his huge arms.

Mike helped the lifeboat passengers off the boat and onto the quay, pleasantly suggesting they go and buy a tide timetable, so they didn't get cut off by the tide again. He approached Foxy and looked at him with concern.

'What's up? I wasn't that long?' Mike often had to leave the climbing centre if his pager went off for a shout.

'It's fine,' said Foxy. 'The centre's covered.'

'What's up then?' Mike asked.

'I just wanted to give you a heads up before you get back. A bloke came in looking for you. About six two, dark hair. Pretty well built, but all gym and steroids, you know what I mean?'

'Yeah. What did he say?'

'Wanted to know where you were, when you'd be back and where you lived.'

'Where I lived?'

'I know. Rang alarm bells for me too.'

'What else did he say?'

'Said he'd be back and that he wanted to surprise you.'

Mike looked puzzled. 'I have no idea who that could be.'

'I wanted to mention it as soon as. Weird, I know, but he didn't seem like he'd be a mate of yours, if you know what I mean? Seemed all arrogance and shit attitude to me.'

Mike chuckled. 'Oh well if he turns up again, you can protect me.'

Foxy laughed. 'If this is an irate husband or boyfriend, mate, you're on your own.'

'OK. I'll be back in ten, I just need to get the gear off.'

Mike hopped back onto the boat to take it back around to the station and wondered who the mystery man was.

Back at the lifeboat station, he changed from his all-weather gear and jogged quickly back to the climbing centre.

Mike was finishing up his last lesson of the day, mindful of the fact that he had a gig in a couple of hours. He was a talented local musician; he played guitar and wrote much of his music, which had a popular folky feel to it. He was careful to keep lots of covers in the mix though, to please the crowd. He finished the lesson and ushered the kids out. Foxy's Alsatian, Solo, took his usual place across the door at the end of the day.

Mike got busy coiling and stacking ropes and Foxy was in the equipment room, pairing up climbing shoes. Hearing a low warning growl from Solo, Mike turned and saw a large man standing outside the doors.

'We're closed I'm afraid,' he called over his shoulder.

'Mike, isn't it?' the man asked. 'Are you going to move this ugly mutt so I can come in?'

Solo was still growling, baring teeth at the man's tone.

'Not my dog, mate,' Mike said pleasantly, but taking an instant dislike to this man. He suddenly remembered Foxy telling him about a man with a shit attitude who had been looking for him. 'He doesn't listen to me. Plus, he lives here so he can do what he damn well likes. As I said, we're closed now anyway. What do you need?'

The man continued to stand outside the door, his fists clenched.

'What do I need?' He shook his head as if he couldn't believe what Mike was saying. 'I need to know where the *fuck* she is,' he said in a low voice.

'Don't know what you mean,' Mike said puzzled. 'Who're we talking about?'

'Liv. Where is Liv?' he said through gritted teeth.

'Liv who?' Mike frowned. 'I'm sorry, I have absolutely no idea who you're talking about.'

'I think you do.'

Foxy had heard Solo growling and had been standing in the shadows behind Mike, weighing up whether to butt in or not.

'Everything good here?' Foxy asked, standing next to Mike. He was coiling up a rope just to have something to do with his hands. He was tempted to throttle the guy for the way he was speaking to Mike.

'Just asking my mate Mike here, where my wife is.'

Foxy looked sideways at Mike. 'You're on your own here,' he said out of the corner of his mouth.

'And I've said to you, *mate*, I don't know who you're talking about,' Mike replied with an edge to his voice. 'I don't know anyone called Liv.'

The man stared at him. 'I don't believe you.' He pointed at Mike. 'I'll be watching you.'

A boy aged about twelve stepped out from behind the man.

'Dad? Can we go now?' the boy asked.

'In a minute,' the man said dismissively, pushing him away.

'Dad. My levels are really low, I need to eat,' the boy said, clutching his phone.

Mike had seen this before with one of his regular climbers.

'You diabetic, mate?' Mike called to the child, who nodded.

'I've got a juice box here if you need it?' Mike turned to get one, but Foxy was already striding towards the boy. He stepped over Solo and handed the boy some orange juice.

'Do you need to sit down?' Foxy asked.

The boy took the carton. 'I'm OK, thanks. This will be fine,' he said awkwardly and drank quickly. 'Thank you. Dad, I need to eat though. Now?'

The man tutted at the boy and looked back at Mike. 'I'll be watching you,' he said. He grabbed the boy by the shoulder and angrily propelled him up the road in front of him.

Mike watched him leave and bent down to stroke Solo's battle-scarred face. He was an ex-forces dog that Foxy had found in the middle of a war zone. He had rescued him and brought him home.

Ever sensitive to moods and situations, Solo licked Mike's hand and sat watching the man disappear up the road, a growl rumbling gently in his chest.

'Who the hell was that?' Foxy asked.

'I have absolutely no bloody idea,' Mike said. 'I don't know anyone called Liv.'

He stared up the road, watching the man and the boy disappear into Maggie's.

'How the bloody hell did he know who I was?'

* * *

Nate had made good progress over the last few days. He had managed to locate most of the kitchen in various boxes, finding a myriad of broken glasses and plates when he unpacked. He moved on to the bedrooms and had, with delight, found all the bedding and was finally able to make his bed. When he finished wrestling the duvet cover on (which he firmly believed should be an Olympic sport), the bed had looked so inviting that he lay down for a moment, and woke up three hours later.

He hung up his clothes in the wardrobe and then opened the next box which was full of Viv's clothes. He sat looking at them, the faint scent of her favourite perfume drifting into his nostrils. He buried his nose in her favourite jumper and breathed deeply. God he missed his wife. He loved his wife; heart and soul love. But he didn't know who the woman was that *looked* like his wife at the moment. The face was the same, but something in her eyes had died. She was a stranger to him.

She had so desperately wanted a child; it had become all-consuming for her. But now… he just couldn't relate to her. Couldn't get through to her. His eyes filled with tears as he remembered seeing her flushed, sweaty, crying and in pain as she was bearing down. Knowing she was giving birth to a baby who was already dead. Knowing that, this would not be like most births, where the agony would be worth it all at the end, when the sheer joy replaced the memory of the pain. He was utterly horrified that women had to endure this and wished with everything he had there was a different way of dealing with it.

He remembered the look on her face when she had seen the baby. And then the look when they had dragged her away to a psychiatric ward weeks later.

He longed for her to come back to him. Bright, feisty, sarcastic, wonderfully dry and witty. He wanted the real Viv. His muse, the person who he talked to about everything. The person who played devil's advocate when he couldn't see sense. She always made him see reason. He wanted the real deal, not the shell of the woman who just looked like her.

On impulse, he fished in his pocket for his phone and rang the hospital. After an age he was put through to Dr Oakley.

'I was just calling to see how she was.' Nate struggled to find the words. Unusual for him as he always knew what to say and how to say it. He'd made an excellent living out of it.

'The therapy is going well. Very intensive. She has been very calm.'

'Does she still hear the baby crying?'

'She hasn't for a couple of days.'

'Can I come and see her?'

Dr Oakley was silent for a moment. 'Why not. Let's not get our hopes up though. Perhaps the day after tomorrow? She's much better just after lunch so maybe aim for that. Can I suggest you bring her something familiar too? Like a favourite piece of clothing or something that will remind her psyche of life before.'

Nate's heart lifted slightly. 'I can do that. See you then.'

* * *

Mike was shattered. He had played an extra half an hour at the gig that evening with a number of encores. He had also secured a booking for a wedding and a birthday, so he was pretty pleased with himself.

He loaded his music gear into his car and drove up through the town towards his flat, which was situated over a popular Italian restaurant. In the winter months, the Italians allowed him to park his car in the rear courtyard. He parked up, grabbed his guitar, shut the tall wooden gates and walked back around the front of the restaurant to his front door. As he passed the restaurant, Isabella, one of the owners' daughters, who waitressed and ran the bar, saw him and beckoned him in.

'Mike, are you hungry? I mucked up a pizza order. You can have this on the house.'

Mike grinned. 'I could kiss you, Isabella, I'm starving.'

'There will be no kissing.' Isabella's mother bustled past Mike, handing him the pizza box and making shooing gestures. 'You need to eat more. You are wasting away. No nice girl wants a skinny man,' she said critically in her lilting Italian accent.

'Better keep these coming then.' He raised the box and winked at Isabella. 'Thank you.'

'No problem.' She smiled.

Mike balanced his guitar and the pizza box precariously as he put his key in the lock. As he opened his front door, a woman stepped out of the shadows from the building opposite.

'Mike?' she said. 'Can I come in?'

Mike almost dropped the pizza, but instead knocked over his guitar.

'Christ you scared me!' he exclaimed as he saw who it was. He struggled to pick up his guitar. 'What the bloody hell are you doing here?'

Olivia stepped forward and her face crumpled. 'I didn't know where else to go,' she said as tears ran freely down her face. 'I just didn't know where else to go.'

'Jesus.' Mike shoved the pizza and guitar in through the open door and pulled her towards him to give her a hug.

'It's OK,' he said, rubbing her back as she sobbed into his shoulder. He tried to remember the last time he had seen her.

'Come on,' he said, drawing away. 'Upstairs. There's a perfectly good pizza here, plus I have beer.'

He pushed open the door and picked up the pizza box and his guitar and gestured for her to go up. Inside, Mike sat her down and grabbed a couple of plates and two bottles of beer.

'Right. Spill,' he said, passing her a piece of pizza. 'How long has it been?'

Olivia wiped her eyes. 'Four years?'

'When did you get back?'

'Last week.'

'Did you sell your parents' cottage?' he asked. Olivia's parents had kept a holiday cottage in the town for years.

'No. I let it out as a holiday let. It's not free now until Saturday.'

'Ah. Hence you being here with nowhere else to go. So, where did you go?'

'Dubai.'

'How was it?'

'Hot and a bit like a prison,' she said, taking a bite of pizza and closing her eyes. 'God, that's good.'

'Why a prison?'

'You know, culture. Everything is high security too. You're escorted pretty much everywhere. Everyone knows where you are all the time.'

'What the hell are you doing here?'

'I came back early. I had some things to do.'

'Sounds very cloak and dagger.'

'I had to get away,' she said quietly. 'I couldn't…'

'Get away from what?' Mike asked.

'Get away from the man I married.'

Mike stared at her. 'I didn't know you were married.'

'Biggest mistake of my life.' She sniffed. 'No scratch that. Second biggest mistake of my life.'

Mike frowned. 'What was the first?'

She looked at him, tears rolling freely down her cheeks.

'Leaving you.'

CHAPTER 4

Steve stood, idly leaning against the wall at the takeaway window for the Loafing About Bakery while he waited for his coffee. Years of habit had him scanning his surroundings with the eye of a policeman looking for things that didn't sit right. Catching movement, he looked up at the building opposite the bakery and watched a larger woman at one of the upstairs windows crooning to a bundle she held in her arms. She looked out of the window and down at Steve, their eyes connected briefly, and she gave him a half smile. His musings were interrupted by his coffee, so he thought no more about it and strolled around to the rear of the bakery, sipping his drink looking for the object of his desire.

He found him sat on an upturned milk crate with a handful of pastries, which he was tucking into.

'Sniffy, sorry to interrupt your breakfast,' Steve remarked dryly.

Sniffy was a small man in his early thirties, who actually looked about sixty. He was a well-known junkie and dosser who was fairly harmless, primarily because he was incredibly stupid and refused to give up the drugs. He routinely raided the bins of the bakery for their daily throw outs. Sniffy narrowed his eyes at Steve's presence.

'What d'you want?' he said grumpily. 'Interruptin' a man's breakfast.'

A variety of noises came from the large industrial bin and Steve raised an eyebrow. Sniffy looked over his shoulder and back at Steve.

'What?'

'Who's in there?' Steve asked.

Steve heard a large whoop from the depths of the bin. A tall thin man who looked to be in his early twenties with unkempt dark hair, a patchy beard, red sores on his skin and a sallow complexion had emerged. He was sporting only one front tooth and was triumphantly holding a whole slightly crushed pie. Steve looked at his one remaining tooth and concluded, dental care by heroin.

'Sniffy, I've found a pie,' the man said delightedly, climbing out and holding it reverently. He shrugged repeatedly and kept jerking his chin up, making noises as he did.

'Good job, Spike,' Sniffy said. 'See if there's anything else for tea, yeah?'

'Yeah. Good job. Good job,' Spike said, ticking as he climbed back into the bin.

Sniffy turned to Steve.

'He's got that thingy,' he said, sniffing and wiping his nose with the back of his hand. 'You know…' He waved his hand around vaguely.

'A drug habit and a penchant for bin juice?'

Sniffy looked confused. 'No, he's got that thing.' He snapped his fingers. 'Lilets… No, Tilettes… that's it.'

'You mean Tourette's?'

'Was 'xactly what I said,' Sniffy said belligerently. 'What d'you want anyway?' He unpacked the contents of a nostril and inspected it closely.

'Do you know this guy?' Steve showed him the picture of the face of the dead man in the woods on his phone.

Sniffy shied away. 'Ugh! Is that bloke dead?'

'He is. Know him?'

Sniffy shrugged. 'No. Spike might. He's not from round here. SPIKE!' he yelled. 'COME OUT.'

When he emerged, Steve showed him the picture. 'Know this guy?'

Spike narrowed his eyes and looked, his chin jutting up with ticks every few seconds.

'Does he have swallow tattoos on his hands?'

'If he did?'

'Might be a bloke I know,' Spike said, ticking and itching his sores. 'Fucking twat,' he shouted.

Steve ignored it. 'Where's he from?'

'Cardiff. Place is full of fucking twats,' he yelled.

'Got a name?' Steve pushed.

Spike screwed his face up, clearly trying to remember. 'Harry something.'

'Daly?'

'Maybe.'

'Who was he?'

'Dunno. Hung around with the Tao crew.'

'The what?'

'Danny Tao. He's a fucking c—'

'He's Chinese? Asian?' Steve interrupted.

'Yup.' He ticked furiously for a minute. 'Fucking Chinaman,' he shouted.

'Danny Tao is into drugs?'

'And the rest,' Spike added, chin jerking.

'When did you last see this guy?' Steve persisted.

'Before I got here,' Spike said.

'Which was?'

'Few weeks.' Spike continued ticking, in between taking chunks out of a roll he'd liberated from the bin.

'Did he work for them? Do jobs for them?'

Spike chewed. 'Dealing, collections. Don't do drugs, they'll kill you,' he yelled. 'Roughing up people that owed money, he helped with that... NASTY NASTY! I worked for them for a bit and then got out.'

'Are the Tao's just in Cardiff?'

'Twats! They're all fucking twats,' he shouted.

He cleared his throat and looked at Steve and spoke without ticking for a moment. 'No. London mainly, getting bigger in Cardiff though. They get a lot of supplies from all around here though, cause the filth haven't cottoned on yet. I hitched a ride here from a delivery van of theirs.'

'Where do they deliver to?' Steve asked, intrigued.

'Dunno. All over.'

'Here?'

'Yup. Some bungalow with some busybody old bag next door who was shouting at me. STUPID OLD COW!'

Steve's phone pinged, heralding the arrival of a text. It was from Murphy.

Call me. NOW.

Steve spoke to Spike and Sniffy.

'If you remember anything else. Call me. It's important. Take this.' He thrust his card at Sniffy who eyed it suspiciously. 'Just take it,' Steve snapped.

Sniffy looked at the card, shoved it in his pocket and resumed his nose picking.

'Take care now,' Steve said over his shoulder as he walked away.

'What's so urgent?' he said when Murphy answered his call.

'I'm sending you a picture,' said Murphy.

'By the way, has our man got two swallow tattoos on his hands?' Steve asked.

'He has.'

Steve's phone pinged as he received the picture. 'Hang on.' He watched as the picture went from blurry to clear while it downloaded. He put Murphy on speakerphone and tried to find a quiet piece of the pavement to have the conversation.

'Is that a…?'

'Yes, it is.'

'Where was it?'

'Throat.'

'He'd swallowed it?'

'No.'

'So… someone put it there?'

'Oh yeah.'

'What's that on it?' Steve was peering at the tiny screen.

'That, my friend, is a Chinese dragon.'

'What?'

'There's something else though.'

'What?'

'There was a message rolled around it. I'm sending it.'

Steve's phone pinged again. Steve downloaded the photo and stared.

'Oh shit.'

'Exactly what I was thinking.'

'Anything else?'

'Nope. That was my starting point. I'll know more later. I'll call.'

'OK. Thanks for the heads up.' Steve ended the call and sighed heavily. His phone rang almost instantly. It was Jonesey.

'Before you ask, I am not bringing you in any food.'

'I wasn't ringing about that, but I think that's a little harsh,' Jonesey said in a wounded tone.

'What then?'

'Harry Daly. Forty-four is the stiff in the woods. He's got some serious form on him. Drugs, organised crime, deadly weapon, assault, GBH. You name it.'

'A fine, upstanding citizen by all accounts then.'

'Yup. Graduated with honours from the school of pond life.' Jonesey laughed. 'What do you need me to do?'

'I need a deep dig into known contacts. I want you to get onto Cardiff nick, ask for Ross Scott, tell him it's for me. I want everything they've got on a Danny Tao gang. This guy was in with them so they might know of him too. See what you can dig up. OK?'

'OK.'

'Also, ask them if they know of a low-level junkie called Spike, he's got one tooth and Tourette's.'

'I'd like to see his tinder profile,' Jonesey quipped.

'I need to go and see Pearl. There's been a development.'

'Oh, what?'

'I'll fill you in later.'

'Be careful there. I still think you're lucky to be alive after last time.'

Steve ended the call and made another. 'Pearl,' he said when she answered.

'Three times in as many days, my husband will think we're dating if this carries on.'

'And I won't live to see another day if he thinks that,' Steve replied. 'I need to come and see you and Mickey. You at home? It's urgent.'

'Yes. We're both here. Now?'

'See you in ten,' Steve said grimly, ending the call.

Steve pulled into the driveway of the beautiful architect-designed house that sat high on the hill overlooking Castleby. Stanley, Pearl's right-hand man, was at the front door to greet him and inclined his head as Steve jogged up the steps.

'Stanley.' Steve nodded to him as he walked through the open door followed closely by Stanley. Steve walked through into the main living area which overlooked the entire bay through a wall of glass. Pearl was in the large open-plan kitchen making coffee.

'Hello, darling,' she said.

'Pearl,' Steve said warmly.

'Coffee?'

'Thanks.' He accepted a cup.

'What's going on?' growled Mickey as he entered the kitchen. 'I thought we were well past home visits from the police.'

'Always a pleasure, Mickey,' Steve said dryly.

'Be nice, darling,' murmured Pearl. 'I'm sure Steve wouldn't be bothering us if it wasn't important.'

'Right as usual, Pearl,' Steve said, producing his phone. 'Pearl, the guy in the woods, I spoke to you about this morning.'

She was instantly attentive. 'The man in the noose.'

'Yes. Didn't put *himself* in the noose by all accounts.'

Mickey scowled. 'So what? Pearl told you we didn't have anything to do with it.'

'A bullet was forced into his throat. Wrapped around that bullet was a note.'

'What did the note say?' asked Mickey.

Steve showed Mickey the picture on his phone.

'What does it say?' Pearl asked when Mickey's face drained of colour.

'It says, "Reap what you sow, Mickey",' Steve said quietly.

Pearl's hand fluttered to her throat and Stanley instinctively moved closer to her.

'The bullet has the motif of a Chinese dragon on it,' Steve said.

'Homemade bullet or manufactured?' Mickey asked, his eyes narrowing.

'I suspect homemade, but we're running checks.'

'Who was he?' Pearl asked.

'Pretty hardcore pond life. Harry Daly. Was in with the Tao gang. Danny Tao from Cardiff.'

Mickey inhaled sharply.

'You know him.' Steve didn't miss a trick.

'Darling… who is—'

'Quiet,' snapped Mickey harshly. 'The Tao's are in London. They've expanded to Cardiff now by the sounds of it.'

Pearl raised an eyebrow. Mickey never spoke to her that way normally. Stanley stepped closer to Pearl and laid a protective hand on her shoulder.

'How did he die?' Mickey asked quietly.

'Is that significant?' Steve asked, picking up the friction between the two of them.

'Do you know or not?' Mickey snapped.

Steve looked at Mickey and then Pearl. 'What aren't you telling me?'

Neither Pearl nor Mickey said anything. Steve tried again, frustrated.

'I thought we were past this after the business with Liverpool,' he said. 'You know more than you're letting on. So come on. Why is how he died so significant?'

Mickey stayed silent and glared at Steve menacingly.

'Mickey?' Steve snapped.

Most other men would have backed down, but Steve was used to Mickey and his ways. Plus he had done Pearl a small favour within the confines of the law, and he knew she would have his back because of it.

'Do I need to repeat the question?' Steve asked.

'When you know how he died. Then we'll talk.' Mickey stormed out of the kitchen grabbing his keys and shouting for Maxim, one of his henchmen.

'When will you be back?' called Pearl.

'Dinner,' Mickey called, and the front door slammed.

Steve turned to Pearl, looking at her questioningly.

'What's the issue with Danny Tao's gang?'

'I've no idea,' she said. 'But I'm not liking it already. I think this was before my time.'

* * *

Hannah Evans placed her precious bundle back down and stopped looking out of the window for the attractive man she had seen watching her from the Loafing About Bakery. She reluctantly went into her bedroom and started dressing for work. Tugging at the zip on her nurse's uniform, she tutted. She must have put it on a hot wash, she thought, it seemed to be shrinking every time she wore it. In truth, she was in denial. She knew she was putting on weight and her friend Anne at work had suggested the previous week that they go on a diet together. She hated diets. She hated any form of keep-fit, but she supposed if she could do it with Anne then maybe it wouldn't be so bad.

Hannah had met Anne, also a nurse, years ago when they had worked at another hospital together. They'd lost touch, but had bumped into each other again at a support group for women who had suffered miscarriages. Both women had lost their babies early on in their pregnancies and being on their own, had sought some much-needed support to get through the experience. They had stayed at the group for a few months until they had both decided to move on when they felt they could continue to support each other.

Hannah finished brushing her hair, got herself ready to go and climbed into her car to head off to the hospital in the next town.

Hannah joined the queue in the coffee shop while she waited for Anne. She knew exactly what Anne would have so it was pointless not getting in the queue when she could. She looked over the displays of cakes, biscuits and crisps and her mouth watered, and her tummy rumbled.

Since losing the baby she had needed to fill the ache she had inside, and food did that for her. She didn't care what the diets said, calorie deficits and all that crap. They could fuck right off, she thought moodily. She could please her damn self and eat what she wanted to eat.

'What can I get you?' the spotty ginger man behind the counter asked her with a smile.

'Oh er, two medium skinny lattes and one of those chocolate muffins.'

'Excellent choice,' he said, grinning. 'Eat in?'

'Please.'

He organised a tray and put the muffin on a plate with a napkin, which he then slid a packet of chocolate wafers under. He grabbed her coffees and put them on the tray, then totalled up the amount and handed the card machine over.

'Wafers are on me today.' He smiled. 'For a lovely lady.'

Hannah went beetroot. 'Oh, thank you,' she stammered. 'You didn't have to do that.'

'I see you nearly every day and I like to see you smile,' he said. 'You've not smiled much lately. Maybe this will make you happy.'

'I think it will,' she said, smiling broadly. Did this bloke fancy her, she wondered? Should she maybe *not* eat the muffin to try and slim down a bit? She picked up the tray and looked back at him.

'Thank you,' she said.

'Welcome,' he said, holding her gaze. 'See you again.'

Hannah spotted Anne who was waving from a table and weaved her way over to her.

'Why are you all flushed?' Anne asked.

'The man behind the counter gave me a wafer,' Hannah said, sitting down and unloading the tray.

'Which man?' Anne asked, looking at the counter. 'The ginger one?'

'Uh huh.' Hannah cast a furtive look over. He caught her eye and waved.

Hannah waved back, embarrassed; beetroot red again.

'You fancy him,' Anne announced, looking at her and then back over at him. 'He looks quite sweet. You should go out with him if he asks, mind you from what I hear, he gives wafers to all the girls. Julie calls him Creepy Ginge.'

'Does he? Oh, well, he won't ask me,' Hannah said, feeling slightly deflated.

'You never know. A free wafer today… maybe dinner tomorrow,' Anne said.

'Shut up. Here, have half this muffin.'

'How's things on the ward?' Hannah asked, digging in and making appreciative noises as she took a bite of the muffin.

'That baby, Lucas, is still crying all the time. The mother is still totally bloody useless. Ignores him constantly! She had the cheek to ask me to take him in another room so she could do a live Instagram post. Honestly, people like her shouldn't have babies. It makes me so mad. She just wants a trophy baby, to go with her wag-like house and her wag-like car and her stupid Botox face and filled lips,' she said bitterly.

'Sounds like a right stupid cow,' Hannah agreed. 'He's such a gorgeous baby. Women like that don't deserve to have it so easy.'

'Absolutely,' Anne said fervently.

'Do you find it hard working on the maternity ward? Now I've lost a baby, I think I'd find it hard. I used to love working on maternity, but I just don't know if I could do it now,' Hannah said.

'I'm getting over it. Perhaps it wasn't meant to be,' Anne said wistfully.

Hannah glanced at her watch. 'How long have you got left, it's half past?'

'I need to go. Maybe see you later?'

Hannah finished her coffee and stood up to follow Anne out. As she glanced over her shoulder, the ginger guy waved and gave her another wink.

CHAPTER 5

Mike Young awoke with a stiff neck. He stretched and wondered why he was sleeping on his sofa and not in his bed. Even in his most drunken state, he pretty much always made it to bed. Then he remembered. Olivia was in his bed. And he had almost ended up in his bed with her. He swung his legs around and sat rubbing his face, trying to wake up. He glanced at the clock. An hour before he had to be at work. Getting up, he padded over to the kitchen where he flicked on the kettle and crept along to the bedroom. In the dim light he could see the unmoving form of Olivia. He pulled the door shut and went for a shower, grabbing clean clothes from the tumble dryer so he wouldn't wake her. He sat at the table nursing a coffee and a bowl of cereal and thought about Olivia's reappearance last night. They had caught up, ended up kissing and almost going to bed. Mike had stopped it, suddenly remembering she was married, which meant she was off limits in his eyes.

It was a struggle, seeing her so upset, but he was struggling more with the *why*. Apart from not liking her husband very much, he had no real idea of why she was so distressed.

As she spoke it had dawned on Mike that the objectionable bloke with the muscles at the climbing centre might have been her husband, but the kid? Surely not. Did she have a kid? She hadn't been gone long enough for the child to be hers, unless this was something else she hadn't told him.

He checked the time on his phone and realised he needed to get moving. Moving over to the sink with his breakfast bowl, he busied himself washing up.

'Morning,' Olivia said quietly. 'You OK today?'

Turning, he tried to ignore how gorgeous she looked in one of his RNLI T-shirts. He'd never look at that T-shirt in the same way again.

'Yup. All good,' he managed. 'You sleep OK?'

'Like a log,' she said.

'Sea air, maybe?' He smiled.

'Maybe. You off out?'

'I am. Work.' Mike gestured to his T-shirt, which read 'Instructor' across his back.

'Ah,' she said. 'What's that? Endure?' she asked, peering at the logo on his front.

'Climbing centre,' he said.

'You work there?'

'Yup.' He clipped his RNLI pager onto his belt, it went everywhere with him.

'What's that?' She pointed to it.

'Lifeboat pager.'

'Still on the lifeboat then?' she asked.

'Yup.'

'Wow.'

'What's so surprising?' he asked.

'Nothing,' she said. 'It's just you're so… sorted. Gigs, lifeboat, climbing. You must be busy.'

He folded his arms and leant against the worktop. 'Yup. Life is pretty busy.'

'Is there a girlfriend in this busy life?'

'Not at the moment,' he said guardedly.

'But there has been?'

'Yes,' he said. 'Why?'

She blushed. 'Just wondered if there was anyone serious.'

'I'm not really looking for serious. Got too much on.' He glanced at his watch. 'I've got to go, or Foxy will have my guts.'

'Foxy?'

'Rob Fox. Owner. Top bloke. Look, there was a guy at the climbing centre yesterday with a boy who was diabetic. Looking for someone called Liv. I'm guessing that's you, despite you hating to be called that.'

She looked tearful. 'He calls me that because he likes it, and he knows I hate it.'

'Nice guy.'

'Oh yeah.'

'I assume the kid isn't yours?'

'No. I couldn't have children with that man.'

'Probably shouldn't have married him then, eh?' Mike said, more bitterly than he intended.

'You have no idea how often I think that,' she whispered.

Mike watched her for a beat and almost said something, but his phone pinged: the alarm he set himself reminding him to leave. When he was engrossed in writing his songs, he often forgot the time.

'I've gotta go. Feel free to stay here.'

'I might. Could we talk later? When do you finish work?'

'I've got a late class at the centre. Be done by eight.'

'OK. I'll see you back here then if that's alright?'

'OK.' He grabbed his bag and picked a key off the hook in the kitchen.

'Spare key,' he said, placing it on the table. 'See you later.'

'Bye then,' she said quietly.

* * *

Steve was regretting his weak moment with the Superintendent where he'd agreed with his idea of public 'drop-in' monthly surgeries. The Superintendent had thought it would be excellent for community policing. He'd suggested that he'd be happy to do it on a regular basis to keep in touch with the local people.

However, Steve now found himself sitting in the church hall with a large takeaway coffee looking dubiously at the line forming. While the Superintendent sat in his office, studiously avoiding all contact with the proletariat that was the local people.

Jonesey was in his element, making tea, offering and eating biscuits. He swept past Steve, putting down a handful of biscuits as he passed by.

'I reckon they're only here for the tea and biccies,' he said, winking. 'Nice easy doss of an afternoon.'

Steve rolled his eyes and bit into a custard cream. He beckoned the first person over.

'What can I do for you today?' he pleasantly asked a lady who looked to be in her late sixties. She was clutching a large bag to her chest like the room was full of handbag snatchers.

'You can speak to the electricity company about my electricity bill,' she said, plonking her bag on the table. She fumbled about inside it and produced a large sheaf of papers. 'I'm sick of talking to them about it.'

Steve frowned. 'OK. You know we're the police, yes? And not your MP?'

'I'm not stupid,' she snapped. 'Of course I know you're the police. Honestly, this is the last straw. I've been in and told you all time and time again. People are stealing my electricity.'

'Right,' Steve said, secretly wishing he'd made a sign that read 'not at home to crazy.' He smiled. 'So exactly how are they stealing it?'

She tutted and narrowed her eyes.

'Are you here because you're the thick one who gets to deal with everyone because they don't want you dealing with anything else?'

'Excuse me?' Steve was affronted.

'You know. The liability copper that they can't sack? Plenty of them about.'

'I sincerely hope not.'

'Well, listen up 'cos I'll say it again. My neighbours are nicking my electricity. I don't know how. But my bill has gone from £500 per year to £5000 a year and let's just say, even with the best will in the world I couldn't use that much electricity.'

'You've told them that?'

She rolled her eyes. 'Are you stupid?'

'No. What did they say?'

'They said the readings were right. I had to pay.'

'How long has this been going on for?'

'At least a year. I'm refusing to pay, and they keep telling me they're going to prosecute.'

'Who lives next door to you?'

'No one now. Mrs Roberts passed over about a year ago. One of her dead-beat grandsons dosses next door sometimes. He's about as useful as a chocolate teapot, I can tell you.'

Steve's ears pricked up. 'Is the house empty?'

'Most of the time. All boarded up. You can't see inside. He appears with his cronies sometimes. They all need a job and a good bath. Mind you, with a mother like that, I'm not surprised. Fat old bag she is.'

'Right. What's your address, Mrs…'

'Mrs Clifton. 14 Woodpecker Lane.'

'Castleby?'

'Yes.'

'I'll get someone to look into it. What's the name of the grandson while I think of it?'

'Well, one was called JJ, but I think he died, and the other is Luke Jones.'

'I know the Jones boys and the mother too.'

'Well then,' she said triumphantly. 'You'll know then.'

'I'll look into it personally,' Steve said.

She arched an eyebrow.

'Hmm… But if you're the thick one, nothing'll get done.' She looked over her shoulder. 'Shall I tell someone else? What about that one over there in uniform? The one who's eating?'

'I guarantee I'll deal with it.'

'That doesn't reassure me. I want a response by the end of the week.'

'Consider it done, Mrs Clifton.'

Mrs Clifton grabbed her bag and stalked off. Another pensioner strode over purposefully, and Jonesey gave him a thumbs up. Steve's phone pinged and he saw another text from Murphy instructing him to call. He stood.

'Jonesey. Take over.'

'But, Guv…'

Steve grabbed the phone and walked out of the church hall as quickly as he could manage without running. He dialled Murphy's number and waited impatiently for him to answer.

'What's up?' he said once his call was answered.

'Got a cause of death for you,' Murphy said.

'Hit me.'

'Don't tempt me,' he said. 'Your man was drowned.'

'Uh huh.'

'And the question you need to ask me is?'

'Er… Was he forcibly drowned, or did he just drown?'

'Excellent. You'll go far. He was forcibly drowned. Held down by the throat, I'd say. Come on, Detective, you need to ask me another question.'

'I'm not sure I like this game.'

'Humour me.'

'What did he drown in?'

'And the prize for best copper goes to…'

'Come on,' Steve said impatiently, trying not to smile.

'Petrol. You man was drowned in petrol.'

Steve exhaled noisily. 'Man. That's nasty.'

'I agree. Wholeheartedly.'

'You seen that before?'

'In another life, ganglands in South America.'

'Nice fellows.'

'Oh yeah. Triads have been known to use chicken blood too sometimes, in place of petrol or water. Some of the more hardcore old-school gangs favour it too. My, my, how creative we've all become.'

'Painful.'

'Exceptionally. I think the petrol was hot, looking at the burn ratios. Not on fire. They like to heat it just enough for it to be very hot, but they don't ignite it.'

Steve shuddered. 'Why?'

'Well, it's excruciatingly painful when it's hot, plus it's the idea that they *could* ignite it that's even more terrifying. As if hot petrol isn't scary enough. So, your man was drowned, hung upside down to drain it out and then strung up in the woods. He was left for some time after he died though, before he was stuck in the noose. Somewhere chilly. He wasn't frozen though.'

'Right.'

'And on that note, I must crack on.'

* * *

Hannah cooed goodbye to her babies and left the flat. As she shut the front door and her eyes flicked over the bakery opposite, she remembered the attractive man she had seen looking up at her the day before. He had been very handsome. She wondered if he fancied her and whether she would see him again. With that in mind, she had decided she needed to start looking her best, so that had prompted her to take some action to get fit.

She had decided to go running. She wanted to try and kick start her system into losing some weight; try and get herself into shape if she could. She knew she'd comfort eaten far too much since losing her baby, but she wanted to try and get fitter and lose some of the extra pounds. She squeezed herself into some brand-new running skins and made sure she had her headphones and set off with purpose to Mutters Moor where she knew it wouldn't be busy.

After parking, she got out and embarked on some half-hearted stretches. Feeling good, she set off up the track. This was exercise on her terms. She had fleetingly toyed with the idea of joining a local fat-busting boot camp, which was run early mornings on the beach, but after peeking over the large stone wall one morning, she had been utterly horrified.

She couldn't believe the number of yummy mummies there in Lycra and with immaculate ponytails. She also couldn't believe the level of activity that seemed to be expected. As she watched them, she felt quite light-headed. She knew that she would most likely keel over and die if she did exercise like that. Feeling quite distressed, she had scuttled back to her flat and calmed herself down with a bacon sandwich.

But today, the sun was out, and it made her feel good. She didn't want to think about work. Didn't want to think about the things that went on there. She tried not to think about the emptiness she felt when she thought about her lost baby.

She closed her mind to it, set her music to play and started jogging.

As she plodded, she sang along, puffing out the words to her female power playlist. She puffed out the first verse of 'Sisters are Doing it for Themselves' as she rounded the corner and started to jog down to the lower path.

Still singing, she jogged past a couple who were sat on a bench with their dog. She half smiled at them wondering why they were looking at her strangely. Her legs were screaming, and her lungs felt like they were bursting. She slowed to a walk, her legs hurting as she slowed down, and she struggled to catch her breath. Despite the chilly air she was sweating profusely. She panted heavily in the hope that this would calm her down and kicked herself for not bringing any water. Her throat felt like sandpaper. As she rounded a corner, her heart sank. There they were.

Two Little Miss Perfects. With their perfect arses, perfect busts, flat stomachs, fully made-up faces. Both pushing 'off road' style pushchairs. She felt a rush of hot wild rage.

FUCKING BITCHES.

She kept her eyes averted as she passed by them and tried not to listen to them talking about their perfect lives with their perfect babies. She felt a rush of hatred and rage for them and clenched her fists tightly. Her anger drove her to walk away quickly, desperate to be away from them.

'Excuse me!'

Hannah ignored the voice. She didn't want to talk to them.

'Hey! Excuse me!'

Hannah stopped and turned around to see one of the Little Miss Perfects jog up with her pushchair and sleeping baby.

She yanked the headphones out of her ears and looked at the woman questioningly, reluctant to speak.

'What?' Hannah asked shortly.

'Sorry to stop you,' the woman said pleasantly. 'But I just said to my friend, you know, if it was me, I'd like, totally want to know.'

'Know what?' Hannah said stupidly.

'That my skins had split all down the back seam, and that my knickers were on show to everyone.'

Hannah wanted to die.

'Sorry,' the woman said, turning her pushchair around and jogging back to her friend. Her ponytail swinging and her perfect arse not moving at all.

Hannah reached behind and felt her skins had ripped completely down the back seam. Her eyes filled with tears, and she tried to stop a sob escaping. She frantically tried to remember which knickers she had on. Was it her weekday ones with teddy bears? Or the big girls' black ones? God, was it the grey ones that were once white? She looked around frantically and couldn't see anyone else, so she started running back to the car. Her face felt hot from embarrassment and anger at the girl who told her. Stupid bitch. Stupid fucking perfect bitch. Bet she fucking enjoyed it. Bet they were laughing their perfect fucking arses off now.

Hannah carefully scanned the area to see if anyone could see her. She imagined what she looked like from the back. Fat and ugly. Fat and ugly with a big ugly arse. She felt tears pricking at her eyes again.

The tears were quickly replaced by rage.

Exactly who the *fuck* did that girl think she was speaking to her that way? Looking at her the way she did? And the totally patronising way she said 'Sorry'. Hannah wanted to hit her. Punch her face until it was a mass of blood and broken teeth. All very good having a perfect figure and perfect arse but if your face was a fucking car crash then it was all for nothing. It was no more than she deserved.

Bitch.

Hannah finally got to the edge of the car park. There were two cars: hers and a Range Rover. Hannah snorted. Of course the stuck-up bitch drove a Range Rover. It would never ever go off road or even up more than a small hill. She would ferry herself and her brattish kids about in it, lording it up over everyone else and looking down her perfect nose. Well, she could fuck right off.

Grabbing a large rock from the edge of the car park she marched up to the Range Rover and she hit the windscreen hard with it. She felt wonderful. She smashed the rock down again and again, feeling the wonderful rush of rage as she did it.

Stupid fucking bitch.

Who did she think she was?

Panting, Hannah stood back and looked at her handywork. Not good enough. She scraped the rock all along the sides of the car, making sure she ruined every panel and then smashed both wing mirrors. Satisfied, she threw the rock into a clump of thick gorse bushes, got into her car, and looked at the ruined Range Rover with satisfaction.

'*Sorry,*' she said to the car in the same tone of voice that the woman had used, and she wheel spun out of the car park smiling to herself. Fucking bitch totally deserved it.

CHAPTER 6

Mike was staring out of the window at the climbing centre, thinking about Ollie when his RNLI pager went off.

'Go,' Foxy said. 'I'll fill in. Don't forget I'm off this afternoon though, so let me know if it looks like a long one.'

Mike grabbed his phone and ran around the corner to the RNLI station. He headed into the locker room to start putting on the gear, nodding to Jesse the mechanic, who was already suited up.

Dan, a chef up at the large hotel, was already there along with Ben and Paul; two brothers also on the crew. Doug appeared at the door already in his gear.

'Reports of a small boy in an inflatable dinghy in the water on the Kirby ferry route,' he announced.

'Who called it in?' Dan asked. 'And what's a kid doing out on an inflatable boat? It's bloody freezing out.'

'I know. Post boat from Kirby Island called it in. Leaving in two!' Doug shouted.

The crew took their positions on the boat as the shrill alarm for launch was sounded and the lifeboat slid down the steep incline, meeting the waves below with a thump. It powered off around the headland with the crew on deck searching for the small blue and white dinghy. Clipped to the rail, Mike looked out with the high-powered binoculars. He spotted something in the distance bouncing along the waves being blown by the unrelenting wind.

'Got it,' he called. 'Port side.'

Doug instructed Dan to turn towards it. 'Slow approach,' he cautioned as they got near.

'Jesse, grab the hook.'

Jesse prepared to try and hook the small boat closer to the large lifeboat without tipping it over. She strained to see an occupant. Finally, she saw a small form curled up in the bottom of the tiny dinghy.

'Child in here,' she called and leant out over the side, deftly hooking the dinghy close. Dan stopped the boat and the powerful engines burbled quietly, ticking over. The crew didn't need to be told what to do. Paul gently lowered himself over the side into the dinghy and hooked a strap around the small boy's upper torso. Mike stepped forward next to Jesse so they could lift the child up and over the rail. They laid him gently on the deck. Paul climbed nimbly back on board and then reeled in the small inflatable boat, affixing it to the deck.

'I know this kid,' Mike said. 'He's a diabetic. He looks freezing.'

'From the climbing centre?'

'Nope. Just saw him outside there yesterday and had to give him a juice box.'

Jesse called for the first aid box where there was a gel pack for diabetics. She managed to wake him up enough for him to take the gel and then wrapped him in a warm blanket. After a few moments he struggled to sit up.

'Hey, buddy,' she said brightly. 'Stay lying down for a bit.'

Mike knelt down next to him. 'Hey, bud,' he said. 'I saw you yesterday, didn't I? Gave you a juice box.'

The boy nodded. Mike frowned.

'Where's your dad? He was with you yesterday, wasn't he?'

'He's at work,' he mumbled.

Jesse looked concerned. 'How old are you?'

'Twelve.'

'What's your name?'

'Eli.'

'Well, hello there, twelve-year-old Eli.' Jesse smiled. 'I'm Jesse, and this is Mike.'

Mike gave a small salute. 'What are you doing out here, buddy?'

He grinned shyly. 'Dad told me to stay in the room, but I wanted to try out my new boat. I can swim.'

'So what happened?'

'I missed lunch,' he said. 'I don't have any money and Dad said to order room service, but the menu was horrid.'

'Where does Dad work?' Jesse asked.

Eli raised his head and pointed to the wind farm in the distance.

'He works in there; he's helping build it.'

'Where's Mum then, Eli?' Jesse asked gently.

'Mum died,' Eli said. 'I go to boarding school. I only come back for the holidays.'

'Is your dad married again?' Mike asked already knowing the answer.

'Yes. To Liv. I love Liv. I don't know where she is though,' he said quietly.

'How do you feel now?' Jesse asked as Eli sat up. 'Are you up to driving the boat now we're nearly back?'

Eli's eyes lit up. 'Yes please. Do you have any food?'

'We don't, but we'll get you some as soon as we get back,' Jesse said. 'Come on then.'

Mike watched Jesse take him down the stairs and ducked into the cockpit to retrieve his phone which he had stowed. Back on deck, he made a quick call.

'Hey, Ollie.' He slipped into her old nickname. 'Call me when you get this? It's pretty urgent.'

Mike's phone rang as the boat was being towed back up the steep ramp to the station. Eli was still below deck exploring and Mike jumped off the boat to answer, calling to Jesse to take Eli to the mess.

'Ollie,' he said as he answered.

'What's up?' she said. 'Sorry, I was in the shower.'

Mike closed his eyes and tried to ignore the mental image.

'It's Eli. Your stepson.'

'What? What about him? Is he OK?'

'We had a shout on the lifeboat, he'd taken a boat and got ill.'

'What? By himself in the middle of bloody winter?'

'Yes.'

'Where the hell is Brian?'

'Eli said he'd gone to work.'

'Is he OK? I mean... his levels.'

'We've given him a gel sachet. He needs to eat though. Are you OK to come and get him? I realise it's awkward.'

'Does he know I'm here?'

'No.'

'They can't know I'm here. He just can't. I can't explain right now. You need to ring Brian. He needs to take some responsibility for once.'

'OK,' Mike said doubtfully.

'Don't judge me, Mike... look, I'll try and explain everything later. I'll cook?' she said softly. 'So we can talk?'

'Alright,' he said, wondering what there was to talk about.

'I need to clear up a few things,' she said. 'Explain myself. Suddenly turning up in a state… seeing you again… wishing we had…'

'Wishing we had what, Ollie?'

'Let's talk later,' she said firmly. 'I'll explain everything.'

Mike sighed. 'Alright. See you later.'

He leant against the wall of the lifeboat station oblivious to the noise and activity around him. He wasn't sure whether his heart could cope with Olivia being back. She'd shattered it into a million pieces the last time she'd left him.

Eli had stayed at the station all afternoon. Doug left repeated messages for his father, informing him of the child's whereabouts, but no contact had been made so far. Jesse, worried about the boy and his glucose levels, had taken him around to Maggie's for lunch where Maggie had fussed over him and fed him until he thought his tummy would burst.

In the workshop, Eli was helping Jesse strip down a small outboard motor, and he was carefully soaking parts in oil and cleaning them gently with a toothbrush. She had kitted him out in an oversized RNLI T-Shirt and blue nitrile gloves. He was loving every second of it.

'How come you're a mechanic and you're a girl?' he asked, focusing intently as he gently scrubbed something tiny in his pool of oil.

'Just cause I'm a girl it doesn't mean can't to do jobs that men traditionally have done,' Jesse said in a matter-of-fact way, stepping carefully over her dog, Brock, who was asleep flat on his back on one of Doug's old fleeces. She glanced at Eli.

'I used to work for the Metropolitan Police, you know. The ones on the river looking after their boats.'

'That's sick,' Eli said. 'Did you go on any chases?'

'I did once as it happens.' Jesse grinned. 'Very exciting and we caught the bad guys.'

'So cool,' Eli said. 'What had the bad guys done?'

'Stolen a very posh boat.'

'And you caught them? Wow.'

'It was pretty awesome,' Jesse said, grinning.

Eli carried on rubbing intently. 'Can I come back here again sometime?' he said in a small voice.

Jesse pulled up a stool. 'If you want to. Your dad will have to be cool with it though. Nessie might even let you help out in the shop. Billy will teach you about the winch for the big boat. Aren't you going to school though?'

'My term doesn't start for a few weeks. So I'm here while Dad works. I think we're living in Liv's cottage from Saturday, so I expect I'll be there most days,' he said gloomily.

'Well, when your dad turns up, we can ask him,' Jesse said brightly, feeling sorry for this poor boy who had been dumped.

Hours later, Eli's father had still not materialised. Doug dropped Eli at the hotel with instructions to the owner regarding Eli's condition and a guarantee that he would be fed.

Mike left the climbing centre and bought a bottle of wine from the small supermarket on the way home. He let himself into the flat and was surprised to see it in darkness and quiet. He flicked on the lights and stood in the kitchen looking at the note folded against a bottle of wine on the counter, his heart sunk, semi-dreading what it was going to say.

'And she does it again,' he said, sighing deeply.

He picked up the note.

Sorry. I'll explain when I can. I meant what I said about the mistake. Always. Ollie. x

Mike stared at the note. He crumpled it up, throwing it in the bin angrily. He thought about how easy it had been to fall back into kissing Ollie. How much he had realised he missed her. How much he still felt for her. But then he remembered she was married. He swore lightly. It was like time hadn't passed at all since she'd left him the same note four years ago.

* * *

Not sure of which key to use, Foxy tried a few before the lock released and the door swung open. He walked in and stopped for a moment trying to control the myriad emotions that assaulted him. Breathing deeply, he tried to focus. He pushed down the rapidly rising grief building deep within him. He closed his eyes. The scent of her perfume lingered in the air and part of him wanted to hear her voice or her laugh. But he knew it would never happen. He heard footsteps, voices behind him and felt a strong hand clap him on the back.

'You OK, mate?'

He turned to see his friend Rudi holding some flat-pack boxes.

Foxy swallowed the tears that were building. 'Yeah, all good,' he croaked.

'Liar,' came a soft voice and he smiled. His friend, or bestie as they called each other, was looking at him with concern. 'It's OK to be sad, you know,' Sophie said quietly. 'I'm still sad when I think about Sam.'

Sam was Sophie's husband who had died a few months previously. It had been an incredibly difficult time for her. Sam was Military Intelligence and had been missing in action for two years until he was found. He had been returned to the UK, but his injuries from being captured and tortured had been so severe, that he had lost both legs. He didn't want to carry on living, so he had tried to take his own life and had never recovered. Sophie and her son had made the difficult decision to let him go.

Foxy had been there for her throughout and their friendship had been forged to a deeper level. However, during this time, Foxy had realised that he was head over heels in love with Sophie. He had never acted on it, not wanting to ruin their friendship.

'I know,' he croaked. 'I just feel…'

'What?' Sophie moved to stand nearer to him. 'What is it?'

'I just feel… alone, I guess. No Charlie, no Carla. They were my whole family. Why do I get to be around, and they don't?'

'Shit, you can't be thinking like that, mate,' Rudi announced as he expertly assembled a box in a few practised moves. 'Drive yourself bloody mad that way.'

'Rudi's right,' Sophie said. 'You can't think like that. Now come on, we've gotta get this packed up.' She stretched up and gave Foxy a kiss on his cheek. 'You'll never be alone, you have us. Always.'

Rudi grinned and clapped Foxy on the back. 'Yeah. What she said. Come on, let's get started.'

The three of them were in Carla's flat. Carla was Foxy's ex-wife and had been staying with Foxy over Christmas. She had unexpectedly fallen very ill with a virus and had rapidly declined. Her death had been unexpected and left Foxy reeling. He'd experienced much loss in a short time, and he was still struggling with the grief of it all collectively.

Always organised, Carla left everything to Foxy, which included her flat in Portsmouth, near the hospital where she had worked. Probate had gone through quickly, and it was up to Foxy to empty it of her personal possessions before he put it on the market. He had decided to leave the majority of the furniture in case a potential purchaser needed it.

'You take the lounge, I'll take the bedroom,' Sophie said to Foxy. 'Rudi, you're on kitchen.'

'Yes, Boss.'

Foxy took a couple of boxes into the lounge along with a roll of packing material. He placed the box down next to the sideboard and looked with interest at the photos she had on display. He had been to the flat a few times but hadn't lingered to look at anything for long. There was a small black-and-white picture taken on their wedding day, and lots of pictures of Charlie, their daughter, through the years. The last one, a copy of the one Foxy had in his home of her blowing a kiss towards the camera, taken just before she died in a climbing accident. He touched her face through the glass, smiling at her.

He saw a picture that Mike had taken of him and Carla in the climbing centre, where he had his arm around her, and she was laughing widely at something. He put it aside to go in his flat.

The last picture had him swallowing back tears. It was a picture taken at sunset of the back of him, on the beach facing the sea, and Solo was sitting next to him. Foxy's hand was resting on Solo's head, and they were both watching the sunset; two almost black silhouettes. He had no idea she had taken it. Let alone had it framed and kept in her flat. He carefully placed it aside and started wrapping things up to go into storage.

Three hours later, the team of three finished placing the last of the boxes in the van that Rudi had borrowed from a friend. Sophie had hoovered and they had 'dressed' the flat as much as they could, ready for the agent to start viewings. The agent had assured a sceptical Foxy that he had a list of people looking to buy in that area, but Foxy was in no hurry, so he signed the paperwork and agreed a date that viewings could begin.

Foxy stared at the boxes as he went to shut the van doors. This was Carla's life, her memories, her possessions, packed into the back of a van in boxes. He felt his throat close and jumped slightly when he felt an arm slide around his waist in a hug. Knowing it was Sophie, he wrapped one of his arms around her shoulders.

'Thanks for today,' he managed.

'Anytime, bestie,' she said. 'I've put the bag of stuff you want in your place in the front, so we don't lose it. Are you OK to go? Or do you need a few minutes by yourself in there?'

Foxy glanced up at the flat and then back to the van. Carla's memory lived inside his head now and the possessions of hers that he would now treasure.

'I'm OK. We can get going.'

'Rudi wants food,' she said, rolling her eyes. 'You in?'

He grinned. 'I'm in.'

CHAPTER 7

Nate walked down the long, hideous pink-coloured corridor and tried to keep the smile that he had carefully arranged on his face. His sweaty hand held a bag. He couldn't believe he was nervous. Why was he nervous about seeing his wife? He watched the back of the nurse as she briskly marched down the corridor, her soles squeaking slightly on the utilitarian vinyl floor.

He had carefully selected what to bring with him, mindful of the advice from Dr Oakley. He had brought her favourite jumper. A soft navy-blue cashmere with a large orange lobster on the front. He only ever remembered her laughing in that jumper. Also in the bag was her favourite navy-blue cotton scarf with big white stars on it, which smelled of her perfume. He remembered burying his face in it, remembering her gorgeous scent.

He had also brought a book. He had given it to her on their first anniversary. It was an A4 printed, blue bound book entitled *Viv's*

Story. He had spent hours with her family and friends collating pictures. It was a timeline of Viv through her life culminating in pictures of them together when they first met to their first wedding anniversary. The last page he had left blank, apart from the words 'To be continued'. The loss of the baby had come about nearly nine months after the anniversary, so none of the pictures were anything baby-related.

The nurse stopped outside of a common room and addressed him.

'If she starts to get agitated, walk away. It's not you.'

'OK,' Nate said.

She opened the door and gestured him in. Nate walked through the door, which the nurse closed gently. He was careful not to make eye contact with the other two patients present. His gaze flicked over them briefly. One older lady was reading a newspaper intently, and then Nate realised it was upside down. She was busy muttering to herself and pointing to pictures as she read. He passed by her, heading for Viv who was sitting on a window seat, facing the garden, and hadn't noticed his arrival.

He passed an armchair and an old frail arm with incredibly wrinkled skin shot out and grabbed him, the strength of the hold belying the old and withered look of the arm.

'No good will come of the move,' the old lady said, her eyes closed.

'Sorry? What was that?' Nate asked.

'I said no good will come of this move. The sea won't heal her. You mark my words. Be careful of what rages within and the storm with the woman's name.' She let go of his arm so suddenly Nate wondered whether he had dreamt it.

He stared at the woman who had spoken. To him, she appeared asleep. He looked at her for a moment, but saw no other signs of her being awake. He glanced over at Viv. She had seen him. She smiled and his heart leapt.

'Nate,' she said, standing and wrapping her arms around him, pressing him close. 'God, I miss you. I thought you'd never come.' She laughed. 'I'm going fucking mad in here… Literally.'

Nate splashed cold water on his face and looked at himself in the bathroom mirror. He winced as he touched his swollen, cut nose and examined his eye, which was turning an angry shade of purple. Remembering the visit, he felt his throat close with threatened tears. It had started so well. Viv had been affectionate and loving, and had seemed almost back to her old self.

She had dived into the bag he carried with delight. She wound her favourite scarf around her neck and pulled on her favourite jumper. She sat in the window seat of the tall window with the light streaming in behind her and for a moment he had felt hopeful. It had surged within him and bubbled up. Perhaps a new life, with Viv recovered, *could* actually happen.

Then she saw the book. She had always loved the book. The proper hardbound printed book of all her memories, as a child, growing up and their early years together. He remembered giving it to her on their anniversary. They had been in a tiny cabin in Scotland, on the Isle of Skye. It had been snowing and they had snuggled into bed and gone through it together, laughing at the memories.

Viv had carefully removed the book from the bag and gone through it, not saying a word. When she'd got to the end, she had looked at him.

'Where are the pictures? The other pages?' she asked quietly.

Nate remembered being confused and replying, 'That's the end of the book. We need to make a new one.'

'No,' she had said firmly. Her fingers had scrabbled at the back pages. 'There were more pages here. Lots more.' She picked up the book and inspected it closely. 'How did you do it? How? How did you get rid of the pages and make it look like you haven't?'

'Viv, darling.' Nate tried to calm her down. 'I haven't done anything to the book.'

'LIAR!' she shouted. 'Where are the pictures of Leya?'

'Viv, darling. There weren't any pictures of Leya in there,' Nate said.

'LIAR!' she had shouted again, scrabbling at the pages. 'There were pictures. When she was born, her first birthday. Her first steps. It was all in HERE!' Her finger jabbed the page repeatedly.

'Viv. Darling.' Nate had been desperate to calm her. 'Viv, Leya didn't live to see her first birthday. She died before she was born. You remember?'

Viv backed away from him, clutching the book to her chest. She had been frantically shaking her head, her eyes full of tears. Her look had been accusatory.

'No. That's a damn lie. You're a liar.'

'No, Viv. It's not a lie. You're struggling to come to terms with Leya's death. That's why you are here.'

'I'm not struggling with anything! I'm in prison!' she shrieked. 'You've put me in prison!' She hurled the heavy book at him, the corner hitting him squarely in the face, his nose exploded. She had launched herself at the bars on the window and tried to pull them off.

'Get me out of this prison!' she screamed, wrenching at the bars.

The nurse who had escorted Nate in entered the room briskly, along with a male nurse who spoke quietly to Viv, and she had become instantly calmer. Quietly, they had led her out of the room. The nurse had looked back at Nate and told him to stay put and that she would be back to escort him out.

Nate remembered sitting in one of the large, slightly plasticky wing chairs and trying to stop his nose from bleeding. He had forgotten all about the old woman sitting quietly with her eyes shut.

'She won't recover,' the old woman had said without opening her eyes. 'She's gone to a place where you can't reach her. No good will come of this. You'll think she's better and then the storm will take her.'

'Quiet now, Gladys,' the nurse said as she returned. She faced Nate. 'Come on. Out.'

Nate remembered standing, suddenly feeling wobbly. He had picked up Viv's book and his bag and followed the nurse out.

'Pay no mind to Gladys. She talks nonsense.' The nurse marched ahead. 'Mind you, I told you to walk away when she got agitated. Here.' She'd handed him a wad of tissues and had gestured to his nose. 'That's gonna hurt later.' She buzzed open the door and gestured him through with her head.

* * *

Steve was knackered. As he drove home, he suddenly remembered Mrs Clifton and her stolen electricity. On a whim, he swung the car around and headed into her road and parked. He stood in the driveway of the bungalow next door to Mrs Clifton and pondered. Inspecting the house, he noticed the boarded-up windows and immediately had a sneaking suspicion of what was going on. He tried the tall side gate and to his delight found it open. Strolling around, he saw all of the windows boarded up and in the corner of the garden, thrown haphazardly, were empty compost and fertiliser bags. Dumped next to the bags was a handful of dead plants, which, to Steve's trained eye, looked exactly like cannabis plants. His suspicions were confirmed.

He walked slowly around the perimeter of the property and finally found the cable snaking under the path to Mrs Clifton's property. He followed it and saw that it fed into a crack in the concrete panel of her garage. She probably had power in her garage but never went in there.

'There's your electricity bill, Mrs Clifton,' he murmured. He peered inside the tiniest of gaps in the blackout coverings, seeing the rows and rows of cannabis plants under the lights.

Pondering his next move, he left the garden, careful to shut the gate, and walked along to Mrs Clifton's house where he rang the bell.

When she answered, she was holding a large frying pan like she was about to go out to bat.

'Oh, it's you,' she said, her eyes narrowing.

'Nice to see you too, Mrs Clifton.'

'What d'you want?' she asked, still holding the frying pan like a weapon.

'Were you expecting someone else?' Steve asked, gesturing to the frying pan.

'I thought it might have been those idiots from next door. They come about now. They knock and ask for stupid things sometimes.'

'Do they now?' Steve said, looking over his shoulder. 'Same time most nights or every few days?'

'Every few days, about now.'

'When they come. How long are they in there for?'

'Few hours.'

'Uh huh. And what do they knock and ask for?'

'Scissors sometimes… oh, a can opener and Sellotape.'

'And what do you say?'

'I say no, of course,' she said, looking at him like he was a moron. 'Why would I lend them anything? I'll never see it again.'

'I see. Can I come in please, Mrs Clifton?'

'Why?'

'So, I can wait to see if anyone turns up next door.'

'How do I know that you're actually police and that you're not pretending to be so you can come in and attack me?'

Steve frowned. 'But you saw me at the police drop-in event. We had a chat about this.'

Huffing, she glared at him suspiciously, still clutching the frying pan.

'Would you like to see my warrant card?' he asked dryly.

'They can be faked.'

'Right. If I was going to attack you, do you not think I would have forced my way in by now? There's no one around to see.'

Mrs Clifton looked confused for a moment. 'Hmm,' she said, eyeing him. 'You can come in, but no funny business.'

'I'm not even sure what constitutes funny business these days,' Steve said mildly, stepping over the threshold. 'Can I watch from in here, please?' He gestured to the lounge, which had a perfect view of next door.

'I suppose you'll be wanting a cup of tea and a biscuit now,' Mrs Clifton said huffily.

'Well, if it's no trouble and you're putting the kettle on.'

'Hmm.' She eyed him. 'I've only got Hobnobs. My chocolate digestives aren't for sharing.'

'Hobnobs are the champion of biscuits in my humble opinion, Mrs Clifton. Thank you.' Steve smiled, trying to keep a straight face.

'You can sit. But not in the blue chair… that's not for…'

'Sharing. I get it.' He looked around. 'OK here?'

She gave him a beady eye. 'I'll be back in a minute.'

'Look forward to it,' he said absently, peering through the lace curtains.

A cup of stewed tea and two stale Hobnobs later, Steve straightened up and peered out of the window as a beat-up old blue van appeared. Four men clambered out and went into the house next door. Steve snapped a few pictures on his phone. After about ten minutes, faint music could be heard. Steve was just about to call it in when a sleek white Tesla pulled up outside. Two men got out and stood in front of the bungalow.

'I've seen those Chinks before,' Mrs Clifton said, chomping loudly on a chocolate biscuit. 'I don't think they're delivering a takeaway, do you?'

Steve refrained from giving the woman a lecture on what was deemed appropriate to say out loud these days. He returned his attention to taking more pictures of the two men as they moved about. They spoke for a moment and then walked into the house, reappearing a moment later with a large duffle bag, which they put in the back seat of the Tesla. Next, they opened the boot and hefted out a large suitcase, which had been wrapped in the kind of tight cellophane that was popular at airports. The case was so heavy that it took two of them to lift it. Together they carried it into the house.

'Reckon that's a body in that suitcase there?' Mrs Clifton said, frightening the life out of him. She was far too close for his liking, her breath hot in his ear.

'Don't know for sure,' he said, trying to inch away.

'I reckon it is. There was that dead girl in a suitcase wasn't there? Down south. Left in a car park of all places! P'r'aps that's a dead girl in there.' She peered at him. 'Shouldn't you go in and be looking?'

'Equally, they might be staying a few days.' Steve took a few more pictures before calling in the number plate. It came back as registered to Tao Enterprises. Steve remembered what Spike had said about catching a lift from a delivery van. Steve took a few more pictures and then turned to Mrs Clifton.

'We need to keep this place under surveillance for a while, to help build a case.'

'What about the dead body in the suitcase?' she said her eyes narrowing.

'We don't know it's a dead body,' Steve said patiently, but inwardly cursing all police crime dramas.

'It was heavy.'

'So's money and some drugs, Mrs Clifton. It could be either.'

Her eyes widened. 'You think?'

'Maybe,' he said sagely.

'Enough to cover my electric bill?'

Steve snorted. 'And then some. Now. I need you to write down my number and call me next time you see the van back. OK? Doesn't matter what time it is.'

'Hmm. Aren't you going to set up surveillance?'

'No budget for it at the moment.' He gave a wry grin. 'You're my surveillance. Do a good job and I'll bring the choccy digestives next time.'

'Hmm. I am very busy you know.'

'Oh, I don't doubt that. But you'll be doing the community a service.' *Bingo*, he thought as her eyes gleamed.

'Will I be on the news or something?' she asked.

'Highly likely. Or the local paper,' he suggested, straight faced.

'Oh well, if I'm doing the community and the police a favour then I better get cracking. Leave your number there and I'll ring next time they turn up.'

'Great.'

'You can go now,' she said, dismissing him.

'Take care now,' Steve said. 'Speak to you soon. I'm going out the back way, I don't want them to see me.'

'Whatever,' she said dismissively, opening a drawer and producing a pair of binoculars. She moved the chair around to face the window and sat down.

CHAPTER 8

Hannah buzzed through the door into the maternity wing of the hospital. Looking along the corridor, she spotted Anne wheeling a baby along in a Perspex crib on wheels.

'Hey, Anne!' she called. 'What are you doing for lunch today? Fancy a coffee?'

'S'pose so.'

Hannah smiled down at the baby. 'Such a cutie,' she crooned. 'Hello there, gorgeous.' She held out a finger and the tiny baby grasped it tightly and gurgled a little. 'Do you remember me?'

'You could have texted me about lunch,' Anne said, 'rather than coming up. Sister will be out in a minute.'

'Don't you love how tiny the hands are!' Hannah gazed down at the baby lovingly.

'I'm on lunch at twelve thirty,' Anne said. 'Shall I meet you in the coffee shop?'

'What? Oh yes. Great,' Hannah said. 'Where are you taking this little one?'

Anne tossed a hard expression over her shoulder towards the nearby ward. 'The mother's totally flippin' clueless. Doesn't know how to look after him, so he's been screaming the place down. I'm taking him on a little walk, and he's calmed right down. To be honest I think she's the problem.'

Hannah looked down into the face of the small baby and felt a tug deep inside her.

'Did you need something, Hannah?' Anne prompted. 'If you can tear yourself away from gaping at the baby for a minute,' she added snippily.

'What?' Hannah said, not looking at Anne and pulling faces at the baby.

'I said what do you need, Hannah? From the ward?'

'Oh… I need a to borrow a breast pump, please. We've got a lady in surgical who needs to express before she goes under the knife.'

'No problem.' Anne swung the crib around and marched off. 'Come on,' she said over her shoulder.

'I'm on late shift for Chrissie tonight.' Hannah rolled her eyes. 'Mind you, I could do with the money.'

'So, you'll pull a double shift tomorrow then?' Anne asked. 'Rather you than me.'

'Oh, I don't mind. I quite like the night shifts sometimes.'

'I hate them. They're creepy.' Anne shuddered. 'I've been swapped to do tomorrow night, which I'm dreading. Shame we're not on together, we could have holed up and started a box set if it was quiet.'

'Well, Chrissie said she might need me for the next night too, so there's hope yet! See you later.'

Hannah wandered back to the surgical ward wondering why Anne had been snippy with her. She realised it was probably harder for Anne than her, since Anne was around babies every day so soon after her miscarriage. Hannah knew Anne had limited support, apart from a few friends. Anne's boyfriend had been short lived, and while she had been happy to see the back of him, she had been much happier to discover she was pregnant. She had always wanted a baby and Dave, the taxi driver, had provided one for her and then promptly left.

Hannah suddenly missed her babies at home. She produced her phone, fiddled for a moment and then activated the small webcam she had at home through an app. The app spooled for a moment and then the screen cleared, and she saw them all waiting patiently for her to come home.

'Mummy be home soon!' she called softly so they could hear. 'You be good now! Mummy loves you!'

* * *

Mike had been stewing about Olivia returning, staying with him, weeping all over him, kissing him and then leaving the 'I can't do this' note. He hated the thought that she was married to the rude tosser he met at the centre. He couldn't bear the thought that this man was intimate with her, shared her life. He tried to shake off the mental image and instead steeled himself, thinking she had made the choice to marry him. She had decided to share her life with this tosser. She had left Mike and gone to Dubai with her brother, with no explanation. No goodbye.

He squared his shoulders mentally and told himself in no uncertain terms that this was not his problem. Deciding to buy himself some dinner from the small supermarket, he walked along the high street, so lost in thought that he didn't hear his name being called until someone grabbed his elbow.

'Mike! I have been calling at you. You are lost in a world of your own, no?' Isabella's lilting Italian accent broke him from his grumpy musings.

'Hey, Isabella. Sorry, I was miles away.' He grinned at her. 'How are you?'

'Hmm. I am OK. You have a lot on your mind, I think,' she said, tilting her head and smiling. 'When you think hard, you have a little line – here,' she said, touching his forehead above the bridge of his nose with a gentle finger.

'Do I?' he said, surprised.

'Yes. When you sing some of your songs too, this line appears.'

'When have you seen me sing?' he asked, slightly embarrassed by her observation.

'Few times. I like your sets. I come if I can get away from serving pizzas.'

She looked different tonight. Her hair was loose, her olive skin was brown against the very pale blue scarf she had wound around her neck. She looked stunning. He wondered why he hadn't noticed how gorgeous she was before.

'You look nice,' he said awkwardly, cursing himself for sounding like an idiot.

'Thank you.' She inclined her head. 'I have been out with a friend, a rare day and night off.'

'Where are you going now?' he asked.

'Nowhere really. I was putting off going home because Mama will give me work to do and it's nice to have a break.' She grinned and giggled. 'That makes me sound awful... yes?'

'Not at all. Look, let's have a drink, maybe something to eat at the pub? You're always giving me food, let me buy you dinner. My treat.'

'OK,' she said, linking her arm through his. 'But promise me, no pizza!'

Mike woke in the early hours with a banging headache. He lay for a moment frowning and then remembered his evening with Isabella. After two bottles of red wine, both of them had been very merry. He looked across the bed at Isabella and wondered if her mother would actually kill him with her bare hands or whether one of her brothers would do it.

She was fast asleep on her front, her brown back on display and her black curls spread out over the pillow. He couldn't help himself as his finger traced the faint lighter line, obviously where a bikini top had been. She shifted slightly and made a small noise. Mike got up and padded to the kitchen. He gulped down two painkillers and a pint of water. He padded back to bed, got in and wrapped himself around Isabella who murmured and snuggled back into him.

When he woke the next morning, she was gone. Propped against an empty mug was a note.

'Jesus, what is it with women and fucking notes?' he grumbled, read it, then smiled.

Ciao, bello. Arrivederci.

Mike knew enough Italian to know she had written something along the lines of, 'Hello, handsome, see you soon.'

He smiled and wandered back to bed, still smelling her gentle perfume as he pulled the covers back over him. It occurred to him that he hadn't thought about Olivia for well over twelve hours.

* * *

Foxy finished arranging the last of Carla's possessions he had saved for himself. He smiled at the photograph of him and Carla in the climbing centre and tried to remember what he had said to get her laughing so much. As he stood staring at the picture, Solo barked and he turned to see Sophie climbing the outside stairs to his flat. She was balancing two coffees and a large brown paper bag.

'Hang on,' he called as he finished folding up the box.

He opened the door and Sophie walked in accompanied by a gust of cold wind.

'Oof! Breezy out there today!' she said, putting down the coffees on his dining table. She bent to make a fuss of Solo, before stripping off her coat.

'Are you not working today? Not that it's not nice to see you.'

'I am, but I have to write a paper, so I'm at home. I had to drop Marcus off early for a school trip, so I figured I'd come and check on my bestie with coffee and a sticky bun.'

Foxy smiled. 'Music to my ears on all counts. Come on, what's in the bag?'

'OK. I've got a choc chip croissant muffin or a maple and pecan plait. Which is it?'

'Let me look.'

She hid the bag. 'Nope. Decide without looking.'

'Hmm. Maple and pecan thing.'

'Done. Chuck me a plate.'

He passed her a plate and she rooted about in the bag and plonked his pastry onto it.

'Is service included in that?' he asked dryly.

'Me thinks you shouldn't be biting the hand that feeds.'

'Well, thank you very much, I'm very grateful,' he replied, lips twitching.

'Is that a new picture?' She stood and wandered over to the shelves where he had just arranged the pictures.

'Yeah. Mike took it. It was in Carla's flat.'

'I love it! What a fantastic picture of you both. Oh, and I love this one of you and Solo. It's perfect. It's so… you and Solo.'

'I never even knew she took that,' Foxy said.

'How are you doing?' Sophie asked quietly as she walked back over to the table and took a seat opposite him. 'You feel OK?'

'Apart from feeling like I'm cast adrift with no anchor now?'

'Is that how you feel? Really?' Sophie frowned. 'I thought you would feel different, you know, you've settled in so well, you're part of the community now. Don't you feel that?'

Foxy chewed thoughtfully. 'I do feel that. Everyone is amazing. But Charlie and Carla were my family. My whole world for a time, they knew me warts and all. Everything about me. They saw me at my absolute worst and still loved me anyway, now there's no one like that. Now it's just me. I just feel like I don't know where my roots are.'

'Rudi, Mack, me, Maggie, we all know you really well. The boys particularly, you served with them long enough.'

'I know.' He shrugged. 'I can't explain it.'

'What can I do?'

'Keep turning up with things like this for a start,' he said, smiling. 'Thank you.'

'It's what besties do,' she said. 'Look out for each other and love you anyway, regardless of everything else.'

Foxy held her gaze. Inside his head a thousand thoughts screamed at him. *Tell her now. Tell her how you feel.* But he remained silent.

Abruptly, he picked up his coffee and raised it. 'Here's to the best bestie ever then.'

'I'll take that.' She picked up her cup and bumped his with it. 'Besties forever.'

Foxy thought the day would never end. He wasn't his usual self and nearly everyone had commented on it. Even Solo, usually chilled out and snoring somewhere in the centre, was following him around with a concerned expression.

Late afternoon, Foxy's phone rang, and he recognised the number from the estate agent dealing with Carla's flat.

'Mr Fox, Henry here from Waites, Brecon and Walker.'

'Hello, Henry, what can I do for you?'

'Well, I'm delighted to tell you I have an offer of the full asking price on the flat.'

'Already?'

'Of course. No chain. Cash buyer. I couldn't have asked for a buyer in a better position. He's keen to move and also keen to have the furniture left and has offered a further five thousand to cover all the fixtures and fittings. Is that acceptable to you, or do you need to think about it overnight?'

'Wow. So quick,' was all Foxy could manage.

'Well, I did say I had a long list of potential clients,' Henry replied breezily.

'Well, yes but you know, you guys say that…'

'So, do you need to think about it? If you instruct solicitors ASAP this could be completed really quickly.'

'Er. Yes. Accept the offer. Thanks, Henry.'

'My pleasure, Mr Fox. I'll email over the relevant details and get the ball rolling.'

Foxy ended the call and thought about the offer. He also thought about Carla's will. He was the beneficiary of everything. Her life insurance policy, her pension and whatever the proceeds were from the sale of her flat. Collectively, he had a nice nest egg, but in reality, he would much rather have had Carla in his life still. They hadn't been romantically involved in recent months, but he loved her deeply and they had a strong bond. More than a few times he had gone to pick up the phone to speak to her and then realised she wasn't there anymore. He missed her counsel terribly.

Mike approached the counter, with two of the kids he had been coaching and booked them in for their next session. As he waved them off into the arms of their parents, he turned to Foxy.

'No offence, mate, you look terrible. I'll close up.'

Foxy thought for a moment. 'OK. Appreciate that.'

Mike peered out the window. 'Why don't you go for a run? Still got an hour or so of light. Solo looks up for it.'

Foxy looked over at Solo who was sitting by the door with an expectant expression.

'Thanks, mate. Appreciate it. See you tomorrow.'

Foxy changed into running gear and locked the door of his flat behind him. He headed down the stairs and towards the beach, Solo at his heels. He inhaled the scent of the sea and enjoyed the coldness of the air and the wind against his skin. He let his mind wander and started running.

CHAPTER 9

Steve nodded to Stanley as he stepped across the threshold of the Camorra's stunning house. Pearl was in the kitchen, immaculately turned out in blue. Mickey was outside on the phone, pacing up and down the side of the large infinity pool, which stretched across the width of the deck.

'Morning, Pearl,' Steve said, accepting a cup of coffee from her and noticing the dark circles under her eyes. 'You OK?'

'Yes, thank you, darling,' she said briskly. She motioned with her head. 'He'll be a minute then you can tell him your news.' She sat down gracefully in one of the large chairs that faced the view of the bay and motioned for Steve to follow suit.

'How are you?' she asked as she sipped her coffee.

'I'm hazarding a guess I'm in slightly better shape than you, Pearl,' he said gently. 'Are you OK? Can I help you with anything?'

Pearl regarded him silently and looked away, blinking suddenly. Steve was sure he saw tears glistening.

'You are really *quite* the darling man,' she said lightly. 'If I was twenty-five years younger, I'd take that offer to mean something else.' She smiled briefly. 'And the way I feel today, I'd probably take you up on it.'

Steve grinned widely. 'I'm flattered. I'd probably not live long enough to see the sun set, but I reckon it would be totally worth it. It's a nice idea while it lasts, isn't it?' He winked at her.

She chuckled softly. 'It's a *very* nice idea.'

The door opened and a gust of cold air blew in making Pearl shiver. Mickey strode over to Steve and stood in front of him.

'How?' he asked bluntly.

Dispensing with pleasantries for Mickey, Steve replied, 'Drowned in hot petrol.'

Mickey inhaled sharply and Pearl made a small murmur of distress.

'You said we'd talk when you knew how he died,' Steve reminded him. 'Now talk.'

Mickey looked at the floor, breathing deeply and shaking his head.

'It's a message for me. Personally.' He looked at Steve. 'No one else.'

'No,' Steve said harshly, standing to face Mickey. 'It's a public message. Yes, it's for you, but I've got a dead guy in the woods. If it was just for you, then they'd hang him somewhere where only you or your guys would find him. I won't ignore this.'

Mickey paced about in barely concealed fury. His fists were clenched, and he seemed oblivious to Pearl and Steve being in the room. Steve opened his mouth to say something, and Pearl held up her hand and shook her head. Finally, Mickey stopped pacing.

'This is a message from someone from my past,' he said quietly.

'Who?' Pearl spoke calmly.

'Before you,' he said shortly, not meeting her gaze. 'I was young. Stupid. In with the wrong people.'

'I said who, Mickey,' Pearl repeated.

'I'm assuming it's a guy called Danny Tao,' Mickey said, going to stand by the window. 'He's the son of a guy called Frank Adams and Lily Tao.' He turned to Pearl.

'Me and Frank used to be close. We used to run protection back in the day. Before you. Before us.' He smiled. 'For Lily. She was like an exotic flower. She was the brains behind it all despite being so young. She was descended from Triads, she liked their principles, their approach, their style. She brought their ideas over here. She was…' He paused for a moment and looked off into the distance remembering. 'Utterly ruthless, but still everyone loved her.'

'What's the significance of drowning?' Steve asked.

'It was Lily's preferred method of dealing with revenge killings. But drown them and then display them as a warning.'

'Is petrol significant?'

'Might be,' Mickey said curtly.

'Is it, or isn't it?' Pearl asked flatly, her usual sunny disposition gone. 'Well?'

'It probably is significant. Yes.'

'How?'

'Because Frank was burnt alive,' he said quietly. 'Someone forced two tyres over his head and then doused him with petrol and set light to him.'

'Why use tyres?' Pearl asked.

'Because they trap your arms, and they burn hotter and longer. It's called necklacing,' Steve supplied.

'And why was Frank burnt alive, Mickey?' asked Pearl quietly.

Mickey leant against the glass to look out to sea. The day had clouded over, and rain had started, mirroring Mickey's mood.

'Because he was in the wrong place, at the wrong time. It was a set up.' He sighed deeply and rubbed his face. 'And I should have been there too.' Mickey stared moodily out of the window and traced a raindrop down the large picture window. 'It was a bent copper trying to muscle in on the action, of which there was plenty. He wanted us out of the way, reckoned he could partner up with Lily.' He swallowed hard. 'She never forgave me for Frank's death. Never. Couldn't bring herself to.'

'Why?' Pearl asked quietly.

'She was blind with grief. Guilt. Wouldn't see anyone, wouldn't speak to anyone. I tried to reach her. But she told me to go.'

'Which you did?' Pearl said. 'Then what?'

'I moved to a different part of London. Diversified. Made more money than I ever dreamt. And then I met you. And life changed for me in a heartbeat. I didn't miss that life. Not for a second.'

'What happened to the bent copper?' Steve asked.

Mickey shrugged. 'I heard a rumour he got sent down, but I'd moved away by then. Probably dead anyway.'

Steve put his coffee cup on the side in the kitchen.

'Touching though all of this is, Mickey, I still have a dead man in the woods and your life is still under threat. So why now?'

Mickey scowled. 'I can't work that out... unless Lily's passed? And it's some sort of delayed revenge from Danny?'

'Do you know Danny Tao?'

'Know of him. Never met him. Not many people have from what I hear.'

'Well, it turns out he's getting his supplies from here.'

Mickey frowned. 'Here? On my patch?' His eyes narrowed. 'What sort of supplies?'

'He's got a bungalow full of bush.'

'What?'

'A bungalow that's a weed factory. I was watching the other night, run by a few of our local pond life. Then who turns up, but a couple of Chinese guys in a white Tesla with a large suitcase. Car's registered to Tao Enterprises.'

Mickey turned and yelled, 'MAXIM?'

Maxim appeared in the room with an expectant look on his face.

'Where is it?' Mickey demanded.

'Oh no. No way. I am busting this lot. Everything is in place to do that. Just waiting for the nod when they're there.'

Maxim turned to Mickey with a disappointed expression. Steve looked at Mickey.

'Depending on what I find and what's in a large suitcase in there, I would reckon Tao Enterprises are all yours.'

'What suitcase?'

'The two Tesla guys rolled in a very heavy-looking large suitcase. By my reckoning, they're either keeping all supplies in one place so this was from another farm, or it's money or worse, it's something like a body.'

'When's the bust?' Mickey asked.

'Probably tomorrow, next day latest. You can't move on the Taos until then.'

'If I live to see that long,' Mickey said. 'Look, I'm not confusing the two things. They've sent me a warning, so they consider me fair game. Your little bush farm means nothing in the equation. I need to put measures in place, so no one gets hurt.' He snorted at Steve. 'Well, no one important anyway.'

'Mickey,' Steve warned. 'Exactly what measures are we talking about?'

'Time for you to go,' Mickey snapped. 'You don't want to hear this.'

'Mickey, what you need to realise is that I have to pursue the Tao crew myself for the murder. I don't want you getting in my way.'

Mickey gave Steve a murderous look.

'Mickey,' Pearl warned. 'Steve has helped us. We owe him. He didn't have to tell us about the bullet.'

'Just keep out of my way,' Mickey muttered, then clicked his fingers at Maxim and walked out.

'Sorry,' Pearl said, watching him go. 'He's been like a different man since that bullet was found. He certainly won't listen to me anymore.' She stood gracefully and walked towards Steve.

'I have a small favour to ask you.'

Steve raised an eyebrow. 'Oh?'

She slapped him playfully on the arm. 'Stop. Now, I have a small request, keep me in the loop with your findings on the Taos. I don't like the sound of this organisation and I need to be watching our back.' She glanced towards the door Mickey had stormed out of. 'I fear Mickey is too busy dealing with old ghosts to focus on what's going on in front of him.'

Close up, Pearl looked exhausted. 'I can do that.' He smiled and kissed her gently on the cheek. 'Look after yourself, Pearl. Out of all the ruthless criminals around here, you're by far my favourite.'

He walked to the door and nodded to Stanley who opened it for him. He pressed his card into Stanley's hand and said quietly, 'I'm worried, Stanley. For Pearl's safety. Keep me in the loop. I don't want anything happening to her.'

Stanley grunted, pocketed the card and closed the door gently.

* * *

Nate was exhausted. He had been training some candidates for a private contractor all day, making use of the local training environments that the MOD allowed them to use. He was frustrated. Only one of twelve candidates had shown any aptitude for hostage and crisis negotiation. The majority of them had been aggressive, unyielding, arrogant and opinionated. Nate had failed all of them; they would do it all again tomorrow.

He thought as he drove home that he would seriously ramp up their training exercises and shock them into thinking differently. He made a mental note to email his colleagues at the training centre HQ and ask for the special resources that they sometimes used. He pondered the afternoon and the one candidate who showed promise. A woman. She didn't have a military background or a police background. But she had worked in social housing for years, dealing with difficult estates and residents and then more recently had been dealing with the Traveller communities. The woman had rough edges, but she was a listener. She listened, considered and tried compromise, but then always fell at the final negotiation hurdle. He wanted to get to know her and what drove her. She had the most potential. In his view, she was the one he would have standing next to him on a difficult job. He didn't see any of the others passing the course. They were too damn arrogant.

He pulled into the drive and rested his head on the steering wheel, wincing as he hit his tender nose. He grabbed his phone from the centre console and let himself into the house. The landline phone was ringing as he opened the front door, and he grabbed it just before it rang off.

'Hello?'

'Ah… It's Dr Oakley. I've been trying your mobile.'

'Oh, sorry. I've been at work. Phone's been off. Is everything OK?'

'I think we've had a minor breakthrough. A new therapist has helped with a different approach and different triggers, and Vivienne has decided that she would like to come and see you for a weekend. The new medication has certainly taken hold and the spells of psychosis are almost non-existent now.'

Nate was filled with a mix of trepidation and excitement.

'That's good news. Did you see her last week though? She lost it over the book.'

'We've replayed that extensively with her, and the triggers and rationale behind it.'

'I need to see her before she can come home. I need to tell her we've moved. Explain. Prepare her,' Nate said with an air of desperation.

'Excellent plan. You can judge for yourself. This intensive therapy and drug combination is really something.'

'When should I come?'

'Day after tomorrow?' Dr Oakley said. 'I think you'll be rather surprised.'

'OK.'

'I'll see you then. I think you'll have your wife home sooner than we anticipated, Mr Bennett. It really is marvellous progress. Goodbye.'

'Bye.' Nate ended the call and put the phone back in the charger. He didn't believe for a moment that she would be well enough to come home. He had to be hopeful and try though.

He dumped his briefcase on the desk and stood for a moment breathing in the sea view. On a whim, he kicked off his shoes, put on his walking boots and let himself out. Walking down the steep castiron steps to the beach, he spotted Jenny with a small dog. He waved and she changed direction, towards him.

'Hey, neighbour.' She grinned. 'How are you doing? I've taken in a parcel for you. Dylan didn't want to leave it on the step.' At his confused look she added, 'Dylan's the postman.'

'Thank you for that.'

'Good day?' she asked as they strolled along the beach. Archie danced around them with his ball, which Jenny was kicking along the sand.

'I've been training all day.'

'What sort of training?'

'Hostage and crisis negotiation.'

'Wow. That sounds full on,' she said. 'No wonder you look shattered. Is that how you got that?' She pointed to his black eye.

He grinned ruefully. 'I am knackered. The lot of them were bloody hard work. And no, this was an accident,' he said, pointing to his nose.

'So, personally, as someone who hates any sort of conflict, what are the main things that make a good hostage and crisis negotiator?'

He looked at her sideways. 'Do you really want to know?'

'I do. It's interesting.'

'OK. Well everyone is different. In my view, it's about being a good listener foremost. Not being aggressive. Being firm. Being articulate and clear, and being intuitive.'

'Are you all of those things?' Jenny asked, smiling.

'I like to think I am,' he said. 'But when it's something personal, something I'm deeply emotional about, then I tend to lose all of these qualities.'

'Do you and your wife argue much then?' Jenny laughed.

Nate couldn't bring himself to reply and rolled his eyes instead.

'How is she?' Jenny asked. 'Is she home soon?'

'Not sure. I'll find out in a couple of days,' he said, not wanting to explain.

They reached the end of the beach and the slipway outside Maggie's cafe. The smell of cooking wafted out and Nate's stomach rumbled noisily. A young man was planting up Maggie's pots and he smiled and waved at Jenny as they approached.

'Hey, Teddy,' Jenny said warmly, and Archie rushed up to greet him. 'How are you?'

'Good thanks, Miss Jenny,' he said shyly. He looked at Nate. 'I can hear your tummy rumbling from here! If Miss Maggie hears it, she'll make sure you eat!'

'Do you reckon she heard then?' Nate grinned at Teddy, who nodded enthusiastically.

'Heard what?' Maggie appeared from the rear of the cafe holding a large flower in a pot and gave it to Teddy. Teddy giggled and pointed to Nate.

'I was just saying to Miss Jenny's friend that if Miss Maggie heard his tummy rumbling that loud, she'd make sure that he had food.'

Maggie looked at Teddy. 'Did you hear his tummy rumbling then, Teddy?'

Teddy giggled. 'I did, it was loud.'

Maggie put her hands on her hips. 'Hmm. Well, I think you should get inside now. Steak and mushroom pie on special today, mash and veggies.'

Nate looked at Maggie. 'Well…'

'Have you got dinner all ready waiting for you at home?' Maggie asked.

'Well no…'

'Inside then. You too, Jenny. You're wasting away and you know your cooking is bloody awful.'

'That's a tad harsh Maggie—'

'Inside!' Maggie said firmly. 'Come on. I might have a glass of wine and join you. Teddy, when you finish those, you come in for your tea OK?'

Two hours later Nate and Jenny walked up the road to go home.

'My God that woman can cook,' Nate said. 'I could happily eat there every day.'

'I know. I think I'd be the size of a house if I did though,' Jenny mused. 'Nate, can I ask you a personal question?' She glanced at him sideways. 'You can tell me to bugger off.'

'Go on,' he said, dreading it.

'Has your wife had some sort of breakdown?'

Nate was silent for a beat. 'How did you know?'

She looked rueful. 'That's about the only thing that keeps people in hospital longer term these days, I think.'

Nate was silent for a moment as they walked together.

'It's OK. You don't have to answer,' she said gently.

Nate took a deep breath. 'We had a baby, she was stillborn. Vivienne couldn't cope. Refused to believe the baby had died. Kept hearing her crying.' He cleared his throat as emotion welled up. 'I had to section her.'

Jenny touched his arm. 'I'm so sorry. That must have been really difficult. Losing the baby is hard enough, but your wife too, not being able to cope. So hard.'

He gave a half smile. 'The doctor's just rung and they're using this new treatment. He says she wants to come home for a weekend. The last time I saw Viv I got this,' he said, pointing to his nose.

'She hit you?' Jenny asked, surprised.

'She threw a book at me.'

'So, let me guess. You kind of want her home, but don't?'

'Exactly.'

'Without wanting to sound like a cliché, is it maybe about small steps? Go and see her. See how she is. Then if you think she'll be OK for a weekend, then do it. She's not coming home for good yet. It's small steps. Bite-sized pieces.'

'Hmm. She's so unstable though.'

'They wouldn't have suggested it, surely, if they weren't sure this was a good next step?'

'Suppose so.'

'Go and see her.'

'OK.'

They arrived outside their houses.

'Nate, anything I can do to help when she's home. Please just say.'

'Thanks, Jenny.'

CHAPTER 10

Mrs Clifton had been operating in a military fashion since Steve had suggested to her that she was the sole person responsible for surveillance on the bungalow. She had adopted war-like rations so she didn't have to go to the shops and for the first time ever had placed a small online order, which, after three attempts, had been fairly successful. (With the exception of the five bags of potatoes it had contained along with the thirty-two rolls of toilet paper.)

She had created a base-camp environment with chairs facing the window, binoculars, a small pad to record comings and goings and a very ancient camera, for which she had found a film, a Thermos and a tin of biscuits. She took position at 6 a.m. and then stayed awake for as long as possible until she had to go to bed. She wasn't particularly bothered about missing anything in the wee small hours since she figured the druggie layabouts didn't look like they'd be creeping about in the night and losing sleep. They usually turned up early evening and then left just after her bedtime.

She heard the rumble of a vehicle and snatched up the binoculars, peering through the curtain. A large white van pulled up next door and she carefully noted the registration. She watched as a man got out, hefted some bags on his shoulder which he dumped by the side gate. He climbed in the van and drove off again.

Hours later, when Mrs Clifton woke from an afternoon nap, she noticed the blue van had arrived and rang Steve immediately. She omitted telling him that she had been asleep in her haste to cover up her poor surveillance skills.

* * *

Steve walked around the scene. The raid had happened, the three men inside the bungalow had been arrested and were now residing comfortably in the local nick. Forensics had left with a promise to return the next day to seize the plants, but there was enough evidence to charge the three who had been looking after the plants. As Steve walked around the bungalow, he mused to himself that this was quite the set up for a weed factory. Growing areas, a drying area, even an area for packing. This was clearly someone else's brainchild, and not the three they nicked. They'd be lucky if they had a brain cell between them.

He snapped pictures as he went, despite forensics doing the job well, he always liked to double up on pictures. He had checked the evidence list for the large suitcase that Mrs Clifton was sure contained a body and couldn't find it anywhere.

Leaning against a door jamb, he pondered where a large suitcase might be hidden in a property like that. He walked through the house again checking all the bedrooms and cupboards, even looking in the roof space. Arriving back at the kitchen, he looked around with a critical eye. This was clearly the packing area. He noted a few air fresheners dotted around the place, and wondered what the point of them was. Walking slowly around taking in the line of the walls, he mentally drew a plan of the property in his head. As he scanned the walls and floor, his eyes settled on a large old-fashioned dresser. In front of it there was a threadbare and dirty rug that seemed out of place on the dated linoleum. Idly kicking it aside, he saw the deep scrape marks where the dresser had been dragged out and moved.

'Gotcha,' he muttered.

He thought for a minute and then rested his phone on a shelf opposite, ostensibly to record himself finding the evidence. He stated the date and time and then began to carefully edge the dresser aside.

There it was, the large suitcase.

It took him a while to manoeuvre the unwieldy case out of the space and finally when it was in the middle of the kitchen, he inspected it carefully. He didn't want to open it, that was a job for forensics. What he did see, on closer inspection, was what looked like long black hair caught in the closing mechanism, trapped now in the tight cellophane wrap covering the case. He chuckled to himself. Mrs Clifton had perhaps been right after all. It looked like there was a body in the suitcase.

Continuing his visual inspection of the case, he heard the front door open and hoped it was forensics returning. He called out.

'I'm glad you're back, I've found something else for you to look at.'

Puzzled at the lack of a response he turned, seeing two unfamiliar men behind him. One of them had a raised arm. Something in Steve's psyche told him the man had a cosh in his hand, but his brain didn't process it quickly enough for him to dodge it. He felt intense pain in his head, and then everything went black.

* * *

Jonesey was looking for Steve. He'd been off radar for a few hours, and he couldn't reach him on the phone. Despite his shift being over, and being desperate to get home for the large takeaway he had promised himself while watching the last few episodes of *MasterChef*, he was worried for the boss. It was very unlike him to go dark.

Jonesy guessed Steve might be at the bush bungalow next door to Mrs Cliftons. He liked to walk the scene after a raid, so Jonesey figured he was still there. As he was about to turn into Woodpecker Lane, a white Tesla shot out of the junction, almost clipping his wing and sped off down the road. Muttering at the driver, Jonesey pulled up and climbed out of the car, noting Steve's car parked further down the road. He approached the front door which was ajar and smelled smoke instantly.

'Steve?' he called but heard nothing. He pushed open the door, wishing he was still in uniform with his cosh handy, but decided the large pebble door stop at his feet was as good a weapon as any. Clutching his pebble, he crept along the corridor, checking each room as he went. At the end of the corridor there was a door inset with 1930s mottled glass and through that he could see flickering light and a dark shape on the floor. He crept along the corridor and pushed the door open slightly, horrified to see Steve on the floor and a fire burning from a pile of cloths on the gas cooker.

'Shit a brick!' He ran over to Steve and frantically searched for a pulse. Steve's face was a bloody mess, and he was unconscious.

'Jesus, Guv.' Jonesey scrabbled around desperately in his pockets for his phone. He stabbed out 999 and called it in, staring at Steve for signs of him regaining consciousness. Realising the fire was still going, he ran over to the sink and looked for a container to fill with water to put out the fire. He found a bucket, filled it and threw it over the cooker. Then realised he actually needed to turn the gas rings off, which he fumbled about doing. Satisfied he'd stopped the fire he ran back over to Steve and tried to bring him around.

'Guv!' he said urgently. 'Guv!' He leant in to inspect Steve more closely. He noted the large suitcase and then caught sight of Steve's phone balanced on the shelf opposite the dresser. Knowing Steve would have probably done this to record himself finding something, he stabbed out the number for the station and waited impatiently.

'Sarge, it's Jonesey,' he said, putting his phone on Steve's chest and pressing speaker phone. 'I'm at the bush bungalow. You gotta get forensics back over here. They missed a suitcase.'

'I'd heard you'd called it in. You clocked off half an hour ago, what the hell are you doing at a crime scene? I'm not paying you overtime, you know,' the duty sergeant snapped.

'I was worried about Guv. I was just checking on him and found him here. He's had the shit beaten out of him. Ambulance is coming.'

'Any idea who did it?'

'Dunno. But a white Tesla left here in an awful hurry as I was coming in.'

Sarge was silent for a moment. 'He called in a plate for a white Tesla the other day.'

'Where was it?'

'Where you are, I think. Tell me about the suitcase, why didn't forensics pick it up?'

'Steve found it, I think.' Jonesey picked up Steve's finger and used it to access his phone. 'Hang on, I've got his phone here, he was recording something.'

Jonesey played it from the beginning and fast-forwarded through Steve moving the dresser aside and dragging out the case. He let it play at normal speed when he saw Steve being surprised by two Chinese men, who beat him with a cosh and kicked him repeatedly. Jonesey winced.

'Jonesey,' snapped Sarge. 'What's happening?'

'Sarge, looks like Steve found the suitcase and filmed himself recovering it. It kept rolling, we know who beat him up.'

'I want that video – now.'

Jonesey tried to send it, but the file was too big.

'It's too big to send.'

'Bring it in then.'

Jonesey saw his dreams of a takeaway drifting off if he had to go back to work. 'But I was gonna go to the hospital with him,' he said.

'OK. I'll send someone to get the phone from you at the hospital.'

Jonesey heard the ambulance sirens and ran out of the house. He flagged it down and ushered in the paramedics who knew Steve well.

'What we got?' Phil the paramedic asked as he walked along the hall with Liz his partner. 'Control said an assault?'

'It's… it's Steve,' Jonesey managed to get out. 'He's been beaten.'

Entering the kitchen, Phil knelt down next to Steve.

'How long has he been like this?' Phil demanded.

'I don't know… Wait.' Jonesey accessed Steve's phone and scrolled back through the recording. 'I think he's been down about thirty minutes.'

'Liz, get the stretcher, we need to get him in. I don't like the sound of his breathing on the left side.'

The ambulance sirens screamed in the quiet lanes on the way to the hospital. Jonesey clutched Steve's phone in one hand and Steve's hand in the other.

'Nearly there, mate,' he kept saying over and over, but Steve remained unconscious for the duration of the ride. Jonesey looked over at Liz who was recording things on a chart; she was biting her lip and looked worried.

'Liz,' he said suddenly. 'How worried do we need to be?'

'Let's see what the consultants say,' Liz said. 'He might just be concussed, which is why he's fairly unresponsive.' She looked out of the window and unclipped her seat belt, stuffing the file under Steve's legs.

'Let's go,' she said and opened the door when the ambulance stopped.

Jonesey had never felt so helpless as he watched Steve being wheeled into Accident & Emergency. He jumped when the phone in his hand rang and he saw it was Kate, Steve's girlfriend, calling.

'Hello?' he said hesitantly.

'Now that sounds like Jonesey to me,' she said, sounding amused. 'Except I can't hear you eating... so is it really you?'

Jonesey gave a strangled half laugh and then missed what she said next as an ambulance screamed past with the sirens on.

'Jonesey?' she said. 'Where are you?'

'Hospital,' he croaked out.

'And why do you have Steve's phone?'

'Kate—'

'What's happened?' she demanded. 'Where is he? Is he OK?'

'He's just been brought in.' Jonesey was struggling to function and felt ridiculously close to tears.

'What happened?' she demanded.

'He was beaten up. At a crime scene.'

'Was he conscious? Talking? When you found him?'

'No... not really.'

'I'm on my way,' she said and ended the call.

Jonesey stood next to the ambulance and felt lost. He wasn't sure what to do. The blast of a car horn made him jump. Jonesey turned and stared. The duty sergeant had come himself to get the phone and, presumably, to see how Steve was.

'Stop standing there looking like a gormless twat and let's get in there!' he roared, pulling up next to the ambulance and getting out.

'I-I don't think you can park there—' Jonesey stammered.

'I'll park where I damn well like when one of mine is in the hospital,' he said, marching in through the door and smiling at a young nurse who approached him.

'Who is going to tell me where my police officer is then?' he said charmingly to her.

'He's being assessed right through there,' she said meekly.

'Right. I'll be having a chat with the consultant then. Thank you.' He reached for her key card and swiped it, then marched through the open doors that read 'No admittance,' dragging Jonesey by the arm as he went.

CHAPTER 11

The hospital ward was quiet, with a few of the patients sleeping. Steve had been moved to a side room and Kate was sitting in the chair next to Steve's bed. She was busying herself with work on her iPad when she heard him stir. She flicked a glance over him and saw he was wide awake, staring at her.

'Hello, gorgeous,' he croaked.

She dropped the iPad in her bag and leant forward to kiss him gently, holding his hands.

'You scared me,' she said quietly.

'I scared me. I thought I was going to die in a hideous 1970s bungalow.'

'Jesus, if Jonesey hadn't found you.'

He shifted slightly and winced. 'Come on then, Doc, what's the damage?'

'Concussion. Three broken ribs. Broken nose. Battered and bruised generally. Your kidneys took quite the beating.'

'Have I had a nose job then?' he asked. 'Am I even better looking?'

'Nope. They've just set it where it used to be. Alas, still ugly.' She glanced down at the bag attached to his catheter.

'Ahh.' He peered over the side of the bed and pointed to a bag of urine. There were spots of blood dancing in it as it filled gently. 'Look, I'm having a wee, and I have no idea I'm doing it.' He frowned. 'Why is there blood in my wee?'

'Because of the kicks to your kidneys. It'll be fine.'

'When can I go home?'

'When your doctor says so.'

'When do you say so?'

'It's not up to me.'

'What if I have things I need to show you that are injured?' he asked innocently.

'I don't think you're going to be up to much in that department for a while,' she said. 'Doctor's orders.'

'Hmm. I'm not happy with these doctor's orders. I might appeal.' He yawned loudly and then winced when his split lip opened up and bled again.

'I'll have a chat with the consultant,' Kate said, smoothing his hair back from his forehead and dabbing his bleeding lip with a tissue. 'Are you tired?'

'I just need to rest my eyes,' he said, half drifting off to sleep. 'Umm, yes, talk to the consultant and let me go home. And I think you should really think about moving in with me. Forever.'

* * *

Olivia had been back in her parents' cottage with Brian for a day and already she was regretting it. She had told Brian that she'd needed time away because she felt her mental health was suffering and that she'd gone to a retreat for a few days to clear her mind and refocus herself. She was relieved when Brian seemed to accept the explanation.

'Olivia. OLIVIA. I hate it when you ignore me. I asked you what your plans were today? Are you going out?'

Olivia placed a bowl of porridge down in front of Eli and turned to look at Brian.

'I've no idea what I'm doing today. I've got some work to do and a few bits to get.'

'What bits?' His eyes narrowed. 'You did a shop yesterday, what bits can you possibly need?'

'I just need a few things I forgot.'

'What things?'

'I don't know… mushrooms. Shampoo.'

'Right, so the greengrocers and Boots then?'

'Does it matter where I get them?'

'Olivia,' he warned.

'Dad, can I go to the lifeboat station, please? Jesse said she'd show me how to build an outboard motor and Billy said he'd show me the winch.'

'No. They won't want an annoying kid around.'

'But, Dad, I was there all day the other day when you were working.'

'I haven't worked out a punishment for you yet for doing that.'

'Wouldn't need to be a punishment if you'd been looking after him properly,' muttered Olivia.

Brian inhaled sharply. 'What was that?'

'Well, it's not his fault. You left him alone in a hotel where he didn't like anything on the menu and then buggered off to work where you couldn't be reached. Hardly worthy of any form of punishment, I think.'

'Oh, so you know what's best for my son now do you?' Brian moved closer to Olivia, and she immediately regretted speaking up.

'Go to work, Brian. I'm not starting an argument.' She tried to put some distance between them, but he held her arm tightly. She knew it would show a pattern of small bruises the next day.

He looked at his watch. 'I'm late now.' He glared at her and Eli. 'You've both made me late.'

'Sorry, Dad,' Eli said meekly.

Brian looked at Olivia expecting a response, and she folded her arms and stared at him. He moved closer and pointed a finger at her.

'I don't know what's going on with you, but you're different and I don't like it.' He grabbed her face and kissed her hard on the mouth, and she suppressed a shudder of revulsion.

'Greengrocers and Boots. That's it,' he said firmly. 'I'll see you for dinner.'

'What about the lifeboat, Dad?' Eli said plaintively.

'I'll sort it all out. You go. You're late,' Olivia said with a forced cheerful smile. 'See you later.'

Brian picked up his rucksack and jacket and walked towards the door. He turned and pointed to her.

'Greengrocers and Boots, Olivia. See you for dinner.'

Olivia stood at the kitchen window and watched him run down the road to the harbour. She hoped he hadn't missed the shuttle; he would come back and be unbearable. She had been fantasising lately about Brian dying in an accident and how wonderful that would be. She turned to Eli who was finishing the last of his porridge.

'I say we go and talk to the lifeboat folk and see what we can work out?' she said, grinning.

'Can we, Mum… sorry, Liv?' He reddened. 'Sorry. I didn't mean to call you mum… it's just sometimes…'

Olivia hugged him hard. 'It's OK. Call me mum if that's what you want. I love it.' She tousled his hair and kissed the top of his head.

'I wish it was just you and me,' he said in a small voice, hugging her hard.

'Me too, sweetheart. Me too,' she said, a surge of affection for this poor boy coursing through her.

They walked down through the town together, with Eli uncharacteristically holding on to Olivia's hand.

'It's this way,' he said, pulling her hand and taking her down the narrow path that led around to the lifeboat station. 'Come on.'

They walked into the lifeboat station and an elderly lady came out of the shop holding a duster.

'Well now, Eli. How lovely to see you back here. Are you coming to help me in the shop again today? You were a godsend helping me get to the high shelves,' she said, her eyes twinkling.

'Hello, Nessie,' he said, grinning broadly. 'This is Olivia.'

'Hello there, Olivia,' Nessie said. 'This young man is wonderful.'

'Is Doug here? And Jesse?' Eli asked, looking around.

Nessie pointed to the lower metal staircase. 'Let yourself into the restricted area and knock on the door. They'll be pleased to see you.'

'Can I help you out again later, Nessie?'

'As long as it's OK with Doug, and Olivia of course.'

'OK!'

Eli dragged Olivia by her hand out of the shop and along the gantry, down the stairs towards Doug's office where he banged on the door and then barged in.

'Hey, little man!' Doug said as he replaced the phone in the cradle. 'How are you today?'

'I'm good, thanks.' Eli beamed.

'How are those levels?'

Eli rolled his eyes.

'Not good enough.' Doug adopted a stern expression. 'What are they?'

Eli held his phone to his arm, scanning his monitor and then waited a second. 'Levels are good.'

'Excellent.' Doug grinned. He looked at Olivia and extended his hand. 'Hi there. I'm Doug. Skipper here.'

Olivia shook his hand. 'Hi. I'm Eli's stepmum. I'm sorry about the other day. I wasn't really, er… here.'

Doug waved it away. 'Ach, he was a joy to have.' He looked at Eli. 'Why don't you pop down and say hi to Jesse?'

'Is Brock here?' Eli asked breathlessly.

Doug chuckled. 'Jesse doesn't go *anywhere* without Brock. So yes, he's downstairs.'

Eli ran out of the door, and they heard him clattering down the stairs calling out to Jesse and Brock.

'Thank you for keeping him here the other day,' Olivia started.

'Not a problem.'

'He seems set on coming back every now and again.'

'I don't have a problem with that as long as Nessie is here in the shop, in case we get called out on a shout. He'll be safe with her if we go out.'

Olivia looked tense. 'Are you sure? Will he get in the way?'

'There's enough of us here to keep him busy for the odd day or so. It'll be good for him. He'll learn and then he'll pass on his knowledge to other kids, and you never know, it might be one less person for us to rescue in the future.'

'Playing the long game, I see.' Olivia grinned.

'Gotta have a plan.' He gestured to the door. 'Come and meet Jesse. She'll have him taking an engine apart by now I expect.'

Olivia waved goodbye to Eli, who was clutching a bright yellow duster and helping Nessie with the window display, and walked quickly up through the town. Switching off her phone she hurried up through some of the back roads until she finally arrived, out of breath, at her destination.

Opening the door, she greeted the receptionist and signed in. Heading down the corridor she entered a room and sat in the chair next to the bed.

She took the lifeless hand of the man in the bed and kissed it gently. The only sound was from the slight hiss of the oxygen helping him breathe. Tears ran down her face and she made no effort to brush them away. She sat there for a long time, thinking. Remembering. Looking for any hint that he would wake up. Finally, she stood and gently brushed away a hair from the man's face. She rested her hand on his cheek.

'I'm so sorry, Gil. Come back,' she whispered. 'Please come back to me.'

Olivia left the room and a few minutes later stepped out into the winter sunshine. The heat from the sun was a wonderful contrast to the dingy room she had left. She turned her face up to the sky, drawing in the warmth like it was essential nourishment.

Walking down the road quickly, she hurriedly switched her phone on again when she reached the main part of the town. She went to the greengrocers and Boots and then on a whim, wanting to prolong being in the sunshine, walked down to the beach by the castle. She bought herself a large takeaway coffee and went to sit on the beach. The sun warmed her face and she closed her eyes, having a nostalgic moment of summer days, lying on the beach dozing the hot sun, listening to the roll and draw of the tide.

'I thought that was you,' a voice said.

She opened her eyes and there he was. Tall and well sculpted in his wet suit, his hair wet, droplets of water sat on the very end of the long eyelashes of his large dark eyes. Water dripped off the bottom of his neat beard. He held a large surfboard, which he threw onto the sand next to her. He carelessly rubbed his face with a towel and scrubbed it over his hair, making it stand up in all directions. Her stomach did a little flip. Christ this man was drop-dead gorgeous.

'Surfing too as well as everything else. However do you fit it all in?' she said dryly.

'I try, I'm a good juggler and a very busy boy.' Mike grinned and watched her drink her coffee. 'Fancy sharing that?'

She rolled her eyes and handed it over. He took a healthy swig and smacked his lips.

'Thought you were long gone,' he said, passing the coffee back and plonking himself down on the sand next her. He stretched his legs out.

'It's complicated,' she muttered.

'No, it isn't. It's as complicated as you wanna make it.'

'Mike, you… you… don't know…you don't know what…' She trailed off staring out to sea, frowning.

He shrugged. 'So tell me. I thought that's what you were going to do the other night, but as usual you bailed, leaving no explanation apart from a note that said nothing.'

'I can't tell you. But I meant what I said in that note.'

He snorted derisively. 'Well, I'm confused. You really need to help me out here, Ollie. You can't tell me anything, but you can turn up after four years, come into my flat, kiss me stupid and then leave me another note, that, just like the last one, didn't leave me any clues.' He faced her. 'Just for once tell me what's going on, so I don't spend another four years…' He stopped himself before he said too much.

'Spend another four years doing what?' she asked, hopeful of what he might say.

'Hey, Mike! Ciao, Bello!'

Mike looked over to the beach cafe and saw Isabella standing there with one of her brothers. He grinned, raising his arm to wave.

'Hey, Isabella! Ciao!'

'See you later,' she called and blew him a kiss, winking as she turned away.

Mike grinned to himself remembering their night together.

'Girlfriend?' Olivia asked snippily.

He was snapped back to the moment.

'Of sorts, yeah,' he said quietly.

'She's pretty.'

'She is. And nice. So, come on. Tell me what's going on. I'm listening.' He lay back on the sand, bunched his towel under his head and closed his eyes. 'I've got about ten minutes in this wetsuit until I start to get really cold.'

'I don't know where to start.'

'Easy,' he said. 'You left me a note and buggered off four years ago. Take it from there.'

She was silent for a moment.

'I had to go. I had no choice,' she said, twisting the coffee cup nervously.

'Yet you couldn't tell me.'

'No.'

'Why not? I thought we had plans. I thought we…'

'We did, but… it was Gil. I had no choice. No options.'

'There's always options. How is Gil?' he said, referring to Olivia's brother.

'He's…' Olivia struggled to form the words and a rogue tear slid down her cheek. 'He's not great,' she croaked.

Mike opened an eye. 'Ollie?' He pushed himself up to rest on his elbows. 'What's happened to Gil?'

'He's in a coma.'

'What? What happened?'

Olivia sighed deeply and turned to face him.

'When I left you, we ran away to Dubai. We had to go. The girl he was with… she was in trouble. Serious trouble. Organised crime kind of trouble. She knew they would come after her. There was a lot of family stuff going on with her and, well, Gil – he loved her and he begged me to go with them. He would have gone anywhere with her. So, we ran. Jade, his girlfriend, went via somewhere else to be safe, to stay with a friend. It was easy to find jobs teaching English over there and tutoring expats. We were raking it in. Free and clear. And then Jade turned up, she'd been hiding out in Qatar with a friend.'

'Wasn't that what Gil wanted?'

'Yes. We were earning good money, we'd got settled. She turned up and wanted to throw it all away and go somewhere else, straight away. But Gil wanted them to have a life there. So he persuaded her to stay. For a while it worked. We earnt well, had a good life. Gil and Jade were happy, he was talking about proposing, the whole deal. Jade's friend was a guy who had just got a job working in Dubai and she introduced us. He was nice, I sort of started seeing him, we were like the fabulous four for a while.' She sniffed. 'I wish we could have stayed that way.'

'What happened?'

'One of Jade's brothers' henchmen turned up, with some Qatari muscle. No idea how they found us.' She exhaled heavily. 'And they came with a whole load of trouble.' She brushed a tear away. 'Jade freaked. We tried to run. I got a car and drove out to the desert to get away from them one night, but they came after us. I was driving…' She gulped in some air. 'They kept chasing and chasing and then a sandstorm hit. And I couldn't see… I just couldn't see.'

'It's OK.' Mike sat up, mirroring her pose and draped his towel around his shoulders. 'Go on.'

'We crashed. I don't know what I hit. The car rolled. I don't remember… anything really. I woke up in hospital and Gil was there too, but he had hit his head on something in the crash, and they couldn't get him back.' She sniffed. 'They still can't get him back.'

'What about Jade?'

'No sign of her. No idea where she went.'

'Where's Gil now?'

'He's here. I brought him here. He's in care up the road.'

'Was that why you were here? Last week?'

'I was bringing him over, yes, and…'

'And what?'

She sniffed again, her eyes two huge pools of tears.

'I was having a termination.' She shuddered. 'I can't have a child with that man.'

'This would be your husband, right?'

She bowed her head and wiped the tears away.

Mike ran his hand through his wet hair in frustration. 'Jesus, Ollie. Why the bloody hell are you with him if you can't stand him?'

Olivia was silent for a long time.

'It wasn't too bad in the early days. He was new to Dubai too. Prior to Qatar, he'd been working in Cardiff and had some sort of bad break-up. Then a work thing went shit-shaped so he wanted to get away. He got a job out there, working on the plans for a big wind farm in Hatta. He was nice back then, I needed someone and he was there. I hate myself. I'm the absolute worst version of myself. I'm with him because he's paying for Gil to stay alive. All the medical bills. I can't afford to do it on my own. Plus, I'm terrified of what he'll do if I leave properly. I'm already suffering just for leaving for a few days. Thank God Eli is around, he's saved me from a proper punishment just by being home from school.'

'Wow.'

'I hate it. I hate him,' she whispered. 'It's like living in a prison. He's… controlling. Violent. He has this over me. All the time he dangles this in front of me. The minute he stops paying for Gil the likelihood is that he'll be moved back to NHS care, and he'll probably be left to die!'

'The NHS won't do that.'

'They will. It's how it'll go. I know it will.' Olivia was sobbing quietly now. 'He threatens me all the time with it.' She looked around suddenly. 'He doesn't know Gil's here. I managed to sell some things and get him moved so he doesn't know yet. He thinks he's still over there; I've got about two months before the change shows up on a bank statement because I've paid cash for the first couple of months.'

'Christ, Ollie.'

'I have to wait until Eli goes back to boarding school, then I need to decide what to do. I can't hurt Eli.'

'I can't stand the thought of you living like this.'

'I have to, for now.'

'You don't.'

'I do. It's my fault he's like this. I was driving.'

Olivia's phone rang and made her jump. She looked at the display and bit her lip. It was Brian. She looked at Mike and then back at the phone before answering it tentatively.

'Liv.' His voice was loud enough for Mike to hear. 'I said Boots and the grocers. What are you doing sitting on the beach?'

'Just having a coffee, enjoying the sunshine. I'm going home now.'

'Why was your phone switched off?'

'Was it?'

'I think you know it was.'

Olivia stayed silent. 'Olivia?' he pressed. 'Answer me?'

'It wasn't switched off,' she said, closing her eyes. She would pay for this later. 'Maybe I lost signal.'

'Tell me again, why you're on the beach and who you are with?'

'I'm not with anyone,' she said. 'I'm just having coffee on the beach and enjoying the view.'

'Promise me.'

'I promise.'

'Well, well,' he said, his voice dangerously soft. 'Isn't Liv quite the little liar. If you're on the beach alone then I'd like to know who the man in the wetsuit is sitting opposite you. See you for dinner, Liv. Go home and think on that.' The phone went dead.

'Shit,' Olivia said to herself.

'Is he like that every day?' Mike asked.

She bowed her head.

'What's he going to do now… later?'

'Don't know. I think I'll be OK because Eli's around, and he doesn't tend to hurt me in front of Eli.'

Olivia's phone rang again; it was Brian – again.

'Hello, Brian,' she said, resigned to his anger.

'Leave the beach now and go home immediately. I will not tell you again. I've told you before, Olivia, I will not have this level of disobedience. Now. I mean it.'

She ended the call and stood, brushing sand off herself.

'Gotta go,' she said lightly. 'See you soon.'

'Wait, Ollie.' Mike grabbed her hand. 'If you need anything. I'm here. If he kicks off, get out, come to me. I mean it. I'll do anything to help.'

She gave him a sad smile. 'Anything?'

He squeezed her hand.

'How about you forgive me? For everything?' she asked.

'I'm working on it.'

CHAPTER 12

Nate found himself nervous about seeing Viv. He had decided that a stroll along the beach would help him get his head straight before going to see her. After the last time, he couldn't get his head around that she would be in a position to come home, even for a few days. He'd been so unsure about it he'd ended up having a detailed discussion with her new therapist and had ended the call feeling slightly more reassured that this was perhaps a pivotal turning point. He understood more about what was happening now. As he strolled and mused, he was almost knocked off his feet by a large Alsatian chasing a ball.

'Solo!' a loud voice commanded, and the dog stopped in his tracks, turned and ran back the other way, instantly abandoning the ball. Impressed, Nate turned to see who was controlling the dog that well and smiled when he saw it was Foxy from the climbing centre.

'Pretty impressive,' Nate said, nodding to the dog. 'Obedient.'

'When he wants to be.' Foxy grinned. 'Good to see you. How are you settling in?' He looked at the dog. 'Fetch.'

'Not too bad. Found most things now. Getting there.'

'Not seen you around much. You been away?' Foxy asked as they strolled together with Solo returning to trot in between them, holding the ball.

'Training job, up on the MOD base.'

'What are you training?'

'Hostage, crisis negotiation. You know… all the usual stuff.'

'Umm. In my experience and very humble opinion–' Foxy gave him a sideways glance. '–it's a bit of a gift. Not something you can really train people to do. You've either got the magic combination or you haven't.'

'What's your take on the magic combination?' Nate asked, intrigued.

'Oh you know, a mixture of being able to listen, compromise, but also having the balls of steel to say no and be able to live with the consequences.'

'Ahh… Yup. I fall down on the balls of steel bit sometimes.'

'Don't believe that for a moment. My mate Rudi thinks he might remember you. He thinks it was you who negotiated with pirates on a tanker where they got nasty and started shooting the crew. Rudi's lot were called in after you told them negotiations were over when they kept putting the ransom up.'

Nate was silent for a moment. 'I remember it. They were all killed, and their boats were scuttled.'

'Rudi's lot were the natural conclusion to it, if the pirates were killing crew and not listening to reason.'

'They were off their faces,' Nate murmured. 'You can't reason with people like that. I still don't think they realised what was coming.'

'Their funeral,' Foxy said matter of factly. 'Any promising recruits on the training?'

'Nope.' Nate grinned. 'Well, one woman showed promise. Out of twelve. But none of them qualified for the next round.'

'Harsh taskmaster you must be,' said Foxy with amusement as they walked up the slipway from the beach. He gestured to the stairs that ran outside up to the top floor of the climbing centre where there was a balcony and a large picture window. 'I'm making coffee before I open up. Fancy one?'

Nate thought for a moment. 'Why not? Thanks.' He followed Foxy up the stairs, all the while being pushed out of the way by Solo who was desperate to get to the top.

'Great space,' said Nate appreciatively as he stood at the end of the flat and looked out of the picture window. 'Great to sit here and watch the weather roll by.'

Foxy grinned. 'Everyone says that.'

'How long have you been here?' Nate asked, watching Foxy make coffee.

'A while now,' Foxy said. 'Feels longer. Feels like I got family here.' He paused for a moment. 'They've helped me through some really difficult times. Amazing people.'

'I'm getting that,' Nate said, accepting a mug from Foxy and making himself comfortable in one of the chairs by the large window. 'Are you here on your own? Wife? Kids?'

A shadow passed over Foxy's face. Intuitive by nature, Nate held up his hands.

'Sorry. Didn't mean to pry.'

Foxy sipped his coffee. He had realised, since living in this close community, that it was OK to share and tell people personal details.

'I came here when I first got out of the service. I wasn't in a great place. Had some issues from being in the military and then my daughter died, and I sort of imploded a bit.'

'I'm sorry,' Nate said quietly. 'What was her name?'

'Charlie.' He pointed to a picture of a beautiful teenager smiling and blowing a kiss at the camera. 'She was fifteen.'

'I'm so sorry,' Nate said. 'Is her mum still around?'

'She wasn't, then she was. Divorced, but we'd made our peace, and we were in a good place. She had come for Christmas. We'd got close again,' Foxy said, looking out of the window. 'Then she caught some virus and died, that was a few months ago now.'

'Jesus, mate,' Nate muttered, staring at this man who had lost his entire family.

'It was quick,' Foxy said, clearing his throat, and Nate knew he was forcing down emotion. 'But she couldn't fight it anymore, I think.'

'I am so sorry,' Nate said.

'Everyone here was amazing. Wonderful. So supportive.' He blinked. 'Sorry didn't mean to go down that rabbit hole and depress you. It's still a bit raw. Anyway, what's the deal with you? When is your Mrs home then?'

Nate glanced at Foxy and figured it was OK to share.

'That's where the balls of steel are missing,' he said ruefully.

'How so?'

Nate settled back in his chair and told Foxy. How the baby had died, how he had to section Viv and what had happened the last time he saw her.

'That must have been tough. Is that where the bruise came from?' Foxy asked. 'I wondered if someone had lamped you. So, this afternoon you're going to see her and decide if she can come home for a few days?'

Nate grimaced. 'Yeah. I don't know what I'm doing though. Stuff I think would be a good idea isn't, I'm frightened I'm gonna mess it up and set her off again.'

'You strike me as pretty intuitive. I'm guessing you just need to read her now she's a little different.'

Nate looked confused. 'Different?'

'Yeah. You're used to her being the Viv she was. What the markers or signs were for happy or sad, when she was pissed off but didn't say it? All the little markers that you learnt subconsciously.'

Nate suddenly realised where he was going with this.

'You're saying that I need to learn her new ones? She's thinking differently, behaving differently. I just need to learn the markers. That's it.' Nate narrowed his eyes at Foxy. 'How come you know this?'

Foxy gave him a rueful look. 'PTSD counselling. Marriage was falling apart.'

Nate pulled a face. 'Hard thing to get over in any situation.'

'Not my finest hour,' he said, picking up the cafetiere. 'More coffee?'

'Thanks, so were you in Afghanistan then?' Nate asked. 'If you don't mind me asking.'

'I was all over,' Foxy said. 'Feels like another life now.'

'And the PTSD… you were captured? Tortured?'

Foxy nodded.

'How long?' Nate asked softly.

Foxy looked out of the window. 'Few months. You lose all track.'

'Bad?' Nate asked.

'Yup. Lucky to get out. Others weren't so lucky.'

'Do you miss being in the forces?'

'Sometimes. Rarely now. I missed the sense of belonging. Family. But I have that here now and I consider myself a very lucky man.'

Solo barked as a blonde woman appeared on the balcony. She knocked lightly on the door and let herself in.

'Hey, Rob… oh sorry. Didn't know you had company,' she said, shushing Solo as he insisted she made a fuss of him. Foxy grinned and stood. He went over and bent to peck her on the cheek.

'Soph, this is Nate. He's moved in next to Jenny. We were shooting the breeze over coffee. Nate this is Sophie.'

'Good to meet you, Nate.' She looked at Foxy. 'I'll come back.'
Nate held up his hand. 'Not on my account. I've gotta go.' He put his mug on the worktop and turned. 'Thanks for the coffee. How about a pint on me next time?'
'You're on.' Foxy grinned. 'Hope it goes well later.'
'Thanks. See you later. Nice to meet you, Sophie.'
'Bye, Nate. See you around.'
Nate let himself out and walked down the stairs, mentally processing what Foxy had said about learning to see new signs, new markers. Fuelled by a little more optimism, he went home feeling slightly more positive.

* * *

Sophie watched Nate walk down the steps. She turned and said to Foxy, 'He seems nice.'
'He is. Poor guy. Got a lot on his plate.' He grinned at her. 'So, bestie, to what do I owe the pleasure this fine morning?'
Her eyes twinkled. They both shared a deep love of climbing.
'I need a climbing buddy. I've got some serious cliff work to do, and I need a point man.'
'Music to my ears. When?'
'Tomorrow.' She tilted her head and reached out to touch his face lightly. 'You OK, bestie? You look sad. You having a bad day about Carla?'
He smiled at her, his heart lurching at her touch. 'I'm OK. It's just one of those tough days, you know?'
'I do,' she said. 'Group hug?'
Foxy enveloped her in a large hug and tried to control his body's response to having Sophie held tight in his arms. He couldn't ever make it known how he really felt; he had once, but then had played it down. Sophie was too important to him as a friend to risk telling her.
She squeezed him and stood back. 'OK?'

He tried to avoid meeting her eyes. 'Yup. I'd better get on and open up.'

'OK,' she said, grabbing her bag, 'See you tomorrow.'

'See ya,' he echoed to her retreating back.

* * *

Mickey Camorra had reached out to his London contacts to find out what the word was on Danny Tao, and more importantly, Lily Tao. He wanted a face to face with one of them to try and find out what was going on, even if it meant he was sticking his head into the lion's mouth, which would mean certain death. A bullet sent as a message was usually fairly non-negotiable in Mickey's book.

Mickey wasn't frightened of anyone. He'd had a harsh, brutal upbringing and had learnt early on that fear was a futile emotion. Better to be ruthless and strike before you got hurt – it had always been his mantra. Take the emotion that was fear, and channel it into something more productive, like violence. The only thing Mickey had real fear of was losing Pearl, or something happening to her. He just couldn't process the thought of it.

His colleague, a Russian named Alexy, who had proved both supremely loyal and a close friend, plus a highly lucrative business partner appeared in Mickey's kitchen and came to stand at the window next to him. He folded his arms and looked out at the view.

'What's the word?' Mickey despised pleasantries.

'Umm. This is difficult nut to open,' Alexy said in his pidgin English.

'How so?' Mickey asked, eyes narrowing, used to interpreting Alexy's confusing phrases.

'They are like…' Alexy searched for the right word and muttered something in Russian.

'What's that?' Mickey prompted.

'Like ghost people,' Alexy said.

'I don't know how that can be, they run a fucking empire. They have to be somewhere,' Mickey snapped.

'They say Lily is not dead. But is like ghost. No one knows where she sleeps.'

'What about Danny?'

'Same. No one knows.'

Mickey exhaled heavily. 'Someone must know where they are.'

'Did you hear about policeman?' Alexy asked quietly.

'What policeman?' Mickey absently scrolled through his phone.

'Steve Miller.'

'What about Steve Miller?' asked Pearl, coming into the kitchen with her coat over her arm.

Alexy looked uncomfortable.

'Hospital. Two Chinese men beat him.'

Pearl looked worried. 'What? Is he alright?'

Alexy inclined his head. 'Broken bones. I am thinking he will live.'

'Where was he beaten?' Pearl asked.

'At drugs house. I am hearing there was body in suitcase there too.'

Mickey narrowed his eyes. 'Who was it?'

Alexy shrugged. 'Don't know. But I will find soon.'

'Who were the two men?' Pearl asked.

Alexy looked at Mickey when he replied.

'Tao industries.'

'Fuck's sake!' exploded Mickey.

Alexy looked at his watch and swore quietly in Russian.

'I go now,' he said. 'We talk later, yes?' He slapped Mickey on the back. 'We will find. Don't worry. Alexy is on the cases.'

Mickey watched Alexy leave and pondered what he had said about Lily and Danny being like ghosts. There must be someone who knew where they were. He decided to put another feeler out to the old patch. As he tapped out a text, he saw Alexy's large black truck wind its way down the road and disappear from sight.

The sound of a loud pop made him look up from his phone. He frowned, trying to place the noise and then a huge explosion shook the window. Mickey looked in horror and disbelief at where Alexy's truck would have been.

'What was that?' Pearl asked, coming around the kitchen counter where she had been making espressos, her line of sight not seeing the billowing clouds of black smoke.

'Alexy—' Mickey began. His phone rang. He looked at the ID – unknown caller – and raised it to his ear. He heard a soft male voice speak.

'Reap what you sow, Mickey.'

The bullet entered through the plate glass window and ploughed into Mickey. The unpredictable winter weather was responsible for its slight shift in trajectory, moving it from his heart to his side.

Pearl screamed as the glass wall shattered. She instinctively dropped to the floor and struggled to drag Mickey by the collar to the other side of the kitchen. They would be hidden from sight behind the huge island, as bullets rained around them.

Stanley and Maxim, their close protection, burst in the door and threw themselves to the floor to help drag them to safety.

Blood pumped from Mickey's side, leaving a wide, bright-red trail across the white terrazzo floor as they dragged him across it. Bullets pinged around them, embedding themselves into the floor and flicking up sharp bits of stone. Finally, they were behind the kitchen island, out of sight.

'Mickey!' Pearl screamed and grabbed her coat to press it against the wound.

'Get that fucker, Maxim,' Mickey said through gritted teeth.

Now they were safe, Maxim rolled over and deftly kicked open a hidden door in the kickboard. He drew out a high-powered rifle.

Bullets whizzed past his head as he moved the final few feet to position himself behind a wall. He ran up the stairs to a different part of the house, stumbling up the last few stairs to the top floor.

Throwing himself on the floor behind a large day bed, he peered through the telescopic sight. He scoped out the hill opposite, carefully, taking his time. He couldn't see anyone.

More shots rang out and then Maxim saw the shooter. He was in the sunken garden of the hotel on the cliff opposite. He had moved his head from the telescopic sight, and he was looking directly at the house, smiling to himself. Maxim exhaled and squeezed the trigger.

The shooter wasn't smiling anymore. He didn't have a face.

CHAPTER 13

Mickey was unconscious, clammy and bleeding profusely. Pearl had bunched her coat into a ball and was pressing hard on his side, trying to stop the blood flow. The once pristine white cashmere coat was now stained a deep crimson.

'How long, Stanley?' she shouted, struggling to keep pressure on the wound as they roared through the lanes.

'Two minutes,' Stanley replied, calmly taking the corner hard and accelerating as fast as he could. He saw the sign for the hospital and turned in, heading directly for the A&E department. The tyres screeched as he skidded to a stop. He jumped out and ran around to the side door.

'You can't park there,' shouted a security guard who had leapt up from his doze at the prospect of some activity.

Stanley ignored him. He wrenched open the door and pulled Mickey towards him. His eyes widened at Pearl covered in Mickey's blood and he looked behind him at the security guard.

'Get a stretcher. A wheelchair. Anything. DO IT NOW!' he roared.

The security guard opened his mouth to say something, but when he caught sight of who it was in the back of the car, he turned and bellowed for help.

A nurse came out with a stretcher and Stanley helped them lift Mickey into it. Pearl grasped Stanley's arm.

'Go. Check on Maxim. Sort the house.'

'I can't leave you, Pearl,' Stanley said desperately. 'I can't chance it.'

'I'll be fine here. Go quickly and come back.'

Stanley was torn. He worshipped Pearl. His sole purpose in life was to keep Pearl safe. He would rather die than let anything happen to her.

'Go,' she said firmly. 'Now. Every minute, we are exposed. Go. I'm relying on you, Stanley.'

As he turned to go, she grabbed his arm and held on tightly, her fingers leaving bloody finger marks on his jacket.

'Be careful, Stanley. I can't bear the thought of losing you too.'

Stanley swallowed the lump in his throat. He loved Pearl with all his bones. He patted her hand and was gone. He hoped to God Maxim had got the shooter.

* * *

Pathologist Jim Murphy left the mortuary, in the lower echelons of the hospital, and headed up to the wards. He knew his friend Steve was there, and he wanted to see for himself how he was. When he finally pushed open the door to Steve's room, he found him sitting on the bed in a pair of jeans, gingerly buttoning up a shirt.

'Well, you're a sight for sore eyes,' Murphy remarked. 'Honestly, I pay a couple of idiots to get rid of you and they end up mucking it up.'

'You wish.' Steve grinned. 'Have you missed me?'

'Like a hole in the head. Are you going home?'

'I'm not going home. I'm going to work.'

'What?' Murphy was incredulous.

'I've got things to do.'

'Have you seen your face?'

'I think I look roguish.'

'Roguish?'

'Not doing it for you?'

'Not particularly. I've told you before, you're not my type. This is verging on harassment.'

'You wish. Some people find this look irresistible.'

'Are they locked up in a psychiatric facility?'

Kate entered the room and smiled at Murphy.

'Hey, Jim. Are you talking him out of going to work?'

Murphy held up his hands in a gesture of surrender.

'I wouldn't dare. I came to see whether he would be needing my services any time soon.' He frowned at Steve. 'Are you seriously going into work in that state?'

'Uh huh,' Steve said, wincing as he tucked his shirt into his jeans. 'What news of the person in the suitcase?'

Murphy tilted his head in amusement. 'Do you ever stop?'

'Well?'

Murphy sighed. 'The body had been frozen absolutely solid. It had really only just started thawing out. What with the suitcase and all the wrapping. Anyway, I'm waiting on dental records. Oh, and it's a she. I'm pretty sure, of mixed heritage. I'd say maybe in her late twenties at first glance.'

'Cause of death?'

'Double tap to the head. From the back. Clean, precise. I'd hazard, she wasn't expecting it. No defensive evidence. Professional job.'

'Bullets?'

'Only one left in there. It has our friendly dragon motif on it.'

'Christ.' Steve pushed himself off the bed and started putting on his jacket. 'I need to go and have a chat with this lot.'

'Please be careful. I don't want to be hacking you to bits anytime soon.'

'I thought you said it was cutting precisely but respectfully?'

'Whatever you want to call it. This is me saying be careful.'

'I hear you. Do you nag your husband this much?'

'Only when he's being a dick.' Murphy turned to Kate. 'Always a pleasure to see you. I've decided I like you much more than him.'

The door burst open to reveal Jonesey holding Steve's mobile phone. He was wild-eyed and panting heavily.

'Steve, it's Stanley…' he gasped and bent over. 'So many stairs… Oh God, I've got a stitch.'

Steve grabbed the phone. 'Stanley?' He listened, frowning. 'What? JESUS! Where are… Here? OK. I'll come now.'

He ended the call. 'Mickey Camorra's been shot. He's downstairs. I'm gonna need the bullet if it's still in him.' Glancing at Jonesey, he said, 'Get a forensics team to their house right now.'

Jonesey was still panting from his exertion. 'I think I need to lie down for a sec,' he said and took a sudden interest in Steve's breakfast tray, still sitting untouched on the side. 'Are you not eating that?'

Steve hurried down the corridor as quickly as his broken ribs would allow him, Murphy strode by his side.

'This way,' Murph said, dragging Steve down a maze of corridors. He opened a door and walked into the rear of the emergency room, his eyes flicking over the board on the wall.

'Cubicle two,' he said, pushing the curtain aside to see Mickey laid on a bed with Pearl clutching his hand, she was covered in blood.

'Steve,' she said weakly.

'It's almost a straight through,' the consultant said, lifting the large surgical pad from the wound. He hummed with satisfaction. 'I can feel it in there. We're going to do an X-ray for other fragments, and some quick surgery to debride and tidy up the wound.' He smiled. 'Nothing much to worry about.' He looked down at Mickey. 'It won't be pretty though.'

He inspected the wound closely. 'I think your husband should consider himself a lucky man, Mrs Camorra,' he said, snapping off his gloves. 'A little more in either direction and it might well have been curtains. We'll get him into surgery in the next hour or so.'

He saw Murphy standing beside Steve.

'Jim? Whatever are you doing here? Hopefully not touting for business?' He brayed with laughter at his own joke.

Steve showed the consultant his warrant card.

'I need the bullet from him, to go to him.' He gestured first to Mickey and then Jim.

The consultant looked between the two men. 'Let's hope we can whip it out then!'

'It's part of an ongoing investigation,' Murphy clarified.

The consultant walked off, issuing a nurse with instructions.

Steve looked at Pearl, she was pale and the dark shadows under her eyes were pronounced. There was a smudge of blood on her cheekbone. He moved to stand next to her.

'How you holding up?' he said quietly, noticing her hands shaking. Painfully, he dragged over a chair next to the bed and guided her into it. She sank down gracefully and squeezed Steve's arm.

'Thank you,' she said. 'He got a call and then…'

Mickey's eyes flew open. His hand shot out and grabbed hold of the rail of the bed.

'Alexy,' he gasped weakly. 'His truck… exploded. Right before…'

Pearl inhaled sharply. 'Alexy?'

The curtain was thrown back and Alexy stepped into the room, staggering slightly. There was a bloody gash down one of his cheeks and more blood covered his face, coming from a head wound. His hands had small cuts all over them, and they were smeared with blood. His trademark black T-shirt was ripped, and Steve noticed huge scuff marks on the shoulder of his jacket and rips in his jeans, with bloody cuts visible beneath.

'Mickey,' Alexy gasped, ignoring the angry nurse who was following him and telling him to sit down because he was bleeding everywhere. 'Thank the God. You are OK.'

Mickey looked relieved. 'I saw the truck explode, I thought…'

Alexy's expression was grim. 'Petrol tank shot. Not good shot first time. Good second time. I jump out and roll and roll.'

Pearl leant over and grasped Alexy's hand. 'I'm so happy to see you.'

He smiled. 'I am thinking you would be missing me if I was dead?'

'Yes, I would.' She smiled. 'You're family to us.'

Alexy looked unusually emotional. 'Alexy is happy to be that.' He sighed deeply. 'Now I am thinking I am the wobbly and I will be sick.'

With that, Alexy dropped into a dead faint at the foot of Mickey's bed.

* * *

Nate arrived at the hospital where Vivienne was staying and was greeted by the same nurse who had escorted him out the last time. He gave her a wan smile as she buzzed the door open and beckoned him in.

'That's a proper shiner,' she remarked, gesturing to his eye. 'Did it hurt?'

'It did.'

'Told you.'

'You are clearly the all-seeing eye,' he said dryly.

Chuckling, she said, 'I've been called a lot worse.' She glanced sideways at him. 'She's good by the way. The fact that she wants to leave here for a period of time is good.'

Nate didn't commit to a reply and the nurse stopped and looked at him with a knowing expression.

'You're scared of her,' she observed.

Nate inhaled sharply at her perceptiveness. 'Not *her* as such,' he stammered.

The nurse rolled her eyes. 'OK, you're scared of her unpredictability. Of the illness.'

'Yes, I am,' he said simply.

'Don't be,' she said. 'That won't help her.'

He stared at her. 'Why does it feel like everyone here talks in bloody riddles?'

She laughed. 'What I'm saying is, that if you're scared of the illness, then you won't be treating her normally.'

'But she isn't her normal self anymore,' Nate said quietly.

'She needs to keep on the meds,' the nurse said firmly. 'That's what's given her a nice even keel. Psychosis is under control. She's been great.' She winked. 'Trust me.'

The nurse swiped her card and shouldered a door open into a small bedroom.

'Nate!' Viv flew across the room and jumped on him, wrapping her legs around his waist. She kissed him firmly. 'Where the bloody hell have you been? I've been waiting to go for ages!'

'Oh… I didn't think I was taking you home today,' he murmured, enjoying the feel of her wrapped around him.

'Course you are… isn't he, Lisa?' She peered around his shoulder at the nurse who was still in the doorway.

'I think you'll have a chat first and then decide,' Lisa said firmly. She looked at Nate and winked. 'I'm next door.'

'OK.'

'Come and sit by the window,' Viv said, dragging him over and sitting cross-legged on the window seat. 'Tell me everything that's been going on. I feel like I've been living in a fog, and now it's lifted.'

Nate sat down and took her hand. He braced himself.

'By the way. Sorry about the eye and nose,' Viv said, pulling a face.

'You remember?'

'Little bit.' She waved her hand. 'It's all part of the treatment. Unpick things to death. I'm sorry, I must have properly lobbed it. Anyway, come on. Tell me everything.'

He took a breath. This was it.

'We've moved,' he said, bracing himself for a huge reaction.

'Cool. Where?'

'By the sea. Remember Castleby?'

'The place you lived as a kid with the brightly coloured houses and those beaches to die for?'

'Yes.'

She clapped her hands delightedly. 'Tell me!'

He grinned and relaxed slightly. 'It's a bright blue house, and it has this amazing little office that juts out over the cliff and feels like you're hanging over the edge with the sea beneath you. We can sit in the lounge and look at the sea, we can lay in bed and see the sea.'

She breathed deeply. 'It sounds like heaven.'

'I've bought it. This is it. I gave notice on the last place.'

Viv was silent for a moment. 'What happened to all our things?'

'All packed up and in the process of being unpacked in the new place.'

She plucked at a loose thread on her sleeve and didn't meet his eye.

'And the nursery?'

He breathed deeply, hoping this wouldn't set her off.

'Nursery is all packed up. I brought it with me. Everything is in the loft.'

She looked thoughtful for a moment. 'Good.' She smiled at him and took his hand. 'It's important we try and move on and make a fresh start.'

Nate almost wept. 'Fresh start,' he said, softly kissing her hand. 'Right, let's see about going home?'

CHAPTER 14

'Olivia... OLIVIA! Please look at me when I'm talking to you.'

Olivia dragged her gaze away from the window to Brian's frowning face.

'What?'

'I was asking you where you were going today?'

'Hadn't thought about it,' she said vaguely.

He tutted. 'Olivia, you know this isn't how we *do* things. You know I would like to know your plans before I go to work. You've proved to me that you really can't be trusted, so I need to know more than ever, where you are going and who you will be spending time with.'

'Remind me why do you need to know?' she said, angry at the injustice of it. Then wishing she hadn't said anything as soon as she uttered the words.

He grabbed her jaw and forced her to look at him, his fingers painful on her soft skin, as they encountered previously bruised areas.

'You know why,' he said through gritted teeth. He released her and pointed a finger. 'Don't fuck with me, Olivia. You know what'll happen. Now I expect an answer. Where are you going today?'

'Eli has a climbing lesson. He wants to call into the lifeboat station too before he goes back to school.' She looked at Brian. 'By the way, are you taking him back to school next week, or am I?'

'You can. I'm not taking the time off just to spend the day on the motorway. Waste of time.'

She shook her head sadly. Eli had been stood in the doorway behind him and had overheard. Brian turned and seeing him there, rolled his eyes.

'You know what they say about people who listen in doorways. They never hear anything good about themselves.' He turned to Olivia. 'I'm working here for a couple of hours this morning; the shuttle is coming later. Don't disturb me.'

Olivia sighed. 'Shall we go, Eli?' she asked, knowing that his lesson didn't start for an hour. 'We'll get some coffee and a sticky bun before we go in,' she whispered.

He nodded enthusiastically.

'Shoes on!' she said, grabbing her coat.

'Olivia!'

She tried hard not to scream in frustration. 'Yes, Brian?'

'Don't think I've forgotten who works in that shabby climbing centre. You won't be speaking to him today, will you?'

'Really?'

'Olivia,' he warned.

Frustrated, Olivia nudged Eli out of the front door and slammed it loudly. Two thirds of the way to the climbing centre she realised she had left her purse behind. They turned around and walked back home, and she told Eli to sit and wait on the outside wall.

'I'll be two ticks,' she said, 'hang on!' She quietly opened the door and crept in. As she fished her purse out of her large handbag, she heard Brian's voice. She crept along the corridor a little more to listen.

'Brian Baker here. This is a message for your administration department. Does nobody there know how to answer a phone? Regarding a patient you have there, Mr Gil Palmer. I will be withdrawing funding with immediate effect. I will need someone to call me and inform me of the next steps.' He reeled off his mobile and landline number, and ended the call. She heard him laughing softly to himself. 'Not that I actually give a fuck what happens to the silly bastard.'

A chill settled over Olivia. She backed out of the house and quietly closed the door. She smiled brightly at Eli, who was sat on the wall swinging his legs.

'Come on, bud. Let's go and see what cakes that cafe has!'

Eli jumped off the wall and slipped his hand onto hers as they walked. She felt a surge of affection for him followed by abject guilt. If she wasn't married to Brian anymore there was no way he would allow her to see Eli. She tightened her grip on his hand, and he nattered away happily about the lifeboat station and how he was going to try and climb the outside wall at the climbing centre.

After their coffee and cake, Eli dragged Olivia into the climbing centre. She smiled at the enormous man behind the counter who grinned at Eli.

'Hey, buddy,' Foxy said. 'How are you today?'

'Good, thanks,' Eli said.

'You feel OK?' Foxy asked. 'I've got juice boxes standing by.'

Eli laughed. 'I'm good. Are you teaching me today, Foxy?'

Foxy tapped the screen of the iPad in front of him.

'Did you book yourself in to try and climb the outside wall?' he queried.

Eli hopped about enthusiastically. 'Yes.'

'Well, I like your style. Yes. It is me then. Go on back and get some climbing shoes on.'

'Yes, Boss!' Eli grinned and ran to the back of the centre.

'Nice little guy,' remarked Foxy.

'Yes, he is,' Olivia said, watching him go.

'Ollie.' Mike said her name quietly and she turned to find him standing there with ropes slung over each shoulder.

'Is it bondage hour?' she asked dryly.

He raised an eyebrow. 'I'm game if you are. Anytime.'

She burst out laughing and Foxy left them to it.

'Still in one piece?' Mike asked, searching her face.

'For now.'

'What are those marks on your jaw?' he said, frowning. 'Is that from him? Ollie, you have to get out.'

'I know,' she said desperately. 'I just need to find out about Gil. What's going to happen to him. Plus, Eli goes back to school next week. Then I'll go. I don't want to leave him there alone with Brian. I just don't trust him.'

Eli stuck his head around the corner. 'Mum…' He reddened. 'Sorry – Liv, I'm going up the outside wall now! Can you film it for Dad?'

'Sure can.' She moved to stand where she could see him. Making herself comfortable, she watched with interest while Foxy patiently took the small group through safety briefings and then a talk on technique. Eventually they were good to climb. Foxy made them patiently look at the wall and mentally try to map out a route via the coloured holds that suited their level before they started. Foxy called Mike to look after the safety ropes for two of the other boys while he focused on Eli and another.

Eli chalked his hands and started climbing, giving Olivia the thumbs up as she started filming.

Olivia followed Eli's progress up the wall as high as he could go. As she tracked him upwards, filming, she saw Brian standing at the top of the wall watching them.

'Dad! Dad!' Eli called and waved, trying to get his attention. 'Look how high I am!'

'Both hands, Eli,' cautioned Foxy, tightening the safety rope.

Brian was looking down the wall at Mike. He looked at Olivia and then at Mike and then pointed to Olivia.

'Dad! Look where I am!' called Eli, but Brian had gone.

Eli's face became a picture of disappointment.

'Eli wins! He gets to the top first! Wahey, buddy! Record time!' Foxy called out, giving Eli some encouragement. Eli gave him a wan smile and climbed down quickly.

'Good job!' Foxy said, giving him a high five.

Mike leant over and high fived as well.

'Eli the Gecko,' Mike said, laughing. 'You're good, Eli.'

'There's a competition tomorrow. You should enter for your age group. I reckon you'd smash it,' Foxy said.

'You think?' Eli said doubtfully.

'For sure,' Foxy said. 'You've got great technique.'

'Great,' Olivia said firmly. 'Where do we sign him up?'

* * *

Brian had moved position. He watched his son dispassionately as he climbed the wall and there was a part of him that wished he would fall and then his burden would be over. He closed his eyes and willed it to happen, but the boy was still there when he opened them again.

He watched Olivia laugh and joke with Eli and the two men, and felt a surge of anger. She said she wouldn't be talking to them. The bearded one was the one in the wetsuit on the beach the other day, he was sure of it. He clenched his fists. The sooner this contract was over, and they could move on, the better. As he continued watching his phone rang. He answered it, not recognising the number.

'What?' he said rudely.

His blood ran cold as he heard the voice.

'You're a difficult man to find. We need to know where the boyfriend is. Then we need to know where the money is. Once we get that and the money is returned then your slate is clean.'

'How did you get this number?'

'We know everything, Brian. Little wifey and son all cosy by the seaside. Clock is ticking. We need to know where the boyfriend is.'

'He's in a coma. He never came out of it after the crash.'

'Your wife must know then.'

'She doesn't know anything.'

'You sure about that?'

He snorted. 'I know everything about her, I'd know if she knew.'

'Perhaps she left the money at the clinic when she had an abortion two weeks ago. I expect an answer by tomorrow. Or we find out ourselves.'

Brian listened to the dial tone. He felt the rage bursting up inside of him. Abortion? She had terminated *his* baby?

He considered what Olivia had done and breathed deeply, trying to control the white-hot rage he felt.

He frowned. They were lying. She wouldn't have done that. She would never have the audacity to terminate *his* baby's life. He clenched his fist and rammed it into the castle wall, not feeling the pain. He imagined Olivia's' face underneath his fist and it gave him a modicum of relief. He breathed deeply.

He had to find out where the shipment or the money was. If he didn't, all of this was for nothing.

* * *

Nate parked the car and grabbed Viv's bag from the boot. She'd got out and was looking at the house.

'Is this it?' she asked with a large smile on her face. 'Is it really ours?'

'It is,' he said, suddenly desperate to show her around. 'Come on.'

Pushing open the front door, he grabbed her hand, and pulled her down the hall and out to the lounge that faced the sea.

'Beautiful,' she breathed, admiring the view. 'Is that ours? That garden?'

'Yup.' He opened the French doors that led out to a terraced garden built on the top of the large rock that the houses sat on. The wind gusted in and made them shiver. She walked out and looked over the edge of the flint wall and shrieked.

'There's even steps down to the beach!'

He grinned and held out a hand. 'Come see the rest.'

She strode lightly back into the house and closed the door. The chilled wind had made her nose red and mussed her hair. She looked like the old Viv and Nate's heart lurched.

'Kitchen?' she said, pointing.

Viv inspected the rest of the house and completely fell in love with it. She insisted that they moved the bedroom around so they could lie in bed and watch the sea, and Nate was more than happy to oblige. She loved everything and then promptly insisted they light the wood burning stove in the lounge and make lunch to eat in front of the fire.

They sat on the floor, backs against the sofa, eating pasta from bowls, staring at the crackling fire.

'So… good decision?' Nate ventured.

'The house?'

'Yup. The move.'

'I think so,' she said. 'I was sick of constantly moving around. This here, it's a wonderful house. I'd like to explore the town a little in a minute?'

'Sure.'

'Have you got to know anyone yet?'

Nate grunted through a mouthful of food. 'The day I moved in, the removal men left, and I was starving, couldn't find anything and the woman who owns the hotel next door came in with a hot pot and a bottle of wine. I don't think I've ever been so pleased to see anyone.'

'That's a nice thing to do.'

'It was. She's nice. She's Jenny and her dog is Archie.'

'Anyone else?'

'I had breakfast with a few locals, had coffee with a Foxy from the climbing centre. He's a good bloke – ex-soldier. And Doug, he's the skipper of the lifeboat.'

'I'm glad you've made friends. I'd like to meet these people.' Viv put her plate down. 'Do they know?' She shifted and then looked at him. 'About me?'

'Foxy knows. He's had some troubles. He understood. Jenny guessed. That's all. They'll be respectful about it. They're sound people.'

'OK,' she said thoughtfully. 'Be good to meet them.'

Nate put his plate down and draped an arm across her shoulders, pulling her in close. He buried his face in her blonde hair and closed his eyes, almost not believing she was home.

'It's good to have you here,' he said softly.

She snuggled into him. 'It's good to be here.'

'How do you feel?'

She looked up at him. 'Good… I feel good. Much stronger.' She sighed. 'This therapy has been brutal… tough… invasive, but effective. But I've realised that we need to be able to talk about it, Nate.'

He was silent for a moment, deciding what to say.

'Truth is, I'm a bit unsure of how to talk about it.'

'Says the king of negotiators,' she teased.

'This is different.'

'I know. We just have to be honest. If I feel wobbly, I'll say. OK?'

He nodded.

'So, what's the problem?' She touched his forehead lightly. 'What's going on in here?'

He looked at her for a moment, overwhelmed with love for her.

'It's just…' He struggled to vocalise what he was thinking.

'What, Nate?' she asked gently.

'You seem so… so normal. Like the old you,' he blurted out. 'Before… you were so different, Viv. You looked like you, but you didn't, if you get what I mean. It's hard to see you like this when, not so long ago you were like that, and not wonder…'

'Wonder if I'm going to go batshit crazy again?' She laughed and then looked serious. 'It must be hard for you.'

'I just want to be sure you're OK. You seemed to get better really quickly.'

'A lot of it was getting the psychosis under control. That had run a bit rampant and was driving everything. Soon as they found the right balance of meds, I felt much more normal. Much more like me.'

'Really?' he said. 'You seem so much better. It's hard to believe that the right mix of drugs can work so well.'

'I think that and the therapy helped a lot. Talking through the underlying issues.'

Nate frowned. 'I need to know what's OK to talk about. What's to be avoided,' he finished awkwardly.

'What do you mean what's to be avoided?' she asked.

He struggled, feeling uncomfortable. 'Are we OK to see babies? Talk about babies? Or does that make you uncomfortable?'

She stared deeply into the fire. 'It makes me sad, Nate. Just really sad. But I'm getting on and trying to deal with it.' Her eyes filled with tears, and she blinked them away. 'It's just…' She wiped a tear away. 'I want to be sure we don't forget her.'

'Of course we won't forget her,' he said, firmly squeezing her hand. 'Never.'

'We'll get there,' she said. 'I've got more therapy when I go back, and if I feel OK, I can come home and be an outpatient for a while.'

'How do you feel about that?'

'Good. I feel good about it. It's about small steps, I think, and being open and discussing how I–' she faltered, '–how *we* feel. I don't want you walking on eggshells or steering me in a different direction if you see a baby in the distance.'

'OK. Everything's on the table then, no matter how difficult.'

She touched his face gently. 'Everything. Anything. You need to check in with me and make sure I'm taking my meds too.'

'Good plan.' He hugged her close. 'OK. So, what's on your list to do next?'

'You,' she said, grinning and grabbing him.

He kissed her. 'Game on.'

Bundled up in warm coats they left the house for a stroll. Nate was very happy. He felt connected to Viv again. Their intimacy had cemented it for him, and she had seemed like the Viv he had always known. He had to be hopeful that the treatment really was working and she was back. She seemed on an even keel to him. As they strolled along he draped an arm over her shoulder, and they wandered comfortably along the street. They headed down towards the beach beneath the castle and he pointed out Maggie's cafe.

'It looks lovely in there,' she said, pressing her face against the window. 'Food looks good.'

'Food *is* good,' Nate agreed.

Viv wandered over to the climbing centre, and crouched to stroke the Alsatian that was lying in the doorway.

'Isn't he lovely?' she said, making a fuss of him. 'Look at his scarred face. Have you been in the wars?' she asked the dog who had decided to expose his stomach for a full belly rub.

'He's supposed to be on guard,' an amused voice said from behind them. They turned to see Foxy holding a large coffee.

'Nate, how are you? This must be Viv. Nice to meet you, Viv, I'm Rob Fox.'

Viv grinned. 'Good to meet you.'

'But everyone calls him Foxy,' Nate interjected. 'Except Sophie, I noticed.'

Foxy laughed. 'She's always called me Rob. I'll answer to most things though. And this is Solo.'

'Why is he so scarred? He's beautiful.'

'I found him in a war zone, buried under rubble so I brought him home,' Foxy said. 'He was an army dog anyway, but we think he got separated from his team and they left him.'

Viv stroked his head and looked into Solo's brown eyes. 'I couldn't have left him.'

Foxy watched the interaction. 'Me neither. So here we are.'

Viv stroked the dog gently. 'This is a nice life for him, after a war zone. Quiet and restful.'

'For both of us.' Foxy glanced at Nate. 'So, is this the grand tour then?'

Nate chuckled. 'Verdict is all good so far isn't it, Viv?'

'Definitely.' She grinned. 'When I'm home properly, come for dinner maybe?'

'I never say no to food.'

'Good,' she said. 'Solo can come too.'

'We'll be there.'

'Right,' Nate said. 'Let's carry on the tour.'

'Nice to meet you, Foxy.'

'You too, Viv. I'll hold you to that dinner.'

She laughed. 'You do that.'

As they strolled away, Viv rested her head on Nate's shoulder. 'I'd like to get a dog if we're living here.'

Nate had been thinking the same thing.

'Deal,' he said. 'Right. Harbour next.'

'Is it too cold for an ice cream?' Viv asked.

Nate tutted loudly and said in a mock stern voice. 'Vivienne, how many times have I told you? It's never too cold for ice cream.'

'OK, OK.' She grinned. 'Oh, and Nate?'

'What?'

'I'm not living with the kitchen being that colour. Just saying.'

'Copy that, Boss.'

CHAPTER 15

Steve sat down gingerly at his desk and almost moaned with relief. The sergeant was bellowing at him about being back at work too soon. Despite the sarge not being Steve's line manager, Steve both respected him and listened to him, but currently he was at his limit.

'Sarge,' he said, holding up a hand to try and stop him in his flow. 'Take a breath for God's sake and do us all a favour.'

The sarge carried on unabated.

'SARGE!' Steve bellowed.

Sarge looked surprised.

'What?'

'Just... stop for a minute,' Steve pleaded. 'Look, I appreciate your concern. But I'm fine. I feel fine.'

The sarge eyed him suspiciously. 'I'm wasting my breath. Your health, your funeral,' he muttered as he stomped out.

Steve slumped in his chair. He was exhausted and had a banging headache, but he needed to get on. The body of an almost headless man had been found in the gardens of the hotel that sat on the cliff opposite the Camorra house. Next to him was a high-powered rifle, together with ammunition embossed with a dragon motif.

Steve knew exactly who had killed the man, but he wanted to know where the man was from. And where he needed to start to track down his employer.

He chugged down a few painkillers, swigging from a bottle of water and ate a stale cereal bar he had found in his desk drawer. Clearly too healthy for Jonesey to have nicked it.

He grabbed his phone and put a call through to an old colleague in Cardiff.

'Ross Scott,' the voice answered.

'Steve Miller,' Steve said wearily.

'Buddy! How you doing? Heard you took a pounding, and not in a good way either.'

'I'm OK. Getting there.'

'Glad to hear it, my friend. Let me guess, you want to talk to me about Tao Industries?'

'I thought I might.'

'Jonesey sent me the stills of the Chinese guys who gave you a once over.'

'Who are they?'

He snorted. 'Couple of Tao henchmen. No one important. Slight delusions of grandeur. But I find that with organisations like these where there is a whiff of Triad involvement, they think they're all hung like donkeys.'

Steve laughed. 'So, who do I nick?'

'Ah and there is the million-dollar question, my friend. You could nick them, but that's only cutting the head off a tiny snake in a whole pit of them.'

'I want the person in charge of the pit,' Steve said grimly.

'Easier said than done. Head honchos are Lily and Danny Tao. She's harder to nail to the wall than fog. No one knows where she is, where she operates from, and the same goes for her boy. He's the top snake charmer if you will. But he's not visible and nor is she.'

'They had a pop at Mickey Camorra. Shot him.'

There was silence on the other end of the phone.

'Jesus,' Ross said. 'Is he OK?'

'Not sure yet. I'm afraid this is going to be all out war though.'

Ross sighed heavily. 'My advice?'

'Bring it on.'

'Stay on the sidelines, let them kill each other.'

'Can't do that, plus I don't want the collateral damage. They sent a message to Mickey. A bullet. Someone wants him dead, and they seem fairly intent on doing it.'

'If you get involved, the likelihood is that you'll be collateral damage too.'

'Me? Nah, nine lives.'

'Eight and a half now. Seriously, mate. Be careful.'

'Do me a favour. Charge the two henchmen anyway? I've got them with a suitcase containing a body, all on film, dragging it into a bungalow full of weed. Suitcase will be covered in their prints. It's at least two less snakes from the nest of vipers.'

'No problem. You want them up to you?'

'Nope. You OK to sort it down there? You've got access to it all.'

'Happy to. I'll call you when it's done.'

'Top man.'

'Take care of yourself, mate.'

'You too.'

Steve ended the call and looked up to find Jonesey lounging in the doorway.

'You look like shit,' he announced, chomping down on an iced bun.

'None taken,' Steve retorted grumpily.

Jonesey made himself comfortable on the chair in front of Steve's desk.

'I think you have a death wish,' he announced with a mouth full of bun. 'First the Camorra's, now the Tao's, who are essentially the Triads.'

Steve snorted. 'Don't be ridiculous. They're just another group like the Camorras, but in a different location.'

Jonesey shot him a disbelieving look. 'These are way worse. Jerry says you need to watch your back.'

'Well perhaps fucking Jerry should stop offloading all his shit to me then,' Steve muttered, shuffling paper around on his desk.

He silently cursed DCI Jerry Reed who headed up the organised crime unit for the area. He had been on Mickey's case for years, largely unsuccessfully. Mickey loathed him and refused to even speak to him, so Jerry had offloaded most of the dealings with the Camorra onto Steve, knowing Steve had a good rapport with Pearl and, on occasion, Mickey. In typical fashion, Jerry seemed to be washing his hands of the current situation and allowing Steve to deal with things again.

'Jerry said…' Jonesey began, stopping as Steve held up a hand to stop him.

'Jonesey, I don't wanna hear it. What I do want is an ID on the woman in the suitcase.'

Jonesey inspected the last piece of his bun.

'That involves you getting off your arse and finding out about it,' Steve added. 'Like… now.'

Jonesey pushed himself off the chair. 'Why are you so grumpy today?'

'A good beating with a cosh does that. You should try it sometime.'

'Tempting, but I'll pass.' Jonesey brushed the crumbs off his uniform. 'Right. What was I doing?'

'Dead woman in a suitcase. Soon to be joined by you unless you get your bloody finger out.'

'Alright, alright. Keep your drawers on. I'm going now.'

'Praise the Lord.'

'Rude,' Jonesey muttered as he left.

* * *

Mickey was out of surgery. Things had gone well, but when he came around he was grumpy and in a lot of pain. Now he was arguing with a nurse about going home.

'*Mr* Camorra,' she said dismissively, speaking over him loudly. 'I've never heard anything so ridiculous in all of my life. There is no way on *earth* you will be allowed to discharge yourself and go home. It's quite ridiculous.' She noted her observations down on a chart and took Mickey's blood pressure. He started to talk, but she frowned and held up a hand shushing him.

Very few people had the audacity to shush Mickey Camorra and if they did, they rarely lived very long afterwards. The nurse, blissfully unaware of this fact, noted down his readings and unwrapped the Velcro cuff.

'Too high,' she admonished him. 'You need to calm down, Mr Camorra. Something's got your blood pressure up. That needs to come down before we'll even think about a home plan.'

Mickey clenched his fists and looked over at Pearl. 'I'm not a fucking pensioner.'

'Darling, calm down,' she said soothingly. 'You'll be home soon enough.'

The nurse bustled off, tutting.

'Alexy?' he croaked out.

'He's OK, a knock to the head, but he's good. They checked him over and patched him up and he's staying at the house now. Maxim is there.'

'Did Maxim get the shooter?'

'He did.' She patted his hand. 'The boys have patched up the house and made it secure. Now, enough. I think you should sleep for a bit. No one is going anywhere. Stanley and Tommy are outside.'

'I need my phone,' he muttered, looking around.

Pearl opened her handbag and produced it. 'Darling…'

'We've got to get ahead of this,' he muttered.

He cleared his throat and made a call.

'Reggie,' he said when the phone was answered. 'It's Mickey.'

'I'm talking to a dead man.'

'Do I sound fucking dead?'

'Word on the street says so.'

'Your street?'

'My street. Others too.'

'How did I die?'

'Danny Tao.'

'What's his beef?'

'Not for me to say.'

'Let's pretend for a fucking minute that it is,' Mickey growled.

'Says you killed someone close to him.'

'Who.'

'Someone close.'

'Lily's still alive?'

'Not heard otherwise.'

'Who then?'

'Dunno. Look, people have been here, Mickey, sniffing around, asking about the old days. Asking who knew who, who was doing who… you get the gist.'

'People?'

'Danny Tao's guys.'

'What d'you say?'

'What do you think I fucking said? Nothing.'

'Not about Frank? Or me?'

'No. But they talked to Mad Maisey.'

'She was crazy even back then.'

'Still is. Nuthin' changed there. Look, Mickey, I've gotta go. I'll be a dead man if they know I'm talking to you.'

Mickey snorted. 'Since when did the Tao's rule your patch, Reggie?'

'Since they took it from me and shot my wife in the face in front of me.'

Mickey was silent for a moment. 'Jesus, Reggie, I'm sorry—'

'Look,' Reggie interrupted him harshly. 'I didn't want to be having to say this. You're way out of touch, Mickey. You might wanna check in on your empire. This lot are like a load of fucking Ninjas in the night. I don't want you to wake up one morning with a knife to your balls and a gun to Pearl's head. There's no fucking happy way back from it.'

Mickey was silent for a beat.

'Thanks, Reggie. As you know, I'm still a dead man for the time being until I can sort this. We clear?'

'Crystal. Have a good death, Mickey.'

Mickey ended the call and looked at Pearl. She'd heard everything.

'We've got work to do,' she said grimly. 'You need to rest. I'll handle this.' She picked up her handbag and moved towards the door.

'This is my problem,' Mickey snapped. 'Keep out of it.'

Pearl whirled around with a murderous expression and jabbed an angry finger at him.

'How *dare* you. This is *our* problem, Michael Camorra. The minute someone thought we were fair game and came after you in *our* home and tried to kill one of our closest friends, they made it my problem too. I will not stand for this. Someone will pay. I don't care how messy it gets.' She glared at Mickey. 'I'm taking over.' She turned and marched out.

'Pearl!' Mickey roared, as she was followed out by Stanley. 'PEARL!'

Tommy, the Camorras' driver, stuck his head around the door and winked at Mickey.

'She's long gone, Boss. She said to stop shouting and get some sleep.'

***

On the next floor up of the same hospital, Hannah looked down into the small face of baby Lucas and smiled, delighted when she received a toothless grin in return.

'Hello there,' she cooed. 'Hello, gorgeous. It's nice to see you again. Yes it is.'

'Hannah, I'm busy. What do you want?' Anne said, sounding annoyed. 'Why are you always so focused on the babies?'

'Oh I didn't realise… I was just checking about lunchtime and meeting in the coffee shop.' Her gaze returned to the baby. 'I think he recognises me from the other day.'

'Of course he doesn't. You could have texted.'

'I'm dropping this back,' Hannah said, holding up the breast pump.

'Oh right. Chuck it in the store at the end of the corridor?'

'Anne, I need you,' the ward sister called.

Anne looked down at the crib she had been pushing. She passed it to Hannah. 'Here, do me a favour, take him back to his mum. First bed on the left on your way out. She's asleep so just leave him next to her. He'll be fine.'

Hannah took the clear crib on wheels and walked slowly down the corridor, cooing gently to the baby. She pulled some faces and he gurgled with happiness. As she walked along the corridor she dawdled, wanting to spend more time with the baby. She chucked the pump in the store and then lingered, playing with baby Lucas. There was a row of chairs outside the ward doors, and she sat for a moment and lifted him out of the crib and into her arms.

She closed her eyes at the feel of the baby's smooth head against her cheek and she breathed in the smell of him. He nuzzled into her neck, and she sat there enjoying the sensation of him.

Her phone rang, waking him suddenly and he let out an angry wail. She shooshed him gently as she answered the phone. It was one of the nurses telling her to hurry back. She popped him back in the crib and wheeled him around the corner to his mum.

Hannah carefully parked the baby next to the mother and looked at her critically. She was a typical yummy mummy. Everything Hannah loathed in a person. Blonde, trout pout, false nails, ridiculously huge false eyelashes. Hannah snorted. She expected that the baby would be taken home wearing a Burberry outfit in a Range Rover or something similar. She felt a surge of hatred for the woman, why did she get to have a baby and she didn't? A pen fell out of her pocket and as she bent to pick it up she saw the woman's Prada handbag on the floor by the bed, open for all to see, her Chanel purse clearly lying on the top. Hannah looked at it for a moment and then turned and walked away. Her fault if anything went missing. Who left everything on display anyway? Stupid fucking bitch.

CHAPTER 16

Pearl closed her eyes and inhaled the scent of the city. She buzzed the window down on the black cab and breathed in the scent of exhaust fumes mixed with light rain and the occasional whiff of coffee and fast food. She heard the noise and bustle of the city, the sirens, the traffic, the quick blasts on horns, the shouts. She had missed it. Not too much. But she had.

'Here will do, thanks,' she called to the driver and handed over a twenty-pound note. 'Keep the change.'

She stepped gracefully out of the cab assisted by the ever-present Stanley, who shut the door and lightly tapped the roof as the cab drove off. Pearl adjusted her coat and glanced at Stanley.

'Back seat today, Stanley,' she said. 'I can't have you breathing down my neck here. People will think I'm important enough to need protection and I don't want that.'

This was a difficult comment for Stanley's tiny brain to process, so he kept quiet. He was her protection though, wasn't he?

'Yes?' she quizzed. He inclined his head, so she carried on. 'Stay outside and don't be lumbering in.'

She walked briskly down New Bond Street glancing in the odd shop window. She trailed a hand lovingly over the shoulder of the bronze sculpture of Winston Churchill and Franklin D. Roosevelt where they sat on a bench sharing a joke.

'Hi, Winnie,' she murmured as she passed them. She carried on down onto Old Bond Street and turned into the Royal Arcade, stopping outside one of the shops. She cast an eye over the collection of rare watches in the window and smiled slightly, shaking her head.

'Stay here,' she instructed Stanley as she pushed the door open and stepped inside.

The carpet was thick underfoot and the air of luxury pervaded. Dark cherry cabinets with highly polished glass tops ran along the edges of the room, with a large display cabinet in the centre. In one corner of the room, two chairs and a low table sat as a viewing area. A tall, dark-haired twenty-something woman with slightly Slavic features stood behind one of the counters.

'How can I help you, Madam?' she asked in clipped tones.

Pearl detested being called madam. It made her feel like a pensioner.

'Is he in?' She turned and looked up at the camera. 'Bernie, come on out, darling.'

'As I live and breathe!' The effeminate voice of Justin De'Silva rang out as he entered the shop via the rear door. 'Pearl darling, you look ravishing. How long has it been?'

'Long enough. How are you, Bernie?'

Justin De'Silva's nickname was Bernie and had been – much to his annoyance – since he was a young man. He bore more than a striking resemblance to business and Formula 1 magnate Bernie Ecclestone, with his bowl haircut and round glasses. He was extravagantly dressed in a purple velvet suit with a bright-red shirt underneath and highly polished black brogues.

'Scraping a living, darling. Scraping a living,' he said, taking Pearl's arm and steering her to two chairs in the corner. He clicked his fingers.

'Zara, coffee now.'

He settled Pearl into a chair and took the one opposite.

'I doubt very much you are scraping a living, Bernie,' Pearl observed. 'Still in handmade suits and shirts. Seems to me you're not starving.'

He raised an eyebrow and said conspiratorially, 'Well one must keep standards up, darling. So… I heard a rumour you had a rare Patek Phillipe that you sold recently. Apparently, it went for a record amount.'

Pearl smiled. 'You know what they say about listening to rumours.'

'These things are never rumours. Darling, why didn't you come to me with it?'

'I'm sure I don't know what on earth you're talking about, Bernie.' She looked around the shop. 'Quite the collection you have in the window. I love the Rolex.'

Zara delivered a tray of coffee.

'The Daytona?'

'Is there any other?'

Bernie chuckled. 'You've always loved an old Rolex.'

'Price is a bit toppy though, Bernie… by about ten grand. Left over from Christmas?'

Bernie looked slightly embarrassed. 'You always did know your watches.'

Pearl smiled indulgently. 'There'll probably be a contingent of foreign tourists in next week, so I reckon you'll be able to offload it then. Tell them a royal wore it once and they'll have your arm off.'

'Banking on it.' He laughed and dabbed his head with a spotty silk handkerchief. 'Now, darling, this isn't a social visit since there is some henchman type outside. Am I in trouble?'

Pearl raised an eyebrow, and brought the china cup to her lips. 'Should you be in trouble, Bernie?' Pearl regarded him closely as he constantly mopped his brow with his handkerchief.

She sipped her coffee. 'Why so nervous? Whatever have you done?'

'Pearl, I've been meaning to tell you.' He looked around. 'I'm so sorry,' he whispered. 'So sorry. They *made* me tell them... *threatened* me. I had to tell them.' He wiped his teary eyes. 'They *hurt* me, Pearl,' he whispered, wide-eyed and then grasped her hand. 'Tell me how I can make it right.'

Pearl was silent for a long time. She spoke coldly and withdrew her hand.

'I thought it must have been you. You broke the rules, Bernie. They came for us in our home. Shot my husband in front of me. You should have warned me.'

Bernie was almost sobbing. He grasped her hand again tightly, his hands clammy.

'Pearl,' he begged. 'They threatened me.' He looked traumatised. 'They *hurt* me, Pearl.' He sobbed as he hunched over her hand. 'Tell me how I can make it right.'

'You know if they'd have been asking around for us, we'd have known. We'd have had warning. This is betrayal of the worst kind, Bernie.'

'I know. I know. I'm sorry. I want to make it right. How can I make it right?'

Pearl snatched her hand away from his sweaty, desperate grasp. She regarded him with a hard stare.

'I want an audience with Lily Tao.'

He stared at her in utter disbelief. 'What? Are you mad? She'll kill you.' He glanced sideways at the girl behind the counter and said in a low voice, 'No one gets an audience with the Tao's.'

Pearl met his stare coldly.

'I want to see Lily Tao. Tomorrow 1 p.m. The Bleeding Stag in Soho.'

'What makes you think I can make this happen?' Bernie said, terrified at the prospect of what Pearl was asking of him.

'You know enough people to make anything happen in this town. I'm sure you still use Jack the Hat as your fixer. Get to it, Bernie, or you will have to suffer the consequences and it won't be pleasant. I feel sure she'll come out of curiosity if nothing else.'

Bernie was quiet for a moment. 'If I can get her there, our slate is clean?'

'I'll think on it.'

'But, Pearl…'

'I said I'll think on it,' she snapped. 'Clock's ticking, Bernie. Better get cracking.' She stood gracefully. 'If this happens again, I won't be so accommodating. Mickey would have torn you apart with his bare hands for this. You will only get the one chance to make it right.' Reaching the door, she turned as an afterthought. 'Oh, and Bernie?'

'Yes, Pearl?'

'I see at least two fakes in the window. You are getting sloppy, my friend. Fakes in the Royal Arcade? That doesn't bode well. That could ruin you. See you, Bernie.'

'F-fakes? I don't deal with fakes? Which…' He pushed himself out of his seat, knocking the small table over in his haste, sending the coffee cups crashing to the floor. He peered at the window display from behind, his face a sheen of panic. The mere hint of a fake would ruin the long-standing reputation of both him and the shop.

'Pearl…' he called after her desperately. 'Which ones? Pearl. Pearl!'

* * *

Danny Tao sat in the car watching Pearl Camorra leave the Royal Arcade. He knew someone from the Camorra would make the link that it was that fucking fairy De'Silva who had given them up. He was surprised though that Pearl had taken it upon herself to come and see him. He watched her walk along the road with that lump of meat who looked like her protection and wondered where she was going. He half expected her to go to Soho to find one of her old cronies. He didn't like it that she was here. In London. He wondered fleetingly if he could just run her over, but he spotted a police car parked down the road and knew he wouldn't get far in the city of CCTV that was London these days.

He rubbed his face, sniffing constantly. He felt sweaty and sick. He knew he needed a fix. Then he could think straight. He dug around in his pockets and found a small plastic bag containing a tiny amount of powder. He licked his finger and ran it all over the inside of the bag and then touched it to his tongue. For a moment he felt wonderful and then it was over. Paranoia crashed in.

Had his mother had him followed? He turned around in his seat craning his neck over his shoulder, seeing if he could spot anything suspicious. What if Pearl was going to see his mother? What if she knew about the suitcase? Would Pearl tell his mother? He wiped his face, he was sweaty, but at the same time cold. His hands shook and he cursed himself for needing a fix so badly. He saw the man with Pearl hail a black cab and help Pearl get in when one stopped.

He couldn't think straight. Did he follow her? Did he want to kill her? He couldn't decide. He wanted to hurt Mickey like he had never been hurt before and that meant harming what mattered to him the most. He wasn't sure if Mickey was dead or not. Even if he was, should he kill Pearl anyway?

Paranoia engulfed him. Was Pearl here to kill him? Was she here pretending to see people and Mickey was actually tracking him? Had he risen from the dead and was after him? He let out a small involuntary moan. What if he was here to make him suffer personally?

Pearl's taxi had driven off and he quickly pulled out to try and follow it, before realising with frustration that it was lost in a sea of black cabs.

* * *

Steve ended the phone call informing him that two of the Tao henchmen were currently residing comfortably in Cardiff nick, and grimaced as he sipped from a cup of cold coffee. He had slept fitfully the night before; lying on the side of his broken ribs kept waking him up. In the end he had left the bed and Kate's warm arms and slept sitting up in an armchair, as he'd concluded it was marginally less painful.

'Coffee?' Jonesey appeared around the door clutching two coffees that were dripping everywhere and a crumpled open packet of custard creams.

'Custard creams?' Steve queried. 'Don't you usually save them for PC Warren? To what do I owe the honour?'

'PC Warren only appears to have eyes for Garland,' Jonesey said mournfully. 'Despite my best efforts.'

'Well, what's he got that you haven't, eh?' Steve said being supportive.

'Well, he's a tad more beach body ready than me,' Jonesey began.

Steve snorted. 'Beach body ready?'

Jonesey shifted in his seat. 'He's all gym and flat abs. I think that's what she likes.'

'Get down the gym then.'

'It's not that simple.'

'Rubbish. Get yourself beach body ready as you say.'

'I want her to love me how I am.'

'But maybe she will if you build up your muscles and develop a six pack.'

'I don't know if that's me though. All gym and no substance.'

'All that time in the gym will mean less time for eating and watching *MasterChef*,' Steve concluded.

'Exactly! See? It's just not me. I'm no gym bunny.' He fiddled with the biscuits and crammed one into his mouth. 'I'm just not cut out for the gym,' he said his mouth full.

'So it would appear,' Steve said. 'We've got two new PCs starting tomorrow. Perhaps one of them might eventually love you for who you are.'

Jonesey helped himself to another biscuit and chewed, dropping crumbs all down his front. 'You think?' he said, slurping his coffee and dripping it all down himself.

'You never know,' Steve said mildly. 'If you can up your eating age from toddler to adult, you might actually be in with a chance.'

'Ha ha, very funny. Oh, by the way, Murphy called. He said he had news.'

Steve stared at Jonesey. 'Could you not have said this when you came in?'

'Oh yeah, probably,' Jonesey said, standing up and brushing crumbs off himself. 'I'm gonna go and talk to Sarge about who's starting tomorrow. Find out if they're fair game.' He waggled his eyebrows at Steve and said in a mock Sean Connery James Bond voice, 'I'd better stock up on my biscuits, Moneypenny.'

'Go away,' Steve said, picking up his phone, 'and shut the door.'

'You're welcome for the coffee and biscuits,' Jonesey said huffily.

'DOOR!' Steve bellowed as he dialled.

'You playing hard to get?' Murphy said as a greeting. 'I gave Jonesey the message to call me ages ago.'

'There's your first mistake,' Steve said. 'Fuckwit central. Come on. Hit me with whatever it is.'

'Two things,' Murphy said. 'One, I got the bullet from Mickey. Surgeon was very accommodating. What we expected with the dragon logo. I also took the opportunity to get Mickey's DNA off the bullet.'

'Er, we kind of need permission to do that.'

'Did you not hear him give it to me in the hospital?' Murphy asked innocently. 'In A&E? You were right there.'

'So that's in the system now?'

'It is.'

'Not sure that'll stand up in court if we need it to. The second thing?'

'Body in the suitcase,' he cleared his throat. 'Er… we've fucked up a bit there.'

Steve sighed and closed his eyes. 'Epic fuck up or "only a bit" fuck up?'

'Not sure. Personally, I think it's a result.'

'Jesus, Murph. What is it?'

'Body is no match for any dental records.'

'At all?'

'Not a whisper.'

'Go on.'

'I ran it through the DNA database and that's where the lab kind of fucked up.'

'Stop talking in bloody riddles and get to the point.'

'The lab ran it against Mickey's DNA before it went into the main system. And er… it was a potential familial relationship to Mickey's DNA,' Murphy said quickly, as if saying it faster made it less of a mess up.

'It was a *what?*' Steve said in disbelief.

'It was a match, for Mickey.'

'They're related?' Steve asked faintly.

'Father and child. The child inherits half of the father's genes, so checking the genetic markers on the father and child is enough to be 99.99% confident that someone is the father.'

'So you're saying…'

'That the girl in the suitcase is Mickey's daughter.'

'Christ alive!' Steve exploded, struggling to process the enormity of what he was hearing.

'She was mixed race. Probably Asian heritage, maybe Chinese.'

Steves struggled to find words for a second or two.

'You still there?' Murphy prompted.

'Yup. Sorry.' Steve tried to process. 'I just can't believe what I'm hearing.'

'It's pretty irrefutable,' Murphy said.

'So, she was killed by a double tap to the head, with a dragon motif bullet?'

'Yup. From behind. I'd hazard a guess maybe she wasn't expecting it.'

'Right. Thanks, Murphy. I don't know what to do with this just yet.'

'Greatest respect, not my problem. I've got a bunch of stiffs to hack about with – those are your words, not mine. Gotta crack on. Take care, mate.'

'Thanks, Murph.'

'No problem.'

Steve chucked his phone back on the pile of paper on his desk and tried to process what he had heard. He didn't know Mickey had children. Surely it would have been mentioned somewhere. On a file somewhere. He decided to play it safe, picked up his phone again and dialled a number.

'Steve, how are you? What can I do for you?' Pearl's warm voice floated from the speaker on Steve's phone.

'Just checking in. Seeing how you guys are,' he said, hoping she wouldn't see through the ruse.

'Mickey is getting better. Alexy is staying at our place for now.'

'And you, Pearl? Are you OK?'

'I'm fine. I'm running some errands in London. I'll be back in a day or so.'

'Pearl, you're not going to do anything stupid are you?' Steve warned.

'When have you ever known me to do anything stupid?' Pearl asked. 'How are those ribs?'

'Promise me, Pearl, you'll stay safe. Tell me where you're staying in case I need to get hold of you.'

'I'll be fine. I'm in Flemings. Mayfair.'

'OK. One more thing, Pearl.'

'Go on.'

'Does Mickey have kids? I assumed you guys never did, but I might be wrong?'

Steve thought he'd lost connection for a second as Pearl was quiet.

'Pearl? You there?'

'We certainly didn't,' she said lightly. 'But who knows what he was up to before we met. I've never been made aware of any.'

'Pearl,' Steve said. 'I—'

'What have you found Steve?' she interrupted. 'You wouldn't be asking me unless you were suspicious of something. Tell me. It might make all the difference.'

'This stays between you and me,' Steve paused. 'There was a dead woman in that suitcase in the bungalow.'

'The drugs bungalow?'

'Yes.'

Ever perceptive, Pearl asked, 'Are you saying that she is or was Mickey's child?'

'I'm afraid so.'

'How old was she?'

'Late twenties early thirties they're guessing.'

'Anything else I should know?'

'They think she was mixed race. Chinese possibly. Not a hundred per cent sure yet.'

'Does Mickey know?' Pearl asked.

'No.'

'Keep it that way for at least twenty-four hours for me?' Pearl asked. 'As a favour?'

'For you, Pearl. But you promise me you won't put yourself in danger.'

'I will do my best. Stanley is with me. Tell me, how did she die?'

'Two bullets to the back of the head. Dragon motif. Call me when you're back.'

'Will do, sweet man.'

'Bye, Pearl.'

Steve ended the call and sat thinking. Jonesey put his head around the door, looking excited.

'FYI. Sarge says one male, one female starting tomorrow. I'm popping out to buy biscuits to feather my nest with. You want anything?'

Steve rolled his eyes. 'Go away.'

Steve was wading through paperwork when his mobile rang.

'Miller,' he said absently.

'It's Mrs Clifton from Woodpecker Lane.'

'Mrs Clifton. How the devil are you?' he said, only half paying attention.

'I've been watching the house again.'

'Oh, there's no need. You saw the raid. No need now.'

'Is that so? Well, I want to know then why a load of chinks—'

'Mrs Clifton, it's simply not appropriate to say things like that.'

'But they are chinks.' She sounded puzzled.

'Yes, but you can't say it.'

'World gone mad. Anyway,' she said dismissively, 'these chinks have turned up with a white van and have loaded all those plants into it.'

'We were supposed to come and seize the plants last week.'

'Well, no one has come except for a couple of chinks a few days ago and now the big van with all the chinks—'

'Mrs Clifton, you can't say that—'

'Don't interrupt me. So they've loaded all the plants in, and I think they've left some sort of orange light on.'

'Call the fire brigade, Mrs Clifton. I suspect the orange light is a fire. Did you happen to get the number plate of the van?'

She snorted. 'What am I? Stupid? Of course I did.' She reeled it off. 'Right. I'd better call the firemen then.'

'Thanks, Mrs Clifton.

'I look forward to reading about it all in the paper,' she said.

'Absolutely,' Steve said, trying to sound convinced. 'I'll make sure they're aware.' Then a thought occurred to him. 'Of course, we'll have to wait until the case is closed and all the culprits arrested. We wouldn't want them to come and seek out their revenge on you, would we?'

Mrs Clifton went unusually quiet. He heard her swallow.

'Mrs Clifton?'

'Am I in danger?' she whispered.

'Not at all,' Steve said breezily. 'But we need to make sure that everyone is safely locked up before we talk about your wonderful surveillance efforts.'

'I think that's a good idea,' she said. 'Anyway. I'd better call the fire brigade.'

'You do that, Mrs Clifton,' Steve said. 'Bye now.'

* * *

Olivia was helping Eli pack. Brian had left his phone on the table when he had stepped out to buy some milk, and she had managed to field the return call from the residential home where her brother used to be. She had almost passed out from relief at the timing of it. She quickly explained that there was no need to worry and that it was all a misunderstanding, and no one needed to speak to Brian. That accomplished, she had replaced the phone exactly where it had been, deleted evidence of the call and took refuge with Eli as they packed for his return to school the next day.

'What's up?' she asked, walking into Eli's room finding him lying on the bed, clothes scattered around him.

He bit his lip. She came to sit beside him.

'What's up?'

Eli threw his arms around her and sobbed. 'I don't want to go back to school. I hate school. I want to stay with you. I hate Dad. Why can't it just be us?'

'Oh, sweetie. I'm sorry you feel that way.'

'Why can't I go to school here?'

'Have you asked Dad about doing that?'

'No, because he'll say no.'

'How do you know if you don't ask him?'

'I would say no. Absolutely not,' Brian said from the doorway. 'You will go to a good school and make something of yourself.'

'I hate it.'

'You need to man up,' Brian said dispassionately. 'Boarding school is good for you.'

'You only want me to go so that I'm not around!' Eli shouted. He pushed himself off the bed and ran into the bathroom locking the door. 'I hate you,' he yelled.

'Eli.' Olivia tried to defuse the situation. 'Eli, come on out,' she called.

'No,' came the muffled reply.

'Leave him,' Brian said. 'He can miss dinner too. Did my phone ring while I was out?'

'Not that I heard.' She turned and began folding clothes so she didn't have to look at him.

Brian stayed in the doorway a little longer.

'You know you never really told me what actually happened in Dubai.'

'Whatever made you bring that up? Of course I did. I told you about the sandstorm and the accident.'

'Yes, but why were you driving out to the desert with your brother? Where was Jade?'

'She was in the car. She wanted to go somewhere.'

'Where?'

'Don't remember.'

'Where did she go? She wasn't in the accident?'

'I don't know.'

'You must have an idea where she went?'

'I don't. I was unconscious. What's with all the questions?'

Brian shrugged. 'Just wondered, that's all. You were in an awful hurry to drive out in a sandstorm.'

'There wasn't a sandstorm when we left, otherwise we wouldn't have gone, would we?' she muttered sarcastically.

'Careful, Olivia,' Brian warned. 'I don't like that tone of voice.'

Olivia smiled brightly at him. 'Are you coming to drop Eli off with me tomorrow?'

He frowned at her. 'Of course I'm not. I've got some really important stuff happening tomorrow, I can't spare the time.'

'Right.'

'It's a day wasted.'

'I'm not the one you have to justify it to.'

'Olivia, I don't have to justify anything to anyone.' He moved as if to go back down the stairs. 'Are you sure my phone didn't ring?'

'I didn't hear it,' she said. 'I was up here the whole time.'

CHAPTER 17

Hannah arrived at work early and snuck up to her favourite ward. She helped the volunteer with the tea trolly through the doors and went in search of Anne. The ward sister said Anne was in one of the side rooms where new parents could change their babies and give them a bath. She stood at the door and watched Anne who was hunched over something that Hannah presumed was a baby. She looked like she was half laying on whatever it was. Hannah pushed open the door.

'Anne?' Are you OK?'

Anne jumped and moved away from a baby, which let out a breathless wail and started crying.

'Jesus, Hannah. You frightened me,' she said, her eyes looking red and her face blotchy.

'Anne, what's up? Are you crying?'

Anne dashed a hand across her face. 'I'm OK.'

'You look like you've been crying.'

'I'm fine.'

'What's the matter with this one?' Hannah said, approaching the baby. 'Why is he crying?'

'He has something stuck up his nose. I was trying to get it out,' Anne said, wrapping up the baby and placing it in the Perspex crib on wheels.

'What did you want, Hannah?' she asked briskly.

'Why do you always ask me that when I come up to see you?' Hannah asked, puzzled by Anne's slightly odd behaviour. 'Can't I just come up and see you?'

'Sister's a cow. Always telling me off if she sees me talking, that's all. You need to go. I'll come and find you later for coffee.'

Hannah watched Anne's back disappear as she swept the crib around in an arc and walked back towards the ward. Hannah wondered at her slightly odd behaviour. Shrugging, she left the room and wandered back to her own ward, pondering why Anne was so abrupt. She wondered whether her friend was really OK after her miscarriage or whether she was struggling to cope. She vowed to ask her if she was doing OK when she saw her later.

As she approached the doors, she passed the entrance to the ward and saw baby Lucas. She crept towards the door and stood for a moment, watching him through the glass and waving at him while the mother lay snoring on the bed.

In the hospital coffee shop, Hannah sat opposite Anne and wondered how to ask the question. Anne was moaning about the ward sister and how she had been saying she needed more nurses on the ward. Hannah's ears pricked up. She had been thinking that she'd like to get back to a maternity ward, so she vowed to email the sister about a transfer later.

'Sorry about this morning,' Anne said, interrupting Hannah's mental career planning.

'It's fine,' Hannah said. 'Look, are you coping? Are you finding it hard working with babies after… you know.'

'Sometimes,' Anne said, and her face hardened. 'It's hard sometimes when the parents clearly don't give a toss about the baby.' She frowned. 'Actually, no it's not hard, it makes me furious, and I really struggle not to say something. They don't deserve it, you know? They don't care about them. It's just an accessory, a new plaything. None of them deserve it, not really.' She sighed. 'But we've said all this before, haven't we? Won't change anything.'

Hannah made noises of agreement, unsure of what to say, and tried to look sympathetic.

'I mean take that baby you took back to the mother the other day. She's still here. Fucking stupid cow,' Anne said bitterly. 'One C-section and she can't even think for herself. Honest to God. She's a pain in the arse. Doesn't deserve to have that baby. Only person she loves is herself.' She snorted. 'Now she's accusing people of nicking her purse that had her engagement ring in it. She reckons the ring alone is worth a good ten grand! Honestly, we say to people don't leave your handbag lying about and she goes and loses her purse! Silly bitch. She had the audacity to suggest one of us nurses took it. Who brings a Prada handbag and a bloody Chanel purse into hospital anyway?'

'That's awful,' Hannah said. 'How long is she in for?'

'Sister said another day or so, something about her stitches and some sort of infection, but she's saying that she can't possibly cope with a baby at home, so she's asked her husband to hire a wet nurse! Honest to God, she's a stupid bitch and doesn't deserve to have a baby. Anne looked at Hannah and reddened. 'Sorry. Didn't mean to rant. She just annoys me.'

'It's OK,' Hannah said quietly. 'I know exactly how you feel, I feel the same way.'

'Do you? I thought it was just me.'

Hannah smiled ruefully. 'No, I think it quite a lot, but that's what they said in group, wasn't it? That it's fairly normal to feel this way. To feel resentment. We just have to learn to control it, don't we?'

'S'pose so. Did you get any more overtime?' Anne asked, snapping a KitKat in half and handing two fingers over to Hannah.

'Tonight's shift. Then maybe another at the weekend.'

'You're not very busy on your ward, though, are you at night?'

'No. Should be easy. Might get to catch up on my soaps!'

'Sister asked me if I'd pull a double today and I said I'd think about it – but if you're on. We could catch up together.'

'Great!'

'Buzz me later.'

'OK.'

* * *

Viv finished reorganising the last of her things in the wardrobe after Nate's poor attempt at unpacking and sat on the bed, gazing out of the window towards the sea. She breathed in deeply. She felt happy here. Her therapy as an inpatient was concluded and she felt good. She felt able to cope. 'An even keel,' was how she described it to her doctors. She was now an outpatient at the nearby hospital and had already met her new doctor and had a session with him. He seemed nice and she felt she could talk to him. She decided that tomorrow, she would email her boss and ask for a meeting to discuss a phased return to work. She marvelled at how a change in approach and meds had helped her turn the corner. She felt… sane again. She felt unbearable sadness when she thought about the baby they had lost, but the therapy and medication had helped enormously.

Her stomach rumbled and she realised she was starving. She knew she needed to eat properly, plus it helped her to maintain a routine. In the kitchen, she made herself some food and wondered what to do with her afternoon. Nate had reluctantly left her as he had some training to finish, so he wouldn't be home until around six.

As Viv washed up her plate, a woman walked past the window and then the door knocker went. She opened the door and came face to face with a woman of a similar age to her, holding a large bunch of flowers and the lead of a small dog that looked like a corgi cross of some type.

'Viv, isn't it?' the woman said.

'Er, yeah,' Viv said, smiling at the woman and then down at the dog.

'I'm Jenny from next door. These are for you. Welcome home and welcome to the neighbourhood.'

'That's so sweet. Thank you,' Viv exclaimed, taking the flowers. 'They're beautiful. Let me guess, you're the lifesaver with the hotpot and wine, aren't you?'

'I am.' She grinned. 'I brought your husband food and wine, but thought you might like flowers.'

'Good shout.' Viv grinned. 'Wanna come in for a cuppa?' She bent to stroke the small dog who wagged his tail enthusiastically. 'He's gorgeous.'

'I'd love a cuppa, but I need to walk Archie along the beach. He's not been out today, and I feel guilty.' She tilted her head. 'Tell you what, come along if you like and we'll get a cuppa from Maggie's to drink on the way. Sound good?'

'Sounds like heaven,' Viv said. 'Bear with me. I'm still trying to find everything. Nate's version of unpacking is to open a cupboard, stuff it full and close it again.' She dug around in a box leant against the wall and produced her walking boots and a coat.

'Right.' She put them on and grabbed her keys. 'Ready to go.'

Together they walked down the street towards the slipway onto the beach. They entered the cafe, which smelt of wonderful food cooking.

'Hey, Mags,' Jenny called out. She glanced over her shoulder at Viv. 'Careful you're about to get "Maggied".'

'Jenny love, how are you?' Maggie said as she bustled over, appraising Viv as she came.

'Mags, this is Viv, Nate's wife.'

Maggie grinned. 'Good to meet you, Viv. He didn't tell me how gorgeous you are. Mind you, he's as nice as a club sandwich to look at, isn't he?'

Viv laughed. 'Well, I don't know if he's as good as a club sandwich… maybe just a cheese sandwich.'

Maggie tittered. 'I like you already. Mind you, you need some fattening up.'

'Uh oh,' said Jenny out of the corner of her mouth. 'Here we go.'

'Oh, shush you.' Maggie nudged Jenny. 'Are you girls in for lunch?'

'No, just takeaway tea twice, please,' Jenny said.

'Two ticks. I'll do it myself.'

Jenny went to hand over some money and Maggie waved it away.

'Tea's on me. Good to meet you, Viv. Give me a minute and I'll get them.'

'Hello, ladies,' said a voice behind them and Viv whirled round to see Foxy's large frame filling the doorway.

'Hello!' Viv said. 'Foxy, isn't it?'

He grinned. 'And you are Viv, Nate's lovely wife who has promised me dinner if I'm not mistaken.'

'Viv, never promise anything related to food to Foxy. He's like an elephant,' Maggie said. 'He'll never forget and hound you constantly.'

'But she promised,' Foxy protested. 'That's a commitment.'

'Oh stop.' Maggie nudged Viv. 'She probably hasn't even unpacked the kitchen yet! Look, how about I get a few of us together for dinner in the cafe? Just us and a welcome dinner for you and Nate.'

'How is that dinner for me?'

Maggie rolled her eyes. 'You, of course, can come if it will stop you hounding this poor woman.'

Foxy leant down to Viv's ear. 'Maggie's cooking is amazing. Say yes and I'll give you free climbing for life.'

Viv chuckled. 'Done. I love climbing.' She turned to Maggie. 'It sounds wonderful as long as you let me come and help you.'

Maggie smiled with satisfaction. 'Lovely. Let's say tomorrow night? Everyone free? I'll see if maybe Will and Suzy are too.'

Jenny murmured to Viv, 'Suzy runs a dog rescue and Will's the harbourmaster. They're brother and sister.'

'Suzy will sound you out to see if you want a dog!' Jenny grinned. 'She totally seduced me with Archie.'

'I reckon I'll be pretty easy then.'

Maggie produced their teas and gave them a small paper bag. 'Little sweet treat for the walk,' she said, winking.

'Thanks, Maggie,' Jenny and Viv chorused.

'Right so 7.30 good for everyone tomorrow?' Maggie asked. She looked at Viv. 'Perhaps come and give me a hand around six?'

'Happy to. See you then and thanks, Maggie.'

'No problem. Look forward to it. See you tomorrow.'

Viv and Jenny left the cafe and walked along the beach. Archie was splashing about in the shallows chasing his ball that Jenny was kicking along.

'Hold this a sec,' Viv said, handing Jenny her tea she peered in the bag. 'Oooh we've got a Welsh cake each.'

'Oh man,' Jenny groaned. 'I've put on a stone since I've been here. The woman is relentless.'

'Well, I'm game,' Viv said. 'Here.' She swapped her tea for a Welsh cake, and they wandered along the beach happily munching.

'Mmm, that's good,' Viv said, licking her fingers.

'Everything Maggie makes is good. Tomorrow night will be great.' Jenny glanced at Viv. 'You OK about it? It was kind of sprung on you.'

Viv sipped her tea. 'I've got to get back to normal,' she said quietly. 'It's going to be a struggle, but all the time I think I can overcome the struggle I have to push myself. I'll probably be nervous as hell before it, but I'll love it when it's happening. I know I just need to push myself.'

'I'm so on the same page as you!' Jenny exclaimed. 'When I first moved here, it was supposed to be with my brother, but he died. It was really hard starting again on my own, but everyone was so wonderful it was like I had a new family. I got invited to something and almost didn't go, but I kind of got bullied into it and it was the best thing I ever did.' She looked back towards the cafe. 'Maggie brings you into the community. She makes you part of her flock.'

'And with the added bonus of being an amazing cook by all accounts,' Viv added.

'Exactly!' Jenny laughed. 'What's not to like?'

The two walked the length of the beach and back again, chatting about everything. By the time they arrived back at their respective front doors Viv felt like she had made a friend. She squeezed Jenny's arm.

'Thanks so much for today,' she said. 'It was totally what I needed. I really enjoyed it. Let me know if I can help with anything in the final rush before you open.'

'Do you know what?' Jenny said. 'Tomorrow I need to finalise the colours and schemes for each room, and I'd really like a second opinion. Just to check I'm not making a massive premenstrual mistake. Do you have a spare couple of hours?'

Viv laughed. 'That sounds like heaven. Definitely. What time?'

'Eleven?'

'See you then.'

* * *

Mickey's recovery was going far too slowly for his liking. The doctors had found an issue with his heart and were keeping him in to monitor it, which in turn was driving up his, already high, blood pressure. He'd not heard from Pearl, and he was worried. Maxim and Tommy were tight-lipped about where she'd gone. But Mickey knew exactly where she was. He knew Pearl. He knew what she'd be doing. He knew she would be after whoever gave them up to the Tao's. He was beyond worried, but he wasn't going to admit it to anyone.

His consultant breezed into the room and Mickey had to refrain from punching him in the face. The man annoyed him intensely as he came across as an upper-class twat, the kind Mickey despised.

'Mr Camorra,' the consultant said, consulting a long piece of paper. 'Simple terms, and I won't mince my words. You have a small tear in your heart, and we need to fix it. Your blood pressure is making the tear worse. It's holding for now but could go at any moment and it would be fairly catastrophic for you if that happens.'

Mickey narrowed his eyes. 'Catastrophic as in…?'

'As in the heart stops working properly, Mr Camorra.' He snorted. 'I'd say that's about as catastrophic as it gets, wouldn't you?'

Mickey clenched his fists under the bedclothes and the machines bleeped an alarm next to him.

'See there it goes again. Too high,' muttered the consultant. 'I'm operating on this as soon as I can. I think I can do it this afternoon. My plan is for it to be minimally invasive, so I only make a small incision, but if something goes wrong, then it's open surgery and there's a long recovery time. You just need to be aware. Are you clear on that, Mr Camorra?'

Mickey focused on him. 'You just need to make sure that nothing does go wrong then don't you, Doctor?'

'What? Yes, Yes,' the consultant said dismissively, half listening. 'I'll see you later, Mr Camorra.'

Mickey watched him leave the room and whipped back the covers to stand. He swayed slightly, feeling light-headed. He needed to get out of there and go and sort this mess out. He shook his head slightly, there was a whooshing sound in his ears, his head began to swim. His head pounded.

His arm started to tingle and then his hand, and he felt the most incredible pain rip through his chest. Gasping, he staggered, vaguely hearing the machines' alarms blaring out. The room spun and he slumped against the bed. In his peripheral vision he saw the consultant run into the room followed by the nurse, and Tommy in the background with a phone pressed to his ear. Then Mickey's world went completely black.

* * *

Brian said a clipped and unemotional goodbye to a sulky Eli that morning as they loaded his cases into the car. Eli didn't want to speak to his dad and was still angry and upset that he was being packed off to school again. Brian, not really caring what his son thought, had said goodbye, picked up his briefcase and site jacket and walked down to the harbour to catch the shuttle out to the wind farm. Eli watched his back as he walked away without a backward glance.

'I hate you,' he had said loudly.

'Come on. Stop that,' Olivia said as she carried a bag out to the car and slammed the front door shut. 'Right. Good to go? Sandwiches? Drink?'

'Yes,' he said. 'But I still want to stay here with you.'

'I'll work on your dad,' she said, tousling his hair. 'Come on, bud. You can DJ.'

'I can?'

'Only if that really annoying song isn't on there.'

'Which one?'

'You know which one.'

As she was about to climb into the car, a van arrived, blocking her in. Olivia shut the car door and approached the man who had jumped out of the cab holding a clipboard.

'Olivia Baker or Mr Gil Palmer, please?'

'I'm Olivia.'

'I've got crate for you. I need some proof of ID. Do you have a passport or driving licence? I need to verify.'

'What crate?' Olivia said, not understanding. 'I've not ordered a crate. From where?'

The man consulted his clipboard. 'You are Mrs Olivia Baker?'

'Yes, but…'

The man flipped through some pages and sighed. 'OK, what do we have…' he said, scanning the document. 'Right. Package was sent by a Jade Tao to you or a Mr Palmer. Instructions were to hold at Qatar for a period and then ship afterwards. So, it's here for you now. For delivery.' He looked at her and then his watch. 'Right now.'

'Right,' said Olivia, feeling stupid. 'What does it say it is?'

'Furniture and artwork. Perhaps Mr Palmer might be able to help instead?' the man said, adopting an irritated tone.

'It's fine. Bring it in then, I guess.'

'Happy to. It's big though. Could you grab your ID for me?' He turned and trotted back down the path. Five minutes later, he returned with a large square wooden crate with steel corners that he was expertly balancing on a sack trolly.

'Where do you want it?' he said. 'I'm telling you now, it won't go through the front door. Garage maybe?'

Olivia pointed around the side of the cottage. 'There's a summerhouse there, will it fit in there?'

He walked around the corner shaking his head. 'Gate's not wide enough.'

She thought for a moment. 'There's a small boatshed that comes with this place, it's just past the row of cottages on the left.'

'Black double doors?' he asked.

'Yeah.'

'It'll fit through those,' he said and started to wheel the crate back down the path. 'You got a key?'

'I'll just grab it.'

Returning, she trailed down the path after him and passed him the keys, watching as he deftly opened the double doors of the boatshed and tipped the crate gently in. He handed her back the keys.

'I'll need that passport?'

'Oh yes.' She dug it out of her pocket. 'Here you go.'

He scrutinised it and her and then snapped a picture of both of them with his phone, which he then presented to her.

'Sign with your finger, please.'

She awkwardly signed it and he beamed at her.

'All done. See you.'

'Thanks.' She glanced at her watch and realised they needed to get on the road. After locking the boatshed doors, she climbed into the car, and forgot all about it.

As they drove through the town, they tooted their horn to Doug when they drove past him in the harbour. Eli hung out the window yelling that he'd be back soon, and Doug grinned, giving him a thumbs up.

'I hate school,' Eli said while he fiddled with his phone. 'I hate Dad too.'

'I know, buddy. I'll see what I can do.'

At the school, Olivia said a tearful goodbye to Eli who was so clingy that he had broken down completely and begged her to take him home. It had taken her at least an hour to settle him back into the school mindset. Personally, she loathed private schools; she felt they bred a society of people that looked down their noses at others and had no idea of how to speak to anyone they considered a lower class to them.

She hated seeing Eli so upset. She had mopped up both his and her own tears, given him one last hug and driven out of the enormous school gates.

Olivia exhaled heavily as she turned towards the motorway for the three-hour drive back to Castleby. She vowed that she would try and work on Brian to get Eli into the local school and then stopped herself. She was planning to leave Brian. It wasn't a matter of working on him. She was leaving as soon as she could get away.

Tears filled her eyes at the prospect of having to leave Eli. She loved him. Genuinely. He was a wonderful, loving boy, and she would miss him. But she couldn't live with Brian for a moment longer. The more she thought about not seeing Eli again, the more upset she became. As she drove, the rain lashed against the windscreen, and she tightened her grip on the wheel.

Her phone rang, but there was nowhere for her to pull over safely. Ignoring it, she carried on driving until she reached somewhere where she could use it safely.

* * *

Brian had stomped down to the harbour and onto the shuttle, annoyed and grumpy. He had heard Eli say he hated him, and he felt very little, apart from anger at his ungratefulness. In truth, he was glad to get him out of the way; he found him annoying and when he was home from school craved peace and quiet until the boy was either out or in bed. As he sat waiting for the boat to depart, his phone rang, the call was from an unknown number. He debated answering and then it stopped ringing abruptly and a text appeared.

Answer the phone, Brian, or we will come to your workplace and talk to you.

The phone rang again almost immediately, and Brian answered.

'What?'

'Hello, Brian.'

His blood ran cold.

'Time's up, Brian. What do you have for us?'

'I'm still trying to find out,' he said, trying to appear normal in front of colleagues.

'You're not doing very well. There's a lot of money gone missing, Brian.'

'I'm fully aware of that particular issue,' Brian said pleasantly, looking around the small boat.

'All of the money from the last shipment.'

'I am aware.'

'So that equates to around £150 million.'

Brian swallowed hard and said quietly, 'I don't know where Jade and Gil went.'

'We took Jade, but she didn't have it. Wouldn't give it up.'

'Ask her again then,' Brian snapped.

'She's dead.'

'Jesus,' Brian exploded and then realised people were looking at him.

'We conclude either the boyfriend or his sister, as in your little wifey, must know. £150 million isn't just a small thing you can tuck into your pocket, Brian.'

'Yes.'

'You have until the end of tomorrow to tell us where it is, or you and your family will be suffering an untimely death. Understand?'

'Understand.'

'Just like Harry. Your contact.'

'Harry? What happened to Harry?'

'Check your local paper, Brian. He went to relax in the woods. End of tomorrow.'

Brian realised he had been sitting listening to dead air when the boat bumped against the harbour wall and they set off. The sea was choppy and the wind was squally, blowing in hard gusty bursts. He stuffed his phone into his pocket and wondered what the hell he was going to do to get Olivia to talk. He had stopped himself asking her about the abortion; he knew he needed information from her and he also knew once she admitted it, the situation would have ended badly – for her. Shrugging into his high visibility jacket he stepped off the shuttle and onto one of the larger support vessels that carried the turbines out to sea and constructed them. He raised his chin to acknowledge the skipper.

'Reckon we're in for a windy one today,' the skipper said as a greeting.

Brian looked out at the sky. 'What's the wind speed? I'm reluctant to do it when it's like this.'

The skipper laughed. 'Chill out. We're not even at a five on the scale yet.'

'You happy to carry on?'

'Course. It's got to be done.'

Brian stepped out onto the deck. He watched as the huge main body, housing the workings of the wind turbine, known as the rotor hub and nacelle, was craned onto the ship, followed by the three massive rotor blades.

Finally the skipper made the call to leave and the huge boat cast off. These boats had always fascinated Brian, from a distance they looked like a floating oil rig, with their huge four legs that could be lowered.

The further out to sea they went, the choppier the waters were. Reaching the location, the skipper skilfully held the boat in position, stopped the engines and the four legs were slowly lowered, so they lifted the boat clear of the water, turning it into a stable platform for them to work from.

Brian ducked back into the bridge to grab the radio.

'Wind is getting too strong,' he said to the skipper.

'Weather report said it's blowing through,' came the reply. 'Stop fretting like an old woman.'

Brian stepped back out onto the deck. The wind was slightly hampering operations and reports were that the wind speed had risen to the limit they could operate the crane in. He watched the nacelle being lifted into position. The crane operator only just managed to secure it in the gusty winds. He watched the crane swing back around and breathed a sigh of relief now the heaviest thing was in place. Just the three blades to go.

As project manager, it was his neck, and job, on the line if there were any more delays. Brian looked up at the crane swinging around to collect the next rotor, and spoke to the operator on the radio telling him to take it easy in the wind. He watched as the crane swung wildly in a gust of wind. The operator managed to control the swing and picked up a rotor blade. A gust of wind swung the blade wider than expected.

'Careful,' Brian shouted to no one in particular. The crane operator was well aware of what was happening and didn't need Brian shouting at him.

The skipper poked his head out of the door on the bridge and made a cutting gesture across his throat. Brian gave him a thumbs up and radioed the crane operator.

'We're pulling it.'

There was no response from the operator.

'Come in,' Brian repeated, but the operator continued trying to move the rotor into place.

Brian fiddled with his radio. His sole focus on trying to get the comms to work. He needed to stop the crane operator. He swore loudly and turned towards the bridge when he heard the sound. He looked up. With mounting horror, he saw the huge blade hanging, the chain broken one side. It was swinging wildly.

'Come in!' he yelled into the radio. 'The chain's snapped! Get clear!'

The sound of groaning metal caused Brian to whip around in time to see the huge rotor blade being blown towards the ship. The screeching sound of metal under intense pressure assaulted his ears. He looked around frantically for somewhere to escape to and started to run.

There was a loud metallic snap. Over his shoulder he saw the massive rotor blade hurtling down towards him.

The blade landed on the bridge, killing Brian and the skipper instantly. The crane arm had snapped and was hanging over the side of the boat. The crane operator had eventually managed to scramble to safety, climb back along the crane's arm and onto the ship to call for help.

CHAPTER 18

Pearl sipped an espresso and watched the bustle of Soho as she sat outside the Italian cafe waiting for her guest to arrive. She was dressed warmly, her preference to take coffee outside and watch the city begin its day. She had been greeted enthusiastically by Marco, the Italian owner. He remembered her well from her younger days and she had smiled indulgently as he paraded photographs of his children and grandchildren in front of her.

Marco appeared with a small plate of biscotti and looked down the length of the street, squinting slightly.

'He's here,' he said and went inside.

Pearl's guest arrived and kissed her affectionately on both cheeks before pulling out the chair opposite and sitting down.

'Still the bloody stunner, Pearly,' he said. 'Sorry to hear about Mickey. When you're over his unfortunate demise, I'll be at the front of the queue. You and me would be good together.'

Pearl raised her eyebrows. 'Ever the charmer, Trilby.' She appraised him. 'Life is treating you well it seems.'

Terry 'Trilby' Tincherra, was the man who knew everything and everyone who mattered in London. He carried the nickname Trilby since he always wore one to match whichever slightly bizarre, yet impeccably presented outfit he wore. He worked closely with local fixer 'Jack the Hat', and together they cut quite the scene with their outlandish hat choices.

Today, Trilby was dressed in a crisp white shirt, a matching dark green tweed waistcoat and jacket combination, and a green tie. His look was completed by velvet, sage-green plus fours and tan coloured lace-up knee-high brogue boots. The pinnacle of his outfit was a sage brushed velvet trilby with a large pheasant feather and tartan ribbon.

Luckily for Pearl, she and Trilby had gone to school together. She knew he had always maintained a lusting for her, and he seemed to be forever hopeful that one day she would turn her affections towards him. He also jumped at any opportunity to be helpful to Pearl in the hopes that this would endear him to her further.

He leant forward on his elbows. 'So, Pearly. You'll be after the deets.'

'I am. No better person than you to tell me, Tril.'

'What do I get in return?'

'Why do you need something in return?' Pearl gave him a long-suffering look.

'Because what I'm going to give you is golden.'

'What exactly did you have in mind?'

He leered. 'I can think of a few things.'

'Can you now?' Pearl wondered how much use he would be to her and whether she should just have him killed. She refused to be held to ransom by anyone.

'Tell you what,' she said, leaning in, 'tell me what I want to know and then I'll think about how best to reward you.' She looked deep into Trilby's eyes and saw hope blossoming.

'OK. You're going to need more coffee.' He clicked his fingers. 'Marco!'

* * *

Danny Tao sat in his car and watched Pearl talk to the twat in the hat. He suspected the bloke she was meeting was the one he'd heard about, called after a hat or something. If it was him, he was well connected. The Camorras were traditional. They had contacts. The cafe was a hot bed of, what looked like, the old-school Italians who the Tao's hadn't managed to dominate yet. He watched her listen with rapt attention and then sit back in her seat and shake her head. What Danny didn't see was Stanley in the cafe across the road, watching Danny watching Pearl.

Later, Danny lay on the stinking mattress and closed his eyes. He had lost Pearl Camorra and was distraught, but the need for a fix overrode every other emotion. He didn't care that he was lying in a mixture of bodily fluids and decomposing rodents. His usual fastidiousness had disappeared as quickly as his drug habit had started. He had always said he would deal, but never partake. He'd seen too many druggie wasters for that. He didn't want to be constantly chasing the dragon – always looking for the next fix.

But that was then. Before he knew. Before he'd discovered the truth. Before he knew what Mickey Camorra had done.

His arm lolled sideways, and he dropped the syringe; it hung out of his arm, and he just managed to loosen off the tourniquet before slipping away into his dream world. He didn't care that he had progressed incredibly quickly up the chain of hardcore drugs. He didn't notice it, wasn't conscious of it. He heard his phone ringing in the background, but he couldn't have cared less. He was flying.

* * *

Stanley knew about Mickey collapsing. His tiny brain was struggling to decide whether to tell Pearl or not. He was also bothered about something else, something he knew he couldn't mention to Pearl. He'd heard that Mickey had been rushed into surgery for a heart repair after he had collapsed. He had been relieved to hear that the procedure had gone well, meaning Mickey's recovery time would be quicker.

Stanley knew that Pearl was preparing for her meeting and that she would get some answers today. He knew it was crucial for her to be focused, so he made the decision to keep his concerns from her until after she had met with Lily Tao. He lied to Pearl and told her the doctors had taken Mickey's phone away because of his blood pressure, but he had assured her Mickey was OK. He stepped into another room away from Pearl and made a call to Alexy.

'Stanley,' Alexy answered immediately. 'Pearl is OK?'

'She is. I've not told her about Mickey yet. She has a meet today.'

'Is she safe?' Alexy asked.

'I need some extra eyes up here, Alexy. Soon as. I've got a watcher, and I don't like it. I can't protect her up here on my own.'

Alexy inhaled sharply. 'I will send Nicholai. He is few hours away.'

Stanley was relieved. Nicholai was Alexy's right-hand man. He oversaw most of the Camorra's supply pipeline and he dealt directly with suppliers and the dealers at the top of the chain. He was utterly ruthless, killed without remorse and adored Pearl. He would protect her with his last breath if asked.

Pearl had dressed carefully. Ever the classy dresser, this was a day she wanted to be subtle but powerful, so her trusty Louboutin's were out, along with her most severe of outfits. One which made her look like a high-powered city lawyer or banker.

She left her room, collected Stanley, and together they left the hotel and got into a waiting cab.

***

Danny Tao felt on top of the world. He had his wits about him, and he was fuelled with a new sense of purpose and revenge. He showered, dressed in a good suit and felt ready to face the day. His phone rang and he answered it. The sentence was brief and he was left listening to a dial tone.

He immediately broke out into a cold sweat and needed another fix like his life depended on it. He looked down at his shaking hands and didn't recognise them. Paranoia raged.

Danny ran to his bedroom, scrabbled about in the wardrobe, and produced a gun from a shoebox. He then moved quickly through his flat, waving the gun wildly and checking behind doors and in wardrobes.

He stood panting in his kitchen, gun in hand, and looked through the massive wall of glass, across the London rooftops from his penthouse apartment. Movement on the rooftop opposite had him throwing himself to the floor in panic, expecting a bullet at any second. When he peered around the corner of the kitchen island, he saw the movement was just a neighbour in their roof garden. Ever paranoid, he crawled into the hall, away from the sheet of glass that was a window into his life, and sat on the floor gently rocking, clutching the gun, wondering what he was going to do.

Danny had finally left his flat, still fuelled with paranoia. He'd managed to source an interim fix and was riding high again. In his mind he was a tall, dangerous, not to be messed with man about town. The London gangster to be feared, nobody messed with Danny Tao.

In reality, Danny had become a joke. His rapid spiral into hardcore drugs had left him and his interests exposed. His mother, unbeknownst to him, had activated some hard-hitting damage control, which had led to a number of unfortunate lessons being learnt, together with a few untimely deaths.

Danny's usual crew had abandoned him. Embarrassed by his actions and behaviour for a so-called London gangster, they had returned to the fold where they had informed Lily of Danny's various activities. They had accepted their punishments from her and been glad to be back in a respectable organisation where they could hold their heads high.

* * *

Pearl climbed out of the taxi with her usual grace and, accompanied by Stanley, entered the restaurant. Stanley spoke quietly to the maître d' and they were ushered into a private dining room.

Stanley pushed aside the heavy red velvet curtain for Pearl. As she stepped into the room, she was stopped by a large man around Stanley's size, who insisted on patting her and Stanley down. He did it expertly, but respectfully. He moved aside and gestured to the round table where a small, very beautiful woman of Chinese heritage sat. She had piercing green eyes, and her hair was long, black and straight. Inclining her head gracefully, she gestured to the chair opposite.

'Mrs Camorra,' she said without a trace of an accent.

'Ms Tao.' Pearl took a seat.

A waiter arrived, poured water for them both and left a menu on the plates in front of them. He briskly outlined the special of the day.

Pearl acknowledged him with a smile and Lily Tao waved him away.

'Well,' Pearl said and took a sip of water. 'I don't know about you, but I'm starving.' She inspected the menu.

'Are we really going to sit here and eat lunch together?' Lily asked, leaning back in her chair and folding her arms.

'Why ever not? We are in a wonderful restaurant. Michael is quite the chef. We aren't at war, Ms Tao.' She met her eyes boldly and gave a small smile. 'Well, not yet anyway. Nor are we men who need to compare the size of certain things in an overly aggressive fashion. So, yes, I do suggest we sit here in a civilised manner, eat a wonderful lunch and discuss our problem.'

Lily sipped her water. 'Out of interest, what do you see as our problem?'

After examining the menu, Pearl looked around and tutted. 'Stanley, be a darling and find me an ashtray, please. Oh, and I'd like a martini.' She looked at Lily. 'Martini?'

'Gin and tonic.'

'Be a dear, Stanley.'

Stanley pushed aside the curtain and clicked his fingers. The waiter rushed over. Stanley gave the order in a low voice and the waiter went off looking embarrassed. He returned a few moments later with an ashtray and disappeared again, quickly returning with the drinks.

'Ah, thank you,' Pearl said to the red-faced waiter whose hand shook slightly as he placed her drink down. 'I'd prefer it if I didn't have to place a drinks order through my friend in the future. Surely the whole idea of private dining is that every whim of ours is catered for as soon as we decide what that particular whim is.' She looked at Lily. 'Isn't that right, Ms Tao?'

Lily gave a slight nod.

'Sorry, Madam,' the waiter said.

'One last thing,' Pearl said. 'I utterly detest being called madam. I am Mrs Camorra, and this is Ms Tao.'

'Yes, Madam.'

'Did you not hear me?' Pearl said.

'Oh. Yes. Sorry, Mada– er… Mrs Camorra,' he stammered.

'And you are?'

He looked confused. 'I am what, Mada– Mrs Camorra?'

'Not very bright,' provided Lily, sarcastically.
'Your name. What is your name?' Pearl persisted.
'Oh. Richard.'
'Wonderful.' Pearl beamed. 'Now Richard, darling, I think we are ready to order and then you can disappear for a little while.'

Pearl watched Richard leave through the curtain and extracted her silver cigarette case from her bag. She offered one to Lily, who declined but produced her own pack of cigarettes. Stanley stepped forward and lit them both.

'Thank you, Stanley.' Pearl inhaled deeply and then regarded Lily. 'Now, you asked me what I saw as our problem.'

'I did. I'm intrigued by you, Mrs Camorra. Not many people insist on seeing me in person. So much so, I felt I had to meet you for myself. I must say, I expected you to be a woman of action, not talk.'

Pearl watched Lily through narrowed eyes.

'Don't make the mistake of underestimating me, Ms Tao. Many before you have and I can assure you, none of them have lived to tell the tale. I am a woman of action when it is justified and warranted. Unlike some of my male counterparts, I like to obtain the full picture before I make the decision to go nuclear.' She sipped her martini. 'Perfect. Now. My *problem* as you describe it, is the fact that someone from your organisation took the liberty of shooting my husband and tried to blow up a close personal friend of mine. I consider that to be quite the *problem*.'

'What makes you think my organisation had anything to do with it?'

'Please don't insult my intelligence.' Pearl took a sip of her martini. 'Now, I'm going to tell you how I came to that conclusion and then you can tell me whether my deductions are correct.'

Lily shifted imperceptibly. Stanley cleared his throat discreetly as Richard appeared with their starters.

'This looks quite wonderful,' Pearl said, putting her cigarette out and inspecting her plate appreciatively. 'Thank you, Richard.'

'Are you ladies in need of anything else at the moment?' he asked nervously.

Lily waved him away and Pearl smiled at him warmly.

'No thank you, Richard, I think we're all good for a little while.'

He retreated hastily though the curtain. Pearl laid her napkin on her lap, picked up her cutlery and sampled her food.

'Delicious!' she exclaimed.

'As you were saying,' Lily said, picking at the food on her plate.

'Ahh yes.' Pearl rested her cutlery on her plate. 'Firstly, our local police find a body hanging in the woods. This poor man had been through quite the ringer. Drowned in hot petrol, which I'm told you're particularly fond of as a punishment, and then someone had carefully placed a bullet wrapped in a note in his throat.'

Lily remained impassive.

'Now, the bullet had a dragon motif, which as I understand it, is widely associated with your organisation.'

'What did the note say?'

'The note said "Reap what you sow, Mickey".' She watched Lily silently for any reaction.

'What else?' Lily asked.

'The man in the woods was a known member of your organisation. The police tell me that the bullet removed from my husband had the same dragon motif. As did the box of bullets retrieved from the man who shot my husband and who tried to kill my good friend.'

'So where is the man who shot your husband? Did you ask him?' Lily enquired.

'Alas no. I think he is busy looking for the rest of his head,' Pearl said. 'My starter is quite delicious. How's yours?'

Lily shrugged.

Pearl sipped her water. 'As I see it there are two issues here. One, you are in full knowledge of everything I have outlined, and you gave approval for the hit. Or two, you genuinely don't know anything about it which you are reluctant to admit since this would suggest, somewhat embarrassingly, that you don't have full control of your organisation.' She leant forward. 'Now which is it?'

CHAPTER 19

Danny sat in his car watching the restaurant. He knew they were in there. That's what he'd been told. He felt the gun in his lap and found its presence reassuring. He was sweating profusely and desperate to know what they were discussing. Why was Pearl Camorra even meeting his mother? What could they possibly say to each other? Was Pearl there to kill his mother? He'd heard she was ruthless. Had she found out about him? Were they talking about him?

He felt around in his pockets and found the bag of white powder. This would have to do. He stuck his pinky finger in, filled the long nail and snorted heavily. He then ran the finger around the inside of his mouth. He felt strong. Invincible. Then he had an epiphany. Why didn't he just go in there and kill them both himself? Then he could have both organisations. People would quake in their boots at the very name Danny Tao; he would be *revered*. The man who killed Lily Tao *and* the Camorras and took their organisations.

No one would mess with him. He scrabbled around in the bag feeding more powder up each nostril, feeling increasingly confident as the idea took hold. He checked the gun for bullets and took some deep breaths. He would do it. He would shoot his mother and then Pearl Camorra. He buzzed down the car window to let in some air and closed his eyes as he felt the breeze caress his face.

* * *

Steve was sitting at his desk, trying to find a comfy position where everything didn't hurt, when his phone rang.

'Miller.'

'Mate, it's Ross.'

'How's it going? Thanks for nicking the Tao boys.'

'Always a pleasure. Organised crime boys are chuffed.' He lowered his voice a notch. 'Look something's come to light and I'm struggling to patch it all together. Your man Jonesey wanted some background on the Taos a while back and the bloke you found in the woods.'

'Harry Daly. The bloke who was hanged as a warning to Mickey,' Steve provided.

'Uh huh. So, we asked them what he did for the organisation and one of them was pretty vocal about his comings and goings.'

'Right.' Steve cast his mind back to Spike from the bins and what he had said. 'Yeah, but wasn't he just dealing a bit and providing some occasional muscle for people who owed them money?'

'He was, but he was also a runner of sorts for them. Or at least, he sourced runners. Rumour was that he was quite gifted at spotting opportunities for new runners, or new lines anyway.'

'Perhaps not quite the waster we took him for.'

'He got them a cracking deal going from Cardiff out overseas with the gear hidden in some sort of industrial parts, wind turbines or something like that. Great green credentials, so no one batted an eyelid. He recruited a runner who was quite the star apparently. Big volume, practically untouchable, in and out of the UK.'

'What happened?'

'Don't know yet. We're still looking into it. They wouldn't say anything else.'

'Pipeline still active?'

'Not sure.'

'Do we know who the runner was or what this company was?'

'Not as yet.'

'Keep me posted. Do we have any idea why he was killed?' Steve asked.

'I've heard a theory.'

'Hit me.'

'There's a rumour he was killed because his star runner went rogue. Organised a massive load to go overseas and then buggered off with it.'

'How's that linked to Mickey?'

'It isn't. Well, not that we can see, but Harry Daly, your corpse in the woods, he was tortured to see if he knew anything and hey presto his number came up at the same time as Mickey needed to be sent a warning,' Ross said. 'So, he was a convenient corpse if you like.'

'Are they connected?'

'Mickey and this deal? Don't see how – Mickey for all his faults is a stickler for an honest supply chain.'

'This isn't adding up to me.' Steve rubbed his chin.

'Me neither. I'll keep at it.'

'OK'

'You feeling better?' Ross enquired.

'Slow progress, but I think so.' Steve didn't bother to mention he was still in a lot of pain.

'I keep saying it. Be careful.'

'You too. Cheers, mate.'

Steve ended the call and closed his eyes. He was exhausted. He felt rough, his head was throbbing, his back ached where his kidneys had taken a kicking, and his side was agony. There was a knock on his door.

'What?' he shouted grumpily.

The door swung open, and Kate stood in the doorway.

'Thanks, Jonesey,' she said over her shoulder.

Kate walked towards Steve and swung his chair around to face her. She placed her hands either side of him on the arm rests, her face close to his.

''Ello, gorgeous,' she said in a mock cockney accent.

'Hello yourself,' he said, smiling.

'You look tired and in pain. I am here to take you home.'

'But…'

'Nope!' She put a hand up to silence him. 'I don't want to hear it. Pick up what you need. You're coming to rest at home.' She put her hands on her hips. 'Sarge said he'll pick you up and carry you home himself if you don't come with me.'

'I feel ambushed,' Steve complained.

'Get over it. Come on, get your things together.'

'I've got stuff to do.'

'All of which you can do at home.'

'But…'

'And I'll be there to tend to your every need.'

Steve raised an eyebrow. 'My *every* need?'

'Maybe… I think this kicking might have affected your stamina though.'

'Perhaps I need another assessment by a medical practitioner.'

'Perhaps you do. I think we might be able to organise that.' She smiled. 'When you're up to it. Home. Now.'

* * *

Olivia was exhausted from both the drive and the emotional upheaval of saying goodbye to Eli. She went straight to bed when she eventually made it home and was awoken the next morning to persistent knocking on the front door.

Confused from being woken from her deep slumber, she gathered her robe around her and opened the door, shivering in the frigid wind.

'Mrs Baker?'

She stared at the man on the doorstep who wore a warm parka with the logo of Brian's company on the front.

'Er. Yes,' she managed. 'Is everything OK?'

'Can I come in, please?'

Olivia rubbed her eyes and pulled her robe tighter. 'Er, s'pose so.'

She opened the door wider and gestured for the man to come in, pointing towards the kitchen. 'Go through.'

The man hesitantly stepped in, ducking his head in the small doorway.

'Has something happened?' she asked, confused by the appearance of this man from Brian's company.

He turned to her. 'Mrs Baker. Could you sit down? I've got some very bad news.'

Olivia sat down. She frowned at the man and said again, 'Has something happened?'

'Mrs Baker, we've been trying to call. I'm really sorry to have to tell you this, but there was an accident yesterday, the wind, well, there was an accident with one of the turbines under construction and your husband. Well… your husband, I'm afraid, is dead.' He finished abruptly, as if he'd run out of words to say.

'What? What accident?'

'One of the wind turbines fell onto the boat. Your husband. Well… he was killed… er… instantly.'

'Killed?' she said faintly. Her mind tracked back to a week or so previously when she had been fantasising about Brian dying in an accident. *Am I dreaming?* She surreptitiously pinched herself hard and gasped.

'Can I call anyone?' the man asked, looking concerned.

'I-I... No. I'm fine,' she said, still trying to process what he was saying. *Is this real or just a test from Brian to see what I'm up to?*

'Are you sure?' she managed.

'Yes. I'm so sorry. I just don't know what to say, er...' he added as an afterthought, 'we will look after you, Mrs Baker. There will be a hefty compensation payment for you, and we have a death in service pay out too. Anything we can do to help with the funeral etc, you must let us help. I'm going to leave the card of one of our colleagues who can support you through this. Once again, I'm so sorry.' He stared at her for a moment and then rose as if to leave. 'Look, can I call someone for you?'

'What?'

'Can I call anyone?' he repeated. 'To come and be with you.'

'Oh... oh, no. That's not necessary,' she said. 'Thank you though.'

He nodded. 'I feel bad. Saying this and then leaving,' he said quietly. 'I don't really know what to say... this is the first time I've had to...'

'Can you tell me what happened?' Olivia asked. 'Sorry, have you told me already? I...'

'It's fine. One of the holding chains on the crane snapped and a large rotor arm fell down into the deck.'

'So it was instant? Brian was on the deck?'

'Yes. It would have been.'

'And you're sure?' she asked, wondering again if this was an elaborate ruse of Brian's.

'Absolutely sure.'

'You've seen the...'

'Well, no, but I've seen the body bags.'

'Was anyone else…?' she trailed off.

'Three other people.'

'Oh God,' she said. 'How awful. For everyone.'

'Yes. Always difficult to construct in the wind.' He cleared his throat. 'It came out of nowhere really. He had a son, I believe?'

Olivia was stunned. She hadn't considered Eli.

'Yes. He's at boarding school. I was there yesterday. I took him.'

'Hard news for him. Being away and all that,' the man said awkwardly.

She nodded, unable to speak for a moment.

'I'll leave you now,' he said. 'Will you be OK?'

'Yes. Thanks. I'll be fine,' she said vaguely, wondering what the hell she was supposed to do now.

At the front door, the man turned and said, 'Again. I'm so sorry.' He closed the door gently behind him, leaving Olivia standing in the hall staring at the closed door.

She sank into a chair in the hallway. *Brian was dead? Actually dead?* She couldn't quite comprehend it.

* * *

Lily Tao regarded Pearl. She wasn't sure how she felt about her. She wondered fleetingly what it would be like to do business together.

'Which is it Ms Tao? Did you know about the hit or is your organisation out of control?' Pearl pushed.

Lily flashed Pearl an angry look. 'I would never authorise a hit on Mickey.'

'You wouldn't. But you know who did. I'm told it was your son, Danny.'

Lily's eyes burnt. 'Danny has his own issues. His own mind.'

Pearl settled back in her seat. 'Ms Tao, your son shot my husband. He has to pay for that. Eye for an eye. You know the rules.'

Lily leant forward. 'Are you telling me that you will kill my son?'

Pearl smiled and then her face grew cold. 'No. I'm saying you must. Otherwise you will both suffer the consequences.'

Lily inhaled sharply. 'You come into my town—'

'It's not *your* town,' Pearl snapped. 'You've lost control. You're deluding yourself. You need to get the power back. Save face. Pronto.'

'How *dare* you,' Lily began.

Pearls eyes glittered. 'How dare *I*?' She pointed a finger at Lily. 'I'll tell you how I dare. Your son shot my husband and tried to kill a good friend of mine. In my home. He is out of control and you, lady, are becoming a laughing stock. We cannot have that, Lily. We are strong women in powerful organisations and there cannot be a whiff of weakness here.'

'I have complete control.'

'You are clinging on by your fingernails. Your son is making you weak.'

'No…'

'Yes.' Pearl raised her voice and said harshly, 'You know it. You just refuse to see it. He is your weakness.'

'No.'

'Yes.'

'He's not himself.'

'So I hear.'

Lily's eyes narrowed. 'What do you hear?'

Pearl leant forward. 'Everyone knows Danny is junkie scum and you are looking the other way. You need to take a stand. Get the respect back.'

Lily snorted. 'Rubbish.'

'Really?' Pearl produced a gun from her pocket and laid it carefully on the table. 'You've even lost the respect and loyalty of your closest men.' She glanced at Lily's minder who had patted Pearl down. 'You can go now, George, thank you.'

George inclined his head slightly to Lily. He turned and left the room. Stanley spoke quietly to him and then returned his attention to Pearl.

'Now. I am prepared to help you save face and sort out your problems, Lily, but this will be in exchange for a significant slice of some of your business activities.'

Lily sat back and stared at Pearl. 'Who exactly do you think you are?'

Pearl smiled. 'You know exactly who I am. I've said it before, don't make the mistake of underestimating me. Nathan White did that, and we now control his empire.'

'I heard that you met Nathan White and then no one saw him again.'

Pearl inclined her head. 'I liked him very much, but he was unwilling to negotiate or compromise, so our dinner date didn't end particularly well. For him anyway. You've got until the end of our lunch to make a decision.'

Lily sipped her drink. 'Why do you want to help me?'

'Because Mickey would expect me to. You shared time together. You meant something to each other.' She leant forward and spoke so softly that only Lily could hear. 'You had Mickey's children.'

Lily inhaled sharply and leant back in her seat her eyes wide.

'How do you know?' she whispered.

'Twins, wasn't it? A girl and a boy?'

Lily raised her chin defiantly.

'You never told him,' Pearl observed. 'You pushed him away after Frank died.'

'I didn't push him away. He left. They told me he orchestrated the kill.'

'Who told you that?'

Lily waved a hand dismissively.

'Mickey swore he wasn't involved,' Pearl stated. 'You kept it from him. He didn't know, Lily. He never knew. You deprived him of children.'

Lily's eyes glittered angrily. 'I didn't deprive him of anything.'

'His children…'

'He left.'

'You drove him away. He said you were sick with grief.'

'But he chose to leave.'

Stanley cleared his throat, heralding the arrival of Richard with their main courses. Pearl slipped the gun into her handbag before he emerged from the folds of the curtain and smiled at him. Richard put the plates down.

'Richard, this looks wonderful.'

'Do you ladies need anything else?'

'I think we're fine, Richard, thank you,' Pearl said.

'Enjoy your meals, ladies,' he said quietly.

Pearl inspected her plate, humming appreciatively. She picked up her cutlery. 'Let's eat.' She ate a few mouthfuls, dabbed her lips with her napkin and sat back in her chair.

'So, I would like to know…' She thought for a second. 'No, I would like to *understand* why Danny shot my husband. The rumour mill says that Danny has been sniffing around Mickey and Frank's old patch asking questions he shouldn't. They say Danny believes that Mickey killed someone who meant a lot to him.'

After a silence, Lily said, 'He's convinced Mickey killed Frank.'

'And he thinks Frank was his father?' Pearl clarified.

Lily nodded.

'Why have you never told him the truth?'

'I had my reasons.'

'Share them.'

'I'd rather not.'

'I think you should.'

Lily sighed. 'I was angry. I didn't know they were Mickey's until they were born. And even then, I was sure Mickey had killed Frank. I wasn't going to tell him that my children were his when I thought he killed his best friend in cold blood.'

'Did you believe he'd really do that?' Pearl asked.

'I don't know. There was so much at play.'

Pearl inclined her head as if acknowledging the point. 'So, Mickey left. And then? Why not find him and tell him later?'

Lily poked her food idly with her fork. 'A few years later, I went to find Mickey, I was going to tell him. Then I decided against it.'

Pearl frowned. 'Why?'

Lily pushed her plate away, the fork clattering onto the plate, and drained her drink.

'Because I saw you both together. I saw how he was with you. He…' she seemed to search for the word, 'worshipped you,' she said bitterly. 'He never looked at me that way.'

Lily extracted a cigarette from her pack and lit it. 'I made a decision to keep up the pretence that Frank was their father.'

'And Danny had no idea?'

'No. He feels that he has been cheated out of a father and that Mickey is solely responsible. He's not thinking straight. He's been on a crusade about it for months.'

'He's out of control, Lily.'

'I'll deal with him.'

Pearl regarded her stoically. 'You need to tell him the truth. Do you know who killed Frank?'

'Perhaps I'll tell him the truth sometime,' she said tightly. 'But I'm still not sure who killed Frank. I have a long list of suspects.'

Pearl was quiet for a moment while she considered something.

'Lily, I have some bad news for you. I didn't want to be the one to tell you.'

'Tell me what?'

'Your daughter.'

'What about her?' Lily said guardedly.

'A body has been found.'

Lily gasped.

'It was a female. She had been put in a suitcase and left. Her DNA is a match to Mickey's. She was part Asian heritage.'

Tears ran down Lily's face, but she retained her composure.

'She was murdered, Lily,' Pearl said quietly.

'How? How did she die? Who did it? Do you know?' Lily demanded.

Pearl watched Lily, impassively.

'She was shot in the back of the head twice. The bullets had a dragon motif. I suspect your son murdered his sister.'

* * *

Danny was flying high. He was gonna do it. Take out his mother with a shot to the face. Take out that bitch, Camorra too. He was invincible. He closed his eyes and felt the breeze on his face through the open car window. He fantasised about running the Camorra and Tao empire. How he would be treated, what people would say about him. He would be feared… loved, respected. Revered. He opened his eyes when he heard a noise by the open window and struggled momentarily to make out the black object hurtling towards his face.

Nicholai looked at the unconscious form of Danny Tao slumped across the front seats of his car. He opened the door and pushed him across to the passenger seat and started the engine.

To anyone watching, Nicholai had strolled up the road casually, his hands in his pocket, crossed the road and opened the car door. The movement of withdrawing a gun and hitting Danny in the face with the butt was so quick and practised that any onlooker would have doubted they'd actually seen it. Nicholai revved the engine gently, checked his mirrors and drove off.

* * *

On the first floor of the restaurant, the man stood at the window and watched Danny Tao being knocked unconscious by a tall dark-haired man covered in tattoos and being driven away. He felt a wave of rage.

FUCK!

Danny was an integral part of his plan. An excellent distraction. A useful decoy. He had been utterly pliable. It had been *so easy*! A few suggestions here and there and before long, a rage and hate-fuelled mission of childhood abandonment and bitter revenge had been born. The added bonus had also been Danny's newfound penchant for hard drugs. He couldn't have planned it any better if he had tried.

He tied the waiter's apron around his waist and screwed the silencer onto the end of the gun. He had known there was a slim chance Danny would fail today, so he was prepared. Holding the silenced gun flat, he carefully laid a napkin over it and balanced a large black tray on top. He made his way downstairs to the dining area. Obviously, he'd have to take matters into his own hands now.

He entered the restaurant and moved around various tables, collecting empty plates and glasses industriously, no one giving him a second thought. He emptied his tray onto a side table and approached the first of the private dining areas. Noting four men in a business meeting, he quickly moved on. Approaching the second private dining room, he noticed a heavy-set bald man, who was standing outside the door guarding the room. He veered back to the kitchen and returned with some sort of sauce in a delicate dish.

As he approached the heavy-set man he said, 'Forgot the sauce.'

Stanley held up a hand. 'Where's Richard?'

'Break.'

Stanley regarded him carefully. 'I'll take it in,' he said finally, holding his hand out for it.

The man awkwardly passed the sauce to Stanley, placing himself so the curtain closed behind him as Stanley opened the door to the private room. At the same time, the man produced his gun and pushed Stanley hard, back into the room, shooting him in the heart before he could react. The suppressor made a loud *pop*. Their positioning in the private room meant the sound wasn't heard in the noisy main restaurant. Kicking the door shut and side-stepping the falling Stanley, he first shot Pearl and then Lily. He glanced at both women, who had fallen to the floor, and then retreated from the private room and out of the front door of the restaurant, tossing the gun into the back of a passing dustbin lorry.

CHAPTER 20

Viv was having a very productive day. She'd had a telephone catch-up with her therapist and she was feeling great. The meds were working, and she was feeling more and more like her old self. She had spent a little time in the loft going through the box from the nursery. She'd forced herself to do it, but she recognised that she had to move on and remember, but to try and do it in a healthy way for herself. Afterwards, she emailed her therapist her thoughts and he had been incredibly supportive and encouraging about her progress.

She had spoken to her boss to arrange a phased return to work, and he had given her a small project to break her in gently. She had then spent the rest of the morning with Jenny, approving her choices for her themed hotel rooms and making further suggestions that Jenny had embraced fully.

Viv was looking forward to the evening at Maggie's but in equal part was nervous about it. She realised she should take something as a thank you for her, so she threw on her coat and grabbed her handbag, with a view to going to the florist to buy some flowers. As she pulled the front door closed and double locked it, she heard a crying baby. She stood completely still for a moment, the key poised in the air, feeling a faint panic washing over her. She was afraid to look around, terrified that the sound was being created in her own mind. She closed her eyes and breathed deeply and still she heard the noise. She mentally checked in on herself and used some of the exercises she had been taught.

Breathe deeply. What day is it? What time is it? How do I feel? Where am I going? What do I see?

She opened her eyes, turned around and sagged with relief against the front door. A woman walked past her with a crying baby strapped to her front, desperately trying to comfort it. Viv blew out a breath and stood for a moment leaning weakly against the door. She was overcome with relief that it was a real baby, having a real cry. She wasn't hearing things. She took a deep breath and steeled herself. Glancing at her watch, she realised she needed to get a move on and hurried off up the high street to the florist before it closed.

* * *

Hannah sat in the nurse's office and watched the last of the episodes of the soaps she had missed during the week on her small iPad. She turned off the screen and walked through the quiet ward checking on her sleeping patients. Her phone pinged. It was a message from Anne saying that she wouldn't be able to get away. Hannah replied with a sad face emoji and wandered through the sleeping ward again. She returned to the office, activated an app on her phone and dialled home. She cooed, gently, when the camera showed them all sat waiting patiently for her.

'Mummy be home soon!' she whispered. 'Mummy loves you!'

Bored, and on a whim, she crept up to Anne's ward to see how she was and try to help out. When she arrived, she couldn't find Anne.

Many of the mums were dozing with a few watching things on small screens. None of them acknowledged Hannah as she walked past. She peered into the office, went to the loos, but couldn't find Anne anywhere. She wondered if perhaps she was ill and had gone home. There was an empty bed but no sign of an occupant, so she assumed Anne had taken a patient somewhere.

Wandering back through the ward towards the exit she spotted baby Lucas. She smiled. He was gorgeous. She crept towards the mother who was fast asleep with her mouth wide open. The baby was awake, but content. He kicked his arms and legs when Hannah approached. He grasped her finger tightly and she smiled down into his little face and gummy smile.

'Hello, you,' she whispered. 'How are you, gorgeous boy?'

He kicked his legs some more and produced, what Hannah thought, was a big smile. Then he frowned and went very red in the face, before relaxing once more. A strong odour wafted up towards Hannah.

'Do you need a new nappy?' she said, smiling at him. She leant in and the smell was overpowering.

'Come on, you. Let's get you cleaned up.'

She gently wheeled him away, cooing and smiling at him in the quiet ward.

'You and me are going to get you cleaned up and then we'll have a proper catch-up and cuddle,' she said softly.

* * *

Dinner at Maggie's was a raucous affair. Everyone had turned up and Viv found herself surrounded by people she genuinely liked. Foxy arrived and he'd brought along Sophie too. Viv took an instant liking to Sophie, they got on well, and when Jenny arrived, the three of them prodded fun at Foxy for most of the evening. Jenny and Viv also gently ribbed Sophie because she spent most of the evening yawning widely. She maintained that she had planned an early night, but Foxy had dragged her there to get her out.

Viv met Will the harbour master and Suzy who ran a groomers and dog rescue, and liked the brother/sister duo immensely. Suzy had been gently probing all evening regarding whether Viv and Nate would like a dog and had been delighted to find out it was something they were thinking about.

Foxy was on form and Viv enjoyed winding him up about his promise of free climbing for life if she had agreed to Maggie's dinner.

People had left the table to clear the plates and Maggie was making coffee when Viv felt a gentle hand on her shoulder. Foxy sat down next to her.

'How are you holding up?' he asked quietly. 'Maggie does love a baptism of fire. I remember mine.'

Viv laughed. 'I'm OK.' Adding, 'Genuinely. I am,' when she saw his raised eyebrow.

'Pleased to hear it.' He sipped his coffee. 'So, when are you going to come climbing? It's fantastic for looking after up here.' He tapped his forehead.

Viv pretended to think. 'Well, the world is my oyster as they say, especially now I've got free climbing for life.'

Foxy rolled his eyes. 'Perhaps I was a little hasty when I promised "for life". You've got a good few years left in you, I reckon.'

'Are you reneging on the deal?'

'Perhaps I am,' he mused.

'Have I got to send in the big guns to make you rethink that?'

'Oh scary stuff.' He grinned then looked serious for a moment. 'Look, Viv, I know you don't know me, but I just want to say, I've had my own mental health struggles. I know what it's like. How it feels. How alone you can feel. So if I can help at all, in any way, all you need to do is say. I'll do what I can. OK?'

Viv looked at this man she hardly knew. He seemed so genuine and honest she became slightly tearful.

'Sorry. Didn't mean to upset you,' he said, noticing her eyes filling up.

She waved a hand. 'It's fine. You haven't. It's just so nice. You're so nice. Thank you. That means a lot.' She squeezed his arm. 'Also, I love your girlfriend, you make such a great couple.'

Foxy looked surprised. 'My…? Oh… she's not… we're not…'

Viv didn't miss a trick. 'Umm, if you say so,' she said, giving him a side eye.

Foxy awkwardly tried to change the subject. 'I mean what I say. Come and climb, talk…' He waved a hand vaguely. 'Or talk then climb. Or talk and don't climb… or climb and don't talk. You get the gist.'

She laughed. 'I get the gist. Thank you. I'll take you up on that.'

'Pinkie promise?'

'Pinkie promise.'

'What are you pinkie-promising my wife?' Nate sat down on the other side of Viv and draped an arm across her shoulders, kissing her cheek.

'That she'll definitely come and climb.'

'You've promised her free climbing for life, haven't you, mate?' Nate laughed. 'Big mistake. She loves to climb.'

'I might have to caveat it,' Foxy said dryly. 'Mind you, if you're that good I might sign you up to do some classes.'

Viv raised her eyebrows at Foxy. 'If you're that good? This sounds like a challenge… is it a challenge?'

'Do you want it to be a challenge?'

'Oohh what am I missing out on?' Jenny sat down opposite Viv clutching a coffee.

'Oh God,' said Nate, lips twitching. 'A challenge. Now you've really started something.'

'What have we started?' Sophie said, sitting down next to Jenny, with an expectant look.

'These two are challenging each other to a climb off, I think,' Nate said.

'I'm always up for a challenge. Reckon you've got the chops?' she asked Foxy.

Foxy burst out laughing. 'I'll give it a go.'

'Game on, big guy.' Viv grinned. 'Let's see what you're made of. See if you're one of those all-mouth-and-no-trouser types.'

Sophie burst out laughing. 'Oh, you're going to fit right in.'

'Who's all mouth and no trousers?' Maggie asked, bustling up with a plate of after-dinner mints.

'We're just establishing that,' said Viv. 'Foxy's challenging me to a climb.'

Maggie looked between Viv and then Foxy and laughed. 'How's that gonna go, Nate?'

Nate grinned and pulled Viv closer to him, kissing the side of her head affectionately. 'She's basically gonna spank his arse, Mags.'

'Well, I for one would like to see that,' Maggie said.

'It sounds a little too good to miss,' Will said, plonking coffee cups down. 'I think you'd better name the time and the place, and we'll all make sure we've got a ringside seat.'

'I reckon we could sell tickets,' murmured Suzy.

'I think you lot are getting ahead of yourselves,' Foxy said indignantly, looking around at the amused faces.

'I say bring it on,' said Viv. 'You chicken?'

'Chicken?' snorted Foxy. 'Nah. Next Saturday 5 p.m. Give you a chance to practice a bit, Viv. Make it fair.'

'What's wrong with tomorrow at 5 p.m.?' asked Viv innocently. 'I'm game if you are.'

'Bring it on then,' said Foxy. 'And you lot can bugger off if you think you're selling tickets.'

Later, after Nate and Viv said their goodbyes and walked home, Nate pulled Viv close as they walked up the hill.

'How did you find it tonight?' he said. 'You looked like you were having a great time.'

'I was. People are lovely. It was nice to be normal. To *feel* normal.'

'So, you feel OK?' he said, looking at her. 'We said we needed to be honest and check in. This is me checking in.'

'Absolutely. In fact, I didn't get a chance to tell you. When I went out to get some flowers for Maggie and as I locked the front door, I suddenly heard a baby crying.'

'What?'

'I heard a baby crying and for a moment I was terrified. Genuinely. I froze. I thought, oh my God, not again. So, I did my exercises, breathing—'

'Then what?'

Her lips twitched. 'Then a woman walked past me with a baby in a carrier who was crying, and I almost died with relief. That's what I heard.'

Nate pulled her to him closely and kissed the top of her head.

'Must have given you a fright.'

'Not gonna lie. It terrified me.'

'Thing is. Look how far you've come. The very fact that you questioned it and are telling me about it is such good progress.'

'It is.'

'You have to tell your shrink. What's his name?'

'Jonathan. Dr Jonathan Lewis.'

'Tell him. He'll be proud of you.'

'OK.'

'Saw Suzy talking to you about dogs,' he ventured.

'I'm totally in on the dog front. I love it here. A dog would be wonderful. Suzy said she's picking one up that might suit us tomorrow. She needs to assess him and check for any issues, but she seemed to think he might be good. He's young and his owner has just been diagnosed with something nasty, so she can't look after him. Suzy said to ring her next week.'

Nate smiled. 'I'll ring her Monday.'

'Good. You're painting that kitchen tomorrow.'

'Yes, Chief.'

* * *

Foxy sat in his flat by the large windows and stared at the bluey blackness outside. Dark shadows in the sky were moving fast, and the forecast said they were in for a few days of stormy weather. On the horizon he saw the lights flashing from the wind farm that was being constructed and remembered the accident he'd heard about.

He sipped his Scotch. Part of him wanted so badly to call Carla. To see how she was and tell her about this evening. He missed her presence and her counsel. He knew they would have chatted about everything, and she would eventually have asked him whether he had told Sophie how he felt.

Months ago, Carla had told Foxy in no uncertain terms that he needed to tell Sophie he was completely in love with her, but he couldn't bring himself to do it. He didn't want those eyes of hers to meet his and for him to see disappointment in them, for overstepping the line. He thought back to Viv's earlier comment, assuming they were together, and exhaled heavily.

Footsteps on the outside metal staircase had Solo rushing over to sit by the door, but Foxy knew it was a friend as Solo's tail was wagging. He got up and opened the door to find Maggie standing outside.

'If that's Scotch, I'll have one, please,' she said, coming in and placing a Tupperware of something on his dining-room table. She shrugged off her coat and sat in one of the armchairs. 'Put that in the fridge, it's leftover pie for your dinner tomorrow.'

'Thank you. Ice?'

'As it comes, please. Only a small one mind.'

Foxy handed her a glass and took his seat again.

'People will gossip, you creeping into my flat at this hour,' he said dryly.

She tittered loudly. 'Your mouth to God's ear.' She chortled. 'I wish.'

'What's on your mind, Mags?'

She took a sip and was thoughtful for a moment.

'I'm just checking in on you,' she said. 'Tonight, you had a look about you I've not seen since you first came here, and it's got me in a worry for you.'

'You don't miss a trick, do you?' Foxy said softly.

'I don't when it's someone who means the world to me,' she said, watching him over the rim of her glass. 'So, what's up?'

He was quiet for a moment. 'I'm just missing Carla. And Charlie obviously. I feel a bit cast adrift, like I'm on my own. You know? Really on my own. They were my whole world and now…'

'Oh, love.' Maggie leaned over and placed a hand on his arm. 'You mustn't feel that way. We are your family now. All of us here.' She patted his arm. 'You really couldn't escape us if you tried.'

He gave a small laugh. 'I know. I'm so grateful to everyone for letting me into the family. But I just feel so…' He struggled to find the words. 'I don't know, so… alone is the only word I can think of.'

'You'll never be alone with us lot around, you know that.'

He smiled at her. 'I know, I'm sure it's just me dealing with Carla. I'll be OK.'

Maggie put her glass down. 'When my husband died. I thought I'd die. Genuinely. I don't think I have ever felt so utterly alone in my life. The person I shared every single thing with, was suddenly gone. The things we laughed about, our secret little jokes and sayings, it was all gone. The man could take one look at me and know exactly what I was thinking, I didn't even have to say a word. I thought I wouldn't feel joy or happiness again. Ever. But I did.

'I felt less alone with time passing, I let people in, talked to them so they knew I wasn't necessarily OK, and I got through it.' She glanced at Foxy. 'So just like you got through the terrible pain of losing Charlie, you'll get through losing Carla, because people will help you, because they love you.' She looked wistful for a moment. 'Not that I wouldn't give everything I have for one more minute with him. But that's just a fantasy... Listen to me. You are loved, and people care and want to help. You know I saw you helping Viv tonight, talking to her. You don't give yourself enough credit for the effect that you have on people. How much you help them. You need to let people help you for a change.'

'Blimey, Mags,' was all Foxy could manage in response.

'I'm off.' She squeezed his arm and got up from the chair. 'I just want you to know you aren't alone, but I need to know that you've listened to what I've said.'

'I listened.'

'So, it's OK to say, I'm struggling today. OK?'

'OK.'

'Night, my love, you stay there, I'll let myself out. See you tomorrow.'

'Night, Mags. Thanks for... you know... all that,' he said. 'Means a lot.'

'No problem. You mean a lot to me. So we're even.'

She opened the door and stepped out into the night.

CHAPTER 21

Stanley couldn't catch his breath. The bullet, at such close range, had knocked him off his feet, but it hadn't punctured his bulletproof vest. He gasped, drawing in air and feeling a crushing pain in his ribs. His slow mind processed what had happened and he looked around the room, eyes bulging, looking desperately for Pearl.

'Pearl,' he croaked, trying to roll onto his side to ease the pain, only to find it came in stronger waves. He crawled on his belly towards Pearl and found her lying on her side with her eyes closed, her face a deathly pale. He touched her face his eyes filling with tears. He loved Pearl with everything he had, she was in his bones. He couldn't compute that he had failed her.

Her eyes fluttered open. 'Stanley.' She smiled weakly. 'I thought... I saw...' She drifted off again.

'Pearl.' Stanley reached in his pocket for his phone and called Alexy. He told him what happened. He needed his contacts. If he called an ambulance the police would come, and he couldn't control their questions in this city. He was almost crying when he spoke to Alexy, he couldn't work out who had talked. Who knew they would be there, and who would want to kill Pearl *and* Lily if it wasn't Danny Tao. (Who he knew was safely being escorted elsewhere.) Alexy promised to sort it and call him straight back.

He struggled to his knees and looked at Pearl who was semi-conscious. He saw a bullet wound in her side and inspected it as gently as he could. She moaned and tried to push his hand away. He grabbed a hand full of linen napkins and held them firmly over the wound. In Stanley's extensive experience, the bullet looked like it had gone cleanly through her side.

'Pearl... Pearl.' Her eyelids fluttered open. 'Hold this for a moment,' he said, placing her hand on his. 'You've gotta keep the pressure up.'

He scooted over to Lily and found that she had been shot straight through the heart. She was dead, her eyes, wide and huge, stared up at him, devoid of life.

Stanley managed to get to his feet. He wasn't sure how he was going to deal with all of this on his own. He needed to stop anyone coming into the room for now. He lumbered over to the door and made sure the large curtains were tightly closed and placed a chair in front of the doors to stop it from being opened from the restaurant side. Then he returned to Pearl and was pleased to see the bleeding had slowed, but she was too pale for his liking.

His phone rang. It was Alexy. He told him to wait and that someone was five minutes away and that they would be taken to a safe place and the area cleaned. This was the usual code for everything removed and some sort of payoff for cleaning and keeping quiet.

The door knocked against the chair, Stanley moved it out of the way and drew back the curtain slightly. Richard was standing there with two ambulance crew.

'They said there's been a call for them from here?' he said.

Stanley stood aside allowing them in. 'I'll speak to you in a moment,' he said to Richard, holding him back firmly. 'Stay there.'

He closed the door on Richard's surprised face and turned to the crew. One of the pair dressed as a paramedic said, 'Alexy said one dead, one injured.'

Stanley gestured to Pearl. 'Looks like a straight through.'

The paramedic laughed. 'We're not medical, mate, we use this get up to get them out fast – no questions. We're taking her to the doc we use now. Ivan is coming to do the clean. We'll go when he gets here.' The paramedic turned to the other one. 'Chair for the dead one, stretcher for her.'

The other paramedic turned and left the room.

The curtains parted and a tall man with very pale skin, dark hair and almost black eyes stepped in and nodded to Stanley.

'I am Ivan,' he said in a heavily accented voice. 'You go with them. I will deal with this.'

Stanley frowned. 'You sure?'

'Alexy is my cousin. He would do anything for your people, and I will do anything for him. I will deal. You go now.'

The paramedic returned with the stretcher chair folded on top of the stretcher. The pretend paramedic neatly flicked open the chair and together they manoeuvred Lily's prone body onto it and placed a blanket around her. Her head lolled to the side, but they buckled her in so that she remained upright. They gently laid Pearl onto the stretcher and tucked a blanket around her.

'I want out of that fire exit,' said Ivan, pointing to the corner of the room and drawing back a large red velvet curtain that exposed a set of fire doors. 'Move ambulance around to here.'

The ambulance man jogged out and Ivan beckoned Richard into the area. He looked around the room, eyes wide taking in the blood stains on the floor and the two women.

'Focus on me,' Ivan said, clicking his fingers in front of Richard's face. 'I will be opening that fire door. I suggest you switch off the alarm for a moment.'

Richard looked confused. 'Oh I don't think I can…'

'You can and you will. I will be doing this in five minutes.'

'I don't. I…'

'Yes. You do not want this being paraded through the restaurant, particularly if we speak loudly about food poisoning. You have four minutes.'

'OK. Yes. I'll do it.' Richard scurried off.

Stanley sat in the back of the ambulance holding Pearl's hand. He had no idea where they were going but Alexy had called and told him everything was ready. He said Ivan had dealt with the restaurant. He also said he was coming up to London to accompany Pearl and Stanley home. He would be with them in a few hours.

The ambulance stopped and the rear doors opened. They pulled Pearl out on the stretcher and wheeled her into a small clinic attached to the side of a large Victorian house. Stanley followed. The doors shut and the ambulance drove off with Lily still inside.

'Where are they going?' Stanley asked the paramedic who had remained.

'Crematorium. They're burning this afternoon, so they'll put her in. We have an arrangement.' He pointed to a chair. 'Wait here. Nothing else you can do. They'll work on her now. She's in safe hands.'

Stanley sank into the chair and closed his eyes. The horror of the day sank in, and tears rolled unchecked down his round face. Pearl had to pull through. He couldn't bear the thought of life without his Pearl.

Stanley awoke to someone shaking his arm gently. It was Alexy.

'Stanley, this is no time to be sleeping, my friend,' he said affectionately.

Stanley blinked and clutched Alexy. Grateful to see him.

'How did you get here so quickly?'

'Heli-chopper. We go back same way. Pearl is ready. We go now.'

Stanley stood painfully and Alexy looked at him with concern. 'You are hurt, my friend?'

Stanley waved a hand dismissively, but Alexy pulled aside his suit jacket and saw the hole where the bullet had gone. He undid the Velcro side of the bulletproof vest and ripped Stanley's shirt open, tutting at the black and purple bruising all around Stanley's front and side.

'You are being the check now. Come. Now.'

Stanley followed him through to the clinic where a softly spoken doctor examined him and took an X-ray.

'Nothing broken, just chest wall and rib cage very badly bruised. Gonna hurt a lot for a few weeks. Take anti-inflammatories, and light duties only,' he instructed firmly. 'Get dressed. We're done here. Careful with her.'

Ivan took them to the helipad in Battersea. They drove in silence. Stanley was watching Pearl anxiously. She was still deathly pale, but the doctor had assured him that she just needed rest. He had treated her wound, given her antibiotics and painkillers, and told her to rest as soon as she was able. She would heal.

As they pulled into the helipad enclosure, Alexy turned to Pearl who was dozing in the rear seat.

'Pearl. Who? Who was it? Who knew you were there?'

Pearl opened her eyes. She had known the moment the man had stepped into the restaurant with the gun who had betrayed her again.

'Justin De'Silva,' she said bitterly. 'He was responsible for giving up where we lived. He set up the meet.'

'He is dead man,' Alexy said flatly. 'Ivan.'

'With pleasure, my friend.'

Pearl looked from Ivan to Alexy and said weakly, 'No one can know Lily is dead. Control the narrative if you can, until we can deal with it. Trilby will help you, and Jack the Hat will help him. I'll call him in a moment. But people must know that betraying us leads to serious consequences. I want Justin De'Silva's death as public as possible and a full rumour mill along with it.' She gasped as a wave of pain shot through her. Stanley touched her arm with concern.

'I'm fine,' she said, grimacing. 'Ivan, Lily's man, George, helped us. Ask him to hold the fort and he will be well rewarded. Keep the narrative that Danny Tao is off the rails. Do we know where he is?'

Ivan nodded. 'We have him safe. No one will find him.'

Pearl looked at the three men. 'How come?'

'He was following us,' Stanley said. 'I wanted him contained. He was a loose cannon.'

'Well done, Stanley,' Pearl said. 'Ivan, thank you for all your help. Alexy said you were wonderful.'

Ivan inclined his head. 'Who Alexy takes into his heart, I also take into mine. I am at your disposal.'

'Thank you. Now if you wouldn't mind dealing with our problem, I would be most grateful. Oh, and if you happen to be around Mr De'Silva's shop, there was a rather nice Rolex Daytona in the window, somebody so distasteful really shouldn't be in charge of something quite so beautiful.'

'Consider it yours, Pearl,' Ivan said.

'Thank you, Ivan. Keep us posted. Come and see us soon?'

'It would be my deepest honour,' he said gravely.

* * *

Danny Tao awoke and couldn't work out where he was. His head was throbbing. His face hurt, his nose was bloody, and he could feel a lump the size of a large egg on his forehead. There was a sound he couldn't place, and he was lying on a metal floor in some sort of circular room. There was a large ladder running up the side of it as far as he could see. Next to him, there were two crates of water, a portable chemical toilet, toilet roll, and large bucket attached to a long rope. There was also a cool box filled with packets of sandwiches and sausage rolls.

His head pounded, he was sweaty, felt sick. He had the shakes. He needed a fix like he had never needed one before. He stumbled to his feet and lurched over towards the bucket, retching until he lay on the floor sobbing. After a while he tried to stand and work out where he was. There was dim lighting around him and up high, out of reach, he could see a small camera blinking at him. He saw a door and staggered towards it, and wrestled with the metal handle. He dragged it open a crack and was forced backwards by the strength of the wind. Rain drenched him instantly as the unforgiving weather assaulted him. Confused, he stepped out onto a metal platform and looked around.

Realisation dawned. He was on a wind turbine with sea all around him and nowhere to go. He had no way out; he couldn't swim, let alone see anywhere he could have swum to. A wave of panic hit him like a sledgehammer, and he couldn't stop screaming.

* * *

The crowd from dinner the previous evening had gathered at the climbing centre for Foxy and Viv's 'climb off'. Sophie, Jenny and Maggie were nattering in the corner and Suzy walked in with Will just as Foxy was chalking up his hands and ignoring the jibes from Sophie and Maggie.

Viv arrived and shrugged her coat off. 'Hey,' she said casually, lips twitching.

'Hey,' Foxy replied with a twinkle in his eye. He was beginning to like Viv for her gutsiness and dry humour.

'Scared?' she teased.

'No. You?'

'Not a jot,' she said, laughing. 'Let's have some of that chalk.'

As she rubbed her hands, she scanned the room and walked over to the large window that showcased the massive outside climbing wall.

'First one up here then?' she asked, arching an eyebrow.

'Whatever the lady wants,' Foxy said, a smile tugging at the corner of his mouth.

'Let's warm up then,' she said, embarking on some stretches.

A few minutes later they both stood in front of the high wall.

'Free climb or ropes?' Viv asked.

'Ropes,' called Nate. 'No *way* are you free climbing.'

She rolled her eyes, stepped into a harness and clicked a rope into a carabiner.

'Who's the timekeeper and adjudicator?' she asked innocently. 'Someone independent surely?'

'I'll do it.' Will volunteered.

'OK.'

'I'll count down,' Will said, taking the stopwatch from Mike. 'Ready? Five, four, three, two, one. GO!'

Viv launched herself upwards gripping one of the high handholds, giving her an immediate head start. The huge wall loomed above them and Viv closed her mind to everything but getting to the top.

She was in the zone. *God it was good to climb!* One, two, three. Constant movements with purpose; large risky moves, but she could do it. She was good at this. This was her in her element. She pushed herself upwards, jumping to a high outcrop of wall giving her a big lead and grasped the handhold firmly, pulling herself up. She felt free. Wonderful. Like it was just her and the wall.

She could see the top now. Hear the cheers. Hear Nate calling her, egging her on. Two metres to go. She braced herself to leap to a higher handhold that she wouldn't normally have gone for and the moment she leapt she heard it. A baby crying. It threw her. She missed the handhold and fell, for split second plummeting down. She screamed. A broad arm caught her, and she swung against the wall, feeling the safety rope tighten.

'I've got you,' Foxy said softly.

Tears sprang from her eyes.

'Viv, I've got you,' he repeated. 'Grab a hold.'

She clung on to the face of the wall breathing deeply. She heard it again. She felt Foxy behind her. He clipped himself to her and loosened her hands. He lowered them both to the ground.

As he lowered them, he said quietly, 'Was it the baby crying? I heard it.'

Relief flooded through her, and she leant against him, drawing in some strength from his solidity. Nate strode over and gathered her into his arms.

'I heard it, Viv. I heard it,' he said, kissing her head.

Unsure of what was going on, Will said, 'She was almost at the top. Massive lead on you, Foxy. She would have spanked your arse.'

'I yield,' he said. 'Viv's the winner.'

Viv realised she needed to try and save face. 'Sorry, folks. Bit rusty. I'll practise and we'll have a rematch.'

'Will we buggery,' exclaimed Foxy. 'I'm not going to have my arse kicked again.'

Viv stayed outside while the others filed back into the climbing centre, she was still shaky and in the distance she could still hear the baby crying. But she knew it was an actual baby crying and not her imagination.

Nate wandered out with her coat and draped it around her shoulders.

'How you doing?' He hugged her. 'I reckon you would have got that; he was way behind you.'

She sniffed and gave a half smile.

Nate pulled her around to face him. 'Sweetie, we've gotta do some work on you going to pieces every time you hear a baby cry.'

'It's hardly going to pieces,' she said, half joking.

'Whatever it is. You need to have this out with Jonathan. See what he says.'

'Yes, Boss.'

Nate pulled her close and together they strolled back into the climbing centre. 'Now come along, Mrs Bennett, you still need to reward me for painting that bloody kitchen.'

CHAPTER 22

Ivan had ensured that Justin De'Silva died a particularly horrible death. One he considered fitting for the level of betrayal he had demonstrated to Pearl and Mickey. He had also made sure that Justin knew, in his final agonising moments, that Pearl was the maestro of his demise. With the assistance of Trilby, and subsequently Jack the Hat, he had also ensured that everyone who needed to know this was Pearl's doing would be in no doubt whatsoever who had sanctioned the kill.

As an added bonus, he had secured the Rolex Daytona for Pearl and a particularly nice vintage Tag Heuer Vanquish for himself. He had then emptied the till and mercilessly torched the shop, ensuring the accelerant he used would burn hot and quick to reduce the level of evidence for anyone interested enough to go picking through it.

* * *

The man who had shot Pearl and Stanley and killed Lily Tao stood in the crowd on the pavement watching the fire brigade fight the raging fire.

He cursed himself for not checking that they were both dead, and for not finding out exactly where Pearl lived before De'Silva was killed. He knew Danny had found out and he kicked himself again for not asking. He'd tried every avenue available to him. He knew roughly which area they were in, but he'd have to quietly ask around. This wasn't over yet. He had heard Pearl made it, and that one of the henchmen had exacted revenge on her behalf.

He had also heard Pearl would be running the Tao operation now and this only made him angrier. There was also a whisper that Mickey wasn't actually dead. He felt his rage starting and struggled to control himself. Despite his best efforts, he hadn't been able to find his pet puppet, Danny Tao, or actually confirm whether Mickey was dead or not. He assumed one of Pearl's crew had taken him, so he suspected that he was either in hiding or long dead by now.

He muttered a curse. In simple terms, he had messed up his own plan and everything was shot to shit. He needed to think of something fast. The Camorras weren't going to get away with anything. Not after all this time. The Tao operation was his. The money it was worth was staggering and he deserved every penny of it, and then some. With interest. It should have been his thirty years ago, he'd worked hard enough to help build it. He was long overdue it.

He felt a rare moment of sadness for killing Lily. He had always loved her. Fantasised about her. Imagined them running the empire together. But the bitch couldn't be trusted. So she had to go. She had looked at him with such loathing when he had made contact after he was released from prison, he had nearly killed her then and there.

But she'd had no idea it was him. A chance meeting in a bar, or so she thought. He'd tried to be charming, buy her a drink in the hope that she'd remember him, but she had looked at him like he was shit on her shoe. It was in that moment he had decided to make her pay and take everything from her.

* * *

In the cafe opposite De'Silva's shop, Ivan had been enjoying a late lunch watching the impressive matinee of his direction. He had also been carefully noting the people who had been visiting the shop and now those that were watching the fire. He knew rumours would start and that the shooter would perhaps come back to find out what he could about Pearl's whereabouts. He knew if he stayed there long enough a face would appear that he would recognise, based on Stanley's description.

And there he was. Delighted, Ivan finished his lunch, snapped pictures of the man and surreptitiously followed him down the road to the nearby Tube station.

* * *

Mickey, still in hospital, had overheard Maxim talking to Tommy about Alexy bringing Pearl home because she had been shot. Mickey had promptly yanked out all his tubes, thrown back the bed covers, and marched out of the hospital still in his hospital gown, roaring at anyone who got in his way. He had to get to his Pearl. He was on a mission. He wanted to satisfy himself that she was OK and then kill whoever had shot her with his bare hands.

Mickey burst into the house, yelling for Pearl who had recently arrived home and gone straight to bed. She was exhausted by the journey and her injury, and dozy from the medication the doctor had given her.

Alexy pointed upstairs and Mickey took the stairs as quickly as his heart could manage in its fragile state. He almost fell into the bedroom and found Pearl lying in bed, eyes closed.

Fear of losing Pearl hit him like an emotional tsunami and he dropped to his knees by the side of the bed.

'Pearl,' he said urgently, his hand trembling as he touched her pale face. 'Pearl.'

Pearl opened her eyes. 'Darling,' she said quietly, grasping his hand. 'Why aren't you in hospital? You need to be in hospital.'

Unable to control the myriad of emotions coursing through his body, Mickey climbed onto the bed, gathered Pearl into his arms and sobbed quietly as she fell back to sleep again.

* * *

Alexy ended the call from Ivan and beckoned Maxim and Stanley over to sit at the table with him.

'Ivan has the face of the shooting man,' he announced and showed them a picture on his phone. 'You know him?'

Both Maxim and Stanley scrutinised the screen and both looked blank.

'Ivan is to follow him,' he said. 'But he thinks he know and will lose him soon, like ghost.'

Stanley enlarged the picture on the phone. 'Looks like filth to me,' he announced, narrowing his eyes. 'He's got that look about him.'

Maxim flicked his eyes over the photo again. 'Hmm.'

'Send it to me,' Stanley said. 'I'll ask Steve. He's sound. He'll do it for Pearl.'

Alexy tapped the phone and sent it. Stanley checked the picture on his phone and went outside, closing the large glass doors carefully behind him.

Stanley wondered how much to tell Steve. He wasn't cut out for lots of layers of deceit. Stanley was a cut and dried man. Black and white if possible.

Steve answered on the second ring.

'Stanley? You OK?' he said, concern in his voice.

'Er. Yeah. I need a favour.'

'What?'

'I need an ID on a man I've got a picture of.'

'Hello?' Stanley said again when Steve hadn't responded for a moment.

'Why, Stanley?' Steve said quietly. 'What's happened?'

Stanley was quiet for a moment. 'Er.'

'Stanley,' Steve warned.

'Someone shot Pearl and killed Lily Tao.'

Steve inhaled sharply. 'Is Pearl…?'

'She's home. She's OK. It was a straight through.'

Steve exhaled loudly. 'OK. So, who is the man in the photo?'

'He's the one who shot her.'

'Send it to me.'

* * *

Steve ended the call. Pearl had been *shot*? He couldn't bear the thought that something had happened to her. He opened the picture Stanley had sent and scrutinised it for a while. He didn't recognise him, but he thought for a moment and then put a call into Toby.

Toby was an old colleague of his in London who he had worked with on a recent case. His call was answered after a few rings.

'Mate, I was gonna call you,' Toby said with amusement.

'How so?'

'I think some of your lot are causing trouble on my patch,' he said, chuckling.

'Oh?'

'Oh yeah. We've got rumours of a shooting at a swanky restaurant in Soho, but no bodies. No evidence, all very tidy. No comments from anyone. A nasty fire and rumours afoot that one of your favourite ladies was involved, not to mention rumours of a turf war takeover. The name Camorra just keeps on coming up.'

'Really?'

'Know anything about it?' Toby asked.

'Very little, mate. We've got much the same here with a shooting, a dead guy and links to the Tao gang.'

'Ahh, the plot thickens as they say.'

'Certainly does. Look, I've got a favour to ask.'

'Shoot.'

'I've got a picture of a guy that I need you to look at. Tell me if you know him.'

'Ping it over.'

'One sec.' Steve forwarded the picture.

After a moment, he heard a sharp intake of breath from Toby.

'You don't know who this is?' Toby whispered; his voice had dropped so low that Steve strained to hear.

'Who is it?'

'Fuck's sake, mate,' Toby whispered. 'It's Graham Curtis.'

Steve was silent for a moment as he scrolled through his memory. 'Wait. *Commander* Graham Curtis?'

'The very same.'

'Shit a brick.'

'I thought he was still inside,' Toby said, and Steve could hear the tapping of a keyboard. 'Let's have a looksie. Well, what do you know. He got out five months ago.'

'I know he went down and was publicly disgraced, but what was he actually done for?'

'He was one of the first senior coppers to be found to be totally bent. Staggeringly bent in fact. They uncovered his involvement in a huge protection racket, drug money, payoffs, bribery, murders, all leading back to him. There were also rumours that he personally murdered a few people in particularly nasty circumstances.'

'Such as?'

'He was pretty fond of a bit of necklacing by all accounts.'

'Frank Adams,' Steve said suddenly. 'Rumours are that he killed Frank Adams.'

'Who was he?'

'He was a gangster about thirty years ago, give or take. Hung out with Lily Tao and Mickey.'

'Rumour mill is telling me that she was shot,' Toby said.

'So I heard.'

'Who shot her then?' Toby asked.

'I heard from a fairly reliable witness that it was ex-Commander Graham Curtis,' Steve said. 'Perhaps he needs to be brought in for questioning.'

'Perhaps he does, my friend,' Toby said with amusement. 'Can't have him being a naughty boy when he's fresh out of the nick. I'll get back to you.'

Steve was worried about Pearl. He tapped out a text to Stanley saying he'd get back to him with news later. Then he chugged down some more painkillers and went to find Jonesey who, as he guessed correctly, was sitting in the mess room stuffing his face with an iced bun.

'Busy then?' Steve said wryly.

'First chance I've had to eat all day,' Jonesey complained. 'I've been searching the woods around the hospital.'

'Why have you been searching the woods?' Steve looked at him blankly.

Jonesey stared at him as if he was stupid. 'Because of the missing baby. Apparently lots of people escape into the woods from the hospital.'

'What missing baby?'

'Haven't you heard? Baby's gone missing from the hospital. It's on full lockdown.'

'Jesus. Who's dealing with it?'

Jonesey rolled his eyes. '"Double I".'

'Christ we're doomed,' muttered Steve, referring to Ineffectual Ian who was dubbed 'Double I' by those who worked with him.

'Exactly,' said Jonesey, stuffing in the last of his bun.

'Find anything in the woods?'

'Few things,' he mumbled.

'Such as?'

'Couple of hospital gowns, but they'd been there a while by the looks of it.'

'Hopefully no one in them?'

'Ha ha.' Jonesey pulled a face. 'A carrier bag of some bits.'

'What sort of bits?'

He shrugged. 'Some sort of diary, some make-up and a purse.'

'Whose was it?'

'Dunno.'

'Where was it?'

'Just over the fence from the staff car park.'

'Have you checked to see whether anything like it has been reported missing at the hospital?'

'I should probably do that.'

'You think?' Steve said, frustrated. 'Did they find anything on CCTV?'

'Double I was there looking. Dunno what he found.'

Steve tutted. 'Is Double I still at the hospital?'

Jonesey nodded. 'He's coming back to look at some more footage, I think.'

'OK. You'd better get back to it then, Jonesey.'

'Guv,' Jonesey said grumpily.

As Steve returned to his office, he was summoned to see the Superintendent, which was never a good thing. After a brief audience with him, Steve stomped back to his office muttering and cursing under his breath. Once inside, he slammed the door. The SIO – Ineffectual Ian – on the case of the missing baby had decided to go into the woods to look for further evidence and the silly twat had fallen down a hill and broken his leg. The case had now landed in Steve's lap.

Steve was pissed off because Double I had actually done very little and did, in fact, live up to his nickname, although Steve had added more than a few expletives to it.

'JONESEY!' he yelled out of the door.

Jonesey came running down the corridor clutching a half-eaten sandwich.

'What? What's up?' he said, looking panicked.

'Tell me where we are so far. Missing baby's been dumped in my lap.'

Jonesey guffawed. 'Oh, Guv. You should have seen Double I go down that slope. I've just seen it. Garland filmed it. Hilarious. He went down like a—'

'Where are we with the CCTV?' Steve interrupted.

'I was just about to look into that.'

'FUCK'S SAKE!' roared Steve. 'Must I do every single thing around here?'

'Alright, calm down. Keep your knickers on,' Jonesey said huffily. 'Do you need more painkillers?'

'Probably, but there's a missing baby. Do you get that?'

'Of course I get it. I was just going to check to see if they've emailed it over. I asked a while ago for it when I realised he was SIO on the case.'

'Oh.' Steve looked embarrassed. 'Sorry.'

'I'll go and check now,' Jonesey said. 'Do you want to split it up or shall I delegate?'

'We'll watch it together. You're good at spotting things and then we'll farm the earlier time frames out to the others if we need to.'

Jonesey disappeared off and a few minutes later an email from him arrived containing the file.

Steve clicked and opened the file. He scrolled through until he found the correct date and time frame from the night before. Jonesey appeared balancing two mugs of tea, a packet of biscuits and a laptop.

'Gotta keep our strength up,' he said defensively when Steve raised an eyebrow at the biscuits.

Jonesey opened the lid of the computer.

'Figured we'd load up the outside footage too, two birds and all that.' He fiddled about and pressed play. 'Right. Hit it,' he said to Steve, settling the laptop down on the desk next to Steve's screen. He picked up his tea, dunked in a Hobnob and then sucked on it noisily.

'You can bugger off if you're going to do that for the next hour or so,' Steve said, not taking his eyes off the screen.

Jonesey rolled his eyes. 'Look, there's the ward. Let's skip through and then go back if we need to.'

The two sat sipping their tea and munching on biscuits as they watched people flit through the ward in quick time. Suddenly the lights on the CCTV dimmed and Steve frowned.

'Bedtime,' said Jonesey knowledgably.

They watched as a nurse appeared and wandered through the ward checking on patients and the cribs next to the beds. She bent over a crib for a while, her back to the camera and then straightened up and disappeared. Later, another nurse appeared and wandered around as if looking for someone. They watched as she walked towards the door and then turned into one of the wards, disappeared behind a drawn bed curtain and then reappeared wheeling a small baby away in the crib.

'Where's she going?' muttered Steve.

'Back into a side room,' Jonesey said. 'There's a room where they wash and change the babies and all that. I think she's heading in there.'

'Where was the baby taken from?'

Jonesey pointed. 'See this first bed with the curtain pulled around? It was taken from there. The wards got a bit of a dog-leg, so the camera view doesn't quite go that far, to all the beds.'

'What's at the end of the dog-leg?'

'A set of doors into another room.'

They watched the ward, which remained quiet. One of the patients rose from a bed, pulled on a dressing gown and walked off out of camera shot. A while later they saw the same nurse reappear, put the baby's crib back next to the patient and then leave.

'Where do I know that woman from?' Steve murmured. He stopped the film at a point where the nurses face could be seen but was slightly blurred.

Steve sat back in his chair exhausted. 'Do we know who was working these shifts? Have we interviewed staff? Did Double I actually do anything?'

Jonesey consulted his notebook.

'Shift list is coming over but from each department so that's likely to be epic. Double I spoke to a few nurses on the ward, but I don't know what they said.'

'Christ.' Steve scowled. The painkillers weren't working and he felt terrible.

'Guv, what have you had to eat?' Jonesey said, eyeing him. 'I think you need to eat something.'

'I've had biscuits.'

'You've had two Hobnobs. That's not enough to keep anyone going.'

'Alright, Mum,' Steve snapped.

Jonesey looked huffy. 'I'm just saying you're popping painkillers, and you shouldn't do that on an empty stomach.'

'OK. I'll get something to eat.'

'Tell you what. Let's swing by Maggie's, grab some food and then go to the hospital and see if anyone knows these nurses. Then we can take it from there.'

Steve rolled his eyes.

'It's a plan,' Jonesey said, avoiding direct eye contact.

'Is this just about you going to Maggie's for food?'

'No,' Jonesey said defensively, inspecting the screen closely.

'Tell you what, go and grab me a cheese sandwich from next door and we'll head to hospital. There's something I need to do first.' He fished his wallet out and gave Jonesey a tenner.

'Yes, you can get yourself one and I want the change.'

'Back in a mo then.' Jonesey started to close the door behind him.

'Don't be all bloody day.'

CHAPTER 23

Jonesey appeared around the door with two sandwiches, two bags of crisps and two KitKats.

'I thought I just said a cheese sandwich,' Steve remarked grumpily. 'I don't remember ordering a fucking picnic for two.'

'Oh shut up,' Jonesey said, passing him a sandwich. 'Does Kate know how hangry you get?'

'I'm not even going to ask what that means.' Steve took a bite of his sandwich. He printed off stills from the CCTV and stared in disbelief at Jonesey who had laid his food out neatly on a paper towel on the corner of his desk.

'Come on,' he said to Jonesey. 'Let's get going.'

'But I'm still eating…'

'Bring it.'

Steve marched off down the corridor towards the car park.

Steve strode quickly into the hospital, closely followed by Jonesey, who was complaining that he hadn't had a proper lunch break. Steve flashed his warrant card at the main reception and informed them that he would be going up to maternity and he needed access to the ward immediately.

Exiting the lift, Steve was faced with a nurse in a Sister's uniform, standing with folded arms and a deep frown.

'You the police officer who has *demanded* access to my ward?' she snapped in a combative tone.

'I am. I'm looking for the ward with the *missing* baby,' Steve shot back, not in the mood for power struggles.

She relaxed slightly. 'I'm Mary Jenner. Sister here. Follow me.'

Steve caught her arm gently. 'Hang on. Firstly, the mother of the missing baby is at home now, not here?'

'Better for her to be there. She's with one of your family liaison people, waiting for news,' Sister said.

'Good. Before we go in. I need to know who these two nurses are.'

Jonesey produced the stills from the CCTV.

She inspected them. 'That's Anne Ford, she's always on this ward and that one is Hannah something... Oh what is it?' She fumbled for her phone. 'Hang on, she's emailed me about a transfer... Here we are. Hannah Evans!'

'Do they work on this ward all the time?' Steve asked.

'Anne does, Hannah is around, but as I said, is looking to transfer.'

'Why? Is that usual?'

'These days it is, we used to specialise, but we're so shorthanded, nurses can pretty much pick where they'd like to be.'

'Do you know this Hannah then?'

'She seems OK. I'll interview her and speak to colleagues before I decide. She's worked at the hospital a while, I think.'

'What about Anne?'

'I've been here a few years, and Anne has always been here.'

'What's she like?'

'OK. Tendency to be lazy without my foot up her backside. I've had to give her a couple of warnings recently for being a bit too vocal with her opinion of some of the mothers.'

'Oh?' Steve raised an eyebrow.

The nurse shrugged. 'She just gets a bit resentful of some of them.'

'In what way?'

'The ones that don't really seem to give much attention to the baby. You know, pay more attention to their hair and make-up or what they're going to post on social media. You know the sort.'

'What does she say?'

'Just that they don't deserve to have the babies, that sort of thing.'

'What does she do when you pull her up on it?'

'Says sorry. Usually cries. She had a miscarriage recently. She wasn't far along at all,' she said dismissively.

'Is she on shift now?'

'No. She went off sick mid shift last night.'

Steve's ears pricked up. 'What was the matter?'

'She didn't say. Said she felt terrible and that she needed to go home straight away.'

'Were you here?'

'No, my colleague was. That's all she said though.'

Steve was thoughtful for a moment. 'I need a home address, please.'

'I'll have to get onto personnel. Come with me.'

'The other one. Hannah. Where might she be?'

'I'll see if she's in, sometimes she pulls a double shift.'

As they followed the nurse through into the lobby before the ward, Jonesey asked, 'Out of interest, have you had reports of any handbags or anything like that go missing?'

The sister turned and stared at him. 'How did you know? Someone reported a purse missing. Squawked about it being taken from her handbag, reckoned the purse alone was worth more than the cash in it.'

'Did you report it to us?'

The sister pointed to a notice that said valuables should not be kept on the ward and that the hospital were not liable.

'As I told her, I've got a ward to run. If she's stupid enough to bring in a Chanel purse that's worth more than what some of my trainees get paid in a month, then it's her own stupid fault. Let alone keeping a ten grand engagement ring in it.' She snorted. 'I'm not surprised it's gone missing. Dopey cow leaves everything lying about.'

'Is the woman who lost the purse still here?'

The nurse rolled her eyes. 'God yes. Talk about high-maintenance. I reckon she'll be here until the baby starts school the rate she's going.'

Steve tried not to smile. 'Jonesey, why don't you go and have a chat and get a description of it, and we'll see if it's turned up.'

As they walked, the sister pointed Jonesey towards the bed where a woman was sitting, posing and taking selfies, while ignoring the small baby crying loudly in a cot beside her.

The sister turned to Steve. 'Right, Anne's address and where Hannah is today. Bear with me.'

Steve leant against the counter and watched the ward for a while. He strolled off down the corridor he remembered the nurse heading towards and saw a large room with changing mats and a large sink. He assumed this was where the nurse had been going in the CCTV footage. He also saw a lounge room with a few chairs and a bookcase full of books and a few magazines lying about. Next door was a small kitchen with a kettle and toaster and a loaf of bread lying on the side.

'Ah, here you are. There you go,' the sister said briskly, handing him a piece of paper. 'That's Anne's address.'

'Thanks. Is Hannah working today?'

'She is. I've asked her to come up. Here she is now.'

Steve turned to see a large woman walking towards him with a quizzical expression on her face. He recognised her face from somewhere but couldn't place it.

Sister pointed to a door. 'Use my office. Hannah, this is Detective Steve Miller.'

Steve faced Hannah and smiled pleasantly.

'Hello, Hannah. I'd like to ask you some questions if that's OK?'

'What's this about?' she asked shyly, reddening slightly as Steve watched her.

'Shall we?' He opened the door and gestured for her to go in. Jonesey approached tucking his notebook into his pocket, and Steve motioned him inside.

'Take a seat please, Hannah.'

Hannah sat down, looking uncomfortable.

Steve had a sudden recollection of where he'd seen her before. It was in the window of the building opposite the bakery.

'You live in Castleby, don't you?'

She looked surprised. 'Y-yes.'

'You were working last night?'

'Yes, on the surgical ward.'

'Anything happen last night?'

'What do you mean?'

'Anything of note happen last night? Anything unusual?'

Hannah frowned. 'No, it was really quiet.'

'Why'd you come up here? To this ward?'

She looked a little surprised at the question. 'Oh well. I'm friends with Anne who works here, and we usually have a cuppa together if we're both working.'

'So, you came up here for a cuppa. Did you arrange that with Anne?'

'She knew I'd come up at break time, we'd loosely arranged it.'

'Did you have a cuppa together?'

'Er. No. I couldn't find her.'

'You've no idea where she might have been?'

Hannah flushed and looked nervous. 'I don't know. I looked everywhere.'

Steve smiled encouragingly. 'How long have you known Anne?'

'Oh, years. We worked together at another hospital years ago and just happened to meet up again at support group.' She flushed. 'We knew each other well before that, but sort of lost touch after I left the hospital and moved away.'

'Tell me about her... husband? Boyfriend?'

'Oh she's lovely, struggling a bit since she...'

'Since she what?'

'She miscarried her baby at six weeks.'

'That must be hard for her, working here.'

'I keep asking her that, but she says she's OK.'

'Boyfriend... husband?'

'No, her boyfriend left when he found out she was pregnant.'

'Nice fella. Was she upset?'

'No, she was just happy she was pregnant, I think.'

'Do you think she was ill last night?'

'I guessed so. I was going to call in on the way home.'

'We watched the CCTV from last night. You stopped at the bed by the door here and then took the baby off somewhere.'

'Oh... little Lucas? He's so adorable.' Her face lit up and she whispered conspiratorially, 'The mother is useless though. He'd filled his nappy and needed changing. She wouldn't have done it. She was fast asleep with ear plugs in. He would have cried and been uncomfortable all night if I'd left him. So, I took him off and changed him.'

'She says someone stole her purse,' Jonesey butted in.

'Well, when I was returning him the other day for Anne, her bag was on the floor with the zip open and the purse on display. That was just before visiting hours so I reckon anyone could have taken it,' Hannah supplied.

'What have you heard about the missing baby?'

Hannah twisted her fingers nervously. 'Just that a baby was taken.' She looked at Steve and then Jonesey. 'You don't think... Wait, you can't think *Anne* would do it?'

'This is what we're trying to find out,' Steve said. 'While we're here, when you were seeing to baby Lucas, did you see anyone else about on the ward?'

Hannah thought for a moment. 'Only the poor lady whose baby died during labour a couple of days ago. I saw her walking down the corridor over there.'

Steve frowned. 'Is that normal for her to be here if her baby died?'

Hannah adopted a rueful expression. 'Sometimes. I remember Anne saying she had a few complications, so she couldn't go home, and there were no other beds in the hospital, so she had to stay here. So awful for the poor lady, being around all of the new babies when hers died.'

Steve made a mental note to also speak to the patient concerned.

'OK. Thanks, Hannah, well, if you think of anything else that might be relevant, give us a call.'

'Oh, thanks. Is that all, can I go?'

'Yup. Don't let me keep you from your patients.'

'OK.'

They watched as she rose and opened the door, looking back over her shoulder and smiling at Steve, blushing a little.

'She fancies you,' Jonesey announced once she closed the door.

'Shut it.' Steve re-opened the door and beckoned the Sister in.

'Tell me about the patient who lost a baby.'

The sister frowned. 'Why do you ask about that?'

'We saw her on the CCTV. She was up and about the night the baby went missing.'

'She was probably making a drink.'

'Still, tell me about her.'

'The baby was born with the cord wrapped around his neck. There were complications and he was without oxygen for too long. We did everything we could.'

'And the mother is still on the ward?'

Sister grimaced. 'It's not perfect. She had some problems, we had to keep her in. We didn't have a bed anywhere else at the time. I didn't want her here, too awful for her.'

'When is she due to go home?'

'Not sure. I haven't finished reading the handover notes. Perhaps today.' She stopped for a minute. 'I haven't seen her this morning, come to think of it.' She turned and opened the door and walked out to the ward. Steve and Jonesey followed her.

She pointed to a bed. 'That's her bay.'

Jonesey tilted his head to one side. 'That's how her bed was on the CCTV, I remember. After she left it. She's not been back.'

Steve put his hands in his pockets and rocked thoughtfully.

'So does this mean we have a missing patient as well as a missing baby?'

'She'll turn up,' Sister said with confidence.

CHAPTER 24

Hannah closed the door to Sister's office. After she had been called in to have a chat with the detective, Sister had asked her to come back to discuss a possible transfer. Hannah had been grilled relentlessly by the sister for an hour, but this still hadn't dampened her enthusiasm for a transfer to maternity. Sister had spoken to Hannah's ward and agreed that she could transfer over to cover Anne's absence as a trial from the next day. Thrilled with the news, Hannah wandered back through the ward, stopping by the bed that baby Lucas was in. He was in his cot crying loudly and the mother was nowhere to be seen. Hannah bent over and made a fuss of him, calming him down and soothing him by pulling funny faces.

'Don't s'pose you wanna a job, do you?' the mother said when she returned. She flopped back on the bed and checked her hair and make-up in her phone.

'Sorry?' Hannah said.

'He doesn't stop crying. I won't be able to cope with that racket at home. I can't have him kicking off when I'm doing my live Insta feeds.' She scrutinised Hannah. 'Maybe you can come and look after him. He seems to like you.'

'But I work here,' Hannah stammered, not sure if the woman was serious.

The woman resumed looking at herself in her phone. 'Whatever.'

Hannah cooed a goodbye to baby Lucas and promised she would see him tomorrow.

* * *

The ward sister from maternity had rung Steve to say she couldn't find the missing patient anywhere and had spoken to the woman's family to see if she had turned up at home. There was no sign of her. Steve ended the call, assuring the sister that he was going to the CCTV suite to see whether that provided any clues.

Steve rolled his neck. He felt stiff, hungry, grumpy and his ribs were killing him. They had been watching CCTV, from different angles, in the hospital security suite for what seemed like hours. They couldn't see the missing patient anywhere; they had tracked the exact time when she had stepped out of bed and then lost her.

'She can't have just gone,' Steve said, frustrated. 'Nobody just disappears.'

'That Lord Lucan did,' Jonesey said, chewing noisily on a toffee that he'd found on the desk in front of him. 'It was a question on a quiz the other day.'

'OK, with the exception of Lord whatshisname.' Steve stared at the screen. 'What aren't I seeing here?'

Steve leant back, thoughtful.

'Do you have any cameras on the roof?' he asked suddenly.

'Yeah. They're not connected though,' the technician said.

'Great. Any other suggestions?'

The technician looked at him, suddenly reminding Steve of a sloth. 'Nope.'

'Where's the camera for the other exits from the ward where the woman went missing, like fire doors?'

'Erm…' The technician frowned.

'I need the footage from there, please. Where do the doors lead to?'

'Staff car parks mostly. I don't think we have footage though. I never really look at that.'

Steve said sarcastically, 'Tell me. Is there ever *any* degree of urgency in your job?'

The technician thought hard for a moment. 'I'd say mostly not.'

Steve scribbled his number in large letters on a pad. 'Call me when you find it,' he said grimly. 'I want the footage from the doors. I'm going up to the roof.'

After a brief argument with a self-important security guard, Steve gave him the benefit of his best beady eye and warrant card, and went up to the roof. To him, it seemed ridiculous that they couldn't locate the missing patient and because he hadn't seen any sign of her throughout the hospital, he concluded she may have gone 'up'.

He pushed open the heavy door onto the roof, tutting at the bunch of security keys left hanging in the lock and stepped out, looking around the large space, his shoes crunching on the gravel. He rounded a corner, walked past some large plant machinery, and his persistence was rewarded.

Huddled in the corner, in an area of rough shelter, the missing patient sat on the floor rocking gently, her eyes glassy and unfocused. To Steve's horror she appeared to be holding a bundle. His stomach lurched at the thought of the child being up there with no food or warmth for so long.

'Hey there,' he said gently, walking slowly towards her. 'My name's Steve. How are you doing up here? You must be cold.'

The security guard rounded the corner and Steve held him back with a hand gesture. He turned slowly to the guard and said quietly, 'I need some blankets up here, please, and a nurse from the baby unit.'

He turned, focusing on the woman again and spoke gently. 'Hey there. Debbie, isn't it?'

She didn't acknowledge him. She stared without seeing, as if in some sort of trance. Her arms tightened on the baby, and he heard a faint whimper. Relief flooded through him. Any noise from the baby was a good sign.

He moved closer. 'Debbie, I need you to come with me. The baby needs to see a doctor.'

'Baby's dead,' she muttered, still staring blindly.

'No. That baby's not dead, I just heard him. He's probably hungry and cold. You look cold, do you want to come with me?' He moved closer and dropped down to his haunches beside her.

'Debbie,' he tried again gently. 'I need you to give me the baby.'

'Baby's dead. No point,' she said again.

'Why don't you let me have him and I'll make sure he gets a proper burial then,' Steve said gently, desperately racking his brains for how to approach this.

The woman blinked. 'I want a white casket. Gold handles.'

'I can do that.'

The security guard appeared with some blankets. Steve took them from him and shooed him back a little. He turned to the woman.

'Now, Debbie, I'm going to put this around you and take the baby. OK?' Then we can talk a bit more.' Steve awkwardly draped the blanket around her shoulders, the exposed skin on her arms was icy cold and he wondered briefly whether the baby would make it.

'So white casket and gold handles,' he said gently, easing the baby out of her embrace. He looked down at the infant as he tried to tuck a blanket around it. He placed two fingers inside the neck of the

Babygro and was relieved to feel that it was slightly warm. He passed it over to the security guard. The baby's face was tinged with blue, under his eyes and around his mouth. Steve sent a silent prayer up that he would be OK.

'Get going. Now.' He pushed the security guard towards the door as a nurse stepped out of the doorway and took the baby from him. Satisfied that the baby was safe he turned back to the woman.

He blinked; she had moved. Movement to his left caught his eye and he saw her at the edge of the roof, her arms outstretched, the blanket draped across her like a cloak.

'Debbie,' he called gently as he walked towards her. 'Come on. Come with me now.'

She turned her head slightly. 'Baby's dead,' she said dully.

'I know. I'm so sorry.'

'I thought I'd dreamt it,' she said. 'But now I think it was real.'

'I'm so sorry.'

'It was the devil; he wanted my baby.'

'Debbie, come back with me, let's go and talk to someone together.'

'No point in going on now,' she said dully. 'No point at all.'

The heavy door banged open and two more security guards rushed onto the roof. Steve turned at the noise and shook his head, gesturing for them to keep back.

Steve turned back to her.

'Come on, sweetheart. Away from the edge,' he pleaded, holding out his hand towards her.

She tilted her head and looked at him, seeming to focus for the first time since he had been on the roof. She looked past him at the security guards, the huge drop behind her.

'In every angel there is a demon hiding. He seeks you when you need the light and he brings the darkness.' She closed her eyes. 'Be careful of the devil. He will take what's most precious to you and leave you with darkness.'

Steve watched in horror as she leant backwards, her arms outstretched, and fell off the building.

'NO!' Steve screamed, darting towards the edge. He made a noise of distress when he saw her splayed out on the ground below.

The two security guards peered over the roof edge next to Steve.

'That wasn't our fault,' muttered one of the security guards.

Steve turned, his face like thunder. 'You fucking tell yourself that, but we all know it was on you. Who was the fucking idiot that left the bloody door unlocked?'

Giving the two guards a disgusted look, he stormed off the roof.

* * *

Foxy's day was not going well. He was on his way to pick up a delivery, only to find that the Land Rover wouldn't start.

'For God's sake,' he muttered, popping the bonnet open.

He climbed out, propped up the bonnet and stood staring at the engine.

'Don't even begin to *pretend* to know what you're looking at,' said an amused voice behind him.

He grinned without turning. 'I'll have you know I've been known to hold my own,' he said, then sighed. 'Sadly, today isn't one of those days.' He turned and ruffled Brock's ears when he rushed up for a fuss.

'And, if it isn't my *most* favourite mechanic at the *most* convenient of times,' Foxy said, giving Jesse a big smile.

'Wait. I'm getting déjà vu here.' She chuckled. 'Haven't I done this before? Come to your rescue when you've been damsel in distress?'

Foxy laughed. 'Would we say damsel? Shall we just stick to *in distress*?'

'Whatever. Why's the bonnet up?'

'Won't start.'

'Ahh.'

'Is this something that all mechanics and plumbers are taught in training? To listen to the problem and then just stand there and say ahh?' Foxy asked in frustration.

'Absolutely. It helps with gravitas. S'pose you want me to have a look?'

'Well, if you're offering.'

She rolled her eyes. 'Tools?'

Foxy strode over to the rear of the Defender and drew out a metal box.

'Turn her over then,' Jesse said, leaning on the edge of the Defender and looking in.

Foxy climbed in and turned the key.

'Oh. I know what it is,' Jesse said confidently.

'What?'

'Well, you need a new battery for a start. How old is it anyway? I didn't think that brand was still around anymore,' she said, peering at an old label.

'Christ it's not that old.'

'Get yourself a spanking new one and it'll work wonders. The Viagra for Land Rovers.'

'Oh stop.'

'Now what's going on out here?' Maggie said, leaving the cafe and crossing the short distance to where Foxy and Jesse were standing.

'Foxy's battery is flat,' Jesse said, deadpan. 'He needs a new one and a bit of a tweak.'

'Ain't that the truth,' he muttered.

'Well, no point moping about is there? Get yourself a new one!' Maggie stated.

'Well, I'd go and get one if the Land Rover actually worked,' Foxy said sarcastically.

Maggie batted his arm. 'Cheeky bugger,'

'I can grab you one. I've gotta go to Pembroke today. I'll get you one there and fit it for you later and do the required tweaking,' Jesse said, leaning in and snapping a picture of it.

'Really?' Foxy looked pleased. 'You're a bloody superstar.' He threw an arm around her shoulders and pulled her in for a hug, dropping a noisy kiss on her head. 'Saved me untold hassle.'

'I can't quite believe what I'm seeing,' another voice chimed in. Foxy and Jesse turned to face the source. 'Jesse and Rob Fox locked in an embrace. How come no one tells me anything? When the hell did this hook up happen?'

'Erin?' Jesse said in disbelief. 'What the *hell* are you doing here?'

'My God!' Foxy said, grinning widely. 'How long has it been?'

The woman called Erin threw her arms around Jesse and Foxy in turn, greeting them warmly.

Jesse turned to Maggie. 'Mags this is Erin, she was my physio at the hospital.' She looked confused for a moment. 'Hang on, how do you two know each other?' Jesse asked, pointing between Foxy and Erin.

'Now there's a story.' Foxy grinned, appraising Erin.

Erin was dressed in running skins and a tight running top that displayed a toned torso. Her trademark ginger hair was tied back in a long ponytail and her attractive face was flushed and rosy from her run on such a chilly morning.

'It's nice to meet you, Erin. Come on, everyone in for coffee,' Maggie announced, herding them across the road into the cafe.

'You look well,' Foxy observed as Erin sat down opposite him.

'So do you,' she said, blatantly eyeing him up and down. She glanced at Jesse. 'You've healed well too. How do you feel?'

'Good as new, thanks to you.'

'I'm very pleased to hear it. You're walking really well.' She glanced at Foxy. 'You too.'

'What the hell are you doing here?' Jesse asked.

'I'm filling in for a friend at her physio practice for a few months. She's poorly, cancer treatment, but still needs the income and wants to keep it going, so I'm here running that. It's local and there's a flat above the clinic that she usually rents out for the holidays, but I've got that now as part of the deal. I got here yesterday, and I start officially in a few days.'

'That's amazing!' Jesse said. 'I lost track of you after your contract finished at the hospital. It's so good to see you!'

'You never used to say that when I was pushing you to do your exercises and get walking properly again. Especially if it was early morning!' Erin laughed.

Jesse grabbed her hand. 'I'll always be grateful for everything you did for me after I went over the cliff.'

'Bet you wouldn't say that to Magda.' Erin laughed, referring to a ruthless German physiotherapist that Jesse had locked horns with on more than one occasion. Magda and Erin had helped Jesse with her recovery after she had been pulled off a cliff by a madman.

'You're right. I wouldn't,' Jesse said, giving a peal of laughter. 'So how come you know Foxy? All this time and I never knew you two knew each other.'

'I did a stint on one of the army bases as a civilian physio, just to help out. That's how we met.' She flicked a glance at Foxy and said to Jesse, 'I dealt with all the difficult patients.'

'Liar,' Foxy said, enjoying himself. 'You were a ruthless taskmaster.'

'And you were hardly a model patient!'

'How long were you working with the army for?' Jesse asked.

'About three years. Long before I started working in hospitals. Plenty of time to get to know all the sneaky habits of this one.' Erin grinned at Foxy.

'Mack's up the road and Rudi lives around the corner. Can you believe it?' Foxy said.

'Mack's still in, isn't he?'

'Yup, Rudi's out, he's a tree surgeon.'

'And you're running a climbing centre, I see.' She pointed at his T-shirt. 'You always said you were thinking about doing that when you left.'

'And here we are. I'm nothing if not a man of my word.'

'Erin, come to dinner at ours tonight,' Jesse said. 'Let's catch up properly.'

'Wait... weren't you with that guy with the amazing eyes? Doug? Now you two are together?' Erin said in reply.

Jesse snorted with laughter. 'No! I am still very much with old blue eyes. This one,' she gestured with her thumb to Foxy, 'is just buttering me up for a new car battery.'

'I am. Completely, ruthlessly buttering her up. Does that dinner include me?' Foxy said.

Jesse chuckled. 'Course. Say, our house. 7.30? That good for you?'

'Good for me,' Foxy said.

'Sounds great!' Erin said. 'I'll look forward to it.'

Jesse rattled off her address for Erin. Foxy's phone rang and he saw it was the solicitor dealing with Carla's affairs.

'Sorry, guys, gotta go. See you both later.' He squeezed his way out and went outside to answer his phone.

CHAPTER 25

Danny Tao's 'cold turkey' was not going well. Alone in the bowels of the wind turbine he had emptied most of the contents of his body into either the toilet or the bucket and was sweating, writhing on the floor, and hallucinating. He had seen his mother pointing at him, screaming at him to be more of a man and then his mother had produced a gun and shot him in the face when she had found out he had killed his sister. He had seen rats running up and down the walls, huge spiders, snakes and cockroaches. There had also been a series of visitations from his dead sister, who kept asking him why he shot her. If he could have torn off his own head with his bare hands to escape it, he would have.

The noise of a nearby boat interrupted his consciousness and sounds from outside had him crawling towards the door. He tried to open it but couldn't, he was too weak and drifted off into unconsciousness again.

When he woke some hours later, feeling stronger, he wrestled open the door to find a bag with more toilet rolls and another cool box with more food and water.

Beside himself with frustration, he sat on the outside gantry and wailed like a small child.

* * *

Pearl was recovering well. Her wound was healing, and she was slightly less exhausted. But she felt weak. Any activity left her completely drained, so she was adhering to the doctor's advice and resting. She had insisted that Alexy take Mickey back to hospital, with a promise to Mickey that she would be in to see him as soon as she was able.

Mickey had no plans to be at the hospital for any longer than was necessary and had only agreed to save Pearl from becoming even more agitated than she already was.

Mickey was worried. On the journey back to the hospital, he had insisted that Stanley tell him everything that had happened in London. He nodded with satisfaction when Stanley told him what Ivan had done to the man who had betrayed them twice. His eyes narrowed when Stanley outlined that they had kidnapped Danny Tao who had been following Pearl and they had him safely ensconced while he detoxed. Mickey had thought for a moment and then called Alexy. He asked him to get Ivan to come down and see them so they could decide on a way forward.

Mickey arrived back at the hospital and went back up to his ward. He was greeted by the nurse who treated him like a small child and invariably made his blood pressure rocket.

'Mr Camorra,' she said in her most snippy voice, 'you will not disappear from hospital without the doctor's or my explicit agreement. I must insist on that.'

Mickey approached her menacingly. 'Oh, is that so?'

Stanley cleared his throat, suddenly nervous for the women's general well-being. 'Is the doctor around?' he asked, stepping in front of a fuming Mickey.

The nurse looked down her nose at Stanley. 'He's on his rounds,' she said haughtily. 'He'll get to you.'

'Great, thanks. We'll just go and wait for him over here. Mickey's keen to get out of your hair.' Stanley guided Mickey over to a chair. 'Thank you,' he said, pushing Mickey down as gently as he could.

'Anything else from her and that's it,' Mickey grumbled.

'It's fine. She can't help it,' Stanley said. 'The doctor will be along in a bit and then we can go home, hopefully.'

After an awkward meeting, the doctor eventually acquiesced to Mickey's request to go home. After examining him, he ran a few more tests and insisted that Mickey return every few days for further checks.

Mickey waited for his medication to arrive and left the ward a few hours later, giving the nurse a sour look as he passed her.

'See you in a few days, Mr Camorra,' she called after him.

'Not if I can fucking well help it,' Mickey muttered.

Stanley insisted Mickey waited at the entrance to the hospital while he went to collect the car from the car park. As he waited, Mickey saw a crowd gathered at the side of the building and police tape keeping them back, and wandered over. He noticed Steve was covering a body with a blanket and speaking to a tall man, pointing up at the roof. Steve clapped the man on the shoulder and headed towards the cordon tape, pulling his phone out of his pocket. Steve met Mickey's eyes and he registered surprise.

'Mickey?' he asked, walking towards him. 'What are you doing here?'

'Discharged,' he said.

'I doubt that very much,' Steve said, his lips twitching.

'Forced discharge… on my part,' Mickey added with a rare half smile. 'You look like shit.'

'Thanks. How's Pearl?' Steve asked.

'Tired.' He paused for a second and then met Steve's eyes. 'Someone shot my girl, Steve.'

'I know.'

'Someone's going to die for that.'

'I get that,' Steve murmured.

'Stanley said he sent you a picture of the man who did it.'

'He did.'

'You know who it is?'

'I do.'

Mickey swore and said through gritted teeth. 'Who is—?'

'Guv!' Jonesey's voice floated through the crowd. 'You got a sec?'

'One sec!' Steve called and turned back to Mickey. 'I need to explain a few things to you both. This is bigger than you think it is. I'll come to you after this. I'll be a couple of hours. OK?'

Stanley pulled up in the car and got out. 'Alright?' he asked, looking at Steve.

'I'm coming to you in an hour or so,' Steve said. 'I've got answers. Get him home. Pearl needs to be there too.'

Stanley flicked a glance towards Mickey who was scowling. 'Come on, Mickey. Pearl's been ringing.'

'Fine. See you later.' He pointed a finger at Steve. 'This better be good though.'

'I wouldn't describe any of it as good, Mickey.'

Steve turned back to the cordon to deal with Jonesey.

* * *

Steve climbed wearily into his car. He was exhausted. Everything still hurt and he was starving.

He knew if he took any more painkillers on an empty stomach he'd feel even more terrible. The tiredness and effects of the pain were becoming insidious, and he was struggling to think clearly. He started the car and drove it around to the front of the hospital where he got out and walked to the coffee shop. He bought a coffee and a sandwich from an empty canteen and wolfed them down with some more painkillers. While he ate, he pondered and then called Ross, his old buddy from Cardiff.

'Hello again,' Ross said as he answered the phone. 'How are things up there? Missing baby, wasn't it?'

'Found. Alive.'

'Phew. Relief.'

'I'll say.'

'Who took it?'

'Poor woman whose baby had died.'

'She in custody?'

'Threw herself off the roof.'

'Shit.'

'I have to be thankful she didn't take the baby with her.'

'Small mercies, mate.'

'Wondered if you had anything new on the Taos?'

'I do. I'm piecing it together from various scrotes I have had the misfortune to lean heavily on.' He laughed. 'Organised crime boys nicked someone high in the chain in Cardiff, and he is singing and singing because he knows he'll die a truly horrible death on remand.'

'What's he singing?'

'You sitting comfortably?'

'I am. Go for it.'

Steve drove towards Mickey and Pearl's large modern house, which nestled high in the cliff face overlooking Castleby. It was a vision of glass, steel and cedar that sat in neatly manicured gardens with a heated infinity pool on the main deck, outside the enormous bifold doors. He was buzzed through the main gates and Stanley met him at the door.

'Stanley,' Steve said, nodding as he climbed wearily up the steps.

'You've looked better,' Stanley said, allowing him to pass through the door.

'You're too kind,' Steve muttered, walking down the hall towards the main living area.

Pearl was sitting on the sofa, a large blanket over her legs, looking tired, but still beautiful. Steve went straight to her and bent to kiss her cheek.

'You had me worried,' he murmured. 'I told you to be careful there.'

'She does what she wants.' Mickey walked over and sat on the end of the sofa. His large hands cupped the outline of Pearl's tiny feet under the blanket. 'She don't listen to anyone.'

'And here's me thinking you and I don't agree on anything, Mickey,' Steve said.

An older woman who Steve had not seen before, placed a tray of coffee gently down on the table.

'Thank you, darling,' Pearl said, gesturing to Steve to help himself.

Steve passed her a cup, took one for himself and sat back in the chair opposite.

'Darling, you really do look quite awful,' Pearl observed. 'Are you in pain?'

'I'm fine.'

'Enough pleasantries,' snapped Mickey, leaning forward. 'Who shot Pearl?'

Steve sipped his coffee and wondered how to tell Mickey he had two children.

'The guy who shot Pearl and killed Lily is ex-Police Commander Graham Curtis.'

Mickey took a second to process what Steve was saying. He shot to his feet.

'Graham Curtis?' he said incredulously. 'Graham *fucking* Curtis had the audacity to shoot *my wife* and kill the head of the Tao empire?'

'As I understand it.'

Mickey narrowed his eyes. 'He went down.'

'He did.'

'Twenty years, wasn't it? I thought he'd died in prison.'

'It was longer than a twenty stretch, I think, but he got out five months ago. Rumours were that he killed Frank all those years ago and had planned for you to be there that day too. Why was that, Mickey?'

Mickey didn't say anything, he strode to the window and stood, breathing heavily. He spun around and directed his gaze at Steve.

'He was always sniffing around. Always making stuff his business. Always looking for a good cut, a way in, a chance for a back hander. Had a thing for Lily. Saw himself and her as the next big partnership. Saw me and Frank as his competition. He was possessed, desperate for money, power, recognition. He loved it. What better front than him being filth with an army of organised crime behind him? Why didn't I think it was him? I thought he was safely banged up for years.'

'He was the first real dirty cop to go down. They made an example of him.'

Mickey snorted. 'They didn't do him for half the things he did.'

'So I heard.'

'So why come after Pearl?' Mickey said, trying to process the events. 'She had nothing to do with me, or Frank, back then. It was before our time.'

'Mickey, as I said, this is bigger than just that. I think you'd better sit down.' Steve looked at Pearl and raised an eyebrow. She nodded imperceptibly.

'When Graham Curtis got out, he befriended Danny Tao,' he began.

Mickey's eyes narrowed.

'He did quite the job, I think. Fed him false information, befriended him, got him hooked on drugs. Made him give up lots of the Tao empire's secrets. He took him on the short journey into a hardcore drug habit. All the time, feeding him a line, that you, Mickey, killed his father. Danny missed having a father. This idea of you taking his father away made him crazy. He became hellbent on revenge. Graham fed him a narrative and he fell for it.'

'Danny Tao thinks I killed his father?'

'Well, he thinks you killed Frank,' Steve said awkwardly. 'Apparently, Lily had washed her hands of Danny. He was a liability. Always high or needing a fix. She pushed him out of the organisation. No one dealt with him anymore. No one wanted to be tainted by him. But he didn't see it.' Steve finished his coffee and put the cup back on the table. 'He arranged your shooting and rumours are that he presumed you were dead. He knew Pearl was in town wanting to see his mother and we are fairly sure that he'd been fed so much hate and loathing, he was going to kill Pearl and his mother, the day they met. But then he went missing.' He paused. 'You wouldn't happen to know where Danny Tao is would you, Mickey?'

Mickey looked away. 'What else?'

'Danny had a sister,' Steve said quietly.

Mickey looked surprised. 'Did he?'

'A twin. She died.'

Mickey blinked. 'A sister? I'd never heard of a sister. How did she die?'

'She was shot in the back of the head with two bullets that had a dragon motif on them.' Steve paused. 'Then she was dumped in a suitcase to rot in one of their drug farms. We're assuming Danny did it.'

'Lily must have had twins then.' Mickey stood, absently, and paced thoughtfully.

Steve looked at Pearl then exhaled heavily. 'Thing is, Mickey, Danny Tao and Jade, his sister, weren't Frank's kids. They're yours. You are their biological father.' Steve braced himself for the explosion.

Mickey turned around slowly to face Steve.

'What?' he said quietly.

'You are their biological father.'

Mickey looked at Pearl, his eyes wide and strode over to her, kneeling next to her. 'I didn't know,' he said quietly, as if no one else was in the room. 'I didn't know.'

'I know, darling. I know,' she said softly, stroking his face.

Mickey sighed and dropped his head down onto Pearl's legs.

Steve felt like an unwelcome voyeur in their private moment. He cleared his throat quietly.

'I'm worried for the both of you. Mickey, you're fresh out of hospital. Pearl, you're getting over being shot. You're not up to fighting off something like this.'

Mickey raised his head and gazed at Pearl again.

Steve tried again. 'Look, Curtis is out there, clearly trying to get some sort of revenge. I don't know the reason behind it, but it must be some sort of retribution. There's a warrant out for his arrest, but it looks like he's gone quiet. You need to be on your guard.'

Mickey tossed him a look that suggested he was well aware.

Steve leant forward. 'Word is that you're planning to take the Tao empire now Lily's dead. You know there'll be resistance.'

Mickey nodded thoughtfully. 'I'm aware of that. The old-school punters will support it though, none of them liked the Taos. They'd probably welcome the change. That'll help.' He pushed himself to a standing position. 'I'll need to go to London and show my face.'

'Hold on a minute,' Steve said. 'People think you're dead and it's Pearl running things. That might be enough to lure Curtis out from wherever he is to confront her if he thinks she's fair game.'

Mickey looked thoughtful at the idea. 'I knew there was a reason Pearl liked you.'

'Here's me thinking it was my good looks and sparkling personality,' Steve said wryly.

Pearl tittered. 'It's all those things, darling. But you might be right about Graham Curtis. He might come calling, so we need to have a plan.'

'I'm assuming, despite knowing that there's a warrant out for his arrest, if you see him, you won't turn him in to me?' Steve said.

'Absolutely right on that.' Mickey grinned.

Steve pursed his lips. 'I guess what I don't know...' he muttered. 'But this doesn't answer the question of where Danny Tao is.'

'Let me worry about that,' Mickey said.

'I need him for questioning on the murder of Jade Tao.'

'If he turns up, I'll let you know,' Mickey said evasively. 'In the meantime, if you hear anything or nick Curtis, let me know.'

'I'm sure he meant to add please to that sentence, darling,' Pearl said in an amused tone.

At that moment, Alexy walked into the room followed by another man Steve didn't recognise.

'Ah! Steve the policeman, you are well after your beating from Chinaman?' Alexy enquired, walking to Steve and shaking his hand as a greeting.

'I'm getting there,' Steve said, smiling. 'How are you, Alexy? Recovered?'

Alexy grinned. 'I have the head that is made of wood or rock,' he said, tapping his head with his knuckles. He turned to the man next to him. 'This is my cousin, Ivan.'

Steve shook the man's hand, who remained quiet. Steve thought for a fleeting moment that he had never looked into eyes so dark or so lacking in expression.

Mickey spoke to Steve. 'We have business to discuss now.'

'I'm off,' Steve said. 'One more thing. If you plan to take over the Tao empire, then I need to know what's happening here. I need to know if the bush bungalow is a one off or whether we have a more serious problem locally. Quid pro quo, Mickey.'

'Of course, darling.' Pearl stood slowly and hooked her arm through Steve's. 'I'll see you out.'

'Be careful, all of you,' Steve said.

As they walked towards the front door, Steve squeezed Pearl's arm. 'I'm not going to lie, Pearl, I'm pretty worried about this.' He stopped. 'I'm pretty worried about you.'

Pearl kissed him on the cheek. 'Such a darling man,' she whispered. 'Don't worry. Alexy and Ivan are here. They will protect us.'

'You'll call me if I can help? In any way?'

'Promise.'

'Hmm.' He stepped out of the front door and turned back to Pearl.

'Keep me in the loop.'

'I will. Take care.'

'You too, Pearl.'

CHAPTER 26

Since the news of Brian's death, Olivia had been in a trance-like state. Not from grief, but more about her not being able to process the fact that she had *wished* he would die and then it actually happened.

She found that she would make herself food and waste hours staring into space, completely lost in thought, leaving it untouched.

She was wracked with indecision about whether to pick Eli up from school and tell him on the way home, or to drive there and tell him and then leave him there. She had no experience of these things and didn't know what the best thing was to do. She didn't even know if she was supposed to be Eli's parent now or whether she would be allowed to. In truth, she loved Eli, but she wasn't even sure if she wanted to be his parent.

The phone rang, interrupting her musings.

'Hello?'

'Olivia Baker, please.'

'Speaking.'

'This is The Pines, we need you to come as soon as possible, please, there's been an incident with your brother.'

'What? What incident?' Olivia stammered.

'If you could just come now? I'm afraid I'm not at liberty to say anything further.'

'Er… Yes, yes. I'll be ten minutes.'

Olivia dressed quickly and threw on her coat. Grabbing her phone and keys, she ran out of the house and thundered down the road. Desperate to get to the care home, her mind full of questions. *Incident?*

She skidded to a halt at the front door, and impatiently jabbed the buzzer as she panted from her exertions. She observed a police car in the car park as she waited for the door to open.

'Mrs Baker?' A tall grey-haired woman in a white blouse and pinstripe grey trousers held open the door.

'Yes.'

'I've been expecting you. Come in. This way, please.'

Olivia followed the woman through the lobby and down a long corridor. The woman glanced over her shoulder. 'I'm the manager here. I don't believe we've met.'

'No. What's this about?' Olivia said, feeling a wave of panic setting in. 'Can I see Gil, please?'

'Please.' The woman stopped at a large door and motioned for Olivia to go inside. Sitting on one side of a desk were two police officers and a nurse who Olivia recognised. The nurse had two black eyes and her arm was in a sling.

'Hello,' Olivia said. 'My goodness, whatever happened to you?'

The nurse regarded her with cold eyes and turned her gaze to the police officers, not responding to Olivia.

'Sit, please.'

Olivia sat down, a sense of dread settling over her.

The manager began. 'I'm afraid I have some extremely unfortunate news for you.'

'What? What's happened to Gil? Is he alright? Why are the police here? Can I see him?'

The manager interlinked her fingers on the table in front of her. 'The police are here because we had an incident last night.'

'Incident?' Olivia asked with desperation, wishing this woman would just get to the point. 'What incident?'

'Your brother's room was broken into and searched, and Karen here was attacked and beaten.'

'What?' Olivia was stunned. 'Why? Who was it? Is he alright?'

'I'm afraid he isn't. I'm very sorry but the doctor pronounced your brother dead a short time ago.'

'What? How is that possible?' Olivia gripped the sides of the chair as she feared she might suddenly fall off it. Her head was spinning.

The manager continued patiently. 'We don't know who it was. They managed to override the CCTV. They seemed to know what they were doing.' She shifted uncomfortably. 'They were looking for something, clearly. The room is a mess. But whatever it was, they couldn't find it. They knocked Karen unconscious, and I'm afraid they did their best to get a response out of your brother.'

Olivia's hand flew to her mouth. 'Oh God.'

'It's very unfortunate. They were clearly trying to bring him around and in doing so deprived him of oxygen for a prolonged period. I am very sorry for your loss.'

Olivia stared in disbelief. 'They stopped his oxygen? Why didn't an alarm go off? Or why didn't anyone hear? He can't be dead.'

'Karen had been attacked and beaten and was unconscious on the floor.' The manager's tone was snippy. 'That's w—'

'If I may,' the male PC smoothly interrupted. 'Madam, I'm PC Garland and this is PC Warren. We were called to attend this morning because of the nature of the break in, but I am now waiting for confirmation that I can escalate this to a suspicious death.'

'Suspicious death?' Olivia said faintly.

'I need to ask you where you were last night?'

'Sorry?' Olivia looked at him in sheer disbelief.

'Where were you last night?' he repeated.

'I was at home.'

'Alone?'

'Yes.'

'You're married, I believe?'

'Um... well, yes. I *was*.' She struggled to form the words.

'May I ask the whereabouts of your husband last night?'

Olivia looked backwards and forwards at the four expectant faces before her and unexpectedly burst into tears.

'My husband died in the accident at the wind farm.' She sobbed, her face in her hands. 'Not Gil. No. Not Gil.'

'I'm so sorry, Madam,' PC Garland said uncomfortably, his eyes flicking to his female colleague. 'Yes, we were informed of that accident. I'm very sorry for your loss... er... losses.'

'Mrs Baker,' PC Warren said gently. 'Can you think of any reason why someone might do this to your brother?'

Olivia stared at the woman. Flashes of the accident skittered across her memory. Vague comments about running, getting away, angry voices, scared faces rushed into her psyche. She tasted sand in her mouth.

'I-I don't know,' she stammered.

PC Garland consulted his notebook. 'You brought your brother over from Dubai a few weeks ago now?'

'Yes, that's correct. We'd been living out there.'

'And you moved back because?' PC Garland asked, pen poised.

'Because we were living here now, and my husband's job moved to the wind farm here.' She gulped. 'I wanted to be near him.'

'Was it an accident that put him in this condition?' PC Warren asked.

'Yes. Car accident. In Dubai. A sandstorm.' She trailed off. She couldn't believe Gil was dead. *Was he really dead?*

'And you can't think of anyone that might do something like this to you or him?'

'No, not at all,' she said faintly. She wondered if she would be able to see Gil soon. *Was that allowed?*

'And no one has approached or threatened you recently.'

Only my husband, a tiny voice in Olivia's head said. She cleared her throat. 'No one's said or done anything like that.'

PC Warren snapped her notebook shut. 'Once again, Mrs Baker, we are sorry for your losses.'

'Could… could I see him?' Olivia addressed the manager directly.

The manager hesitated and glanced at PC Warren, who said, 'Yes, but I'm afraid you can't touch him. We will need to do a post-mortem and we need to preserve any evidence. One of us will have to accompany you.'

Olivia allowed herself to be escorted to Gil's room where PC Warren watched her like a hawk as she stood looking at him.

Tears rolled down Olivia's cheeks. She felt so alone. She realised as she stood there that she had subconsciously said goodbye to her brother properly when the accident first happened. She had been hanging on to a false hope since then. This shell of a body just looked like her brother.

'Love you,' she whispered. 'I'm so sorry.' Her shoulders heaved and she held a hand to her mouth to cover the sound of her wracking sobs, which seemed so loud in the quiet room. Unable to cope she turned and ran down the corridor and out of the front door.

Olivia ran. She didn't know where she was running to, but she needed to get away. Away from the cloying smell of the care home and the smell of the cottage that still smelt like the aftershave of her dead husband. She gulped in air and slowed down to a walk, breathing heavily, trying to calm herself down. She saw the beach and took the path down to it. It was deserted apart from a few dog walkers. She walked for a while and then sat on the sand, burying her face in her knees, and sobbed. She sobbed for her brother and sobbed for the boy who had just lost his one remaining parent.

Evening was falling and Olivia was still sitting on the beach. She was at a complete loss. Never before had she felt like she didn't know what she was doing. She felt like she was stumbling around in a dark room and couldn't see or feel anything. She felt alone in the world. Since their parents had died, Gil had always been her anchor. She genuinely had no idea what she was going to do, now it was just her. Tears of self-pity sprang from her eyes.

She stood up, feeling stiff and cold and watched the sea. She shivered. The air temperature had dropped, and her breath formed clouds in the air. She looked around. How long had she been out here? She trudged back along the beach still wondering what to do. The lights were on in Maggie's cafe and they looked warm and inviting. Olivia stepped inside and ordered a hot drink. She sat in the corner, nursing the mug and staring off into space.

* * *

Maggie had been out and had returned to the cafe about an hour before Olivia had come in. She had spotted Olivia on the beach and Maggie had recognised despair when she saw it, but knew Olivia well enough to leave her alone for a while.

When Olivia finally appeared, looking pale and wan, Maggie watched her surreptitiously from the kitchen and then made a quick decision.

'Hold the fort,' she said to one of her staff. 'I'm just popping over the road.'

Slipping out of the back door, she walked briskly across the road to the climbing centre. Mike was at the counter taking payment from some people and booking them another session. He thanked them and bid them goodbye, his face breaking out into a wide smile when he saw Maggie.

'Hey, Mags,' he said. 'You good?'

'Yes, my love, but Olivia isn't.'

Mike frowned. 'What?'

Maggie told him she had seen her on the beach sobbing and that she was in the cafe staring into a hot drink, looking terrible.

'Do you think she's OK?' Mike asked.

Maggie huffed. 'I'm *telling* you so you can go and blimmin' ask her,' she said, her hands on her hips. 'I think she needs a shoulder to lean on. Plus, I reckon your shoulder will be infinitely more preferable to mine. Go and see her.'

'What's this?' Foxy asked, dumping a cardboard box on the desk.

'Olivia's in bits over in the cafe,' Maggie said.

'That's your ex, right?' said Foxy. 'The pretty one.'

Mike looked embarrassed. 'Maggie thinks I should go and see what the matter is.'

'Wasn't there an accident out at the wind farm? Three people killed?' Foxy said. 'Didn't her husband work there?'

Mike stared at him. 'Seriously?'

'Yeah. It's not official or anything. I just heard some guys talking on the quayside from the shuttle boat when I was chatting to Will yesterday morning.'

'Christ,' Mike said.

'Better get over there. Polish up that armour,' Foxy said.

'I've got half an hour of shift left.'

'Go. Go on. See what's up with the lovely lady.'

Mike smiled. 'Cheers, Foxy.'

He shrugged his jacket on and walked over to the cafe.

'Hey, you,' he said, sliding into the seat opposite Olivia. He was shocked at her appearance. 'Ollie? What's up?'

Olivia raised her eyes from the cup she had been staring at and focused on him.

'Hi,' she said dully.

'I said, what's up?' he pushed, worried that she didn't seem particularly lucid.

'I…I…' She tried to get it out and then her eyes welled up with tears.

'Ollie?' Mike said, taking one of her hands. It was like ice.

'Gil's dead,' she sobbed.

'Oh God. I'm so sorry.' He moved to sit next to her and pulled her to him for a hug. 'Are you alright?'

'I don't know. Everything's changed now. I don't know what to do about anything,' she said in a small voice.

'What do you mean, everything's changed?'

'Brian's dead,' she said softly, staring at nothing, trance like again.

'What?'

'An accident,' she murmured. 'Funny really. I wished that he'd die the other week and now he has. Do you think I did that?'

Mike frowned at her. She wasn't making any sense. He'd seen her like this before after her parents had died in a skiing accident. She couldn't process it then, didn't know what to do or how to be. He stood up and pulled her hand.

'Come on. You're coming home with me. Food and something to warm you up. We need to talk this out.'

He pulled her up, still worried at her lethargic responses. He led her out of the door, and she went with him like an obedient child. As they walked to his flat, he noticed she was shivering and becoming more unresponsive. Her hands were like blocks of ice and she was trembling erratically. Her lips were tinged with blue. Arriving back at his flat, he gently pushed her up the stairs. He sat her on the sofa, went to the bathroom and ran her a hot bath.

When he came back, she was exactly where he had left her, staring into space. He pulled her up and helped her take her coat off.

'Come on. Hot bath for you, you're freezing.'

As he led her down the hall to the bathroom her teeth were chattering so loudly it reminded him of one of the little plastic wind-up sets of red and white teeth that kids played with.

He slipped off her shoes and socks, pulled her shirt and jumper over her head and eased her jeans down her legs, which were damp from sitting on the sand for so long.

'Ollie, can you manage the rest?' he asked, trying not to look as she stood there in her underwear.

Olivia didn't answer him, she just continued staring into space and shivering.

Mike tutted and unhooked her bra and slid her underwear off, trying to do the gentlemanly thing. He pushed her towards the bath, and she stepped in and sat down. The water and bubbles closed gently over her.

'Back in a minute,' he said. In the kitchen he went to the fridge and dragged out a dish of leftover pasta bake. He shoved it in the microwave and set it to heat up. He went to the bedroom and found a pair of warm tartan pyjamas. His mother had given them to him for Christmas a few years ago, despite his protestations. He grabbed a towel from the cupboard and stuck his head around the bathroom door.

'Ollie, don't fall asleep,' he said sternly as he watched her eyelids droop. He left her in the bath and set the pasta back on for another couple of minutes. He grabbed a warm pair of socks and an extra jumper.

Back in the bathroom he stood her up, helped her out of the bath and draped a towel around her shoulders. He rubbed her down like she was a small child before helping her into the pyjamas and the jumper. He shoved the woolly socks onto her feet.

Once she was dressed, he led her by the hand back into the kitchen and sat her at the table. He made her a cup of hot, sweet tea and put a bowl of pasta in front of her.

'Eat,' he commanded. 'Right now.'

Olivia picked at the pasta, eating mechanically. Mike watched her. Worried. She wasn't aware of anything. It was like she was in a trance. Concerned, he rang Foxy and asked his advice about whether to take her to hospital.

'You've warmed her up, fed her?' Foxy asked.

'Yup.'

'So put her to bed. Let her sleep. If you can't get her warm after a few more hours, then take her in. I reckon you've done everything right, mate. A lot of it is the shock, I reckon.'

'Thanks, Foxy.'

'No sweat. Take care.'

Mike went back into the kitchen. Olivia was staring into nothing, but the pasta was almost finished.

'Drink your tea, Ollie,' he said, and she picked up the mug and drank it down in one go.

'Come on.' He led her by the hand into the bedroom and threw back the duvet cover, helping her into bed. He tucked the duvet around her and clicked off the bedside light.

'Sleep for a bit,' he said and kissed her cold cheek and went back into the kitchen.

Mike finished the pasta and caught up on some emails for a while then decided to check on Olivia. He crept into the bedroom and saw she was fast asleep, in the same position as when he had put her to bed. He felt her hands. Still cold. He grabbed a blanket from the cupboard and draped it over her, tucking it around her.

* * *

Foxy was thoroughly enjoying dinner with Jesse and Doug. He'd turned up with Solo and two bottles of wine, which Jesse had happily grabbed and opened immediately. As usual, Solo settled himself down next to Brock, guarding the pack together. Erin arrived and they sat around chatting and teasing Doug before he produced his trademark chicken dish with a flourish.

Foxy was enjoying reconnecting with Erin, she was smart and sassy and teased him mercilessly, which he secretly enjoyed. He was standing by the counter opening another bottle of wine, when Jesse waved her wineglass at him and asked, 'So, what happened to you to warrant receiving Erin's ministrations?'

'Classified,' Foxy replied, smiling.

'What rubbish,' Erin said, chuckling. 'If you must know, he fell from a chopper, broke his leg and did his back in. He was out of action for a while.'

'Ouch.'

'How did that happen? Unlike you to fall out of anywhere I imagine,' Doug asked, amused.

'I didn't fall that far. I just fell onto rocks, that's what did it. I was training some newbies. Bloody idiots. One of them almost fell out of the chopper, and I dragged him back in. He was a gibbering idiot and tried to get away, in the scuffle to stop him falling out again, I went out of the door. I was clipped on, but the harness snapped. So down I went.' He shrugged. 'Stuff like that happens. Nasty break and I blew a disc in my back out.'

'Bet you were in a lot of pain,' Doug said sympathetically.

'Oh yeah, and then some.'

'Made him very grumpy,' acknowledged Erin.

'Yet now I'm sweetness and light, and almost never grumpy,' he declared, returning to the table. 'So why here, Erin? You could get a placement that offers you the big bucks surely, why take over a clinic?'

She looked rueful. 'I'm a bit sick of travelling if the truth be known. I just wanted a rest, somewhere I liked for a few months before I decide what I'm doing. I figure I had a few months to figure out where I go next. I loved this place when I did the contract at the hospital, and although I wasn't living here, I'd come when I could, so I figured I'd spend some proper time here.'

'Would you work for the forces again?' Jesse asked, standing and clearing plates.

'Maybe. I was offered a stint helping out doing rehab in Germany, but I don't know…'

'What don't you know?' Foxy asked.

She flicked a glance at Jesse and Doug who were stacking the dishwasher and getting dessert ready.

'I just don't know what I want to be doing. Germany, you know. It's hard. Some of the guys are so… broken. Anyway, tell me about you. The climbing centre looks impressive, you've done well setting that up.'

'Thanks. It's going great so far.'

'I heard…' She glanced at him quickly and then down at her wineglass. 'I heard about your daughter and Carla. I'm so sorry.' She reached out a hand and placed it over his, her thumb stroking his thumb joint. 'Are you OK? Must have been so hard.'

Foxy stared at her hand on his for a moment and then took a swig of wine. Suddenly he felt ridiculously emotional, blinking furiously, he managed a croaky response. 'Thanks. Yeah. It was. It is. Excuse me for a second.'

He got up and ducked out to the downstairs loo and stood for a moment, his hands resting on the sink. He splashed water on his face and stared at himself in the mirror.

'Get a fucking grip,' he muttered.

He opened the door to find Erin leaning against the wall.

'You OK?' she asked. 'Sorry, it was insensitive of me. Just wanted to check you were OK.'

'I'm good,' he said, easing past her.

'Well, sorry if I upset you.'

'You didn't. It's fine. Don't worry.' He walked back into the kitchen where Jesse was just delivering a large dish of dessert to the table.

'That's mine, what's everyone else having?' He grinned, sitting down again.

An hour, and a further two bottles of wine, later, Erin and Foxy said drunken goodbyes and strolled down the road.

'I'd like to see the climbing centre,' she said, looping her arm into Foxy's as they walked.

'Now?' he said. 'In the dark?'

She laughed. 'We could put the lights on, silly.'

'S'pose,' he agreed as they weaved their way along the road.

'Do you live above it?'

'I do.'

'Do I get a tour of that?'

He was casual. 'If you want.'

'Do you have coffee?'

'I do.'

'Well, we can have coffee then.'

'What the lady wants and all that, I'll try and be accommodating.'

'You're very obliging.'

'I am, aren't I?'

As they wandered down towards the harbour, Erin smiled.

'I see why this place has such a draw,' she said. 'The people are lovely, it's gorgeous to look at, the beaches are amazing, what more could anyone ask for?'

Foxy chuckled. 'I've learnt over the years that it's the simple things that matter.'

'I'm beginning to see that,' she mused.

'Here we are at my humble climbing emporium,' Foxy said, unlocking the front door. Solo pushed past to get inside and went to sit by the door leading up to the flat.

'Wow, this is amazing!' she said as Foxy flicked a few lights on.

He walked to the back of the centre and flicked the outside lights on to light up the massive climbing wall that reared up towards the castle.

'Now that's impressive,' she said.

'Why thank you,' he said, giving a mock bow. 'Now, if I recall, the lady required coffee.'

'That would be lovely.'

Foxy opened the door and gestured with a sweeping movement upwards. Erin peered up the staircase.

'Is this the way into your lair?' she said, laughing.

'It is.'

'I'd better brace myself then.'

Foxy had left a small table lamp on that gave the flat a warm soft glow. Solo got comfortable on his bed by the door to the balcony.

'Right, coffee,' Foxy said, standing in front of the machine.

'Yes please.' She came and stood next to him. 'This is nice. Very… you.'

Foxy turned to look at her and raised an amused eyebrow. 'Very me?'

'Uh huh.'

His eyes searched her face for a moment. The need to suddenly be close to someone almost overwhelmed him. He felt his heart quicken.

'Decaff or full strength?' he asked, gesturing to the coffee machine.

'Why would anyone bother with decaff?'

He shrugged as he continued staring at her. 'Some people think that full strength might keep them up all night.'

She moved closer to him, and he inhaled the scent of her heady perfume.

'That's not necessarily a bad thing,' she whispered. 'Being kept up all night.'

He raised an eyebrow. 'To be honest, my memory is a bit hazy there.'

She took the cup he was holding from his hand and put it gently on the counter. She leant up and wound her arms around his neck.

'Why don't I help you with that,' she said and kissed him.

Foxy's senses went into overdrive. The feel of a woman pressed against him, the sense of arousal and his need to be close to someone overwhelmed him. Fuelled by wine and abandoning all good sense, he kissed Erin deeply and allowed himself to be led to the bedroom.

CHAPTER 27

Hannah's first day on her new ward had gone from bad to worse. The sister had followed her around picking fault with everything and baby Lucas had been sent home too, so she didn't get to see him. She was bereft. Everyone was talking about the woman who had jumped off the roof.

The baby the woman had taken had been reunited with his parents and was in the baby unit with mild hypothermia, but was improving gradually. At the end of the day, the sister had summoned Hannah into her office and told her that unless she improved significantly, she would be sent back to the surgical ward. She had produced a list of all the things she felt Hannah needed to improve upon and had told her in no uncertain terms that she needed to 'up her game'.

Hannah left at the end of her shift, depressed, tearful and despondent. She sat in the car and looked at the list of things the sister had written. *Be more active, move faster, be nicer to the mums, get a uniform that fits properly, anticipate what's needed, don't always expect to be told, think for yourself. Take the initiative!*

She crumpled up the paper and hurled it across the car. 'Fucking bitch!' she screamed. 'Stupid fucking rude bitch!'

Starting the car, she drove around the one-way system towards the exit. All she wanted to do was to get home to her babies. She could be calm there, appreciated and loved. They loved her for who she was. She smiled as she thought of them. Hannah stopped at the barrier, and the sister walked into the car park. She rapped on Hannah's window, which was open a few inches.

'I wouldn't be smiling if I were you, Hannah,' she said waspishly. 'I've given you plenty to be thinking about. I'd be going home and spending my days off thinking about how I can improve. See you in a few days.'

Hannah's fingers curled around the wheel. She tried to push down the rage, but she felt it building. She slammed her foot down on the accelerator, shot out of the car park and drove down the lane. She pulled into a small layby to wait. Within minutes the sister's car passed her by, and Hannah followed her home.

She was fuming. What fucking right did that stuck-up cow have to tell her off like that? Who the hell did she think she was? Hannah watched the sister pull into a small lane and drive up it slowly. Following at a distance, she noticed a sign outside a cottage that offered bags of manure for free. She stopped the car, and opened the boot. She hefted two of the bags into the boot, and carried on. Slowly passing by Sister's house, she noted her car was on a hard standing area to the side, where it couldn't be seen directly from the house.

'Perfect,' she muttered. She carried on, then did a quick three-point turn and drove slowly back along the lane, switching off her headlights until she was as close to Sister's car as she could get.

She parked, opened the boot, dragged out a bag of manure and emptied it all over the car. To her delight, the sister had left the car unlocked so she gleefully opened the driver's door and emptied the other bag of manure into it.

'Job done,' she muttered. 'Teach you to fucking speak to me like that, you stupid fucking bitch.'

She climbed back into her car and drove home singing along to the radio cheerfully.

Hannah awoke to the knowledge that she had three days off work and that the sister would have found her car full of horse shit that morning. She giggled and snuggled under the covers, enjoying the sensation.

She had plans for the day. She was going to go to the police station and see if she could talk to the nice man about Anne. She was still missing. She'd called into Anne's on the way home again last night, and there was no answer, and she still wasn't answering her phone. Then she had some shopping to do. She roused herself, washed and dressed, and said good morning to all of her babies. She cooed over them for a while, then grabbed her handbag and left.

At the police station, she asked the person on reception for a word with Detective Miller and was delighted when he appeared a few moments later.

'Hannah, isn't it?' he said briskly, frowning slightly, a stack of files under his arm. 'You know we found the baby?'

'Yes. Yes. He's doing well too,' she said in what she hoped was a knowledgeable tone. 'I wanted to say, that… well… Anne appears to be missing.'

'Anne…' he said, clearly wracking his brains. 'That would be… Anne Ford. We saw her running across the car park on CCTV if I recall.'

'Yes. She's not at home or answering her phone…' Hannah trailed off as Steve looked at his watch. 'It's unlike her,' she added. 'I'm worried about her.'

'When was the last time you saw her?'

'The day she left the hospital. When we had a drink over lunch. I've been calling, been to her house, there's no answer either.'

Steve looked thoughtful for a moment. 'Do you have her mobile number?' he asked. 'I'll see if there's activity on that as a start.'

Hannah dug in her bag for her mobile and read out Anne's number.

'OK,' he said. 'I'll have a look.'

'Can you let me know? You know, if she's OK?' Hannah stammered, feeling dismissed. 'You'll need my number.'

He scribbled it down as she reeled it off. 'Oh, and I live at Flat 2, Harbour House. You know, opposite the bakery.'

'Right,' Steve said. 'Well, thanks for coming in. I'll be in touch.'

'Oh OK. Well. Good luck. Speak to you soon,' she said brightly as he swiped himself through the door back into the main area of the station.

Steve walked back around to behind the reception desk to watch Hannah head off across the car park.

'She's got a thing for you,' PC Warren announced dryly. 'I was watching her. Bet Kate's quaking in her boots.'

'Do us a favour and see what activity there is on this mobile number will you?' he said, handing over the piece of paper.

'How long for the mobile activity?'

'Last five days.'

'No problem. It'll take a while.'

* * *

Mike woke with a stiff neck from being asleep on the sofa. He tried to loosen off the muscles and groaned when he moved. He rubbed his eyes and noticed Olivia wrapped in a blanket sitting in the armchair opposite him, holding a mug of tea, watching him.

'Morning,' she said, looking amused.

'Hey,' he said, feeling embarrassed. 'How are you feeling?'

'Better, thanks,' she said. 'I think I need to thank you for last night.'

He raised an eyebrow. 'You think?'

She pulled a wry face. 'I don't really remember much about yesterday apart from Gil being dead.' Her eyes filled with tears again and rolled down her cheeks. 'It's all a bit of a blur.'

'Ollie, I'm so sorry,' he said. 'Tell me what happened.'

Mike had the day off, so once he had assured himself that Olivia was much better, he walked her home. As they turned into the lane where her cottage was situated, they saw a police car parked outside and a PC who Mike didn't recognise by the front door, talking into a radio.

'What's going on here?' Mike asked, approaching the PC.

'And you are?' the PC said.

'I live here,' Olivia said indignantly.

'Alright, Mike?' Jonesey said as he stepped out into the street. He turned his attention to Olivia.

'We've been trying to track you down. Neighbour called in that they heard the place being smashed up. Said they saw a white car and then noticed the door was wide open, so they called us.'

'What time was this?' Mike asked.

'Around five this morning.'

'What's happened in here?' Olivia asked, walking up the steps.

Jonesey stuck an arm out. 'It's trashed. Whole place. Forensics are in there.' He sucked in his cheeks. 'It's awful. They've ripped it apart.'

'Why?' Olivia was dumbfounded.

'Dunno. In my experience, I'd say they seemed to be looking for something.'

PC Garland walked out of the cottage. 'Mrs Baker,' he said. 'Remember me from yesterday? I think you have something that someone wants. They've come here looking for it.' His radio burbled and he walked away speaking into it.

'We've been trying to call you,' Jonesey said. 'To let you know.'

Olivia pulled her phone out of her pocket; the battery was dead. 'Oh,' she said. 'Can I at least plug this in?'

'One sec.' Jonesey disappeared for a moment and then reappeared. 'SOCO says you can use the kitchen – that's all done.'

Olivia ducked into the house and plugged her phone into the charger in the kitchen. Mike and Jonesey followed her in. A crime scene officer in a white coverall suit nodded to her as he walked past.

Olivia looked around. The kitchen cupboard doors were open, crockery was smashed, chairs were upended, the contents of the fridge had been raked out.

'What the hell?' Mike said, frowning.

Olivia's phone bleeped telling her she had a voicemail message, and she called it absent-mindedly while Mike and Jonesey picked their way around the kitchen.

She listened to a message from Brian's company telling her that they would be dropping off his personal possessions shortly.

The second message was Eli's school telling her Eli had gone missing from an away rugby match the day before. They had notified the police.

The final message was chilling.

'You have something of ours,' the voice said in a quiet tone. 'So now we have something of yours. You will give it to us, or the boy will die next. This is the final warning.'

At the end of the message, Olivia heard a small voice scream her name. Olivia made a small sound of distress and slumped to the floor.

'Ollie. Ollie.'

She heard her name being called urgently and realised she had fainted. Mike was kneeling on the floor next to her, his hand under her head, looking concerned.

'Ollie?' he repeated, looking closely at her.

Jonesey was holding Olivia's phone, replaying the messages.

'Your face went white as a sheet and then you passed out. Sorry, this sounded serious I thought it might be connected. I think we really need to get the Guv here,' Jonesey said.

He left the kitchen, his phone pressed against his ear, Olivia overheard him before he stepped outside. 'Guv, you need to get down here pronto…'

'Eli. They've got Eli.' Olivia sat up quickly and the room spun again.

'Careful,' Mike said, holding her arm steady.

'I'm OK. I need to stand up,' she said.

She stood and swayed slightly. Mike dragged over a chair.

'Sit,' he commanded.

Olivia put her head in her hands, feeling close to tears again. Mike dropped down on his haunches next to her and took her hands.

'Ollie, this is some heavy shit. This has to be connected to Dubai? You have to tell them what happened.'

She blinked. 'But I don't *know* what happened!'

'Well, you need to tell them what you can then.'

Jonesey reappeared with a carboard box. 'Some bloke just dropped this off.' He dumped it on the floor next to Olivia's chair. 'He said it was your husband's things.' He paused for a moment. 'Sorry and all that,' he said sheepishly.

Olivia looked down into the box and picked up Brian's phone. She switched it on and used her finger to access the phone and disabled the passcode. There were ten missed calls and a variety of texts showing as notifications. She scrabbled in the box to find the charger as it was showing a low battery.

Mike raised an eyebrow. 'Surprised he let you have access to his phone.'

'I did it one night when he was asleep. Only way to find out what was going on.'

She opened the texts and almost dropped the phone. There were pictures of Eli tied to a chair, wide-eyed and sweaty, eyes red from crying. The texts were giving a deadline to find the money.

'What money?' she muttered, scrolling through the texts. 'What money?'

Brian's phone rang suddenly, and she almost dropped it.

'H-hello?' she began.

A soft male voice spoke.

'Since this isn't Brian, I'm assuming this is the lovely wife.'

'Y-yes...' she stammered. 'Who is this?'

Mike grabbed the phone off her and put it on speaker, he then put his own phone on record.

The caller sighed heavily. 'Why is that husband of yours getting you to answer his phone? Is he frightened to speak to us?'

'He's dead,' Olivia said flatly. 'Accident at the wind farm.'

There was long silence.

'Then I am your new best friend,' the voice said. 'Brian owed us money... a lot of money.'

'I don't know anything about that.'

'Your brother did.'

'He wouldn't have known anything either.'

'Oh, but he did. He knew everything because Jade told him,' the voice said. 'Naughty little Jade. Naughty little Brian. Quite the pair they were. Hiding out in Dubai.'

'I don't know what you're talking about,' Olivia said desperately.

'I'm talking about a missing shipment and one hundred and fifty million pounds owing.'

'What shipment? Shipment of what?' she said, her voice rising in frustration.

'Well, well, well. Perhaps little wifey is clueless after all, or a very good actress,' the voice said.

'I don't know what you're talking about. I don't have any money. I don't know anything about the money,' she said. 'What shipment are you talking about?'

'Think on where that money is, little wifey. You have two days.'

'Wait. Eli. Where's Eli?'

'He's safe. We'll keep him safe.'

'He's a diabetic.'

'He's safe. For now.'

The call ended.

'Christ,' Olivia said tearfully, her head in her hands.

'Hello, everyone,' Steve said from the doorway, sipping a large coffee. He addressed Olivia. 'I think we need to have a chat down the station.'

Mike accompanied Olivia to the police station, and they were shown into an interview room. Steve arrived carrying some files.

'Right,' he said as he put down the files. 'Olivia, you're not under caution, we are just fact finding at this stage, but I do want to record this. That OK?'

Olivia nodded nervously. Steve rattled off the details for the recording.

'I need you to go through the events of the last few days, please. I need to get the timeline straight.'

Olivia took a deep breath. 'I took Eli back to school, the day before yesterday. Dropped him off.'

'Eli is your husband's son; he goes to boarding school?'

'Yes. He hates it.'

'Where is it?'

'Winchester.'

'So you took him back and then what? Came back here?'

'Yeah, it was a long drive.'

'How come his dad didn't take him? If you don't mind me asking?'

Her lips twisted. 'He saw it as a waste of a day.'

Steve pursed lips for a moment. 'OK. What did you do when you got home?'

'Went to bed. It was late.'

'Where was Brian?'

'He wasn't at home. I assumed he was working late.'

'Does he often do that?'

'He stays on the support ship sometimes.'

'OK, so you went to bed. The next day? What happened?'

'I got a knock at the door; it woke me up. It was a man from Brian's work, come to tell he had died the day before in an accident.'

'Do you know what sort of accident?'

'Rotor blade from the turbine fell onto the deck. Three people were killed.'

'I'm sorry.'

'Please. Don't be.'

Steve tossed a quick look at Mike, who raised his eyebrows.

'Then yesterday I got a call from my brother's care home to tell me there had been an incident.'

Steve consulted his notes. 'Is this The Pines?'

'Yes. My brother's room had been searched; a nurse beaten up. I think they tried to wake him up.'

'Tried to wake your brother up?'

'Yes, he was in a coma.' Tears rolled down Olivia's face. 'They… deprived him of oxygen.'

'I'm sorry.'

'He was pronounced dead a few hours after that, I think.'

Steve made a note to chase up the post-mortem results with Murphy. He knew there had been a suspicious death, but he hadn't made the connection between Olivia and the victim until now.

'What happened after that?'

'I don't really remember,' she said a little sheepishly. 'I lost the plot a bit. I ended up at Mike's yesterday. Then we went over to the cottage this morning and found it had been wrecked, and then I got the messages about Eli…'

Steve turned to Mike; eyebrows raised. 'You want to jump in?'

'So, Maggie saw Ollie on the beach yesterday. She said she'd been there nearly all afternoon. I found her at the end of shift, and she was cold, totally out of it. Just spaced out. In shock, I think, freezing cold. I warmed her up, fed her and put her to bed.'

'Nice of you.'

'Me and Ollie go way back,' Mike said. 'Check with Mags.'

'I will.'

Steve leant back in his chair. There was a knock at the door and PC Warren poked her head in.

'Guv, DI Scott's here.'

Steve beckoned, and she opened the door and gestured him in.

'Thanks, PC Warren. Do you mind rustling up some drinks, please?'

'Yes, Guv.'

Ross came in and settled himself in the chair next to Steve.

Steve said, 'This is DI Ross Scott from Cardiff. Ross here has been doing some digging on the Taos in Cardiff and I think we're just beginning to join the dots together here.'

Steve focused on Olivia.

'Olivia, I understand you were in Dubai? Tell us more about that.'

Olivia sighed. 'Gil got involved with a woman called Jade.'

'Jade Tao?' Steve asked, seeing pieces of a jigsaw sliding into place.

Olivia nodded. 'I don't think she was from Cardiff though. Gil met her in London. She'd got into some sort of trouble with her family. Something to do with her brother. I don't know the details. She found out something she shouldn't have and decided to take something of value, I think. I don't know what before you ask.'

'Go on.'

'One day Gil turns up in a state, keeps ranting on that we're in danger. He was terrified about something. Apparently, they'd threatened him and me too, trying to get to Jade.'

'Who are they?' Steve asked, knowing in his bones.

'Apparently it was Jade's family. The Taos. Gil wanted to run. He was worried about Jade; her brother was a psycho by all accounts. Kept threatening to kill her. So we ran to Dubai. Jade went to Qatar first, I forget why. She told Gil she had a friend there. She hid out in Qatar for a bit, then joined us after a while.'

'Why Qatar specifically? Just because of the friend?'

'No idea. We got to Dubai, settled in quite quickly. Everything was good. Jade appeared after a while and came to live with us. She introduced us to her friend Brian who was working out there. He'd also been in Qatar, I think. Me and him got along and one thing led to another. We always seemed to be together as a four, so we became a couple.'

'You got married.'

'Uh huh. After a time. I wasn't keen, but the way things are out there, it was easier to be, so we had a small ceremony and got married, yes,' she said, averting her eyes from Mike.

'Then what happened?'

'Then a guy from Qatar came looking for Jade. Followed by men from her family.'

'What did you do?'

'Gil and Jade, they panicked. I've never seen Jade like that. She was genuinely terrified. I kept saying, we can sit down and talk it out with them, but she wasn't having any of it. So we all ran.

'Brian was away at some seminar or something. We drove out of the city, hoping to get into the desert and hide in one of the villages there, but they were really serious. They kept coming. I'd never seen anything like it. It was like…' She searched for the right word. 'It was surreal, like something from a movie or something. Before long, it had turned into this mad car chase.' She gulped in air as she remembered.

'They were behind us in the car, shooting at us! So close. Relentless, trying to get to us. We were terrified. I don't think I've ever been so frightened. Then in the distance we saw it. This huge sandstorm, we knew we'd never escape it, so we hoped we'd drive through it. Jade screamed at me to go faster, so I did.'

She stared down at her hands and said quietly, 'I didn't see it. I didn't see the rocks.' Her voice shook. 'I hit this outcrop of rocks buried in the sand, I must have been doing eighty? Ninety? Maybe. It felt like it completely ripped the chassis off. The car sort of flew up in the air and turned and then rolled and rolled. I remember being hit in the face with stuff flying about in the car as we spun and then nothing.'

'Go on,' murmured Steve.

'I don't recall much about it,' she said, meeting Steve's eyes. 'I remember hearing noises, men's voices and the sound of a car. When I woke up, me and Gil were in hospital and there was no sign of Jade. I never saw Jade again after that.' She gulped. 'Gil… He never recovered.'

'I'm sorry,' Steve said. 'What were these men after?'

'I don't know!' she cried. 'They never told me. Said it was best I didn't know. Safer that way. That I had to trust them. But someone's got Eli now and I don't know anything! How am I going to get him back?'

'Tell me what they said on the phone, I only caught the last part.'

'I recorded it,' Mike said, dragging his phone out of his pocket. He laid it on the table and pressed play.

Steve listened.

The call ended and Ross motioned for Mike to play it again. When it had finished Ross spoke to Olivia.

'It seems they think you have one hundred and fifty million pounds, and they want it. In two days.'

***

Foxy had awoken with a bit of a wine hangover. He lay for a moment thinking about the previous evening and his eyes flicked over to see the curve of Erin's naked back. Her hair cascaded over the pillow, and he could smell her perfume lingering.

Memories of the previous evening flashed across his mind. He had enjoyed the night with her very much, the presence of a warm body next to him had soothed his soul. This morning though, he thought about Sophie and how he felt about her and realised that he was being unfair to Erin. He felt incredibly guilty for sleeping with her; like he had betrayed Sophie.

His rational internal voice had interrupted his stream of consciousness and told his musings that he was a free man and could do what he liked. Particularly as he had made a decision that he wasn't going to tell Sophie how he felt, so in reality, he was free to do what he wanted.

Next to him Erin stirred and then stretched languorously like a cat. She rolled over to look at him.

'Good morning,' she said.

'Good morning to you.'

She rubbed her face. 'Ow. I have a hangover.'

He smiled. 'I have a touch of wine head too.'

She propped herself up on her elbows. 'I need coffee, food and two paracetamol, then I'll be all set.'

He eyed her with amusement. 'You could do with one of Maggie's heart attack in a roll. Superb hangover fodder.'

Her eyes sparkled. 'What on earth is that?'

'Bacon, egg, sausage, portobello mushroom and a hash brown. All in a bun.'

She closed her eyes in ecstasy. 'That sounds amazing.'

'It is.'

'Let's do it. Blimey, this place is increasing in its appeal by the minute.'

He raised an eyebrow. 'Is it now?'

She nodded, her lips twitching with amusement. 'Yeah. Amazing place, amazing beach, nice locals, accommodating climbing wall owners that aren't too shabby in bed, great cafes—'

'Hold up a minute… back up a bit there. Not *too* shabby in bed? What the hell sort of comment is that?'

She turned to face him. 'OK, maybe I'll use the word… proficient.'

'Proficient? *Proficient*? It wasn't a fucking bike test,' he spluttered. 'Shit. If I'm not too shabby, no scratch that, only *proficient*, in the sack, then I must be rustier than I thought.'

She bit her lip. 'Didn't think you were the sensitive type.'

'A man has standards he needs to adhere to,' he said loftily. He turned on his side to face her fully. 'I think we need to work on what I need to do to go from proficient to bloody excellent.'

She grinned widely. 'I'm game if you are.'

'Well, breakfast is going to have to wait,' he growled, grabbing her.

CHAPTER 28

Ross opened a file in front of him, scanned it and then looked at Olivia.

'How much did you know about Brian's life before he went to Dubai?'

Olivia shrugged. 'Not much, he was quite tight-lipped about it, he always just wanted to have fun, muck about. Nothing like he was when we got here. He changed just after the accident.' She was quiet for a moment. 'He used to work in Cardiff, I think, but don't quote me on that. I think he said the job went sour, then he had a messy break-up, so he got a job as an engineer on the wind farm at Hatta. He always said he just needed to get away.' She looked between Steve and Ross. 'Why do you ask? And how is this helping Eli?'

'How did he know Jade?'

She looked blank. 'I have no idea. It never came up. It was always a thing that they knew each other. I never questioned it or thought to.' She looked at Steve through narrowed eyes. 'What aren't you telling me?'

Ross cleared his throat. 'We have reason to believe that your husband was a talented "runner".'

Olivia looked confused. 'A what?'

Steve held up his hands. 'I think I need to start at the beginning. A few weeks back there was a man found dead, in the woods. He had been murdered in a certain way. Anyway, to cut a long story short, this man worked for the Tao organisation—'

'Tao *organisation*?' interrupted Olivia. 'As in Jade Tao?'

'As in the Tao organisation, one of the most powerful organised crime firms in London and Cardiff.'

'What?' Olivia said faintly. 'Jade was part of this? And these people have Eli?'

'This man who was found dead, Harry Daly, he spent his time working for them, looking to recruit runners.'

'I don't know what a bloody runner is,' snapped Olivia.

'A runner is someone who runs drugs from one place to another. In some cases, one continent to another, or country.'

Olivia blinked. 'Are you saying that *Brian* was a runner?'

'I am.'

'A runner for an organised crime family?' she said faintly. 'Running how? Where? What?'

'So far, we think running drugs from the UK to other countries, using the cover of wind turbine parts and components.'

'I've never heard anything so ridiculous,' Olivia said in disbelief.

'It's quite clever, really,' Ross said. 'Fantastic green credentials. Huge plant to transport, easy to stuff with drugs. From what we hear, one last shipment left the UK en route to Qatar and never showed up the other end. The Taos seem to be of the opinion that Brian went bad, and him and Jade took the shipment *and* part of the payment.'

Olivia burst out laughing. 'You have to be kidding! The man could barely make a sandwich! Let alone come up with some James Bond-type plan like this.'

'I think you're underestimating him. From what we hear, he was quite the talent,' Steve said.

Ross grunted in agreement. 'We've heard from a variety of sources that he was quite the innovator in how to get drugs out of the country and into others.'

'I just can't get my head around it.' Olivia exhaled heavily. 'I really didn't know him at all, did I?'

Steve and Ross glanced at each other. 'We've got the major issue that they have Eli. They want their money.'

'But I don't have it!' Olivia said tearfully. She sobbed again, her face in her hands. 'I just don't know what to do!'

Steve turned to Ross. 'Do you know if the Tao's work independently within cells or groups or is it all driven from above?'

Ross frowned. 'Now Danny's not around – Christ knows where he is – and Lily is rumoured to be dead, I'm not sure.' He turned back to Olivia. 'Now's the time to tell us what you know, or the likelihood is that you won't see Eli again.'

'I don't know! I don't know!' moaned Olivia. 'I can't bear the thought that he's alone and scared.'

Ross sighed. 'OK. Let's come at this a different way. The shipment was cocaine. High grade. Uncut. That makes it expensive and highly desirable. There was a lot of it. It was packed in with turbine components, destination Qatar. The boat arrived, but the shipment wasn't found. There are a lot of people who are very unhappy about it. The Taos who sent it and the Qataris who put up the money.'

Olivia's eyes were wide. 'I don't know what to do.' She whispered. 'I just don't know what to do. How do I get Eli back?'

'We need to look into Brian's affairs,' Steve said. 'We'll obviously go through his phones, computer, and see if there's anything at all that might give us an idea of who took Eli, or who might have been dealing with about that shipment' He thought for a moment. 'We need to find out from Interpol if they know of any big deals that went down around that time. That might help.'

'I'll get onto them,' Ross said. 'I've got a contact there. I can be here for a couple of days, the more insight I can get into this the better. I'll go through everything to see if there are any leads.'

'OK,' Olivia said. 'I've got no idea what to look for.'

'I'll get started,' Ross said, standing. 'I'll take you back to your cottage and we'll go from there.'

Steve's phone rang.

Ross waved Steve away. 'Mate, I've got this, you crack on. We'll catch up later. I'll go with Olivia.'

Steve stepped outside the interview room and answered his phone. He was pleased to hear Doug's voice, the skipper of the lifeboat.

'Hey, mate! How are you?' he asked, knowing Doug only usually called in office hours with concerns for the police.

'Can you talk?' he asked. Steve heard the wind buffeting Doug's phone.

'Yeah. What's up?'

'I've got the strangest thing here, hence the call.'

'Oh?'

'We were called out to a shout, some twat in a speedboat was racing around the wind farm; said he thought he saw a guy on one of the platforms, waving at him. Said he looked crazy, so he didn't want to stop. We turn up and there's a guy who's been dumped there, food, chemical toilet, water, you name it. Practically gibbering with craziness. Stinks to high heaven. Says he's being kept prisoner and he can't swim!'

'He with you now?'

'Yeah, going on about being kidnapped. He's not making any sense. Looks like he's been there a while.'

'Got a name?'

'Danny Tao.'

Steve swore softly. 'Shit. This guy is serious business. Don't radio this in. Take him to the lifeboat station. Don't let him leave. I'm going to send two uniforms to take him back to the station for his own safety.'

'That serious?'

'That serious. Thanks for the heads up.'

'We're about ten minutes out.'

'I'll send Jonesey.'

'See you, mate.'

Steve ended the call and bumped into Jonesey in the corridor.

'Get Garland,' he said quietly. 'Two of you go down to the lifeboat station, pick up the guy they're bringing in. I want this hush-hush. Blue lights there and back. I want him straight into a cell. Secure. Comprendo?'

'Absolutely.'

'No stopping at Maggie's for a sarnie.'

'Really? But it would only take a min—'

'Nope. There and back. No stops.'

'Guv,' Jonesey said sulkily.

'Now. GO.'

Steve watched Jonesey hurry off. He stuck his head back into the interview room and beckoned Ross outside.

'Danny Tao has just turned up,' he said quietly. 'I've got uniform bringing him back here into custody. I'm off to see Mickey. If they're taking over the Tao empire, they might know who has the boy. It's a long shot.'

'OK. I'll start trying to find some pointers to the shipment or the cash.'

'Good luck trying to find something.'

Steve headed towards the custody suite to brief the custody sergeant about the impending arrival of Danny Tao and then walked out to his car.

As he drove, he pondered. He wondered whether to tell Mickey that he had Danny Tao or not. Perhaps he'd get as much from Danny as he could and then see. He was still Mickey's son. Quite how Mickey felt about that he didn't know. He stopped at the gates and waved at the camera. The gates opened for him.

Stanley stood at the door waiting for him.

'Stanley,' Steve said, nodding.

'Steve.'

'How's Pearl?'

'Mending,' Stanley said, lumbering after him.

Ivan, Alexy and Mickey were sitting at the large table in Mickey's kitchen. Ivan and Alexy were drinking vodka, but Mickey was on coffee. Steve caught the end of their conversation.

'This man. He is like ghost. He see me and then go.' Ivan made a sweeping gesture with his hand. 'I cannot find him.' He sighed. 'This… it worry me, very much.'

Alexy nodded sagely. 'You say he return to shop of watch man. Perhaps he look for way to find here?'

Mickey snorted. 'It's not rocket science, is it? People know we're in this area, all they need to do is scout around for a while and they'll find us. It's not some big mystery. They just need to invest time and effort.'

'We should go. To be safe,' Alexy said.

'No,' Mickey said firmly. 'I'm not running from him.' He glanced at Alexy and Ivan. 'I want to look him in the eye before I kill him.'

'Gentlemen,' Steve said as he came into the room.

Ivan muttered something unintelligible. Alexy spoke quietly in his ear, and he melted off to another room.

'We are popular,' Mickey said. 'What now?'

Pearl appeared and she was looking better. 'Hello, darling, thought I saw your car,' she said. 'Is Mickey being nice to you?'

'Of course not.' Steve grinned.

'What do you want?' snapped Mickey.

'I have a bit of a problem. Involving a small boy who's been taken.'

'Well don't be looking at me for it,' Mickey growled. 'We don't mess with kids here.'

'He's been taken by someone in the Tao organisation.' Steve paused. 'Well, I assume it's them.'

'Darling, sit down and tell us,' Pearl said. 'I can't abide anyone doing anything to children so we will help wherever we can.'

Steve outlined what he knew, from the missing shipment and money, to the connection to the dead man in the woods.

'So she doesn't have the money or the shipment?' Pearl asked.

'Says she has no idea.'

'Oh, poor thing. And that poor boy,' Pearl said.

'I'll get on it,' Mickey said. 'I need to be resurrected anyway. Perhaps now is a good time to start resetting the rules and make an appearance.'

'Perhaps it is,' Steve said in agreement. 'Look, soon as you can, I need news of the boy. He's a diabetic too, so he's at high risk. I'll see myself out.'

He turned towards the door and saw Maxim, Ivan and Stanley standing in the hall, checking ammunition in each of their handguns.

'Come on, guys,' Steve said, frustrated. 'I don't want to be seeing that.'

'Sorry,' Stanley said. 'Here, I'll get the door. Ivan put that in the car?'

Stanley opened the door and Ivan brushed past Steve to step out. Stanley joked with Steve as they grew level.

'Suppose you'll be wanting to see our firearms certificates?'

Steve laughed and Mickey appeared behind Maxim.

'Steve, I need a name if you can from the source who was nicked in Cardiff. That's a starting point. They'll have an idea of who might have taken the boy and might be dealing with this.'

'I'll see what I can do.'

In the open doorway, Ivan turned to say something to Stanley, there was the sound of a large pop and a bullet entered Ivan's head from the rear. It exited through his left eye, burying itself in the wall next to Steve. Ivan crumpled to the floor. Steve and Stanley were covered in a mist of brain and blood matter. Steve looked in horror at Ivan's fallen body.

'Get down!' Steve yelled.

He dropped to the floor, pushing Stanley out of the way and frantically looked around for the shooter. He turned to look through the house, down the hallway, and saw Alexy usher Pearl away to another room, producing a gun as he did.

Another bullet whizzed by and hit Stanley in the arm causing him to drop his gun, which skittered over towards Steve. Maxim, swearing loudly, had grabbed a different gun from somewhere and returned fire. Mickey disappeared into the kitchen to get his own gun – a collection of which was hidden under the kick boards around the kitchen.

Steve risked a look and raised his head slightly to see over the prone form of Ivan. There was a man in the garage opposite. He fired again and the bullet whizzed past Steve's ear, grazing his cheek.

'Garage,' Steve yelled.

Maxim stood in the doorway and opened fire towards the garage. Maxim hit the man dead centre three times. Although the man stumbled backwards, he still managed to produce another gun and return fire. The semi-automatic flooded the doorway with bullets, catching Maxim in the stomach. He dropped to the floor groaning, his hands over his stomach.

'FUCKER!' Mickey screamed running up the hall, shouldering a semi-automatic weapon and spraying the garage with fire. The man was nowhere to be seen.

There was silence for a moment and the smell of blood, cordite and smoke filled the air. Steve's heart was thumping so loudly he was sure everyone could hear it. He scrambled forward to try and see what was going on. Dragging out his phone, he dialled the station and left it on speaker on the floor in front of him.

'This is DCI Miller,' he shouted over the gunfire as it started again. He tried to reach the gun that Stanley had dropped, drawing his hand back as a bullet buried itself into the floor next to where his hand had been.

'I'm at Mickey Camorra's house, there is a gunman and casualties. I need an armed response team and ambulance.' Steve couldn't hear the tinny response over the sound of gunfire.

He pushed the phone away and he saw the shooter come out from the garage and stride towards the front door, shooting back at Mickey who was ducking behind the door and intermittently returning fire.

A bullet whizzed past Steve's temple and he felt instant pain and hot blood rush down his face. He raised a hand to his face and looked at his bloody hand in disbelief.

'Your time's up, Camorra,' the man roared and opened fire again, this time catching Mickey in the right shoulder. 'You'll pay for everything you ever took from me.'

The bullet spun Mickey around and he slipped on the bloody floor, falling onto his side. His right arm was useless. He scrabbled around trying to get his gun up to return fire as the man approached the doorway.

The shooter had blood pouring from his arm, it was dripping down his hand, but he didn't seem to notice, his focus was entirely on Mickey. His eyes were narrowed and the look on his face was one of pure malevolence. The shooter stepped over Ivan's prone form and viewed Maxim dispassionately. He kicked his gun away and stepped towards Stanley who was trying to reach his gun. The man hadn't looked to the right of the doorway where Steve was, waiting for his chance.

* * *

Ex-commander Graham Curtis looked down at Mickey on the floor. He placed a foot over Mickey's hand which was trying to reach his gun.

'Mickey Camorra, I'm going to take everything you have. You owe me for nearly thirty years. Everything you have, should have been mine. Everything. In a moment, I'm going to finish everyone here, then me and your Mrs are going to have a little fun, then I'm going to gut her like a pig. I can't decide whether to make you watch or whether to end you now.'

He tilted his head. 'I think I'll end you now.' He produced a handgun and pointed it at Mickey.

'Reap what you sow, Mickey. May you rest in hell.'

The sound of a single bullet being fired rang out loudly in the hallway.

Pearl's scream was blood curdling.

CHAPTER 29

Hannah was enjoying her shopping spree. She had told herself that she could have a special treat and she had popped into the Loafing About Bakery and bought a box of six small cream cakes of differing types. This was her reward for working so hard and starting in a new ward, she told herself. The town was fairly quiet, which she always enjoyed, and she looked in various windows of shops as she strolled about. She was walking back up towards her flat from the harbour when she saw it.

The pram was parked outside the coffee shop on the pavement. In the window, two women were sat chatting and showing pictures to each other on their phones. Hannah realised with a shock that the baby had been left outside. The baby in the pram was releasing strong, very loud, angry wails.

Unable to help herself, Hannah approached the pram and realised with a stab of joy that this was baby Lucas. His eyes were wet, his face red and screwed up tightly as he cried. His little hands were tight fists, and his legs were kicking angrily. He looked freezing, he had no socks on, and his hands felt ice cold to the touch.

'Hey, hey, hey!' Hannah said, leaning over him. He stopped crying instantly and gulped a few times then suddenly gave her a gummy smile.

Something shifted in Hannah. She stretched her hand out and he grasped it tightly and then looked into her face and gave her another gummy smile.

'Hello, gorgeous boy,' she crooned. She risked a look into the cafe and saw the mother and her friend with their backs to the window chatting to someone. She remembered the useless bitch from the hospital. Hannah made a decision. She checked around quickly, saw no one else looking her way, let the brake off the pram and wheeled it quickly up the hill.

* * *

Viv liked her kitchen makeover very much. The paint colour was a huge improvement, and she had taken full advantage of Nate in DIY mode and made a few other changes. She had been rearranging some of the cupboards and sorting out the remains of some of the moving boxes when she had first heard the baby crying.

She closed her eyes and breathed deeply. She went through her mental checks. She listened again. There it was. Still there. She moved to the window, which looked out onto the street, and saw a pram outside a cafe further down the road. She realised that the crying was probably coming from there. Relieved, she told herself off and carried on with the kitchen and turned up the radio.

Nate arrived back with a bag full of shopping.

'Can you believe someone has left a poor baby parked on the street down there? It's bawling its eyes out, poor little thing,' he announced, dumping the bag. He pulled Viv towards him, kissed her firmly and shoved his cold hands up her jumper.

'Oi! Bloody hell your hands are cold!' she said, jumping away.
'Ah yes. Cold hands, warm heart.' He grinned. 'Come here.'
'No!'
'Yes. I insist!'
'Nope.'
He tilted his head. 'You OK?'
She risked a look out of the window. The pram was still there. She looked back to him, wondering whether to say anything.
Nate narrowed his eyes. 'Wait. You heard the baby crying, didn't you? Did you wonder again?'
She nodded and sagged with relief when he pulled her in close to him.
'Jonathan said to do your checks. Didn't he?'
'Yes.'
'So you did your checks and the baby was still crying?'
'Uh huh.'
He kissed the top of her head. 'It's OK. It's just gonna take time.'
'I know.' She snuggled in close, seeking his solidity. Without warning he shoved his cold hands up her jumper again.
'You bugger!' she gasped, breaking free and darting out of the kitchen.
'Come here, wife!' Nate demanded, a twinkle in his eye. 'I have hands to warm up!'

Nate and Viv were wrapped around each other in the lounge in front of the fire when the doorbell rang shrilly, interrupting their post-coital doze.
'Shit, who the bloody hell is that?' Nate said, struggling back into his jeans and chucking his jumper over his head. He glanced at Viv, who was wriggling back into her jeans. 'Expecting your weekend boyfriend?'

'I put him off for a couple of days. Won't be him.' She grinned as the doorbell rang again.

Nate strode to the door and opened it. A young male police officer was on the doorstep looking cold in a bright yellow jacket.

'Ah. Good evening, sir,' the PC said. 'We're just conducting door-to-door enquiries.'

'What's the matter?' Nate asked, looking past the PC down the street to where there was a police car parked across the road.

'A baby has been taken from outside the cafe down the road.'

'Not the baby I saw in the pram earlier. Crying its head off, left outside in the cold?'

The PC's eyes widened. 'What time was this, sir?'

Nate turned. 'Viv! That baby we heard has been taken! What time did we hear it?'

Viv approached the door and smiled at the PC. 'It was out there for a while.' She frowned. 'Probably about three o'clock? But it was crying for a long time.' She looked at Nate. 'You came home about half three, quarter to four?'

The PC scribbled frantically. 'You didn't see anything suspicious?'

'With respect, the only suspicious thing is the sort of mother who would leave their baby outside a cafe in the cold for that long,' Viv said angrily.

'Do you recall when you stopped hearing the baby?' the PC asked.

'When my husband got home, we went to the back of the house. Can't hear much from there.'

'Right,' the PC said. 'If I could just have your details for a follow up?'

* * *

Steve sat in the back of an ambulance as Liz the paramedic fussed over a temporary dressing for his head. He was trying to calm his thudding heart and stop his hands from trembling. It had been a while since he had been so up close and personal to a gunfight.

'Plastic surgeon should be doing this,' she muttered. 'It's a deep wound, needs proper stiches.'

He bravely pasted on a smile and tried to sound normal.

'It'll be fine. Stop fretting,' Steve said. 'I'll look roguish with a scar.'

'I think your face has taken enough of a beating lately,' Liz said. 'This is the second time I've had you in the back of my rig lately.'

'Don't let Kate hear you talk that way,' Steve quipped.

'Stop it.' She slapped his arm playfully. 'I mean it. Too many near misses and then it becomes a hit and not a miss.'

'Nag, nag, nag,' Steve said. 'We done?'

'That'll do for now,' Liz said. 'But you need to get it sorted.'

'Refer to my previous comment,' he said, standing up. 'Thanks, Liz.'

Back in the house, Steve met Alexy in the kitchen watching the crime scene techs process the scene with a watchful eye.

'Alexy,' Steve said. 'You doing OK? I'm so sorry about Ivan.'

Alexy took a moment to compose himself. 'I am the A of the OK as you say,' he said sadly. 'But Ivan was my most bestest cousin. I will be missing him.' He sighed. 'You, my friend, are brave man. I am thinking Mickey owe you big debt.'

'Just doing my job,' Steve said, thinking it would be quite likely that he might lose his job from this shitstorm.

'In my country, if you save life. That person has to repay debt. It is the way. I am thinking Mickey need to be a bit nicer? No?'

Steve gave a bark of laughter. 'I'm not expecting miracles, Alexy. Right, I need to get back. I'm going to go and find out how they all are.'

'Tell them I have everything in the hand here,' he said.

Steve tried not to smile. 'Will do.'

Steve was exhausted. He had been through a gruelling few hours of post-incident investigations. It had been recognised and supported by the myriad of statements collected from Mickey, Alexy, Maxim and Stanley that Steve had acted lawfully to protect them, and was also acting in self-defence when he had killed Graham Curtis with a single shot.

Steve was starving and operating on very little sleep. Everything hurt. He just wanted to lie down and sleep for at least twenty-four hours. He opened the door to his office, slammed it behind him and slumped into his chair, yawning widely. He picked up his phone and rang Pearl.

'Darling,' she answered. 'You are rapidly becoming my hero.'

He chuckled. 'Christ don't tell Mickey that, I won't live to see another day. Just checking in. How are they all? And more to the point, are you hanging in there?'

'*Such* a darling man. Maxim is in surgery, but they aren't too worried. Stanley's sitting here next to me, his arm is all sorted, and Mickey is having the bullet removed and something about a clavicle.'

'Alexy says to tell you it's all under control.'

'Poor Ivan.'

'Do you need anything, Pearl?'

She sighed deeply. 'I need some peace, Steve. It feels like it's been a constant battle lately, what with Nathan White and now this. Perhaps someone is trying to tell me to give this game up and do something else.'

'Pearl,' Steve scolded, 'you'd be bored senseless within an hour, and you know it.'

She gave a small laugh. 'Maybe you're right. Look, I need to go, the surgeon's here, darling. Speak soon.'

'Bye, Pearl. Go carefully.'

Steve ended the call and closed his eyes for a moment. He was just drifting off when the door swung open and Jonesey appeared.

'Been looking for you!' he said. 'Jesus! What's happened to your head?'

Steve tried to calm his thudding heart from being jolted awake by Jonesey. 'You didn't hear?'

'Hear what? I've been doing door to door in town down by the harbour.'

'Why?'

'Baby stolen from outside a cafe—'

'Christ. Which cafe?' Steve demanded.

'The Fat Gannett. The mother left the baby outside in his pram and turned her back. Then the pram was gone. No one saw anything. She'd only just come out of hospital too. Day before we were there.'

'What? When was this?'

'This afternoon. Where've you been?'

'Shoot-out at Mickey and Pearl's. You didn't hear?'

'Shit! Ooh, while I remember, Warren was looking for you, something about some phone data,' Jonesey said.

'Where's Warren now?'

'Reception desk.'

Steve picked up the phone. 'PC Warren,' he said. 'You have something for me?'

'Yes, Guv, that mobile phone data for Anne Ford came through about quarter of an hour ago. I'm just looking at it.'

'What's it saying?' he said with an air of desperation.

'Phone records are showing that it's been at the address the whole time.'

'Sure?'

'Yes. Since the early hours of the 14th, where we knew she left the hospital. Phone shows as being at her home address ever since.'

'Thanks.' Steve ended the call.

'With me, Jonesey,' he said. 'Get Garland.'

They arrived at Anne's address, parked and walked around the small house. Steve knocked loudly, he lifted the letter box flap and heard the sound of voices. Knocking even more loudly, he called out.

'POLICE.'

He continued to peer through the letter box and saw some movement in the hallway approaching the door. It swung open and a woman wrapped tightly in a duvet stood there, leaning weakly against the door jamb. She looked terrible, pale skin, hollowed eyes with lank, greasy hair.

'Hi,' she said weakly. 'What's happened?'

Steve introduced himself. 'This is a welfare call, Madam. Your friends and work colleagues are concerned for you. Are you alright?'

She sagged further against the door. 'I've had something like flu. I've felt so awful I haven't even been able to get out of bed. My phone was downstairs. I just couldn't even make it down the stairs. I've only managed to get upright about an hour ago.'

'Do you need an ambulance?'

'No. I think it's just bad flu.'

'Well, as long as you're OK. Can we call anyone for you to help out?'

She shook her head. 'It's fine. Thanks. When you live alone it's one of those things you have to deal with. I'll be up and about soon.'

* * *

Hannah sat in the chair, feeling the happiest she had felt in a long time. She felt the warmth of baby Lucas against her breast. He was happy and content and sleeping soundly. She had fed him, bathed him and wrapped him up warm in the clothes she had borrowed from her other babies. She stared at his small face as he slept. Perhaps this was what it was supposed to be like? she wondered. Was she supposed to feel like this? She felt a pull of something, deep inside of her, but she didn't know what it was. It was like an ache, but not pain. She didn't know.

Raising her hand, she admired the large diamond engagement ring on her finger. She enjoyed how it looked and sparkled when she moved her fingers. She imagined the handsome detective turning up at her flat and presenting it to her, asking her to marry him. She'd put it away safely in a moment, but she enjoyed the weight of it. Plus, she liked to indulge in the small fantasies about a good looking man professing undying love and giving it to her.

She'd heard her doorbell rung repeatedly and seen the police up and down the street. She knew they were looking for him. She pulled him tighter to him. Well, it was too late. That useless fucking bitch had forfeited any chance she had to keep him. He was hers now, and she would be a proper mother. Not like that fucking silly bitch.

Lucas grunted and moved, and Hannah realised in her anger she had been squeezing him hard. She shushed him gently and kissed his head and rocked him back to sleep. He was hers now. No one else's. She deserved it. She'd earnt it.

She had finally heard from Anne, who had confessed to feeling ill and not being able to get out of bed. She said the police had been around and Hannah admitted to asking them for help. Anne said, now she was up and able to cook for herself, she was feeling much better. They had chatted for a while, Hannah filling her in on the poor lady whose baby had died and how the handsome detective had saved the baby, but the woman had jumped off the roof.

She purposefully hadn't told Anne about her taking baby Lucas, she wasn't sure how Anne would react, so she kept it quiet.

They had giggled as they discussed what a bitch the sister on the ward was and Anne had said she was going back to work in a few days, but she wasn't looking forward to it. Hannah had repeatedly apologised for getting the police involved when she couldn't find her, but Anne had said she was very touched that someone had cared enough to do it. She'd got quite tearful at that point and had said she was glad to have Hannah as a friend because she had never felt quite as lonely as she had in the past week. Anne said she was feeling better every day and was planning to head out maybe the next day to get some fresh air. They said goodbye, promising to talk soon, and Hannah hurried off to the large cupboard and got Lucas out. She had put him in the laundry basket in there in case he kicked off while she was on the phone. She settled him back in the room with all the other babies and set about tidying up her flat.

* * *

There was a frustrated, tired trio at Olivia's cottage. Olivia and Mike had tried to sort the chaos a little, while Ross had busied himself collecting phones and laptops – anything that might provide some evidence of Brian's activities.

Before sending them to be analysed, Ross had been through both of Brian's phones and had found nothing that meant anything to him at all. The same with his computer. All he found was that Brian had been fond of online gambling and on occasion, rough porn. He'd bagged them all up and sent them to the station.

'Anything?' Olivia said as she went through some more of Brian's papers from his briefcase and desk.

'Nothing that I can see,' Ross said. 'Let's think about this a different way. After the accident, what happened to all your things? Your brother's and Jade's things?'

Olivia thought for a moment. 'Brian's company sent them all over. Part of the relocation package. They're in the loft now, I think. When Brian came with Eli, he shoved a load of junk up there.'

'Guess we're going in the loft then.'

Ross went up to the loft and found the shipped boxes, right next to the loft hatch opening, where they had been clearly shoved. He passed them down to Mike so they could go through them. They took them into the kitchen and Olivia opened each one until she found a box that contained papers.

'Maybe there'll be something in here,' she said, scanning the papers as she pulled them out.

After a while of scanning each one, she said, frustrated, 'This is just junk. Old statements, post, rubbish. There's nothing here.' She yawned.

'We've been at this for hours,' Mike said, mirroring her yawn. 'I'm gonna call it a day soon. Why don't we get a few hours kip and then you guys start again early?'

'Good idea,' said Ross. 'I'm pretty shattered. Let's meet here in the morning and start again. You might think of something in the night.'

His phone rang, interrupting them, and he saw it was Steve. He gestured that he'd take it outside.

'Hi, Steve. Got anything?' he said, stepping out and closing the door behind him.

'Not yet. What a day. I walked into a shoot-out, and I've been dealing with that.'

'You alright?'

'Few scratches and three hours post-incident grilling.'

'You shot someone?'

'It was me or him, I reckon.'

'Jesus!'

'Any luck there?' Steve asked.

'Squat diddly.'

'Look, Mickey may be able to help with whoever might have taken Eli. I need a couple of names of the guys dealing with the drugs side of things for the Taos. Will your bloke give that up?'

'Probably, I'll get onto it. When are you going to interview Danny Tao?'

'Duty doc said I'm not allowed until he's got a clean bill of health. Maybe tomorrow.'

'I'll get onto those names,' Ross said.

'I'll ask Danny tomorrow too. We'll see if the same names come up.'

'Let you know as soon as I get anything. I'm calling it a day now.'

'Where you staying?'

'Hotel next to the station.'

'See you tomorrow, mate.'

* * *

Foxy was in his flat, making curry and whistling tunelessly to an old Rolling Stones track when a knock at his door made him jump. Turning, he saw Sophie outside and he gestured for her to come in.

'Hey, you!' she said, breezing in. 'That smells amazing! What is it? Curry?'

'Yup. Fancied cooking. You eaten?'

'No, but Marcus is cooking spag bol later, so depending on whether that's edible or not I may well come back to ponce some curry. Yours are usually amazing.'

Foxy smiled as he stirred. 'You want a coffee?'

'Go on then.'

He set about making her a coffee, while she stripped off her coat. She pulled out a chair to sit at the table, and picked up a jacket that was hooked over the back of one of the chairs.

Foxy approached her with a mug.

'Thanks,' she said, holding up the jacket. 'This looks a bit small for you.'

He saw the jacket that Erin had been wearing the night before.

'Probably.' He returned to his curry, not wanting to be drawn into it.

'Whose jacket is it?' she asked, sitting down.

He hesitated a moment and then decided that honesty was the best policy.

'An old friend turned up yesterday, and we went for dinner at Jesse and Doug's. Then she came back here to look around the climbing centre.' He said it in a rush, desperate to get it out and not dwell on telling Sophie any further details.

'That's nice,' she said brightly. 'Army friend?'

'She was a civilian physio, helped me out a lot when I busted my back and broke a leg. She worked on Jesse too after her accident. That's how we both knew her. She's here running a practice for a friend for a few months.'

Foxy watched Sophie's face as she drank her coffee, which seemed annoyingly neutral to him.

'Well, that's nice,' she said brightly. 'Was it a good evening with Jesse and Doug?'

'Always is. Bit of a wine head earlier.'

'Did Doug do his chicken?'

Foxy chuckled. 'He did.' Desperate to change the subject, he asked. 'Everything OK?'

'Everything's fine!' she said. 'I just popped in to return that climbing equipment you loaned me. It's in the car.'

'There was no rush for it.'

'I needed to get out of the house if the truth be known. Dad's doing my head in, and Marcus isn't helping. The carer's there for another hour or so, so I bailed for a bit.'

Foxy turned down the heat under the curry and faced her, folding his enormous arms as he leant back against the worktop.

'Soph, you're going to have to think about something else for your dad. He needs more at night.'

She held up a hand. 'I know. But I can't go there yet.'

'You're running yourself ragged. Not sleeping. You're exhausted.'

'I know. It's been a tough few months. I just...'

'Just what?'

'I just can't pack him off to a home.'

'What if it's the best thing for him? And you? His condition is getting worse. Marcus said he left the gas on the other day, forgot to light it and filled the kitchen with it. He was oblivious and was having a nap in the next room. Have you any idea how bloody dangerous that is?'

'Rob, I'm not having this conversation today,' she said in a warning tone.

'You need to have it sometime and you know it. You're just denying the inevitable.'

She drained her cup and put it down too heavily on the table, it banged loudly.

'Soph, I'm only saying this for your own good,' Foxy said gently.

'What if I don't want to hear it?' she said angrily, standing up. 'What if I'm sick to the back teeth of everyone weighing in on the matter and telling me what to do?'

'No one is doing that, sweetheart…'

'It feels like they are. I'm sick of it.'

'People just want what's best for you. You're shattered, people can see that, they worry about you.'

'Oh! So people are talking about me behind my back are they?'

'No, Sophie, it's not like that—'

'Bloody sounds like it.'

'People just mentioned that you looked shattered and were yawning your head off at Maggie's the other night, that's all.'

'Oh really? Well, perhaps I need people to butt the hell out,' she shouted, her face flushed with anger. 'And mind their own bloody business.'

'We care about you. Everyone does. We just want what's best for you.'

'All I get are endless lectures from people about what I should do. Like I can't decide anything for myself. You seem to do nothing but lecture me lately,' she shouted. 'I'll be the one to decide. I'll say when. It's my life and he's my dad.'

'No one's disputing that. Calm down, everyone's just concerned that you've had such a lot on, what with losing Sam too.'

'Everyone is so sure they think they know what's best for me. People keep telling me what they think I should be doing,' she shouted. 'No one has any idea how I feel, or what I want or what I need.'

'Sit down and tell me all of those things then,' he said, trying to sound soothing.

'What's the bloody point? No one is listening. About anything. All I get is everyone thinking they know best and lecturing me. I've had enough.' She grabbed her jacket and marched towards the door. 'I just need everyone to leave me the hell alone and keep out of my business. And that includes you too!' she shouted, wrenching the door open and marching down the stairs. 'Especially you!'

Foxy watched her go, feeling slight disbelief at her tirade. He followed her out, down the outside steps. She opened her car door and dragged out the climbing stuff, leaving it dumped on the ground.

'Soph,' he called in desperation, as he reached the bottom of the steps. 'Come on. Come back and we'll talk about it.'

'I meant what I said. I want you to leave me the hell alone!'

Glaring at him, she yanked open the driver's door and got in.

Foxy laid a hand on the car window. 'Soph, come on. Don't be like this.'

Ignoring him, she started the car and drove off, tyres squealing as she pulled away.

Foxy watched the brake lights flash at the top of the road and her car disappear around the corner. Sighing and shaking his head, he bent to pick up the climbing gear and hooked it over his shoulder.

'Uh oh, whatever have you done to piss her off?' a breathless voice said behind him.

He turned to see Erin in her running gear, clearly just off the beach. Her face was flushed, and she had a rosy glow.

'I've genuinely no idea,' he said ruefully. 'How's your hangover?'

'Gone. How's your wine head?'

'Gone. Your jacket, however, is still residing upstairs.'

'Oh, I forgot all about that. Can I grab it?'

'Sure. Come on up.' He turned and climbed the stairs, and she followed him.

'Mmm, that smells good,' she said as she stepped inside.

'You eaten?'

'Nope.'

'Want some?'

'You bet.'

CHAPTER 30

Mike watched as Ross walked out of the house to answer his phone.

'Are you staying here tonight or at mine again?' he asked Olivia.

She looked around the cottage and thought for a minute. 'What if they come back? That terrifies me. Could I crash at yours?'

'Sure. I'm gonna head off now though, I've got an early class tomorrow morning.'

'OK.'

Ross reappeared and bade them goodnight. Olivia arranged to meet him at the cottage again in the morning.

'See you, Ross,' called Mike to him. 'You good to go?' he said to Olivia.

She nodded and pulled the door, jimmying it shut with a small piece of slate she found.

As they walked towards Mike's flat, she nudged him and said, 'Thanks for everything. You know, last night and today.'

'No problem.'

'I don't deserve your help.'

'You're so right,' he said, lips twitching.

'Oi.' She nudged him and they walked in silence for a while. 'Do you think Eli's safe?'

Mike shrugged. 'Way I see it. They want their money. He's their bargaining chip. I'd imagine he's the safest kid in the world at the moment.'

'Bloody hope you're right.'

Mike opened the door to his flat and they went upstairs.

'You hungry?' he asked. 'I'm starving. He opened the fridge and then the cupboards.

'Beans on toast?' he said glumly.

'Bring it on. Would it be OK to go and grab a quick shower?' she asked.

'Go for it.'

Mike busied himself and Olivia hopped in the shower quickly, desperate to wash away the smell of the day. She found the pyjamas she had worn the night before and got into those and brushed out her wet hair.

'Ollie! Food's ready,' Mike called.

'What a nice wife you'd make,' she joked.

'You're not the first person to say that.'

'Oh?'

'My culinary talents are legendary.'

They ate in silence for a while.

Mike laid his cutlery down. 'Have you thought what you're going to do if you get Eli back safely. Are you going to bring him up?'

'I have no idea,' she said, chewing. 'Brian had a sister, I think, but I don't know where she is or even who she is. I think she was much older than him though.'

She finished her food.

'I guess I need to think about that.' She looked rueful. 'I don't know what to do about anything.' She yawned widely, which set Mike off.

'You go to bed,' Mike said, clearing the plates. 'After yesterday and today you must be shattered.'

'Let me help.' She took her glass over to the sink. 'I just don't know where to look for what they want. I'm so tired I can hardly think.'

'Just go to bed,' he said as he started the washing up. 'I'm gonna have a shower and then crash.'

'OK. But I'm on the sofa, you take your bed.'

'Nope.'

'Yes.'

'Ollie,' he warned.

'Hit the shower,' she said, shaking out a blanket that was hung over the arm of the sofa. She switched off the lights and lay on the sofa while he stood there frustrated.

'Goodnight,' she said. 'Go to bed, Mike.'

Mike tried to clear his mind in the shower. If Olivia stayed now Brian was dead, what did that mean for them? Could they pick it up again? He pondered as he washed the lather off himself. He knew how he felt about Olivia, that hadn't changed in the years that had passed. But she obviously hadn't loved him enough to stay. Could he live with that? Always knowing that? Always wondering whether she would leave again.

He stepped out of the shower, dried off and slung a towel around his waist. He brushed his teeth, gathered up his clothes and went to the bedroom. He moved about in the dark; the only light was the glow of streetlights through the window. He turned at the sound of the door opening and saw Olivia standing in the doorway.

'Mike,' she whispered, walking towards him slowly.

She laid her head on his bare chest and slid her arms around his waist. He worried momentarily that she'd hear the frantic thumping of his heart.

'Ollie, I'm not sure this a good idea…' he whispered.

'Shush,' she said, reaching up on her toes to kiss him.

She ran her hands over his back and then hooked her fingers into the towel around his waist and dropped it on the floor.

'Much better,' she said, pushing him backwards towards the bed.

* * *

'Who was that stomping off?' Erin asked. She was sitting at the table, sipping a glass of water.

'My friend, Sophie.'

'What did you say to her?'

'Something she didn't want to hear. That's all.'

'Is she a friend with benefits or just a friend?' Erin asked. 'I don't want to step on any toes here.'

'Just a friend. Weirdly both of us are recent widowers.' He shook his head. 'Never understood that term. Widow? Widower?' He flicked a glance towards her. 'You alright with rice?'

'Yup. I'll eat anything,' she said, grinning widely.

'I like a woman like that. Can't stand a fussy eater.'

'Perhaps you're warming to me then,' she said, raising an eyebrow.

He turned and gave her a disarming smile. 'Now that would depend.'

'On what?'

'Your continued use of the word proficient.'

'Ahh, we're back to that again, are we?' she asked as she drained her glass. 'I wouldn't say "continued" use.'

'I won't be letting it go anytime soon.'

'I see. What do you suggest we do about it?' she asked innocently. 'You know, you being *proficient* and all that?'

Foxy chuckled to himself as he stirred the rice.

'I feel sure we'll think of something.'

* * *

Viv woke in the early hours to a loud banging sound. She looked over at Nate who was sleeping soundly and roused herself from bed to try and find the source of the noise. Shrugging into a warm robe, she headed downstairs.

The banging was their back gate in the strong wind that was blowing, so she slipped a big coat over her dressing gown and went outside to secure it. The wind whipped around her forcefully as she closed the gate and then she heard a noise and froze. Not again. She leant against the gate and breathed deeply. Do your checks, the voice inside said.

Breathe deeply. What day is it? What time is it? How do I feel? What do I see? Where am I going?

She opened her eyes and listened. Seagulls cried as they whooped and swerved though the gusts of wind. Had she heard a seagull? There it was again. The sound. She wasn't going mad. She *could* hear a baby crying. She tried to rationalise her thoughts. Maybe, someone lived nearby with a baby, and she hadn't heard it until now. Why did she think the worst? She heard it again and tried to work out where it was coming from. Back inside the house, she moved to the kitchen. The cries were louder in there. She opened the front door, the light from the house casting a warm slice onto the dim street. Stepping out into the street, she pulled her coat tightly around herself and tilted her head to listen. She could hear it quite clearly, faintly, but it was there. Frowning she stepped back inside and jumped when she saw Nate standing there rubbing his eyes.

'What time is it?' he asked sleepily. 'I wondered where you were.'

'The gate was banging in the wind and then I heard a baby crying and wondered where it was.'

Nate rubbed his eyes sleepily. 'Where was the baby?'

'Don't know. I think it's stopped now.'

He shivered. 'Come on. Back to bed.' He grinned. 'I think my hands need warming up again.'

Nate lay awake in the dim light. Viv had fallen asleep again. He was worried. Had she really heard a baby? He tried to rationalise it. She was functioning perfectly normally. She was back at work, albeit with a light workload, she seemed happy and content. She was checking in with her therapist regularly. She was taking her meds; he'd seen her do that. Was she OK? He vowed to call her therapist in the morning and try to chat through his concerns. He wanted to ask about signs to look for in case she was becoming unwell again. He couldn't see her like that again. He needed to know if she was OK or whether this was the start of another episode.

* * *

Hannah was furious with baby Lucas. He had cried nearly all night. She had managed about an hour's sleep, and she was exhausted. She wondered angrily how he could *so* ungrateful when she had saved him from such an awful life.

'Shut up, SHUT UP!' she had screamed at him in the very early hours, and this had set him off again crying even louder. At one point her elderly, reclusive neighbour banged on the wall, and Hannah had gone around and yelled a torrent of abuse and threats through the letter box back at the old woman. She was pleased that the rest of the flats in her block were holiday lets and therefore empty.

She went through the bag that had been on the pram and found a large carton of powdered baby milk, so she fed him. He had hungrily taken the whole bottle and had then promptly fallen asleep.

Hannah had sighed with relief and set about tidying up and folding up the pram. She had made him a cot from a laundry basket and set it on a small table amongst the others. It was the perfect place for him. She placed him down in his makeshift cot and went to make a cup of tea and have one of her treats.

The doorbell rang shrilly through the quiet flat and Lucas let out a wail. She rushed in and calmed him down, popping the dummy she had found in the bag into his mouth. He sucked contentedly and fell asleep again. She closed the door on him firmly.

Peering through the spyhole, she saw with horror it was Anne.

She opened the door a fraction. 'Anne? Whatever are you doing here? It's seven thirty in the morning.'

Anne smiled and held up a big bunch of flowers. 'I'm feeling so much better. I came out for groceries, and I just wanted to give you these. They're for being such a good friend.'

'You didn't have to do that,' Hannah said awkwardly, trying to keep the door shut.

'Yes I did. Can I come in?' she asked. 'I'm gasping for a drink of water. I'm so thirsty since I had this flu.'

'Er. Oh... yes.' Hannah opened the door and gestured her through to the lounge where the cakes sat on the table.

Anne eyed them and turned to Hannah. 'Oh, those look nice! Special occasion?'

'No, I just fancied them, you know, couple of days off, treat myself and all that.'

'Why not, eh? Is it OK to grab that water?'

'Sure, hang on.' Hannah hurried off.

Anne followed her, talking. 'The police are outside. All over the high street. There's a car down near the harbour too. Apparently there's another missing baby. Stolen from outside a cafe of all places. I caught it on the news. Can you believe it's that silly bitch from the ward and the baby you really liked?'

'Anne, I really need to get going,' Hannah said desperately, handing her a small glass of water.

'Thanks, where are you off to then?' Anne drank deeply.

'Nowhere interesting.'

In the other room a loud wail was heard.

'What's that?' Anne said, frowning. 'What's that noise?'

Lucas emitted another wail and started crying again.

'Oh, that's my neighbour's baby. She asked me to watch him,' Hannah said hastily, wishing Anne would leave.

'You always said your neighbour was an old woman.' Anne narrowed her eyes. 'Yes. You told me that once.' She strode out into the hall and listened.

Hannah stood for a moment and tried to control herself. She followed Anne out to the hall.

'Anne, I'd like you to go, please.'

'Hannah, you don't have a baby.' She stared at Hannah in horror. 'Oh my God, did you take that baby? Is that baby Lucas in there?' she asked, pointing to the door that Lucas was behind.

'I can't let you go in there,' Hannah said quietly.

'Don't be silly, Hannah. Did you take him? You can't do that, and you know it. Come on, let me take him to the police.'

'Anne, I've warned you,' Hannah said through gritted teeth.

'Come on, Hannah,' Anne said urgently. 'We can just say you went a bit mad for a minute.'

'I've said you can't go in there.'

'I need to take the baby to the police, he's not yours, Hannah. We can get you some help.'

'No.'

'Come on, let me take him then, I can just say that I found him. I don't have to say anything about you.'

'No.'

'Hannah, be reasonable.'

Lucas let out a long wail.

Anne took Hannah by the shoulders. 'Hannah, I'm taking the baby. I won't say anything about you. You can't steal a baby.'

'You're not taking him.'

'I have to, I can't stand by and know this is happening.'

Anne turned and walked towards the door.

Hannah raised an arm.

'I told you, but you wouldn't listen. I can't let you go in there. I'm sorry, Anne.'

She brought the heavy glass paperweight down hard on the back of Anne's head and kept hitting until Anne was lying on the floor, wide-eyed and unmoving. Hannah glanced at her dispassionately and stepped over her to get to Lucas.

'Coming, darling!' she said sweetly and cooed to the others as she lifted him out of the cot. She was oblivious to the splattering of blood she had all over her from Anne's head wounds.

* * *

Olivia woke and wondered where Mike was. Switching on her phone, she saw that in the night she had received a photograph of Eli tied to a chair in front of some sort of wooden shelving unit. Unsure of what to do and acutely aware of time running out, she immediately sent the picture to both Steve and Ross.

She dressed quickly and left the flat heading for the cottage, hoping Ross might have some news. His face on her arrival at the front door where he was waiting with a coffee, suggested that he had no news.

'Nothing?' she asked.

'Nope. I got the picture. You? Any ideas?'

She bit her lip. 'Nothing. I just don't know what to do.'

'Steve's on the case. He might be able to help get Eli safe.'

Ross had managed to get a colleague to extract a few names from his source in the Tao organisation overnight and had sent them through to Steve in the hopes he could ask Mickey to look into it further. Steve felt the shooting might delay any trips to London for Mickey in the immediate future, but he'd get Pearl on the case.

* * *

Sitting in his office, Steve viewed the photograph of Eli with distress. The poor boy looked terrified. He was tied to a chair in front of some wooden dresser type shelving. Something pricked the back of Steve's consciousness but didn't present itself, so Steve focused on his impending interview with Danny Tao and collected the files he needed.

Steve regarded Danny Tao with interest as he sat down, wondering which interview route to go down with him. Physically, there was no resemblance to Mickey at all. Where Mickey was tall, with a very broad chest and shoulders, Danny was slight and less than average height. Steve concluded Danny favoured his mother's side.

Danny had greasy black hair, nails bitten to the quick and the skin and pallor of an addict. Steve asked him one more time if he was sure he didn't want a solicitor present. Danny refused again.

After pressing record, Steve whipped through the preliminaries for the purposes of the recording.

'Danny,' he said pleasantly. 'I know you have been cleared by the duty doctor, but I'm obliged to ask you if you feel well enough to have a discussion with me. You have also waived the right to a solicitor.'

Danny nodded, his foot jigging; he was sweating profusely and kept yawning widely. Steve recognised the signs of withdrawal.

'Can I get you anything?'

'No. I just want to go,' Danny said in a low voice. 'I wanna get out of here.'

'Not at the moment,' Steve said. 'You're here for a while helping us with our enquiries, I'm afraid.'

'But I was kidnapped,' Danny whispered. 'And left… left in a wind turbine!'

'I understand,' Steve said, 'and we will get to the bottom of that. But we want to talk to you about your other activities. We also want to talk to you about your family and your connection to a Harry Daly and a Brian Baker.'

Danny blinked, sweat glistened across his brow and his leg jigged to a crazy rhythm only Danny could hear.

'W-who?'

'Harry Daly and Brian Baker. Would you like to see some photographs?' Steve asked. 'For the record I am showing Danny Tao photographs numbered E102, E103 and D101. This is Harry Daly.' Steve laid down a photograph of Harry Daly taken on the mortuary slab and then Harry Daly as he was when he was hanged from the tree.

'Recognise him?' Steve asked. 'Oh, and this one. Brian Baker.' He laid out a picture of Brian Baker that had been taken from Brian's recent employee file.

Danny Tao blinked at the photographs and looked away, chewing the end of his fingers.

Shrugging, he said, 'Dunno. Got any food?'

'Got the munchies, Danny?' Steve asked dryly. 'Do you just wanna get out so you can go and score? Must be difficult, all that time in the turbine and not a fix in sight.'

Danny's eyes widened at the suggestion of a fix. 'Dunno what you're talking about.'

'Let's talk about Harry Daly.'

'Who?' Danny looked over Steve's shoulder avoiding eye contact.

'This guy here,' Steve said, tapping the photograph. 'We have a reliable witness who tells us he was quite the talent at picking runners for you. He was very well thought of in the organisation as I understand it.'

Danny snorted. 'He was junkie scum.' He sniffed and wiped his nose on his sleeve.

'Takes one to know one doesn't it, Danny?' Steve asked mildly. 'So, you knew him then?'

'What?' Danny narrowed his eyes.

'You knew him. You see, we have a reliable witness that tells us that, you,' Steve pointed to Danny, 'headed up the Cardiff operation.' Steve sat back in his chair. 'Are you not the big man then, Danny? Do I need to be talking to someone up the chain of command? Someone more important?'

'You can talk to me. I head up the whole Tao organisation,' Danny hissed.

'I see,' Steve said. 'So, you are the man in the know.'

Danny preened and then realised too late that Steve had led him down a path he didn't want to go down.

'Do you admit that you knew Harry Daly and that you do, in fact, head up the Tao organisation?'

'I didn't say that.'

'Actually, Danny, you did. Do you want me to replay the tape for you?'

Danny looked away. 'I was kidnapped. I want to make a complaint. Press charges.'

'OK. No problem. Who kidnapped you, Danny?'

'I don't know.'

'Who would you like to press charges against?'

'It's for you to find out, isn't it?'

'Is it? Quite frankly, I've got much better things to do, like find out who put two bullets into the back of Jade Tao's head and who has taken a small boy hostage because of a missing shipment and some money.'

Steve watched as Danny sweated. His hands had begun to shake, and droplets of sweat rolled down and gently dripped off his chin.

'You hot, Danny?' Steve asked.

'No comment,' he muttered, folding his arms.

'Let's talk about Brian Baker,' Steve said brightly. 'Good old best runner in the game, Brian.' Steve leant forward conspiratorially. 'Stroke of genius it was, transporting the drugs in the wind turbine parts. Absolute genius.'

Danny looked away, a half smile playing on his lips.

'Except they had a tendency to go "poof" and then disappear, didn't they?' Steve said. 'As if by magic!'

'No comment.' Danny scrubbed an arm across his sweaty face.

'Now, a little birdy told me that Jade had been a naughty girl. That she helped herself to a big old chunk of cash and then took the shipment for herself.' Steve watched Danny. 'Tell me, was little sis getting a bit greedy?'

'No comment.'

'Perhaps she was getting good enough to head up the organisation—'

'She needed reining in,' Danny interrupted, sneering. 'She was out of control. Bringing shame on the family. Carrying on. Wanting more money, more control, more power.'

'Did big brother not like that? Or was it little brother?' Steve leant forward. 'Was she big sister or little sister? These things matter, Danny, especially with twins.'

'No comment.'

'I reckon she was big sister. Did she have the guts and wanted too much of the glory? Was she a threat to you, I wonder? Did Mummy love big sister more than little brother?'

'You watch your mouth.' Danny's head whipped around, and he looked at Steve with narrowed eyes. 'She was a pain in the arse.

Reckoned she could grow the organisation bigger and better than it ever was. She was deluded. Reckoned she could take over from the other gangs in the county and then move overseas. She wasn't ambitious. She was crazy.' He shook his head. 'Mother liked the idea.' He laughed a maniacal laugh. 'She encouraged her! Ridiculous!'

'Why did she steal the shipment?'

'There was a falling out. She chose to leave. She wouldn't listen.'

'What was the falling out about?'

'None of your business. She fucked us over though. It was all part of her plan. Steal the shipment, stop the pipeline into Qatar and Dubai, make them desperate. Make them want to pay more for another shipment to feed their growing market. She planned to set up on her own. She needed the shipment and the money she stole for that. She would meet them and offer them exactly what they needed and be able to provide it instantly. She'd control the pipeline from there. She had the contacts. She took the runner with her.'

'Ah, this is where Brian comes in.'

Danny looked away. 'No comment.'

Steve folded his arms. 'I've got a bit of a problem here, Danny.'

'Oh yeah? What's that then?'

'Someone from your organisation has taken a boy. A small boy, who's just lost his dad and wants to use him to barter for the shipment and the money.'

'I don't know anything about that.'

'No idea who that could be?'

'No comment.'

'Because if that boy is harmed, or worse, then I will hang it on you.' Steve leant forward. 'As the head of the Tao organisation, obviously.'

Danny swallowed hard. 'I don't know anything about it.'

'You'll know where he is.'

'I don't know anything!' Danny picked his fingers. 'I-I was pushed out.'

Steve's ears pricked up. 'Pushed out?'

Danny rubbed at the surface of the table with his finger, refusing to meet Steve's eyes.

'Would this be when Graham Curtis appeared on the scene?'

Danny inhaled sharply; his eyes widened.

'I'm guessing it was.' Steve watched him. 'He played you like a bloody fiddle. Frank wasn't your father, Danny. Never was. You never even knew the man.'

'What do you know about my father?' he sneered.

'I know who your father is. I know Graham Curtis shot your mother.'

Danny's eyes widened. 'My mother? My mother's dead?'

'Sorry for your loss,' Steve said flatly.

'He shot my mother?' Danny said in disbelief, blinking furiously.

'He did. Then I shot him,' Steve said.

'He shot my mother?' Danny repeated in disbelief. 'I thought he loved my mother.'

'Perhaps that's what he wanted you to think.'

'What do you mean, you know my father wasn't Frank?'

'I know he wasn't. DNA tells me.'

'Who is it then? Who is my father?'

'Mickey Camorra,' he said quickly.

Danny screamed and launched himself at Steve. Steve dodged him and moved swiftly around, catching Danny and pushing him face down on the table. He held him secure with his arm up behind his back.

'Calm down,' Steve said through gritted teeth.

Danny was wide-eyed. He was breathing heavily, and a line of spittle was hanging from his mouth.

'You fucking bastard,' he shouted as he struggled. 'He's not my father. That bastard is *not* my father!'

'Interview suspended,' Steve said. 'You're going back to the cells to calm down.'

CHAPTER 31

Steve watched as PC Garland dragged Danny Tao down the corridor back towards the cells. Danny was red-faced and screaming at Steve, calling him a liar, threatening to kill him, and explaining how he would die a horrible death.

'Yeah, yeah,' he muttered. 'Get in line.' He glanced down at his phone that had been on silent. He noticed a missed call from Mrs Clifton of Woodpecker Lane and rolled his eyes at whatever it was she would be ringing him about. Kate had also sent him a text asking when she would be able to see his latest swellings and he tapped out a response instantly, grinning broadly.

'You're thinking about sex,' Jonesey announced as he stood in front of him chewing on a chocolate bar.

'What?'

'Your eyebrow does that funny thing when you're talking to Kate or sexting her.'

'I am not sexting her.'

'You totally are. Anyway, bloke from the hospital has got the CCTV loaded up from the car park. He says you need to go and have a look at it.'

'Can't you go? Can't he email it over?'

'He can't strapolate it or something,' Jonesey said. 'But he says there's something on there you should see. Anyway. I'm very busy looking for the baby.'

'That so? Very busy here, eating chocolate and looking for the baby?'

'Yup. I'm on a break.'

'Bollocks. You're with me. Two sets of eyes will be quicker than one. We need to close this out.'

'I haven't had my lunch break yet,' Jonesey said indignantly.

Steve gave him a look.

'OK, OK. I'll get my coat.'

'Outside, two minutes.'

Steve cleared Jonesey's absence with the sergeant and headed out to the car park, telling Jonesey he'd see him out there.

Jonesey climbed into the car clutching an iced bun and two coffees.

'Why must you make everything some sort of fucking picnic?' Steve muttered as he started the car.

'You're welcome,' Jonesey said, digging in his pocket and producing a KitKat for Steve.

The CCTV footage was not the golden goose Steve had hoped it would be, despite viewing it numerous times. It just showed a person leaving from that door and walking off. There was a glimpse of the side of a face of a person dressed in dark clothing.

'I thought you said this was something of interest. Can we not make it clearer?' he asked Sloth – the name he had privately given the CCTV technician.

'Probably,' Sloth said slowly.

'How about doing it now?' Steve asked.

'Oh, yeah.' Sloth fiddled for a bit and peered at the screen. 'Better?'

'No different,' Jonesey said. 'All I see is a white blob for a face.'

'Our guys could maybe have a go at tidying it up, at least try to improve the resolution. Can you send it to me by email?' Steve said, going through his pockets for a card.

'Send it here.' He passed the card to Sloth.

'It's too big to send,' Sloth said, frowning.

'Upload it to the cloud and create a link,' Steve said, frustrated.

'Oh yeah,' Sloth said. 'S'pose so. Anyway, does it really matter now 'cause you found the baby up on the roof, didn't you?'

Steve tried not to explode.

'Yes, it does matter because there was a bag in the woods with an empty purse that was nicked from a patient. That purse had a wodge of cash in it and a ten grand engagement ring, which is also still missing. So, I'm interested to see whether anyone lobbed it over the fence from the car park and if so, who it was, because the chances are this isn't the first thing they've nicked from a patient, and I'd like to identify them and have a discussion about it. Is that a good enough reason?'

He waited for Sloth to register what he was saying. 'Now, have we seen all we can from the door that leads to the car park, from the hospital building?' Steve craned his neck to look at the plan on the wall. 'Block D?'

'Didn't we look at that?' Sloth said.

'No, we didn't,' Steve said with exaggerated patience. 'You said you were going to retrieve it. Did you forget?'

'I guess I did,' Sloth said. 'Sorry.'

'Do it now,' Steve demanded. 'I swear to God, if this gives us what we need and it's been on here the whole time, I'll string you up by the b—'

'Guv,' Jonesey said. 'Your phone's going.'

Steve looked across the desk to where his phone was flashing, forgetting that he'd put it on silent when they entered the CCTV suite. He saw Mrs Clifton's number and swore under his breath. He grabbed the phone.

'Miller,' he barked into it.

'Don't think there's any need to take that tone with me,' Mrs Clifton said. 'It's Mrs Clifton from Woodpecker Lane.'

'How are you, Mrs Clifton?' Steve tried not to sigh too loudly.

'I've already left you a message, but here I am ringing you again. I feel like I'm performing a public service here.'

'Sorry, Mrs Clifton. Things have been very busy.'

'We're all *busy*,' she said snippily.

'What can I do for you, Mrs Clifton?' Steve said, exasperated.

'Well, I don't know if you want to know.'

'Know what, Mrs Clifton?'

'That those chinks are back.'

Steve drew in a large long-suffering breath.

'Mrs Clifton, you cannot use terms like that. It's simply not appropriate these days.'

''Tis the world gone bloody mad,' she muttered. 'Chinks is what they are. I say what they are.'

Steve rolled his eyes. 'Mrs Clifton, are you saying the Chinese men are back next door?'

'You thick or something?' she asked. 'I forgot you weren't the sharpest knife in the drawer. How many more times? The chinks are back here in the bungalow next door,' she said slowly as if speaking to someone very stupid.

'Since when?'

'Few days now. Got a boy with them, I think. Could have been a girl though. Can't tell these days with boys having longer hair. I tell you it's not right. In my day it was short back and sides and that was it. You'll have these boys not knowing if they're Arthur or Martha if they're allowed to grow their hair willy nilly.'

Steve closed his eyes at the staggering level of inappropriateness Mrs Clifton displayed.

'Anyway,' she continued. 'I'll be in for the rest of the afternoon keeping watch if you decide you want to come by. I haven't got any biscuits for sharing, mind you, if you were going to call in. Besides you said you were bringing the biscuits next time. So, if you are coming you need to bring biscuits.'

'Right then.'

'Are you?'

'Am I what, Mrs Clifton?'

'Coming and bringing biscuits.'

Steve's exhausted brain kicked into action. 'Mrs Clifton, sorry, I'm a bit tired. Can you describe the boy?'

'I said I *think* it's a boy. He's got blond hair. Long. Too long for a boy in my op—'

'Mrs Clifton, what was he wearing?'

'Oh, one of those red top things with a hood that's got them letters on it. Oh… Hang on, it'll come – GP,' she said triumphantly. 'It says GP and is red.'

'Could that be GAP, Mrs Clifton?'

'That's what I said.'

'Mrs Clifton, I need you to watch that place like a hawk. Call me the minute anything changes. I'm on my way, but don't do anything.'

'Right.'

'That means no afternoon naps.'

'I don't…' she spluttered.

'Keep watching.'

'Don't forget the biscui—' she said.

Steve ended the call and turned to Jonesey.

'What's that?' Jonesey asked.

Steve eyed Sloth still picking away at the keys on his computer and said quietly, 'Mrs Clifton from Woodpecker Lane. Says the Chinese are back and that they have a boy with them.'

'The bush bungalow?' Jonesey said in disbelief. 'I thought there was a fire?'

'So did I,' Steve said grimly. 'We need to get over there.'

'We need to get backup,' Jonesey said. 'Especially after what happened to you there last time.'

'Call it into Sarge. I want this quiet. No sirens. Wait until it's dark. We'll go in then.'

'OK.'

Jonesey left the CCTV suite. Steve stood by Sloth, who was still picking away at a keyboard as if he was in slow motion.

'I want that footage from Block D emailed over in an hour,' he said. 'Otherwise, your life won't be worth living. Do you understand me?'

Sloth nodded; his eyes wide.

Steve grabbed his jacket off the back of the chair and left the suite. Jonesey was on the phone.

'Jonesey,' he said sharply and turned to leave.

Steve stepped out of the hospital and got a face full of dust and debris from the wind that had blown up in the last few hours.

'Christ,' he muttered, spitting out bits of dust, wrestling his jacket on in the wind.

Jonesey stepped out, ending his call.

'Whoo!' he said. 'Surf's up! Is this the end of storm what's her name?'

'No idea,' muttered Steve. 'I need to call Ross.'

He rang a number on his phone as he walked back to the car, Jonesey trailing after him.

'Ross mate, you need to get back to the station and wait for me.'

'Hang on a minute, I can't talk,' Ross said and Steve waited, hearing a rustling and then a door close.

Ross was back on the line. 'Right, Olivia can't hear me now. What news?'

'Get back to the station. We think we know where the boy is. He was wearing a red GAP hoodie, wasn't he?'

'He was. Housemaster remembered it clearly because Eli got a detention for it, not school colours.'

'Gonna wait till it's dark and go in with backup. I'll see you there.'

'OK. When are we interviewing Tao?'

'Later. He's asked for his brief now anyway. I want the boy safe first. Not a word about this. Say you've been called to the station for a meet.'

'OK. See you shortly.'

Steve ended the call, and unlocked the car so that Jonesey could get in. He made another call, leaning up against the outside of the vehicle.

'My favourite policeman.' Pearl's warm voice made him smile.

'How you doing, Pearl?'

'We are all healing. Mickey's sleeping. I've put some feelers out about the boy, but I think it's a slow process. I'm waiting to hear back from George, who was Lily's version of Stanley.'

'They could never be another Stanley.'

'You're right, but we won't tell him that,' she said lightly.

'Look, I might have a lead on the boy, but I'll see how it plays out.'

'Well, do let me know. While I have your ear, I have a small issue and wondered if you could shed some light on it.'

'This wouldn't be Danny Tao related, would it?'

'How did you guess?'

'Pearl, come on. I'm not that stupid. Pretty genius prison though, if I do say so.'

'You're too kind.' She cleared her throat and dropped her voice slightly. 'Is he well?'

'He is. Currently residing at the station.'

'Does he know?'

'He does.'

'How did he take it?'

'Not as well as we might have hoped,' Steve said mildly. 'Curtis fed him too many lies.'

'Ahh.'

'I don't think he's getting out anytime soon, Pearl. Too much to unpick that he's linked to.'

'Keep me posted?'

'Take care, Pearl.'

'You too.'

Steve climbed into the car with Jonesey.

'Who are you being all secret squirrel with?' Jonesey asked, putting on his seat belt.

'Pearl,' Steve said, starting the car and pulling out of the car park. 'She's put out some feelers about who might have Eli.'

'You tell her we think we know where he is?'

'Nope.'

'You don't tell anyone anything, do you?'

'Not if I can help it.'

* * *

Foxy had been trying to call Sophie all day, unsuccessfully. She was avoiding his calls and when he had finally gone to her house, there was no sign of anyone home. He wasn't sure what to do. She had been so angry. He couldn't recall ever seeing her like that. He figured that maybe he would give her a few more days to calm down and then try again.

Unusually for him, he felt quite torn. He'd enjoyed his impromptu dinner with Erin the previous evening. She had been good company and Rudi had ended up appearing too, so the three of them had reminisced fondly for most of the evening until Erin announced she was off home. Foxy had surprised himself by feeling slightly disappointed that she wasn't staying again, but had kissed her cheek and sent her off with Rudi, who gave her a lift home.

Foxy pondered as he walked along the beach with Solo. He was deeply bothered about the row with Sophie, but he was trying to unpick how he felt about the whole situation. He wasn't sure what the position was with Erin. He liked her, he enjoyed her company, in and out of the bedroom, but he wondered if he was being fair to her, getting involved when he knew how strongly he felt about Sophie. He had no idea what Erin was looking for or whether it was just a one off or a casual thing. Sighing deeply as his mind veered back to Sophie, he walked off the beach and headed for the pub.

The pub was warm, full of conversation and delicious smells. Foxy eased himself around a woman dithering at the bar and winked at Genevieve, who was serving. As Genevieve patiently handed over the card machine so the woman could laboriously type in her card number, she winked at Foxy.

'Usual?' she asked him.

Foxy gave her a thumbs up.

'Go sit while there's a table. You eating?'

'Yup.'

Foxy threaded his way, with Solo following, to a small table he had spotted. Solo settled at his feet. He was pondering the menu when Genevieve delivered his pint and took his order for food.

'Won't be long.' She grinned at him. 'You doing OK?'

'I am. You?'

'I'm fine. Worried because Mack is away again.'

'Better get used to it if you insist on dating a soldier,' Foxy said.

She snatched the menu from him good-naturedly. 'Not helpful.' She nudged him. 'I was looking for some words of wisdom here.'

He grinned at her. 'I'm all out of wisdom today. Try tomorrow.'

'Uh oh. Like that is it?'

'Little bit.'

'Oh dear. Well in that case, your pint's on me.'

'Have I told you you're my favourite here?'

'Oh stop,' she said, laughing. 'Dinner won't be long.'

He watched, amused, as she returned behind the bar. While he waited for his food, he sipped his pint and absently stroked Solo's head, letting his mind wander.

'Hello there!' A familiar voice interrupted his thoughts.

He looked up into the smiling face of Erin.

'Hello!' he said warmly, pleased to see her. 'Fancy seeing you here.'

'Well, you know, I'm getting acquainted with the place. So that means trying out all the pubs.'

'Sounds like a brilliant plan to me,' Foxy said. He was about to tell Erin that there was a man behind her trying to get past, when she turned slightly and spoke to him.

'Mark, this is Rob Fox. Foxy this is Mark.'

Foxy looked in surprise at the tall dark-haired man who reached around Erin to shake his hand in greeting.

'Hi,' he said pleasantly. 'Good to meet you. You knew Erin in Germany, didn't you? She fixed up your back. She mentioned she'd seen you and someone else who'd been a patient.'

Foxy raised an eyebrow at Erin and smiled widely at Mark. 'Yup. I was definitely a patient. I think I was quite grumpy though, by all accounts.'

He laughed. 'She can cope with it. It's actually how we met.'

Foxy gave him a smile. 'She certainly can cope with it. So, Mark, do you live around here?'

'No. Just down for a quick visit. I do contract work, mainly abroad, so I'm back for a couple of weeks and thought I ought to make an appearance to keep the missus happy!'

'Is that so?' Foxy said, flicking an enquiring glance at Erin.

'Yeah. Well, working away is tough, but it won't be for much longer, then we'll decide where we're going to settle.' He smiled. 'You never know, we might pick here! It's certainly a lovely place. Perfect to raise a family.'

Foxy's eyebrow raised further as he addressed Erin. 'A family, eh? Sounds like the future is all mapped out.'

Mark laughed and threw an arm around Erin's shoulders. 'Well, she's been on at me for years to start a family, so we've made a deal that this time next year, we'll both stop doing contract work and settle down.'

'Well, that's certainly a good goal to have,' Foxy said firmly.

'Excuse me, folks.' Genevieve squeezed past Erin and Mark. 'Here you go, my lovely.' She put down a plate. 'Hope you enjoy.'

'Thanks, Gen.'

'Well, we'll leave you to your food,' Mark said, slipping an arm around Erin's waist. 'Good to meet you.'

'Appreciate that. Good to meet you, Mark.'

'See you around then,' Erin said cheerfully as they moved off.

'Yup. See you around.' Foxy watched her as they moved towards the door of the pub. Just before she left, Erin turned around and gave him a large smile and a wink.

Foxy stared at the door. 'Exactly what the bloody hell is that supposed to mean?' he asked Solo, who was watching the proceedings with interest now the food had arrived.

CHAPTER 32

Olivia had heard Ross take a call and crept towards the door, listening as he closed it. Frustrated that she couldn't hear anything, she tried a different approach when he came back in the room.

'Everything alright?' she asked with an air of desperation. She was getting restless. Her two days were almost up. She prayed that Eli was still alive and well.

'I'm needed back at the station,' he said.

'What for? Is there news?'

Ross looked at her oddly. 'No. Just interviewing a suspect, that's all. He might be able to shed some light on it.'

'Right. I'll carry on looking then. Will you be back here tonight?'

'Probably not. If you find anything or hear anything, call me.'

'Will do.'

After Ross left, Olivia was sitting in the kitchen staring into space when her phone rang. She dreaded it ringing and reluctantly looked at the screen. She was relieved to see it was Mike.

'Hey, you,' she said. 'How are you? Busy day?'

'I'm knackered. I forgot to say that I've got a gig later, and it'll be a late one, so if you want to crash at mine that's alright.'

'I don't have a key,' she said.

'I put one on your key chain this morning before you woke,' he said quietly. 'Look, Ollie, last night was—'

'Wonderful,' she whispered.

'I don't know how to…'

'Let's just see where it goes,' she said.

'Maybe I'll see you later then. Now you have a key.'

'Maybe you will,' she said. 'Good luck tonight.'

'See you later.' He ended the call.

Darkness had fallen and Olivia was standing in the boathouse with a crowbar in her hand and the door firmly locked. She glanced at the door as the wind rattled it fiercely on it on its hinges. The bare lightbulb swung about in the draught whistling through the gaps in the door. She was relieved Ross had finally gone. He was beginning to irritate her.

She appraised the crate that sat in the middle of the floor. She had forgotten about it completely with Brian and Gil dying, and had only remembered it's presence when she had come across the key to the boatshed earlier. She had hurriedly hidden it from Ross, unsure of what the crate would contain.

She gently prised the lid off the crate. Laying down the crowbar, she removed handfuls of the straw-type packing until she saw the top of a large object. It was square shaped and was covered in a glossy thick red lacquer.

As she uncovered more of it, she saw it was a cabinet of some sort. It had gold flowers on a vine painted on it, reminding her of Japanese blossoms. She realised she would need to pry off one of the sides to see it and get inside. As she went to pick up the crowbar, she noticed a sheet of paper loose in the crate, and pulled it out. It was a delivery note with instructions and the description of the item. 'Chinese wedding cabinet and artwork.'

Carefully prising off the front panel of the wooden packing crate, she admired the red and gold square cabinet with double doors that had a large round brass lock in the centre. After turning the delicate key, she opened the doors gently. There was more packing inside. Once she had removed that, she saw a large brown leather tube with a cap on each end, which were connected by a worn leather strap. To wear over the shoulder, she supposed.

Looking over the tube carefully, she popped the end off and drew out a rolled canvas that looked worn and cracked. She laid it down gently on the lid of the cabinet and unrolled the canvas, admiring it. It was an old painting, even she could see that. Two men sat at a table playing cards, with a bottle of wine between them. She frowned and looked inside the tube to see if there was anything else. Empty.

She sat for a moment looking at the painting, noting the edges that looked like they had perhaps been cut out of a frame with a sharp knife. She wondered what it was and who it was by.

She picked up her phone, googled the picture and stared in disbelief at the phone and the picture.

'No way,' she whispered. 'No *fucking* way, Jade.'

Her phone was telling her that the tiny, oil-rich nation of Qatar had purchased a Paul Cézanne painting, *The Card Players*, for more than $250 million. The deal, in a single stroke, set the highest price ever paid for a work of art. This said piece of art had been reported stolen from the gallery at the royal palace, only a few weeks after the purchase.

Olivia stared at the painting in disbelief. She ran her fingers over the canvas, lightly feeling the hardness of the paint and the tiny eggshell-type cracking through age. Was that *this* painting? How the bloody hell did Jade get her hands on it? She knew Jade had been in

Qatar for a time but had no idea why she had chosen there to hide out.

She guessed Jade knew they would come for her eventually, so had sent the painting to the cottage knowing that at some point either her or Gil would eventually turn up. Her eyes filled with tears at the thought of Gil. As she looked at the exposed edges of the crate, where she had pried away the front, she caught sight of thick polythene, and wondered why the sides of the packing crate were so thick. With difficulty, she managed to lever off the outside skin of the crate and then stared in disbelief. The crate sides were packed with flat bundles of money. American dollars.

Panting, she clumsily managed to move the Chinese cabinet out of the crate and set to work, prying the remaining two sides apart.

The whole thing was lined with money. In total, she counted nearly a hundred bundles of money. She calculated it roughly in her head. In each strap of bills there was $10,000 dollars, which meant she was holding a million dollars in cash.

Hearing a noise outside, she rushed to roll up the painting, slipping it back into the tube. She pondered where the safest place was to keep it, and in the end, she put it back in the cabinet, which she managed to drag into a corner where she threw an old tarpaulin over it.

The money was sitting in a pile on the floor. Looking around, she saw an old suitcase in the corner. Hauling it over, she emptied the old clothes from it and dragged it over to the cash, cramming in as much as she could. She put the case back in the corner, with the cabinet, under the tarpaulin and kicked the clothes into a pile on the floor against the wall. Grabbing the various bits of the crate, she leant it all up against the cold stone wall as best she could.

Her mind racing, she turned off the light and headed back to the cottage. She let herself in and checked her phone in case there was any news, all the time wondering what to do with the painting and the cash.

* * *

Steve was standing inside Mrs Clifton's house looking out of the window monitoring the bush bungalow. He had made the assumption it was a reasonable cover to park on her drive and go straight in carrying a shopping bag, particularly as he always wore a suit and not a uniform.

He knew the two men who had beaten him up and could therefore identify him were safely on remand, so he assured himself he was fairly safe. Just out to visit an elderly person with some shopping to anyone watching.

As soon as Mrs Clifton had called and told him she'd seen a boy in the bungalow, Steve's memory had clocked into place and shown him the wooden dresser that Jade Tao's body had been found behind. He had seen that same dresser behind Eli in the picture that had been sent to Olivia. He cursed himself for not realising it sooner.

'What's going on?' Mrs Clifton said, her breath hot in his ear as she peered over his shoulder.

'Jesus,' muttered Steve, stepping away slightly.

'Don't think much of your biscuit selection,' she complained. 'Half of them are broken.'

'They were mainly a prop, Mrs Clifton. I wasn't concerned with quality at the time.'

She frowned. 'A what?'

'A prop. You know, to make it look like I was bringing you something if anyone was watching.'

'But you were bringing me something.'

Steve looked at his watch. The team were due to go in any second. He had stepped back and handed over command; he was just a spectator. Armed response would be going in first to clear the property.

He watched as a group of figures in black emerged from the shadows and positioned themselves around the property. From when he'd briefed the team earlier, Steve knew they were entering from the rear.

From his vantage point, he saw a bright flash. A man ran from the bungalow and was tackled to the ground almost instantly. He heard a single shot and a few minutes later the radio burbled with the 'all clear' announcement.

'Stay inside, please, Mrs Clifton,' Steve said as he stepped outside and walked towards the front of the bungalow. As he walked towards him, the Operational Firearms Commander ripped his helmet off and breathed heavily, nodding to Steve.

'One ran. The other produced a bloody Glock, started waving it around like an idiot.'

'Dead?'

'Yup. They're bringing the boy out now. He's fine.'

Steve turned as one of the team led the boy out. Steve looked at his tear-stained face and wondered what sort of ordeal he had gone through. He went over and crouched in front of him.

'Hi, Eli. I'm Steve. I'm a policeman. How are you? Are you hurt?' Eli looked pale to Steve.

'No, I need food though. My levels are low. I feel funny,' he said in a trembling voice.

'We've got an ambulance on the way.' He looked over and saw Jonesey and PC Warren chatting.

'Jonesey, Warren, over here.'

They both trotted up with expectant faces.

'Guv?' Jonesey asked.

'Jonesey, you can get back to the station. Warren, I need you to stay. Before you go home, Jonesey, cast an eye over that CCTV from the hospital. I'd like to know whether it was someone we know who might have left by that door at least. Or even better, slung the bag over the fence.'

'Guv.'

'Where's Ross?' he asked, looking around. 'He didn't come with you?'

Jonesey shrugged. 'Not seen him.'

Steve frowned. 'Warren, can you get Eli settled in the car while we wait for the ambulance and act as a chaperone when I talk to him.'

Eli appeared to have been treated relatively well, apart from a poor diet and hating the smell of smoke that permeated the property. His levels were checked, and the paramedics gave him the all clear, but told him he needed a proper meal. Overhearing this, Mrs Clifton ushered Eli into her house and started cooking for him. Steve watched in amazement at the change in her as she sat him in the kitchen and clucked about feeding him. PC Warren sat quietly in the corner, observing.

Eli looked shattered. He said they had just tied him to a chair for photographs and that he had mostly been watching TV with one of them guarding him the whole time he was there. He said they'd been nice but hadn't spoken to him much. He did say that they had been on the phone a lot and whenever they had a call, they invariably took a photo of him tied up.

Steve asked Mrs Clifton to give them a moment and he spent some time asking Eli how he felt. He was trying to get more details out of him about how he had been treated in case he needed to contact a specialist who could help him talk to Eli.

'They told me my dad was dead,' he said mournfully. 'They said it would happen to me too. Is my dad dead?'

Steve bit his lip. He was way out of his comfort zone.

'He is, buddy. I'm sorry. There was an accident at the wind farm.'

Eli visibly brightened up. 'Does this mean I can stay with Liv?'

'I don't know. I'm not sure.'

'Can I see Liv?'

'Of course. Will you be up to answering some questions tomorrow?'

'Yes. I just want to see Liv and go to bed. There wasn't a bed there.'

'OK. I'll take you now.'

Eli turned to Mrs Clifton who was wiping up. 'Thank you very much for my tea, Mrs Clifton. It was lovely.'

Mrs Clifton smiled. 'My pleasure, my love. You come back and visit anytime.'

'Really?' Eli said.

'Really.'

'Thanks, Mrs Clifton,' Steve said. 'Really appreciate it.'

'Next time you're passing, I'll have some decent biscuits, please, not the cheap rubbish you brought today.'

'Yes, Mrs Clifton.'

'Take this poor boy home to bed.'

'Bye, Mrs Clifton.' Eli gave her an impromptu hug, and Steve left when she started to make excuses about having something in her eye.

PC Warren sat in the back of the car with Eli. 'Do you feel better now?' she asked him.

'A hundred percent,' he said. 'I'm just tired now.'

'We'll have you home in about ten minutes.'

Steve pulled to a stop outside Olivia's cottage and the door swung open immediately. Olivia ran out. Steve had called her from Mrs Clifton's and told her that they had Eli.

'Eli!' she cried, dropping to her knees to gather him into a hug. 'Thank God!'

Steve watched as Eli and Olivia hugged. He had a momentary longing of wanting to be a dad and wondered how Kate would feel about having kids. He knew she had lost a baby, but he hoped she would perhaps want to try again at some point.

'Guv.' PC Warren nudged him out of his reverie.

'What? Sorry.'

'Who had him?' Olivia asked.

'Not sure yet, we think it had something to do with the Taos. We've arrested one man, and we'll question him later, or tomorrow.' He looked past Olivia. 'Is Ross here?'

She looked surprised. 'No, he went to the station. Said he had to interview a suspect.'

Steve frowned. 'I must have missed him,' he said. 'Find anything that might point us to a shipment or the money? I doubt they'll stop looking, you know.'

Olivia bit her lip. 'Er, nothing. I've no idea what he might have done with it.'

Steve spoke to Eli, hanging on to Olivia's arm. 'I need you to come into the police station tomorrow, Eli. Can you do that?'

Eli's eyes widened. 'Will I get to be in a police cell? Like a prisoner?'

Steve smiled indulgently. 'That sounds like you want to be in a cell.'

'Yeah!' Eli was bright-eyed.

'OK. I'll take you into the cells.'

'Promise?'

'Promise. As long as we don't have anyone in them.' He looked serious. 'I'll need to talk to you properly about the last few days. It's nothing to be worried about.' He spoke to Olivia. 'I'll need you there too.'

'What time?'

'Let this guy have a lie in. About ten?'

'We'll be there.'

'Bye, Eli. See you tomorrow.'

'Bye.'

Steve and PC Warren returned to the station and Warren went to find Jonesey. As Steve walked into his office Garland rushed towards him looking panicked.

'Guv, heads up. Sarge is on the war path,' he said out of the corner of his mouth, looking behind him.

'Oh Christ. What now?'

'MILLER!' roared the sarge, stomping down the corridor.

'Sarge, what can I do for you?' Steve said pleasantly, not terrified at all by the overbearing sergeant who put the fear of God into most people.

The sarge was red in the face. 'I won't have toffs from other stations taking my prisoners without the appropriate paperwork and then pulling rank on me by saying they'll report me to the super. I won't have it,' he hissed, stabbing a finger in Steve's direction. 'I dunno who your mate thinks he is and where he gets off speaking to me like that—'

'Whoa.' Steve held up his hands and stepped back from the sarge's wrath. 'Let's back it up a little here. Who the hell are you talking about?'

'Your mate from Cardiff. Ross Scott.'

'What about him?'

'He's gone.'

'Right.'

Sarge rolled his eyes. 'He took Danny Tao. Back to Cardiff. Said his guvnor wanted him back with Danny Tao to question him there. Threatened to report me to the super.' The sarge's eyes bulged. 'The fucking super!'

'Wait,' Steve said. 'He took Tao? When?'

'While you were out raiding the bush bungalow.'

Steve closed his eyes and thought for a minute. He didn't want to believe where his mind was racing to.

'Oh no,' he said with an air of resignation. 'Sarge, put out an alert for his motor.'

'Why?'

'Because he shouldn't have taken him. There's no need to take him unless…' He scrubbed a hand over his face. 'Look, I don't want to believe the reason why I think he would take him.' Steve eyed the sarge. 'Let's get on it,' he snapped, marching into his office and slamming the door hard.

Ross? Bent? On the Tao payroll? Steve couldn't believe that might be the case. He leant on his desk breathing heavily and tried Ross's number. Straight to answer phone. In frustration he rang Cardiff police station and asked to speak to Ross's guvnor.

'Sir,' Steve said as he was put through. 'It's DCI Miller from Castleby. Ross has been helping us with the case involving the Taos.'

'Ah yes. Nasty business. What can I do for you? How much longer is Ross going to be with you?'

'Thing is, sir, I just want to check. Have you given the instruction to bring Danny Tao back to Cardiff?'

'I've not spoken to him. What are you saying? That he's bringing Danny Tao back here?'

'What I'm saying, sir, is that Ross took Danny Tao while I was elsewhere, with no paperwork, telling my custody sergeant that you had requested it.'

'I've requested no such thing.'

'This is why I'm checking, sir. I've put out an alert for his car. It might be nothing. I just want to be sure.'

There was silence from the other end of the phone for a few moments. 'I hope it is nothing, but experience suggests otherwise. I'll kick some arses this end to be on the lookout. Keep me posted, Miller.'

'Yes, sir.'

CHAPTER 33

The sun streaming through the window woke Mike. He turned his head to avoid it and realised he was fully clothed and asleep on top of the bedclothes. He yawned, stretched and sat up. At first, he wondered where Olivia was and then he remembered she was at the cottage with Eli. He wandered out to the kitchen and saw an envelope propped up against the kettle with Olivia's handwriting across the front. Something shifted within him, and he felt a rush of sadness, followed swiftly by a wave of anger. He stood staring at it for a while, half dreading touching it. Finally, he picked it up, part of him not wanting to know the contents, the other part of him needing to know whether she had gone again.

Sighing deeply and opened the letter. He stared at the contents for a long time and then threw it on the side and stomped out of the room.

* * *

Steve was at the station preparing for Eli to come in and give his statement. He looked at the clock, it was almost ten. He'd come in early, checking for reports of Ross's car being seen. The Cardiff police station hadn't seen him return or been able to reach him by phone.

Steve's phone rang, and he dug it out from beneath a pile of papers and answered it, hoping it might be Ross.

'Miller.'

There was a loud rustling sound and then a sniff.

'Tis Sniffy,' a voice said, which was then followed by more sniffing.

'Now why would you be ringing me, Sniffy?' Steve asked, amused.

'There's a woman in our bin.'

Steve burst out laughing. 'You on a bender, Sniffy? This a wind up?'

'There's a woman in our bin.'

'What's she doing in your bin, Sniffy? Stealing what you consider to be yours?'

'She's dead.' More sniffing.

Steve stood up. 'Dead?'

'Yeah.'

'In your bin?'

'In my bin.'

'Don't touch anything. I'll be straight down.'

'Not likely to want to touch anyfin' now, am I? Dead blimmin' woman in my bin,' he huffed. 'Ruined my breakfast that has.'

'Stay there, Sniffy. Don't let anyone near it. I'll be five minutes.' Steve shot out of his seat and rushed to his car; PC Garland was in the corridor.

'Reports of a dead body at the Loafing About Bakery. I'm going now. Follow me with another uniform to secure the scene.

'Guv.'

Steve climbed in his car and drove off, using sirens and lights. He arrived in three minutes. Sniffy was standing in the entrance to the alley with his arms folded, looking self-important.

'Show me,' demanded Steve, snapping on some nitrile gloves.

Sniffy pointed at the large industrial bin.

'Was the lid up or down when you got here?'

'Down.'

'Who put it up?'

'Me.'

Steve grabbed a plastic milk crate and upended it to stand on. He peered into the bin. A woman stared back at him. He recognised her as the nurse from the welfare call the other day. He wracked his brains for her name. Then it came, Anne Ford. She was lying awkwardly, her arm sticking up at an odd angle.

Steve heard sniffing behind him.

'I've not had my breakfast coz of her,' Sniffy announced.

'How the devil did you end up here?' Steve muttered to the body. He heard the screech of tyres and two car doors slamming behind him.

'Guv, where do you want the cordon?' asked PC Garland.

'No one in or out of the alley,' called Steve.

'Guv.'

'Where will I get my breakfast?' whined Sniffy. 'I don't want anyfin' from in there now.'

Steve looked carefully at the woman. Leaning in he could see the side of her head, which was bloody with matted hair. He looked at the woman's hands. 'No obvious defence wounds, broken nails,' he mused.

Stepping back and snapping off the gloves he made the various calls needed to enable forensics to come and process the scene and for the removal of the body.

Steve stood at the entrance to the alley and looked around. It was quiet with very few people about. He could hear a radio playing somewhere, a dog faintly barking and a baby crying. Anyone could have put the body here. It was always open. He looked for CCTV and saw two cameras up the road pointing in both directions. He called the station and asked for Jonesey or Warren and was put through to Jonesey.

'Whassup, Guv?' Jonesey said, chewing loudly on something.

'Sounds delicious,' Steve said wryly. 'I need you to source the CCTV from Silver Lane.'

'Why's that? I'm just about to finish the hospital stuff.'

'You were supposed to do that last night.'

'Sarge had me doing something else, sorry, Guv. I'm on it now.'

'Sniffy's found a dead body in the bakery bins.'

'Oohhh you at the bakery?'

'No, I won't get you anything. Can you get the CCTV for the last twenty-four hours, please? Rigour has set in, so maybe focus initially on early hours?'

'I can do that.'

'Get Warren to finish the hospital stuff? She knows what she's looking for, yes?'

'Guv.'

'Eli and his stepmum been in yet?'

'No. What time were they due in?'

'Ten.'

'Can you check to make sure they're not waiting and stick them in an interview room with a drink?'

'Uh huh. How long will you be?'

'Half an hour or so. Call me with anything from CCTV.'

'Guv, couldn't you get me even just a small—'

'Bye.'

Steve returned to the station to discover Eli had never arrived. He tried Olivia's mobile which went straight to answer phone. He tried Ross's phone and that went to voicemail too. On a whim he got in the car and went to Olivia's cottage. No answer. Peering through the window he saw no movement or signs they were there. He heard a door banging in the strong wind. It had whipped up the day before and was still battering the town relentlessly.

Steve had heard the weather warning for later in the day on the radio and he hoped for Doug's sake that him and the crew weren't called out. He walked down the lane and stood in front of a small boatshed. The large door had come open. He peered in and saw packing material blowing haphazardly around the floor. He noticed with interest, pieces of what looked like a packing crate stacked up against a wall.

Frowning, Steve walked in and looked at the pieces of the crate and the crowbar next to it. Attached to one of the sides of the crate was a clear sticker envelope that contained a folded piece of paper. Steve peeled it off the crate and looked at the shipping note. He frowned when he saw it was addressed to Olivia Baker sent by a Jade Tao from Qatar. He scanned the document for the contents of the crate and all the description said was 'Furniture and artwork'.

Steve stood in the boatshed for a while. Had Olivia had this all along? Had she known about whatever it was that was here while Eli was missing? Donning a pair of gloves, he walked towards an object covered by a tarpaulin and whipped it off, seeing a beautiful Chinese cabinet beneath it. The cabinet was empty. He scanned the garage, there was a pile of old clothes dumped on the floor. He kicked them about to see if they were hiding anything but came up with nothing.

His phone rang, cutting through his musing. 'Miller.'

'It's Superintendent Harris from Cardiff.'

'Sir.' Steve stood a little straighter. 'What can I do for you?'

'I feel it's only right to inform you that we have located DI Scott.'

'Ahh good.'

'I'm sorry to tell you that we found DI Scott, with his girlfriend, dead this morning in his car, in a popular spot for couples if you get my drift.'

Steve swallowed hard and he silently cursed Ross. 'Any idea how they died, sir?'

'Throats were cut.'

'And I suspect the prisoner is nowhere to be seen?'

'Absolutely correct, Miller. Mr Tao is a wanted man. Now more than ever. So if you are able to think of anything that could shed some light, I suggest you do so.'

'Will do, sir.'

'I'm sorry. I know he was your friend.'

'I'm sorry too, sir.' Steve thought for a minute then said, 'Sir? I really thought he wouldn't have gone down this route.'

'We're looking into it. I suspect he had no choice. The scene looks set up from what I hear. I think the girlfriend has been dead longer than him.'

'Right.'

'I'll keep you updated. I didn't want to assume he'd gone bad either. He was a good officer.'

'Thanks for letting me know.'

Steve felt sadness for his friend. He looked down at the shipping note, stuffed it back in his pocket and got back in his car. He sat thinking for a minute and then drove to the climbing centre.

The place was busy, and Foxy had his hands full kitting out a group of teenage girls with harnesses and shoes.

'Hey, mate!' Foxy seemed genuinely pleased to see him. 'How you doing?'

'Good. Bit pushed. Mike in?'

'On the wall. Tread carefully, I think he's nursing a broken heart.'

Steve walked outside and spotted Mike guiding an attractive young woman down off the large outside climbing wall.

'Mike?' he called. 'Got a sec?'

Mike unclipped the woman and said something to her that made her smile widely. He walked over to Steve coiling a rope as he did.

'This about Olivia?'

'It is. Know where she is?'

'Nope.'

'Thought you two were a thing again?'

Mike snorted and stared at the floor for a moment, shaking his head slightly.

'Yeah well, so did I but I now have my third "Dear John" note from Olivia, plus the award for biggest fucking idiot of the year. I think it's safe to say I'm pretty much done,' he said bitterly.

'Are you OK?'

Mike bit his lip. 'She fucking played me. The whole time. What a sucker.'

'You sure?'

Mike scrubbed his face. 'Not completely, but feels like it. She did the big seduction scene the other night and then off she goes again.'

'She left a note?'

'She did.'

'What did it say?'

'What it always says. Sorry.'

'I'm sorry, mate.' Steve looked sympathetic. 'Shitty thing to do.'

'You're sorry, she's sorry, I'm sorry. Everybody's sorry. Doesn't stop me feeling like a dick though,' Mike said.

'You've no idea where she's gone?'

'Nope. She taken Eli?'

'Seems so. You know anything about a crate in the boatshed?'

'What boatshed?'

There's some boatsheds along the lane from her cottage, one of them has an empty crate in it. Delivered days ago by all accounts.'

'To Ollie?'

'Yup. Addressed to her. From a Jade Tao in Qatar – sent months ago but instructions were to hold for a period of time.'

Mike eyed Steve. 'What do you think was in it?'

'No idea. It just said Chinese dresser and art. Sure you don't know anything about it?'

Mike shook his head. 'I think we can safely assume I'm just collateral damage here.'

Steve felt bad for him. 'OK, mate. If you hear anything…'

'I know. Call you.'

'Cheers, mate.'

'See you.'

Back at the station, Steve marched into the briefing room.

'Updates?' he barked. 'CCTV from Silver Lane?'

Garland grimaced. 'Nothing.'

'What? Can't see anything?' Steve demanded.

'Not working.'

'Jesus! What's the point?' Steve said, frustrated.

'We're doing door to door though. Although we covered a lot of these people when we were looking for the missing baby,' Garland provided.

'News on that?'

'Still nothing new.'

'What the *hell* is going on around here?' Steve muttered. He had a sudden thought. 'Anne Ford was friends with Hannah Evans, the nurse. She lives directly opposite. Anyone spoken to her yet?'

'Don't know, Guv.'

He turned to Jonesey, who was eating a bag of crisps noisily. 'CCTV footage from the hospital? Anything? I need to cover this off at least.'

Jonesey knew better than to argue with Steve in this mood. 'I couldn't open some of it, I think it's corrupted. I'm waiting for the tech bloke to re-send it, Guv.'

Steve marched over and pointed a finger at Jonesey. 'Well get onto him and kick his fucking arse then!'

'Guv,' Jonesey said, standing up and hurrying off.

CHAPTER 34

Hannah was exhausted. Baby Lucas was still crying all the time and her mood was getting progressively worse. She was starving and grumpy. Her exertions to get rid of Anne in the early hours of the morning had been taxing. In the end, she used Lucas's pram to shift Anne's considerable weight across the road into the alley, after she had hefted and half dragged her down the stairs from her flat.

From the window, Hannah had seen the police find the body, and when they rang on her bell, she had fed Lucas so he wouldn't scream and give her away. She had also hidden in the lounge in case they looked through her letter box.

Peering through her curtains, she saw the attractive detective on the street and wondered whether he was single. He really was quite gorgeous, she thought as she watched him stride about talking to people and giving orders.

She was frustrated that Lucas wouldn't stop crying. His skin was red and blotchy, and he was hot. He had been screaming so hard he was almost purple. She tried to remember what to do. Why couldn't she remember? She was hungry, sleep deprived and struggling to cope. Was this what it was like? How did people cope? She ran a hot bath for him and then just as she was putting the squalling baby in, she remembered that it should be cool, to try and get his temperature down. Dumping him down on a towel, where he screamed even louder, she let the plug out and then started to add cold water.

Finally, the bath was cool and she gently lowered Lucas into it. His screaming took on a new level and he screamed so much his face went purple. She persisted and, after a while, he calmed down a little and eventually resigned himself to a few whimpers.

'There! That's better, isn't it?' she cooed. Lifting him out, she laid him on the towel, where he started screaming again even more loudly than before.

'Oh for goodness' sake!' she shouted. He stopped his noise instantly. He stared at her with wide eyes, before resuming crying again.

She dried him off quickly, put him in his cot with his dummy and shut the door firmly, desperate to get away into the kitchen to grab some food and make up some milk for him.

Through the wall and hallway, she could hear him screaming. She hoped he would exhaust himself and fall asleep soon. She opened the fridge and saw the cake box still there. She made herself a cup of tea, took the cakes into the lounge, shut the door firmly and switched on the television.

* * *

Mike locked the main door to the climbing centre and stood for a moment looking through the glass at the rough sea. The wind was high, the sea was raging in. He compared his current emotional situation to the sea state and rested his forehead on the glass for a moment, closing his eyes.

'I know it's not helpful, but I'm sorry she did a proper number on you, mate,' Foxy said. 'Are you alright?'

Mike turned and gave Foxy a wan smile. 'Apart from feeling like a prize dick?'

'Happens to us all.'

'Some more than others it seems.' Mike sat on one of the long benches in reception. Foxy sat next to him.

'Were you hoping to pick up where you were before she left last time? Maggie said you two had quite the big romance.'

Mike exhaled heavily. 'I dunno. I guess part of me hoped. I can't believe she'd do this to me. After…'

'After?'

'We'd kind of got close again.'

'Ahh,' Foxy said quietly. 'And you're wondering maybe whether it was genuine or part of her plan?'

'Don't know. I'd like to think she wouldn't treat people like that.'

'Will you be OK?'

'Probably. Mental note not to trust a woman ever again.'

Foxy nudged him. 'Come on. You can't say that. I'm sure Isabella wouldn't do anything like that to you, she's way too sweet.'

'Hmm.'

'Anything I can do?' Foxy asked.

'Nothing for me. But in light of how *I* feel, I would say, you should be true to you.'

Foxy looked puzzled. 'What do you mean?'

'Come on, mate. If nothing else, this has made me realise you have to grab happiness while you can. When it feels real, and you can see a future. When are you going to tell Sophie how you feel? Life is way too short not to. You of all people should know that. You love her and from what I see, she loves you. So why not give it a go?'

'Not going there,' Foxy warned. 'Besides, she's not even talking to me.'

'Carla thought you ought to.'

Foxy inhaled sharply as a wave of grief hit him at the mention of his late ex-wife.

'Yeah, and I told her to butt out as well, so take note.'

Mike raised his hands in surrender. 'Whatever. But think on it. You could have a future with Sophie, a new start. How fantastic would that be? For both of you?'

'I think you need to stop interfering and go home,' Foxy warned. 'I'm done talking about this.'

'Fine. Think on it though. You don't want to be here in a year's time, when she brings her new boyfriend in to meet you because she's decided it's time to move on and you've kept quiet about how you feel.' Mike stood up. 'Sorry to say it. Now I'm gonna head off before you punch me.'

'Wise man.'

'See you tomorrow, Boss.'

* * *

Hannah awoke suddenly with a stiff neck. She looked at the clock and saw it was past midnight. She'd fallen asleep while she had been watching TV.

Easing herself out of the chair, she walked out into the hall. Opening the door to Lucas's room, the smell hit her. Ripe and heavy. Tutting she lifted him out of the cot, laid him on the floor and tried to get his nappy off, wondering what the big red rash was on his torso. She assumed it was maybe from all the crying. She studied it for a minute. She remembered learning about meningitis during her training.

She stared at him; it couldn't possibly be that. He wouldn't have that. It was just a fever, she decided, and that rash was only because of his crying. She cleaned him up and felt his head. He was very hot. He opened his eyes and started screaming again, in an odd high-pitched tone. He needed some paracetamol to bring his fever down. She put Lucas back in his makeshift cot and quickly googled the nearest 24-hour chemist. She found one just around the corner. In her hurry, she grabbed her purse and left the flat, forgetting to drop down the night latch on the door.

* * *

Viv was still awake and watching the sea from the lounge. She couldn't sleep, her mind was full of work, Nate, plans for the future, the dog they were going to see and a myriad other things. The wind was noisy, gusty and relentless, and the sea was raging; crashing against the rocks at the foot of their garden steps. Every now and again a huge spray of surf would rear up. Viv loved weather like this. She could watch it for hours.

She went into the kitchen to get herself a hot drink and heard the cries of a baby again. The cries seemed loud, high and relentless. Viv frowned. This baby had been crying for hours. She knew it was a real baby because it had stopped, started and stopped again. She had done her checks and when she had been out that day, she hadn't heard it at all.

Viv was confident she wasn't imagining it. She knew Nate was worried. She had overheard him on the phone to her therapist asking what he needed to look out for and whether he needed to be worried.

The screams were louder in the kitchen. Viv opened the front door and listened, stepping out and standing in the street. The wind gusted, whipping her hair around her face, scattering loose bits of litter up the road.

The sounds of a baby in such distress affected Viv deeply. She felt something stir in chest, an ache, almost a physical reaction to the cries. She walked further up the quiet street trying to identify the source of the noise. As she moved, the cries became louder and more insistent.

Viv was worried. No one would let a baby cry for this long and not do anything about it. The baby sounded ill to Viv with this amount of crying. Agitated at the prospect of a baby being on its own or at risk, Viv strode purposefully up the road desperately trying to locate where the sound was coming from. She wondered whether she should go and wake Nate and then dismissed it. Too late now.

She stopped outside a double-fronted Victorian-style three-storey new build, which housed six flats. Most of the flats had cards or posters in the window advertising them as holiday lets. All the windows were in darkness except one. Viv could hear the baby clearly now. The main door was ajar, so she pushed it open and walked slowly up the stairs, hearing the baby's cries getting louder as she ascended.

Stopping at a door, she could clearly hear the baby. As she knocked, the door opened slightly. Thoughts raced through her mind. Where the hell were the parents? Were they OK? Maybe they were ill? Her heart was thumping so loudly, she was convinced someone was going to step out and confront her. Tentatively she walked down the hall of the flat, thinking that perhaps one or both of the parents might be unwell or unconscious.

'Hello?' she called out. 'Anyone here?'

She opened the door where the cries were coming from and saw the baby, in a blue sleepsuit lying in a plastic laundry basket. He became her sole focus. He was bright red in colour and crying so hard he was almost choking.

'Hey hey, little one,' Viv said, her heart breaking at the sight of him. She went into the room and picked him up.

'Shush, shush,' she said, holding him against her shoulder and tapping his back. The baby gulped and quietened, making high-pitched grunting noises.

'You feel so hot.' Viv held the baby away from her slightly and he started crying again immediately.

'Shush, shush,' she said, leaving the room. She walked around the flat looking for anyone who might be hurt or ill. The flat was empty.

Viv wondered what to do. She looked at the baby; it looked too hot and there was a rash spreading up his neck. She remembered her antenatal classes and the talk about meningitis. Panicking, she looked for a phone, but couldn't see one. She felt the baby against her, he was becoming floppy. What did that mean? She wracked her brain.

She decided she needed to get an ambulance. Holding him gently, she moved down the stairs and out into the street as quickly as she could. She jogged lightly down the street and pushed open their front door, rushing into the kitchen.

'Nate!' she yelled. 'Wake up!'

Grabbing the phone, she called for an ambulance, gave her address, and said that she thought the baby had been left on its own. She couldn't answer any of the questions about the baby's name or age. She said she had heard it crying and found it on its own in a flat around the corner.

***

Steve was almost sleepwalking and had been just about to leave for the night when the tech working on the CCTV footage was put through to him.

'I can't find Jonesey, but I've tidied up the face from that CCTV,' he said. 'Jonesey said it was urgent, so I stayed late. He sent me the new footage that wasn't corrupted, so I had a go at both of them. You have a slightly clearer face now.'

'You, my friend, deserve a pint on me,' Steve said.

The technician laughed. 'So, it's a hit for you. I've also managed to lighten up the footage from a back door of the hospital building. We've now got a clear face and can place that person leaving from that door, then appearing in the car park. Same person. I'm emailing now.'

'Appreciate it, mate,' Steve said.

Steve's email pinged, and he clicked the first file to open it. As the file loaded on the ancient system, Steve found himself looking into the face of Hannah Evans. The nurse who was Anne's friend. Steve opened the second lot of footage and watched as Hannah opened the door, peered around it and zipped up a black hoody. Pulling up the hood, she walked towards the fence and flung a carrier bag over it and into the woods.

He made a note to go and see Hannah first thing in the morning.

Shattered, he decided to go home. Everything still hurt from his beating, and he genuinely felt like a dead man walking. As he was walking through the station, one of the new PCs stuck her head around the door.

'Guv, don't know if its relevant, but just heard a call for an ambulance from a woman who rang because she found a baby unattended in a flat.'

Steve frowned. 'Where was the flat?'

'Opposite the bakery where the crime scene is. Flat number two, Harbour House. The woman said she'd taken the baby back to hers.'

'Her address?'

The PC rattled off the address and Steve was instantly alert.

'I want backup at that address pronto. Quiet arrival. No sirens. Yes?'

'Yes.'

Steve's mind clicked into place. Hannah Evans. There were too many coincidences at play. Hannah Evans knew Anne Ford. They worked together at the hospital. He'd just seen Hannah Evans lobbing a bag, that was most likely the one containing the empty Chanel purse and other bits, into the woods. Now Anne Ford had been found dead opposite Hannah's flat, when she had been talking to Steve not more than twenty-four hours previously. Plus, the baby who was missing belonged to the woman who had lost the purse. It would be a hell of a coincidence, he mused.

He didn't believe in coincidences.

Steve pulled out of the car park with a screech of tyres, driving fast, but no sirens. He didn't want to scare or warn anyone. He turned into the road where the bakery was and pulled to a halt outside the flats. Then he remembered. In a flash he had an image of Hannah standing at the window holding, what he had assumed to be, a baby. Frowning to himself, he noticed the front door was open and ran in.

He found the door to Hannah's flat wide open and walked slowly in, quickly snapping on some nitrile gloves, treading carefully. He checked the lounge and poked his head into the kitchen, noticing a knife block on the floor with an empty space for one of the bigger knives.

* * *

In Viv's kitchen, the wind howled outside, and she heard the thump of the waves as the power of the sea hit the beach in a relentless rhythm. She looked down into the face of the baby and had a sudden flashback of holding her dead child. She pushed the memory away and focused on the baby she was holding.

He had cried loudly for a time and then had suddenly become quiet. He whimpered slightly and moved, and she felt a flood of relief. She strained to hear the sound of an ambulance siren and willed the baby to hold on.

'Give him to me,' a quiet voice behind Viv said.

Viv jumped and turned around. Behind her, a large woman was brandishing a long-bladed knife, wearing a murderous expression.

Viv stared. 'Who are you?'

'Give him to me,' the woman replied insistently. 'Give the baby to me. He's mine.'

Viv held the baby closer to her. 'I've called an ambulance. He's really ill. Can't you see that? I think he's got meningitis.'

The woman scowled. 'What the fuck do you know?' she said roughly. 'He's just hot and needs medicine.'

Viv breathed in, trying to control her fear.

'He's been screaming for hours. I could *hear* him. He's got a rash. He's gone floppy. He needs an ambulance,' Viv said, trying to reason with the woman. 'It's on its way.'

'I said, give him to me. He's mine.'

'You left him. The flat was empty.'

'What business is it of yours? Give me my baby.' The woman stepped forward with the knife.

'Not until I know he's OK,' Viv said, moving further away from the woman who was approaching her from the doorway. 'I'll give him to you once the paramedics have checked him over.' She silently hoped they'd take the baby to hospital to solve the problem.

'I said, GIVE ME MY FUCKING BABY!'

'NO,' Viv shouted at her.

The woman swiped at Viv with the knife, a murderous glint in her eye. Viv raised a hand to try and protect the baby, and the knife sliced through her palm. Blood poured out of the wound. Viv grabbed a tea towel and awkwardly wrapped her hand in it as she walked in slow circles around the large kitchen table. The woman followed her and tracked her every move, the table the only solid barrier.

'NATE!' Viv screamed, as the woman leant over and swiped again, narrowly missing Lucas's head.

'I *said* give me my *fucking baby* or it's the last thing you'll ever do, BITCH,' the large woman spat out.

'This baby is *ill*,' Viv said desperately. 'Don't you want it to get better? Let's wait and see what the paramedics say? They might have some medicine?'

'If he dies then he dies. That's what's supposed to happen. That's *the way*, it's how it's meant to be.'

'What?' Viv said in disbelief, clutching the baby to her chest. 'But you can save him. All you need to do is give him to the paramedics.'

'Maybe he needs to be with the others,' the woman said. 'Maybe that's the bigger plan. He'll be safe then.' She nodded to herself. 'Yes. He'll be safe with the others, then he won't ever get sick.'

'How can you say that? He can be helped. We have to at least try.'

The woman stared at Viv as if seeing her for the first time.

'*We?*' she sneered. 'Who the fuck is *we?*' She looked around the room. 'Look at you. With your perfect life. Your perfect face. Perfect figure. I *hate* people like you. You have it all. Bunch of fucking do-gooders you are. I'm going to give you one last chance and you're going to hand over the baby or I will gut you like a fish.'

Viv held the baby tight. She risked a look at him. His breathing had become laboured, and his colour had changed; he was suddenly very pale.

'He's very ill,' Viv said desperately. 'I'll give him back to you when the paramedics have seen him.'

'No.'

'But he might die,' Viv choked out.

'Fine. Then he'll end up with the others. They'll look after him. He'll be safe with the others.'

'Who are the others?' asked a soft voice in a conversational tone from the doorway.

The woman turned around in surprise. Looking confused, she brandished the knife at Viv again and then at Nate who was stood in the doorway.

'Don't come any closer to me! I'll kill all of you!'

Ignoring the knife, Nate walked in and sat at the kitchen table. He casually inspected a plate of chocolate muffins that Viv had baked that evening. He carefully selected one and bit into it, making an appreciative noise. He sat casually and draped an arm over the back of the chair next to him and looked at Hannah.

'Tell me about the others,' he said as he took another bite. 'I'm interested. I'm Nate by the way. You keep talking about the others. Who are they?'

The woman stared at him. 'Who the fuck are you?' she asked incredulously.

'I'm Nate. Come on. Tell me about the others. How will he be safe with them?' he asked pleasantly and took another bite. 'Mmm, good muffins by the way. Still a bit sticky.' He threw a subtle glance over at Hannah, who was eyeing the muffin hungrily. 'I'm so sorry, I'm being rude. Do you want one?' He selected one and held it out to her.

Hannah looked around and quickly snatched the muffin from his hand. She bit into the top of it, her eyes closing as she tasted the rich cake.

'What's your name?' he asked gently.

'Hannah,' she managed through a mouthful of muffin.

'Who are the others you're talking about, Hannah? Tell me about them.' Nate continued in a soporific voice.

Hannah pointed the knife menacingly towards Viv and then focused on Nate.

'The other babies,' she said. '*My other* babies.'

CHAPTER 35

Prowling Hannah's flat, Steve checked the bedroom and a bathroom and then stopped at a door, looking closely at it. It looked like there was dried blood splatter up the walls and over the door. He gently opened the door, pushing it back to its open limit and stepped inside, carefully checking there was no one there.

He stood, a chill settling over his shoulders. He took in the makeshift cot made from a plastic laundry basket and the baby paraphernalia scattered across the floor. He turned slowly, sensing something behind him and stared with mounting horror at what he saw.

Behind him, sat rows of life-sized baby dolls. There must have been at least twenty. Each baby doll was in a Babygro, but each baby had a photograph of the face of a real baby, cut exactly to size and fixed carefully to the plastic face of the doll. The effect was utterly chilling.

'My God,' Steve whispered, staring, the hairs on the back of his neck standing up. For a split second his brain had tricked him into thinking they were real babies. *Who were these babies? Had she killed them? Kidnapped them? And then what?*

As he turned, his foot nudged a new baby doll, still in the box, and a blue sleepsuit fell off the box, complete with a photograph of baby Lucas's face.

Steve felt a surge of fear for the missing baby and ran out of the door and around the corner. He tried to run lightly to keep the sound of his feet pounding on the pavement quiet.

Breathlessly, his heart thudding with fear for the child, he reached the house where the woman had called from and saw the front door was ajar. He waited, trying to keep his breath quiet, and listened, the storm carrying the sounds from inside away on the wind. Carefully, he pushed open the door and crept in further, finally able to hear voices talking.

'My babies,' Hannah said, lifting her chin in a defiant gesture. 'They're all safe.'

'Are you keeping them safe, Hannah?'

'Absolutely. Yes, I am.'

'Safe from what?'

'Safe from a life where they weren't loved. Weren't looked after. Weren't cared for properly.'

'And you saved them from that?'

She took another bite of the muffin and nodded.

'Of course I did. They're part of my family now. I love them, look after them. Cherish them.'

'Did you take this baby to save him and give him a better life?' Nate asked softly.

Hannah looked at Lucas.

'I did. I knew him. From the hospital,' she said. 'His mother…' She snorted. 'Useless fucking bitch. Left him outside a cafe! Who leaves a baby like Lucas *outside* a cafe these days?'

'We heard him crying, didn't we, Viv?' Nate agreed.

'We did,' Viv said quietly, meeting Nate's eyes and understanding where he was going with the conversation.

'We were very worried about him, we wondered who would leave a baby outside a cafe,' Viv said quietly.

'Exactly!' Hannah said triumphantly. 'I took him because *she* didn't care! I *saved* him.'

'Is that what happened with the others?' Nate asked.

'What others?' Hannah said belligerently.

'The babies that you've been telling me about. The ones you saved.'

'I've helped them be loved,' Hannah said. 'I love them now. They'll be happy.'

A chill passed over Nate. 'And what about this little one? We should try and save him, shouldn't we?'

'But he's not loved!' Hannah burst out over Nate's calm voice. 'I can save him from a life of unhappiness.'

'He could be loved though, couldn't he?' Nate said gently. 'If the mother can't look after him then he might be adopted by someone who can. Someone who would love him and look after him. You would have given him a second chance, Hannah. Like he was reborn.'

Hannah inhaled sharply and stared at Nate, wide-eyed, her stance, holding the knife, relaxed slightly.

'Reborn? Do you think that's possible?' she whispered.

Nate nodded slowly. 'I do. But we need to give him the chance, don't we? To try and make him better so that we can help him be reborn.'

Hannah's eyes were glassy, her face flushed, and she started nodding furiously. 'Yes. Reborn. I like that. Yes. That would be good for him.'

'So, we should try and help him shouldn't we, Hannah?' Nate said gently, standing slowly. 'We should try and make him better. Will you help me to try and make him better?'

Hannah was transfixed, staring at Nate. She bit her lip. 'But how will we know? I won't know if he's had a better life. He won't be with me. I won't know. How will I know?' she asked desperately.

'We can find out. Ask for news, pictures, reports on how he's doing.'

'Can we do that?' Hannah was incredulous.

'Sure, we can. We'll know if he's safe.'

Viv turned her head at the sound of a siren in the distance.

'Ambulance is here,' she said quietly. 'He's not conscious.'

'Hannah,' Nate said abruptly with authority. 'Look at me.'

Hannah stopped staring in the direction of the window and looked at Nate as if she was in a trance.

'Hannah, let's save baby Lucas together? Yes? So, he can be reborn?'

Hannah bowed her head and stepped aside. 'Yes. You take him. Not her,' she ordered, gesturing at Nate with the knife. Nate stepped towards Viv.

'Hannah, can you put the knife down? I'm worried baby Lucas will be hurt by it.'

Hannah put the knife down obediently.

'Pass me the baby, Viv.'

Viv passed Nate the baby and he tucked the blanket around him, he floppiness reminding him of their own baby. He stifled a wave of grief that lodged in his throat. He knew this was what Viv had been thinking. His heart ached for her.

Nate focused on Hannah.

'I'm going to take him outside, Hannah. He's really poorly.' Nate tarted to walk slowly out of the kitchen. He saw Steve standing in he open doorway, flagging down the ambulance. Steve held up his warrant card and gestured for Nate to go past him.

After Steve had a brief discussion with the paramedic, Nate handed over the baby and said they suspected meningitis. Nate helplessly watched as they rushed the baby into the back of the ambulance.

Viv appeared in the doorway, breathless. 'She's gone out the back door. The tide's at the steps. I'm not sure where she'll go.'

Nate and Steve ran back into the house, hearing the ambulance siren howling over the wind. At the back of the house, they saw the back gate was open but there no was sign of Hannah in the rough sea that was crashing onto the beach. They both leant over the wall to look down, but saw nothing in the swirling white mass of angry water.

Back in the kitchen, Nate found Viv washing her bleeding hand under the tap, sobbing quietly.

'Viv, she's gone. Come here.' Nate wrapped his arms around her as she continued to wash her hand.

Viv said tearfully, 'She said she had to get back to her other babies. What did she mean, Nate?'

On hearing this, Steve ran back out of the front door towards Hannah's flat. His backup had arrived, and he motioned them to be quiet and follow him in.

* * *

Hannah had arrived home via the back door. She had run down the steps from Nate's to the beach and struggled through the raging sea and back up through someone else's garden, a few doors along from Nate's, and then around to her flat.

She was cold and wet, but she didn't care. She had rapidly concluded that perhaps it was time to move on again, particularly with Anne in the bin over the road.

Now she was organising. She hummed to herself as she opened cupboards and started packing her babies' clothes.

Suddenly hungry, she decided to treat herself to another cream cake. When she walked out into the kitchen though, she came face to face with two uniformed police officers; Steve was standing behind them.

'Get out of my flat,' she said, narrowing her eyes. 'You have no right to be in here.'

One of the police officers took a breath. 'Hannah Evans, I'm arresting you…'

Hannah was escorted to the police car. As she left the flat she called out, 'Be home soon, babies! Love you!' and then remained silent.

* * *

Steve drove home. He was exhausted. Parts of him still ached and he felt like he was running on a few hours' sleep. It was only when he looked in the mirror that he was reminded it was only recently he had been beaten by members of the Tao gang and endured the shooting at the Camorra's. He wondered what had happened to Danny. Either way. No news was never a good sign.

Letting himself in the front door, he found Kate asleep on the sofa. He looked down at her and felt a surge of love. Her glasses were sitting haphazardly on the end of her nose and there was a medical journal balanced on her chest. The TV burbled quietly in the background. He gently took the medical journal away and closed it before he picked the glasses off the end of her nose gently and put them on the coffee table. He knelt next to her and smoothed her hair back off her face.

'Hey, you,' he whispered. She stirred and opened sleepy eyes.

'Hey, you,' she said, smiling, and reached up to stroke his face. 'You OK?'

'Yes. I want you here. Move in,' he said. 'I don't want any of this without you. For keeps.'

'Alright.' She grinned. 'Soppy twat.' She pretended to think for a minute. 'One condition though.'

'Anything,' he murmured.

'That I get to see your swellings whenever I want.'

'Done,' he said, pulling her close. 'You strike a hard bargain, but I'll give in just this once.'

Steve was driving to work the next morning, singing loudly along to an old Beatles track on the radio when his phone rang.

'Miller,' he said cheerfully.

'Oh, hello. This is Matthew Winters, the headmaster at Eli Baker's school. I wonder if you could help me. Do you remember we spoke recently?'

'I do remember.'

'It's so nice to have him back safe and sound. But we're having some trouble contacting his stepmother. I feel slightly embarrassed asking, but do you happen to have her number? The one we have has been disconnected.'

'Disconnected?'

'Yes, it says it's no longer in service. I only ask because I understand she resides locally to your police station.'

'She left. A day or so ago now as I understand it. With Eli.'

'Yes, she returned him here. He's very upset and we need to reach her. Do you know where she went?'

'I don't, I'm afraid. I still need to interview Eli about his abduction. He was due to come in yesterday.'

'Oh goodness, was he? Well, I don't know what to do. Thing is, she's Eli's only contact now. We need to have more than one contact, it's policy.'

'I'll see what I can do, Mr Winters. See what we have in the system. I'll call you if I find anything.'

'I'd appreciate that.'

'I do recall she mentioned that Eli also had an aunt. I'm not sure if he knew her, but with that in mind, I'll see what I can dig up.'

'Appreciate that. Bye now.'

Steve ended the call, concerned that something had perhaps happened to Olivia. But then why would she have taken Eli back? Had the Taos caught up with her? He fretted that although they had found Eli, they still weren't clear on what happened to the shipment or the money. He thought about the crate in the boatshed and wondered what was in it and whether something had happened to Olivia.

When he arrived at the police station, he shouldered his way past two uniforms wrestling an unkempt man in his twenties towards the custody suite. He grabbed a coffee and headed for his office, sighing with satisfaction as he sat at his desk. His mobile rang again – it was Pearl.

'Pearl, nice to hear from you. How are you?'

'We're good thank you, darling. I've just come back from London. Mickey will be back in a day or so, he's dealing with a couple of things. How are you?'

'Been a bit frantic, truth be told.'

'I heard, frightful business. Anyway, darling, I just wanted to tie up a few loose ends, in the spirit of information sharing.'

'Oh?' he said warily. 'Do I want to know this?'

She chuckled. 'Of course. The men behind taking Eli have been dealt with. Most severely.'

'Will they be appearing any time soon, intact or in pieces?'

'No. They got what they deserved, elsewhere. Public service and all that. Poor boy. We're now trying to clear up the mess and get to the bottom of the missing shipment and money. That organisation wasn't particularly well run. Lots of small empires, working independently and fighting each other. Not our style at all.'

'I'm guessing that stops now, Pearl.'

'You guess correctly.'

'Within reason, let me know anything you can on the shipment or the money. Is there any news of Danny? The copper that took him has shown up dead in Cardiff with his girlfriend.'

'Danny has gone to ground, as they say. We can't find a whiff of him anywhere. I suspect he's crept off to lick his wounds. We need to put some wider feelers out, I think. I wouldn't put it past him to be holed up in somewhere like South America.'

'Hmm. Laying low for a bit, you mean?'

'Perhaps. Feeding his habit maybe. Anyway, darling, something else, a little bit odd but didn't know whether or not it was relevant.'

'Shoot.'

'Let's use another word, darling.'

'Go for it.'

Pearl cleared her throat. 'I have an old friend in London who is quite the oracle. He knows everything that's going on, nothing happens in London without him knowing. He's a curator of rumour and gossip. Terribly well informed. Type that tells you your marriage is over long before you know it yourself.'

'He sounds useful.'

'He is. Anyway, there's a woman putting feelers out in the London art underworld.'

'Oh?' Steve's mind flashed back to the packing crate.

'She has an extremely valuable painting, but has no provenance for such a piece.'

'And?'

'I'm no art expert, but rumours are that she has a Paul Cézanne.'

'Hang on.' Steve typed Paul Cézanne into Google. 'Any idea which painting?'

'One from the set of the card players, I'm told. I think perhaps the one stolen from Qatar some time back.'

Steve added 'the card players' which produced some images and then he clocked 'news' and read the headline.

'No way,' he breathed.

'I know,' Pearl said. 'So, darling, I am presented with two choices, which I won't bother you with because they relate to certain activities, but my question is, does this woman have the boy?'

Steve's heart sank. 'She dumped him back at boarding school and got rid of her phone.'

Pearl inhaled deeply. 'So, she abandoned the poor thing?'

'It seems so.'

Pearls voice hardened. 'Just to clarify *precisely*, she chose a painting worth millions over the boy.'

'It certainly seems that way.'

'Hmm. The way I see it is, our friends in Qatar would be *most* grateful for their property being returned. It would pave the way for us to be able to do business in that region again and they would trust the organisation is now being managed differently.'

'That's a decision for you, Pearl.'

'Do you want to know how the situation is resolved, when it is?'

'I'm not sure I do, but I think I'm obligated to know.'

'OK, darling. Another public service I'll be performing. Perhaps one day I'll meet the King and he'll commend me for my services.'

'I wouldn't buy a hat for that just yet, Pearl.'

'Darling man.' She chuckled. 'Speak soon.'

'Bye, Pearl.'

* * *

Mike woke to the sound of his mobile ringing. Too tired to get up to answer it he turned over and went back to sleep again, drifting off to the sound of the wind howling outside, warm and cosy and content in his bed.

An hour later when his alarm went off, he shuffled into the kitchen, flicked the kettle on and saw he had a voicemail from a number he didn't recognise. He accessed the voicemail and put it on speaker while he made himself a tea.

'Mike.' Olivia's voice filled the room, she was speaking in an urgent tone. 'It's me. Look, I just wanted to say goodbye. I'm going away, somewhere new. I'm just finishing off some stuff here and then I'm gone. Sorry it didn't work out—'

Mike ended the call abruptly. He didn't want to hear it. He had shut himself down. He wouldn't fall for it again. He needed to forget about Olivia and move on.

'Buongiorno,' Isabella said in her lilting accent. She was leaning against the doorway wearing one of his T-shirts.

'Morning yourself,' he said. 'Coffee?'

'Yes please.'

He eyed her long legs. She walked over to him and draped her arms around his neck, pressing herself against him.

'You have this line here again,' she said, stroking his forehead. 'Like you are thinking hard. Tell me, what are you thinking about?'

He pulled her close and kissed her gently.

'Everything's fine. I'm thinking that T-shirt looks good on you.'

'Does it?' She giggled.

'It does.' He kissed her again. 'I'm also thinking that you look much better without it,' he said, peeling it gently over her head.

'Is that so?'

'Most definitely,' he said, pushing her gently back towards the sofa. 'Much, much better without.'

'But it is cold, and I will freeze.'

'Well, I'd better see about warming you up then.'

CHAPTER 36

Olivia paced the floor of the empty warehouse, fuming, her heels echoing as she stomped angrily.

'You were only supposed to ransack the room, not torture him,' she said angrily. 'I didn't want him hurt.'

'We did what you asked. He didn't know a thing about it.'

'Not fucking good enough. It wasn't what I wanted. He would have suffered.'

'He didn't know anything about it. He was a cabbage anyway, you knew it. It took the spotlight off you though, didn't it?' The man tutted. 'We did what we had to. It looked good, convincing. The copper and his girlfriend put up a fight though.'

'Where did you dump them?'

'In a car near a dogging spot. People will think it was a robbery gone wrong. I quite liked the irony of a copper in a dogging spot.'

Olivia sighed. She marched over to a large bag and produced a bundle of money which she threw it at him. He caught it deftly.

'Take this,' she snapped. 'There's extra in there because I don't want to see you again. Ever. Understand me? We've never met.'

'OK.'

'Go.'

She waited for the tall man to leave, watching as he slipped out of the door silently.

She turned and walked over to a car parked in the corner of the warehouse. She opened the boot. Danny Tao lay inside, hog tied. He was terrified. His skin was slick with sweat and his hair was wet. Gaffer tape was secured tightly over his mouth. Sweat had soaked through his clothes. His body odour permeated her nostrils and made her recoil with distain.

'Mr Tao,' Olivia said, looking down at him. 'Finally, we meet.'

He struggled against his bonds.

'Please don't struggle, Mr Tao. Do you know who I am?'

He blinked at her and shook his head frantically, making pleading sounds in his throat.

'No? Shall I tell you? I'm Gil's sister. Don't know who Gil is? Gil was Jade's boyfriend. You know, the one she ran away with to get away from you. Anyway!' she said brightly, picking up a petrol can and unscrewing the cap. 'Let's get on! I just wanted you to know it was me who was going to light the match, so to speak. You effectively killed my brother by sending your thugs out to get Jade and Gil, and well… here we are now. They always say, revenge is a dish best served cold.'

She splashed petrol on him as she talked, spreading it around the boot and over the sides of the car. She made sure there was a trail to the petrol cap which she unscrewed. She stuffed a rag inside it and drizzled some more petrol over the rag.

'I'm not going to get into an endless boring debate about who did what to whom, and whose fault it was. I just want you to know that *this*,' she struck a match, 'is for my brother.'

She threw the match into the boot of the car and watched with satisfaction as the flames engulfed Danny Tao.

'Bye bye,' she said, smiling as she watched his body burn and writhe in pain. 'Bye bye now.'

* * *

Foxy had tried again to talk to Sophie, but she was avoiding his calls and not returning his messages. He concluded that perhaps she just needed time. He opened the doors to the climbing centre and left Solo in the doorway while he popped over the road to see if Maggie had spoken to Sophie lately.

When he returned, complete with coffee, a bacon roll and no news of Sophie, he found Erin in running gear, fresh off the beach, crouched down, stroking Solo.

'Morning,' he said.

'Morning. How are you?'

'Good thanks.'

She gave Solo a final pat and stood up.

'So… last night. In the pub,' she said.

'Yes. That.'

She pulled a face and laughed. 'Bit awkward, wasn't it? I probably should have said something.'

'About being married?' he said. 'Probably should have, yes.'

'Yeah well.' She shifted from foot to foot.

'Well, what?' Foxy said. 'Would have been good to know.'

'Would it have changed anything?'

'Most probably.'

'Well, for me it doesn't change anything. We have an open marriage.'

Foxy raised an eyebrow. 'Oh. One of those.'

'What do you mean, "one of those"?' she asked.

'In my experience, an open marriage invariably means that only one party is happy with it being open. There's always a discontented partner in the wings somewhere.'

'We're both cool with it. It's how we roll. But I wanted to drop by and say that for me, it doesn't change anything.'

Foxy tilted his head. 'What do you mean, doesn't change anything?'

'Between you and me. We can carry on having a bit of fun. But only if you want to.'

Foxy was a little surprised, unusually, he was at a loss for words. 'Oh,' was all he managed.

She grinned. 'Yeah. We can carry on being friends with benefits, work on moving up that "proficient" chart if you like.'

Foxy struggled to find a response. 'Well, that's certainly something to think about.'

'It is. Anyway, I've gotta go, I've got patients! Have a good day!'

'See ya,' he said and watched her jog lightly up the road.

His eyes moved to the beach cafe to see Maggie standing in the doorway giving him a long-suffering look and shaking her head.

'What?' he called.

'I hear she's married,' Maggie said, giving him a side eye.

'What's your point, Mags?'

'If you need me to say it, you're stupider than I thought,' she called. 'I don't like trollop behaviour. I know her game. Can't stand women that want all the candy in the window and the shop as well, and don't save any for anyone else.'

'I don't even know what that means, Mags,' he said, lips twitching.

She made a dismissive gesture and marched back inside the cafe, muttering.

Foxy's phone buzzed with a message from Sophie. He opened it immediately.

Rob, please stop hounding me. I just need a bit of distance from everyone. I need to work through some stuff. I'm sorry I shouted, but I did mean it. I'd appreciate it if you could give me some space to work through losing Sam, and Dad's situation too. I want to make decisions of my own and I'm sick of people trying to do it for me. Hope that's OK. It's me, not you. I just need time to think and process that's all. Are you able to respect that? Hope so. X

Foxy read the message twice and wondered how to respond. At a loss, he just replied:

OK. X

As he wandered back into the climbing centre he mused over Sophie's text and then his most recent conversation with Erin.

The part of him that was fairly philosophical, agreed that under the current circumstances, it was a pretty bloody tempting offer from Erin. But the honourable part of him didn't want to betray how he felt about Sophie, because ridiculously, he had felt unfaithful after spending the night with Erin.

However, the warmth and closeness of a female body had been a comfort to him, and now he wanted more of it. He made a decision. If anything happened again with Erin, then so be it. They both had their eyes wide open, and the rules had been set, so he figured he'd enjoy it for as long as it lasted, and try not to feel bad about Sophie.

However, something Mike had said to him kept picking at his mind. It had stayed with him, and he was unable to get it out of his mind. *'Imagine being introduced to her new boyfriend, because she's decided it's time to move on. And all this time you've kept quiet about how you feel.'*

Foxy sighed heavily. He couldn't kid himself; Erin was a nice distraction, but his heart belonged to Sophie. Even if he wanted to say something, she wasn't even talking to him at the moment. He would just have to keep quiet and see what panned out.

* * *

Olivia was standing in the plush hotel room looking out of the window. She glanced at the time on her watch. She had a plane to catch. Her luggage was all packed and waiting by the door. The money was in her bag, but she had a contact at the airport who would help her get it through and onto the plane. The painting was hidden with a number of other paintings in a roll; she was an art student travelling across Europe. The painting would be given to the buyer in Rome. It was all sorted. The deal was done. She was home free.

Part of her was relieved that the policeman had found Eli before she'd had to give up something. She simply wasn't prepared to part with either the money or the painting. She'd known if she hung on in Castleby long enough something would turn up. She'd overheard Jade telling Gil that she would always send something to the cottage if they got separated and to wait for it there. No one really knew about the cottage as it was mainly a holiday let. Olivia had no real idea of where the drug shipment went, or most of the money, but she had a painting worth millions and a hefty chunk of cash, so she'd happily offload that and disappear. Hanging on and playing dumb while she waited had paid off.

She felt guilty about Mike. On a whim, she dialled Mike's number from memory. It went to voicemail, and she left a message saying she was sorry and that she was leaving.

Olivia didn't hear the door opening silently. She didn't see Mickey Camorra behind her as he stepped into the room quietly and shot her with a suppressed gun directly in the heart.

In agony, from her position on the floor, she watched him. Blood pumped from her heart and created a near perfect circle of red on the cream coloured carpet. She watched, croaking out desperate silent words as he picked up the leather tube and slung it carefully over his shoulder, before picking up the bag with the money in it. In her final throes of death, she saw him standing, watching her dispassionately with his bright blue eyes, as she bled out.

* * *

After charging her, Steve interviewed Hannah a number of times. During each interview he saw a different Hannah. One minute it was kind and caring Hannah. The next she was grumpy and rude, and sometimes it was the Hannah that swore like a scaffolder and threatened to kill him. Then there was the Hannah that chilled him the most; the one who believed she was the saviour of unloved babies.

Hannah had been charged with the abduction of baby Lucas. He was still very ill, but had made a slight improvement. Steve had also charged Hannah with Anne Ford's murder after finding trace evidence of Anne's skin and blood under Hannah's fingernails and in her flat. Footage from a Ring doorbell also showed Hannah wrestling a large object into the alley behind the baker's, on a pram..

Steve had found Hannah's DNA on the missing Chanel purse, which he had seen her lob over the wall of the car park. Plus forensics had found the stolen engagement ring in her flat, along with a selection of other rings, which Steve fully expected were also stolen.

Steve had been trying to put names to the photographs of the babies' faces that had been stuck to the macabre collection of dolls in Hannah's flat. The team had backtracked to previous hospitals where Hannah had been employed, and it had emerged that some of the babies were ones Hannah had a connection with.

When the team dug deeper, and spoke to staff who had worked with or managed Hannah, and looked at the social media postings of parents around the time, the narrative had started to become clear. Things started adding up.

He discovered her dislike of parents who weren't interested in children, her hatred of what she called 'yummy mummies'. At previous work places, she had received repeated warnings due to her attitude. Steve also found photographs of some of the babies and parents, away from the hospital, outside of their homes, in playgrounds and parks. He concluded that Hannah had been stalking the families long after they had been sent home from hospital.

She strongly believed that the pictures of the babies' faces on the dolls she had, were the actual babies themselves and that she was keeping them all safe from a life of neglect. She believed them all to be real.

Hannah's solicitor was pushing for an insanity plea and the CPS were resisting strongly.

Steve called in on Nate and Viv one afternoon when he was free of interviewing Hannah.

When Nate opened the door, Steve was almost knocked off his feet by the large dog they had taken possession of that afternoon.

'Suzy's got to you then?' Steve said, raising an eyebrow.

'The women's impossible to resist!' Nate laughed.

'Who's this then?' Steve said, scratching the dog behind the ears.

'This is Iggy and he's a long-haired German pointer,' said Viv, coming up behind Nate in the hall. 'And he's got absolutely no recall because everything is way too exciting!'

'He'll be fine,' Nate said and gestured Steve through.

'How are you both?' Steve asked, following them into the kitchen. 'That on the mend?' he said, pointing to Viv's bandaged hand.

'Fine. Ten stiches. I think I was lucky,' she said.

'Look, I've come with some news,' Steve said quietly. 'I thought you'd want to know that baby Lucas is still very poorly, but showing a small improvement.'

'Meningitis?' Viv asked.

'Yeah. He was dehydrated, and it really took hold. Everyone's hopeful he'll pull through.'

'I hope so.' Viv sat down heavily. 'Poor sweet boy.'

Nate pursed his lips and said thoughtfully, 'Anyone pressing charges against the mother for neglect?'

'I'm trying, but the CPS aren't keen. Social services are all over it though. What you did, Viv, was so brave and I just wanted to say how amazing I thought that was. You could have walked into anything, but you went and rescued that child. So, no matter what the outcome, you did a good and incredibly brave thing.'

Steve turned to Nate. 'I was pretty impressed with the way you talked her around too. How did you know to take that approach?'

'Trade secrets.' Nate grinned. 'It was a snap judgement. Can't really explain it. I saw her, made a judgement, which in my job we have to do instantly sometimes. I tried something, hoped to God it would work and then went with it. Thankfully, it did work. At least enough for me to take the baby. You arrested her though?'

'I did,' said Steve. 'Shortly afterwards.'

'My brilliant husband.' Viv grinned. 'Be still my beating heart.'

'What happens to her now?' Nate asked.

'She's pleading insanity. There's quite a bit of history of her thinking she knows better than lots of mothers.'

'Poor woman,' muttered Viv. 'What happened to make her that way?'

'Not sure. We're still digging. Right. I'd better be off.' Steve stood. 'Thanks again for everything you did that night.'

'No problem.'

'Maggie's talking about having one of her legendary parties soon, so I expect I'll see you there. Take care, guys. See you around.'

Steve left the house, chuckling at the sounds of the dog barking and Viv shrieking.

He wandered along to get himself a coffee from the Loafing About Bakery. The crime scene tape still fluttered from a lamp post, and he ripped the last bit off and stuffed it into his pocket. He stood outside the bakery, sipping his coffee and revelling in the smell of cinnamon buns cooking, when he felt his phone vibrate in his pocket.

'Miller.'

'Hello, it's Matthew Winters, Eli Baker's headmaster.'

'Ah hello. Has my constable not been in touch with the aunt's contact details yet?' Steve enquired pleasantly.

'Oh yes. Thank you. PC Warren's been wonderful. We've made contact and she's coming up to see Eli at the weekend, although sadly, she's in no position to have him live with her full time it seems. I just wanted to ask whether you were aware of something; not that I'm looking a gift horse in the mouth or anything,' he said slightly desperately. 'But I've received a letter this morning from a Mrs Camorra, who I understand lives in your locality, and she has paid Eli's fees in full and provided him with a substantial allowance for the duration of his time here with us.'

Steve's lips twitched. 'And the issue is?'

'I don't know anything about this lady. I wondered if you could shed some light.'

'Mrs Camorra is a good friend of mine. She can be very… *benevolent*, when given the opportunity. She would only have the best of intentions. She can be very philanthropic sometimes.'

'Ah, that's wonderful to hear. I shall write and express my thanks.'

'Perhaps ask Eli to as well.'

'Excellent. Yes, I'll do that. Thanks very much. Bye now.'

Steve ended the call and stood there, smiling.

'Pearl Camorra, you're going soft in your old age,' he murmured to himself. 'Who'd have thought it?'

* * *

Newly thirteen, Eli Baker sat in the empty common room at the expensive boarding school where he'd been unceremoniously dumped and abandoned. An incredibly bright boy, he had done extensive research and discovered that Olivia had been found dead in a London hotel room and he had also cleverly made the connection between her and a missing painting worth millions of dollars. He had concluded that she had given him up and abandoned him for the money. He snorted. She deserved to die then. Cold-hearted bitch.

He had also read an interesting article about drugs being shipped to some Arab counties in parts of wind turbines, and he had spent a long time thinking what a genius move that was and wondering whether his father had been responsible for that. If he had been, then Eli felt proud.

His mind wandered to who was responsible for the events of the last few weeks. His father dead in a work accident. Him being abandoned and Olivia being shot. Although he sometimes hated his dad, deep down he had loved him deeply and had been desperate to please him. He always loved it when he had his attention and praise, which had seldom occurred. He was burning with anger that someone had robbed him of that. Unfairly.

In his mind, they had to pay. He'd been told his aunt was coming to see him, but couldn't have him full time. He'd also been told that some unknown woman had paid for his fees and given him a whopping allowance. He didn't care, he didn't know her from Adam.

In his mind, from what he could understand, the Taos were responsible for everything. His father's death, his complete abandonment. He couldn't find anything out about the organisation, but he vowed to seek his revenge and keep looking for information.

Producing his penknife, he picked open the blade. He closed his eyes and drew the blade across his palm feeling the sting of the cut and the warm sticky blood. He clenched his fist.

'I will avenge the death of my father,' he said firmly. He wrapped a handkerchief around his palm and closed his penknife, slipping it back into his blazer pocket.

He knew he couldn't do anything now; he was realistic. But he could watch, find out more. Wait and plan, and when he was ready, he would take his revenge on everyone who was involved in the death of his father, and it would be all the sweeter for the wait.

* * *

Hannah sat on the plastic covered foam mattress on the bunk in the custody cell. She picked some imaginary fluff off the sweatpants she was wearing, which had been issued by the police upon her arrival. She knew she was being moved today, and she hoped that Steve the detective would be the one to accompany her. She couldn't stop thinking about him. Every time he interviewed her, she found herself fantasising about him and a future together. She imagined him walking into the interview room and saying to her, 'Hannah, I've managed to get all the charges dropped because I've realised I'm in love with you and we need to be together.'

She sighed deeply. Wouldn't that be wonderful?

It suddenly occurred to her that she really needed to get out of the cell, and back on the maternity ward. Last time she had been on the maternity suite, there had been two mothers in for pre-birth monitoring and they would have probably had their babies by now. She'd already made a note of their addresses and gone to look at their houses. In her opinion, neither woman was fit to be a mother. They were far too self-obsessed, so she needed to be there for the babies and check they were being looked after.

If they weren't, then she'd just have to take matters into her own hands. She would spend some time checking on them, to make sure they were being treated properly. If not she'd just have to step in. She was there to keep the babies safe and make sure they had a good life.

As the viewing hatch snapped open, she smoothed back her hair and smiled serenely. All she needed to do was tell Steve she needed to get back to work and she was sure it would happen. She was sure he'd look at her, smile, and say it was OK. Perhaps he'd tell her how much he loved her too.

Hannah felt anxiety building in her chest. She wondered if her babies at home were being looked after. No one was telling her anything. She would have to pop home and check on them. She glanced at the door, hearing voices outside and keys rattling. She really had to go. She needed to get back to hospital urgently. Someone had to look after the babies that people didn't care about. Didn't they? Who else would do it?

She knew now that if she planned it carefully enough, she could take the ones that weren't cared about and keep them for herself. What was it that man had said? He said she'd be saving them; giving them a second chance. They'd be reborn. All because of her. She was their saviour. She was the *only* one that *really* cared anyway.

The End

Thanks for reading this book and I hope you enjoyed it. As an independent author I really value all the reviews I get, so if you could take a couple of minutes to review this on Amazon, I would be eternally grateful.

ACKNOWLEDGEMENTS

It seems like only yesterday that it was publication day for *Sea State*, the first in the series, and I still can't quite believe that we are on the fifth in the series and I have already made a start on the sixth. Yes! Castleby is carrying on!

Getting a book out is a big team effort, despite it mostly feeling like a massive solitary undertaking. So as usual there are very nice and extremely important people to thank.

My usual first readers – you know who you are so thank you, you lovely people.

A huge shout out has to go to my wonderful 'dream team'. My editor, Heather Fitt, for her insight, guidance, knowledge sharing and for continuing to indulge my last-minute fretting periods. Abbie Rutherford for her attention to detail, wonderful forensic eye, for putting up with my endless questions. Thank you for going completely above and beyond.

Thanks to Peter at Bespoke Book Covers for interpreting my mad ramblings and pictures and for nailing the cover every time, I know this one was a struggle!

The lovely girls at Literally PR who are so wonderfully efficient, hugely supportive, and an absolute joy to work with. Their excitement for the next instalment always makes me smile.

Love and thanks go to Julie for doing a final read through and also the amazing Kerry Bird for picking up all the things that fell through the net. I am hugely grateful.

A big shout out to Anna Bolton. You took a chance on me, and I will be forever grateful. Thank you for all the time you spend helping me with various bits of research and answering my questions.

Love and thanks as always goes to Jane Bateup – for being a gorgeous ray of light in my world and being such a supportive and wonderful human being.

Huge love goes to my amazing sister, for all of her promotion efforts (love your work), and for being engaged, supportive and hugely enthusiastic since I first had the idea of writing a book. We agonised together (for what seemed like days!) over the title for this book, and this was her suggestion. She continues to be one of my biggest advocates and I will be forever grateful and deeply moved by her support.

Love, thanks and gratitude go to my friends. For *still* pretending to look interested and for being supportive. Your lovely comments, texts and feedback mean the world.

I genuinely couldn't do any of this without the amazing support and understanding from my crew. My two beloved (well, most of the time) teenagers who are largely oblivious of the writing journey and all it involves (primarily because it's not on TikTok), but they make all the right noises when they are supposed to, and look suitably enthusiastic when prompted.

The wonderful Mr S deserves a medal. He puts up with me disappearing into my head for weeks on end. He tries not to be frustrated at my habit of always seeing the potential for a body to be found (literally anywhere, even in the most romantic of locations), and waits patiently for me to finish my frantic note scribbling when I think of a plot line. He endures my grumpiness and frustration through the editing process and often mops up the tears, with emergency Maltesers or wine, after the endless rounds of soul-destroying rejections. What a keeper.

His recent comment of 'I think you should write a book based in Shetland and the Faroe Islands so we can go on a research trip there,' was music to my ears. I genuinely couldn't ask for more from my muse, 'research' partner and 'cell mate'.

Finally, huge thanks to my readers. Your love of the series make the hard struggle of self-publishing worth the slog. I love that some of you have taken the characters into your hearts and really feel invested in their lives and the storylines. It is your love of the books that make me want to carry on creating more for you.

Huge love, respect and enormous gratitude go to the lovely reviewers on the blog tours and those fabulous bloggers that will read my book because I've asked you to! I am so grateful and Castleby wouldn't be what it is without you all, your love and your promotion of the books. You all deserve a medal for giving up your time to help a small author like me get my work out there and I am so grateful for it. If I could, I would write and dedicate a book for each and every one of you.

So! Thanks again to all those who read this, stick around, and stay on the journey with me – there's much more to come!

Printed in Great Britain
by Amazon